THE RESTLESS GHOST

and other Encounters and Experiences

chosen by Susan Dickinson

illustrated by Antony Maitland

COLLINS

William Collins Sons & Co Ltd
London · Glasgow · Sydney · Auckland
Toronto · Johannesburg

First published 1970
This reprint 1984

ISBN 0 00 195272-2
Printed in Great Britain by
Redwood Burn Ltd, Trowbridge, Wilts

Contents

Encounters

Experiences

Acknowledgments

The Editor and Publishers are grateful to the following for permission to reprint copyright material in this anthology:
Winant Towers Ltd for *The Restless Ghost* by Leon Garfield © 1969 by Leon Garfield;
J. M. Dent and Sons Ltd and the Executrix of the Quiller-Couch Estate for *A Pair of Hands* from *Old Fires and Profitable Ghosts;*
Hamish Hamilton Ltd for *Feet Foremost* from *The Collected Short Stories of L. P. Hartley* © 1968 by L. P. Hartley;
A. P. Watt and Son and the Executors of E. F. Benson for *The Bus Conductor* from *The Room in the Tower* by E. F. Benson;
J. M. Dent and Sons Ltd and E. P. Dutton and Co. Inc. New York for *August Heat* from *The Beast with Five Fingers* by W. F. Harvey © 1947 by W. F. Harvey and E. P. Dutton and Co. Inc. (U.S.A.);
Charles Lavell Ltd for *Coincidence* by A. J. Alan from *The Best of A. J. Alan* © 1926 by A. J. Alan;
The author for *Ghost Riders of the Sioux* © 1970 by Kenneth Ulyatt;
The author for *Feel Free* © 1968 by Alan Garner;
A. M. Heath and Co. Ltd for *Minuke* by Nigel Kneale © 1949 by Nigel Kneale
The Executors of William Croft Dickinson for *The Witch's Bone* and *His Own Number* from *Dark Encounters* published by the Harvill Press © 1963 by William Croft Dickinson;
Curtis Brown Ltd for *Lucky's Grove* by H. R. Wakefield from *The Clock Strikes Twelve*;
Scott Meredith Ltd for *The Moon Bog* by H. P. Lovecraft;
A. P. Watt and Son and the Executors of H. G. Wells for *The Red Room* from *Collected Short Stories*;
Edward Arnold (Publishers) Ltd for *The Haunted Dolls' House* from *Collected Ghost Stories* by M. R. James;
A. M. Heath and Co. Ltd for *The Apple of Trouble* by Joan Aiken © 1968 by Joan Aiken.
Every effort has been made to trace the ownership of copyright material in this book, but in the event of any question arising as to the use of any material, the publishers will be pleased to make the necessary correction in future editions of the book.

Foreword

The remarkable revival of interest in ghost stories at the present time is curious, for ghost stories traditionally belong to that great age of story telling: the 19th century. And yet, despite the distractions of the television screen, ghost stories are much in demand, particularly among the young. I hope that this new selection, which has fallen neatly into the two parts of *Encounters*, and *Experiences*, will find favour with the young audience for which it is primarily, though by no means exclusively, intended. For here you will find examples of ghost stories ranging from R.L.S. and J. S. LeFanu in the 19th century, to H. G. Wells, Sir Arthur Quiller-Couch, M. R. James; to A. J. Alan, who read his stories on the radio in the 1920s; to Nigel Kneale, William Croft Dickinson, who first introduced me to ghost stories, and L. P. Hartley. But this particular selection also has stories by the most contemporary of contemporary writers for the young: Alan Garner's account of the boy and girl's visit to the Fun Fair; Leon Garfield whose story of the drummer boy titles the collection; Joan Aiken who has contributed probably the funniest story here and Kenneth Ulyatt who wrote me a curious half-ghost story which is based on fact.

Some of the stories are truly spine-chillers; some of the ghosts are gentle, some are not; but the collection should provide plenty of ghostly "pleasure."

I should like to thank the authors, or their representatives, who have given permission for their stories to be reprinted. And I particularly want to thank Kenneth Ulyatt who wrote his story especially for this collection. I am also grateful to Gillian Avery for telling me about J. S. LeFanu, and the friend who reminded me of A. J. Alan's bedtime stories.

SUSAN DICKINSON

The Restless Ghost

Leon Garfield

D'you know the old church at Hove – the ruined one that lies three-quarters of a mile back from the sea and lets the moon through like a church of black Nottingham lace?

Not an agreeable place, with its tumbledown churchyard brooded over by twelve elms and four threadbare yews which seemed to be in mourning for better weather. A real disgrace to the Christian dead.

Twice a month the vicar used to preach briefly; then be glad to get back to Preston. For he, no more than anyone, liked the villainous old crow of a sexton.

A mean, shrivelled, horny, sour, fist-shaking and shouting old man was the sexton, a hater of most things, but particularly boys.

Some said the reason for his ill-temper was a grumbling belly; others said it was bunions (on account of his queer bounding limp when chasing off marauders and young hooters among his tombs); and others muttered that he was plagued by a ghost.

D'you remember the ghost? It was a drummer boy who used to drift through the churchyard on misty Saturday nights, glowing blue and green and drumming softly – to the unspeakable terror of all.

But that was twenty years ago. Then, two years after the haunting had begun, a certain band of smugglers had been caught and hanged – every last one of them in a dismal, dancing line – but not before they'd made a weird confession. They said the ghostly drummer had been no worse than a foundling lad, smeared with phosphorus to glow and gleam and scare off interruption while the smugglers followed darkly on. For the churchyard had been their secret pathway to the safety of the Downs and beyond.

But that was eighteen years ago. The foundling lad had vanished and the smugglers had all mouldered away. So why was the old sexton such a misery and so violent against idly mischievous boys? What had they ever done to him (save hoot and squeak among his graves), so that he should rush out and threaten them with his spade and an old musket that was no more use than a rotten branch?

An interesting question; and one that absorbed two pupils of Dr Barron's school in Brighthelmstone to the exclusion of their proper studies. Their names? Dick Bostock and his dear friend, R. Harris.

"What say we scare the dying daylights out of him on Saturday night?" said Bostock to Harris on the Wednesday before it.

Harris, who was a physician's son and therefore interested in all things natural and supernatural, nodded his large head. Harris was thirteen and somewhat the more intellectual; but Bostock, though younger by a year, was the more widely profound. Even separately, they were of consequence, but together they were of sombre ingenuity and frantic daring.

So it was that, during three long and twilight walks to their separate homes, they hit on a singularly eerie scheme.

And all the while, in his cottage by the lych-gate, brooded the savage old sexton, unknowing that his angry days were numbered; and that two formidable pupils of Dr Barron's had cast up their score.

"I'll give him something to moan about!" said Bostock, deeply.

"That you will," agreed Harris, with a gloomy admiration . . . for his part in the strange scheme was limited to fetching its wherewithal.

They met for the final time on the Saturday afternoon – as the light was dying – in an obscure lane two hundred yards to the north of the church.

They met in silence, as became their enterprise; but with nods and smiles, as became the success of it.

They walked for a little way till they came to a break in the hedge that led to a spot of some secrecy. There they unburdened themselves of their bundles.

"On a misty Saturday night . . ." murmured Bostock, drawing out of his bundle a scarlet and black striped coat.

". . . There walked among the graves," whispered Harris, producing an old grenadier's cap.

"A fearful, ghostly drummer boy," said Bostock, bringing forth the necessary drum that rattled softly as he laid it in the long, stiff grass. He paused, then added:

"Glowing?"

"Blue and green," nodded Harris, holding up a small stone pot, stolen from his father's laboratory.

In this was the phosphorescent paint – the eerie mixture of yellow phosphorus and pigmented ointment – furtively compounded by Harris from the recipe he had copied out of the condemned smuggler's confession.

The clothes they had borrowed off a brandy merchant whose son had gone for a soldier and not come back – were exactly as the smugglers had declared. ("We dressed him as a grenadier, yer Honour. 'Twas all we had to hand.")

Hurriedly – for the day was almost gone – Dick Bostock put the garments on. As he did so, he felt a strange, martial urge quicken his heart and run through his veins.

He took up the drum, slung it about his neck – and could scarce prevent himself from rolling and rattling upon it then and there.

Instead of which, watched by the silent Harris, he marched stiffly up and down as if possessed by the spirits of all the valorous youths who'd ever gone to war. Indeed, so brightly gleamed his eyes, that he might well have done without the ghostly paint; but Harris, whose masterpiece it was, now offered it with a trembling hand.

"Now the sea mist's come, it'll not be dangerous," he

murmured, shivering slightly as a heavy damp came drifting through the hedge.

"Dangerous?" said Bostock scornfully.

"Moistness is necessary," said Harris, stroking the pot. "It takes fire or burns in dry air. But the mists will keep it damp . . ." Then, clutched with a sudden uneasiness, he muttered urgently: "Bostock! don't be overlong."

"Come Harris! Open it up! Paint me, Harris. Make me glow and gleam. I'll be but half an hour in the churchyard. More than enough to frighten that dismal pig out of his wits. Then I'll be back with you safe and sound. I'll not outstay the mists – I promise you! Don't shake and shiver, Harris! D'you think I aim to stand among the tombs till I take fire and frizzle like a sausage?"

Harris continued to shiver; but even so, his more cautious soul was shamed before Bostock's valour . . . which appeared even more striking by reason of the grenadier's cap a drum.

He opened the pot. And from it, as if there had been something within that had been sleeping – a monstrous glow-worm, maybe – there came slowly forth a pale, evil gleaming . . .

Little by little, this uncanny light increased, shedding its queer radiance on the boys' peering faces – and beyond them to the dense hawthorns that clustered about, touching the tips of the twigs with the bright buds of a Devil's Spring.

"Paint me, Harris," breathed Bostock.

So Harris, with a spatula stolen from his father's dispensary, began to smear the weird ointment on to the drummer's coat, his cuffs, his grenadier's cap, the fronts of his breeches, the tarnished cords of his drum, the drumsticks, and –

"My face, Harris. Dab some on my face!"

"No, not there, Bostock! Not your face! There may be danger from it . . ."

"Then my hands, Harris. You must paint my hands!"

Once more, Harris was overcome. With the spatula that shook so much that the evil substance spattered the grass with its chilly gleaming, he scraped a thin layer on the young skin of Bostock's hands.

To Bostock the ointment felt unnaturally cold – even piercingly so. The heavy chill of it seemed to sink into the bones of his fingers and from thence to creep upward . . .

With a scowl of contempt at his own imagining, he seized up the shining drumsticks – and brought them down on the drum with a sharp and formidable sound. Then again . . . and again, till the sticks quivered on the stretched skin as if in memory of the ominous rattle of war. And he began to stalk to and fro . . .

Harris fell back, transfixed with a terrified admiration. Glowing green and blue, with bony rattle and a shadowy smile, there marched the ghostly drummer to the very mockery of life.

"Am I fearful?" whispered Bostock, stopping the drumming and overcome with awe at the terror in his companion's eyes.

"Horrible, Bostock. Did I not know it was you, I'd drop down stone dead with fright."

"Do I walk like a ghost?" pursued Bostock.

Harris, who'd never viewed a ghost, considered it would need a pretty remarkable spectre to come even within moaning distance of the grim and ghastly Bostock. He nodded.

"Then let's be gone," said Bostock, as hollowly as he might. "Watch from a distance, Harris. See without being seen."

Again, Harris nodded. Whereupon the phosphorescent drummer stalked eerily off, drumming as he went, toward the silent church.

*

The sea mists were now visiting among the elms of the churchyard, sometimes drifting out like bulky grey widows, for to peer at the inscription on some tumbled altar-tomb, before billowing off as in search of another, dearer one . . .

The light from the sexton's cottage glimmered fitfully among the branches of one of the yews – for all the world as if the angry old man had at last given up human company and made his home in that dark, tangled place.

Bostock – watched by fascinated Harris from the churchyard's edge – smiled deeply, and stalked on.

Drum . . . drum . . . drum! the battalions are coming! From where? From the mists and the shuddering tombs . . . platoons of long dead grenadiers pricked up their bony heads at the call of the old drum; grinned – nodded – moved to arms . . .

Or so it seemed to the phosphorescent Bostock as he trundled back and forth, uneasily enjoying himself and awaiting the sexton's terror.

Now the sound of his drum seemed to echo – doubtless by reason of the confining mists. He must remember to ask Harris about it. Harris knew of such things. (Also the banking vapours seemed to reflect back, here and there, his own phosphorescence, as if in a foul mirror.)

Sea mists were queer; especially at night. But he was grateful that their heavy damp eased the tingling on his hands. The ointment was indeed a powerful one.

There was no sign yet of the sexton. Was it possible he hadn't heard the drum? Could the horrible old man have gone deaf? With a touch of irritation, Bostock began to drum more loudly, and stalked among the tombs that lay closest to the cottage.

He hoped the mists and elms had not quite swallowed him up from Harris's view. After all, he'd no wish to perform for the night and the dead alone (supposing the sexton never came). Harris ought to get some benefit. Besides which, a most gloomy loneliness was come upon him. A melancholy loneliness, the like of which he'd never known.

"Harris!" he called softly; but was too far off to be heard by the physician's son.

Suddenly, he must have passed into a curious nestling of mists. The echo of his drum seemed to have become more distinct. Strange effect of nature. Harris would be interested.

"Harris . . ."

There seemed to be layers in the mist . . . first soft and tumbled, then smooth.

These smooth patches, he fancied he glimpsed through shifting holes. Or believed he did. For once more he seemed to be reflected in them – then lost from sight – then back again . . . glowing briefly blue and green.

"Harris . . ."

Now the reflected image stayed longer. Marched with him . . . drummed with him . . .

Yet in that mirror made of mist, there was a strange deception. No ointment had been applied to Bostock's face, yet this shadow drummer's narrow brow and sunken cheeks were glowing with –

"*Harris!*"

But Harris never heard him. Harris had fled. Harris, from his watching place beyond the graves, had observed that his gleaming friend had attracted a companion. Another, palely glowing grenadier!

"*Harris – Harris –*" moaned the painted Bostock as the terrible drummer paused and stared at him with eyes that were no eyes but patches of blackness in a tragic, mouldered face.

Suddenly, the terrified boy recovered the use of his legs; or, rather, his legs recovered the use of the boy. And wrenched him violently away.

In truth, he did not know he'd begun to run, till running he'd been for seconds. Like a wounded firefly, he twittered and stumbled and wove wildly among the graves. All his frantic daring was now abruptly changed into its reverse. Frantic terror engulfed him – and was doubled each time he looked back.

And the phantom drummer was following . . . drumming as it came . . . staring as if with reproach for the living boy's mockery of its unhappy state.

Now out of the churchyard fled the boy, much hampered by his ridiculous costume and overlarge drum, which thumped as his knees struck it – like a huge, hollow heart.

Into the lane whence he'd come, he rushed. He might have been a craven soldier, flying some scene of battle, with his spectral conscience in pursuit.

At the end of the lane, he paused; groaned "Harris!" miserably once more; but no Harris answered; only the drum . . . drum . . . drum! of the phantom he'd drawn in his wake.

Very striking was its aspect now, as it drifted out of the shadows of the lane. Its clothing was threadbare – and worse. Its cap was on the large size . . . as were its cuffs that hung upon the ends of its bone-thin fingers like strange, frayed mouths.

And on its face was a look of glaring sadness, most sombre to behold.

Not that Bostock was much inclined to behold it, or to make its closer acquaintance in any way.

Yet even though he'd turned and fled, trembling on, the tragic drummer's face remained printed on his inward eye . . .

"I'm going home – going home!" sobbed Bostock as he ran. "You can't come with me there!"

But the sound of the drum grew no fainter . . . and the spectre followed on.

"What do you want with me? What have I done? I'm Dick Bostock – and nought to you! Dick Bostock, d'you hear? A stranger – no more!"

Drum . . . drum . . . drum! came on behind him; and, when the boy helplessly turned, he saw on the phantom's face a look of unearthly hope!

"This is my home!" sobbed the boy at last, when he came to the comfortable little road he knew so well. "Leave me now!"

He stumbled down the row of stout flint cottages till he came to his own. With shaking fingers, he unlatched his garden gate.

"Leave me! Leave me!"

Drum . . . drum . . . drum! came relentless down the street.

"Now I'm safe – now I'm safe!" moaned Bostock, for he'd come to the back of his house.

There, under the roof, was his bedroom window, in which a candle warmly burned.

Of a sudden: the terrible drumming stopped. "Thank God!" whispered Bostock.

He drew in his breath, prayed – and looked behind him.

"Thank God!" he whispered again: the phantom was gone.

Now he turned to his home and hastened to climb up an old apple tree that had ever served him for stairs. He reached the longed-for window. He looked within. He gave a groan of terror and dismay.

In his room, seated on his bed, looking out of his window – was the horrible drummer again.

And, as the living boy stared palely in, so the dead one stared out . . . then, it lifted up its arm and pointed.

It pointed unmistakably past the unhappy Bostock . . . over his shoulder and towards the churchyard whence it had come.

There was no doubt of its meaning. None at all. Bostock must fill the place left vacant in the churchyard. His own had just been taken.

Never was a live boy worse situated. Never had an apple tree borne whiter fruit . . . that now dropped down, dismally phosphorescent, to the cold, damp ground.

The miserable Bostock, phosphorescent as ever, stood forlornly under the apple tree. The phantom had caught him and trapped him most malevolently.

To appear as he was, at his own front door, was more than his courage or compassion allowed.

His father and mother's fury on his awesome appearance, he could have endured. But there was worse than that. Would they not have died of fright when they faced his usurper – the grim inhabitant of his room – that other shining drummer boy?

Tears of misery and despair stood in his eyes, ran over and fell upon his tingling hands.

Harris! He must go to Harris, the physician's large-headed son. Wise old Harris . . .

He crept out into the road and ran deviously to a prosperous house that stood on the corner. Candles were shining in the parlour window and the good doctor and his lady were sat on either side of their fire. But Harris was not with them. Bostock flitted to the back of the house. Harris's bedroom was aglow. He had returned.

"Harris!" called Bostock, urgently. But Harris's window was tight shut, against the damp air . . . and more.

"Harris! For pity's sake, Harris!"

No answer. Harris had heard nothing save, most likely, the uneasy pounding of his own heart.

Desperately, Bostock cast about for pebbles to fling at the

window. With no success. What then? The drum! He would tap on the drum. Harris would hear that. For certain sure, Harris would hear that.

And Harris did hear it. Came to his window aghast. Ever of a studious, pimplish disposition; his spots burned now like little fiery mountains in the ashes of his face. Not knowing which drummer he was beholding, he took it for the worse. Bostock would have shouted; Bostock would have thrown pebbles at the window . . . not beaten the evil drum!

He vanished from his window with a soundless cry of dismay. His curtain was drawn rapidly and Bostock – faintly shining Bostock – was left, rejected of the living.

So he began to walk, choosing the loneliest, darkest ways. Twice he frightened murmuring lovers, winding softly home. But he got no pleasure from it . . .

Glumly, he wondered if this was a sign of slipping into true ghostliness.

This mournful thought led to another, even sadder. He wondered if the phantom in his bedroom was now losing its weird glow, and generally filling out into a perfect likeness of the boy whose place it had stolen.

Very likely. Nature and un-nature, so to speak, were disagreeably tidy. They cared for nothing left over. Vague and confused memories of Dr Barron's classroom, sleep-provoking voice filled his head . . . and he wished he'd attended more carefully. He felt the lack of solid learning in which he might have found an answer to his plight.

Ghosts, phantoms, unquiet spirits of all denominations stalked the earth for a purpose. And until that purpose was achieved, they were doomed to continue in their melancholy office.

This much, Bostock had a grasp of: but if ever Dr Barron had let fall anything further that might have been of help, Bostock could not remember it. Neither tag nor notion nor fleeting word remained in his head. He was alone and shining – and his hands were beginning to burn.

Of a sudden, he found himself in the lane that wound to the

north of the church. Back to the churchyard he was being driven, by forces outside his reckoning.

"Good-bye, Harris," he whispered, as he stumbled through the broken hedge and across the grass toward the night-pierced bulk of the ruined church. "Good-bye for ever".

The thick grass muttered against his legs and his drum grumbled softly under his lifting knees.

"Good-bye, light of day; good-bye Dr Barron; good-bye my mother and father; good-bye my friends and enemies; good-bye my cat Jupiter and my dear mice . . . Oh Harris, Harris! Remember me! Remember your young friend Bostock – who went for a ghost and never came back!"

And then, with a pang of bitterness the thought returned that the spectre would have become another Bostock. Harris would have no cause to remember what Harris would never know had gone.

When he found himself among the elms the anger vanished. Instead Bostock sadly, resignedly surveyed his future realm.

There lay the graves, all leaning and tumbled like stone ships, frozen in a stormy black sea. The mists were almost gone and the starlight glimmered coldly down. What was he to do? How best discharge his new office? The drum, that was it, beat the drum and drift uncannily to and fro.

So he began, drum . . . drum . . . drum! But, it must be admitted, he tended to stumble rather than to drift; for, where a phantom might have floated, Bostock trod. Many a time he caught his bruised feet in roots that were more uncanny than he. But there was yet something more frightening than that. His hands were burning more and more.

He tried to subdue the pain by thinking on other things. But what thoughts could come to a boy in a dark churchyard save unwelcome ones?

He gave several dismal groans, even more pitiful than a wandering spirit might have uttered. His poor hands were afire . . .

Water – he must have water! He felt in the long grass for such damp as the mists might have left behind. Too little . . .

too little. He ran from grave to grave, laying his hands against the cold, moist stone. To no purpose. He looked to the ragged, broken church . . . Of a sudden, a hope plucked at his heart.

There was to be a christening on the morrow. A fisherman's child . . . Already, it had been delayed for two months on account of a chill. Harris – interested in all such matters – had sagely talked of it. ("In my opinion, they ought to wait another month. But there's no arguing with superstitious fisherfolk! They'll douse the brat on Sunday, come snivel, come sneeze, come galloping decline!")

The font! Maybe it was already filled?

Bostock began to run. A frantic sight, his luminous knees thumped the underside of the drum setting up the rapid thunder of an advance. His luminous sleeves, his gleaming cuffs with his distracted hands held high, flared through the night like shining banners. And, as he passed them by, the old cracked tombs seemed to gape in amazement – and lean as if to follow.

At last, he reached the church; halted, briefly prayed, and crept inside.

All was gloom and deep shadows, and the night wind blowing through rents in the stone caused the empty pews to creak and sigh as if under the memory of generations of Sunday sleepers . . .

Bostock approached the font. Thank God for Christian fisherfolk! It was filled.

With huge relief, he sank his wretched, shining hands into the icy water. They glimmered against the stone beneath the water like nightmarish fish . . . But oh! the blessed stoppage of the pain!

He stood, staring toward the altar, upon which, from a higher hole in the roof, such light as was in the night sky dropped gently down.

He started; and, in so doing, scraped the drum against the font. It rattled softly through the dark.

What had made him to start? He was not alone in the

church. A figure was crouched upon the altar step. A figure seemingly sunk in sleep or prayer or stony brooding . . .

On the sound of the drum, the figure turned – and groaned to its feet.

It was the sour and savage old sexton. Bitter moment for Bostock. Too late now to get any joy out of frightening the old man stupid. Bostock, his hands in the font, was more frightened by far. Unhappily, he awaited the old man's wrath.

But the old man only stood and stared at him. There was no rage in his withered face; only wonderment and fear. Nor was it a sudden fear, such as a man might betray on first seeing a ghost. It was the deep, abiding fear of a man to whom a ghost came often – to plague him on misty Saturday nights. For in the shadows of the church, he took the glimmering Bostock to be that phantom that had troubled him this many a long year. Yet . . . with a difference –

"Into the church?" he whispered. "Even into the church, now? What does it mean? You never came in the church before. Is it – is it forgiveness, at last?"

Bostock stared at the shrivelled old sexton – that terror of marauding boys. Very miserable and desolate was the ancient wretch. Very pitiful was the hope in his eyes –

"Yes!" cried the sexton, with misguided joy. "It's forgiveness! I see it in your eyes! Pity! Blessed, blessed pity!"

Fearful to speak, or even to move, Bostock gazed at the old man who now hobbled toward him. There was a look of tarnished radiance on his face as secrets long knotted in his heart began to unravel and give him peace.

"At last my treasure, dear spirit! Now I can go to it! It's all right now? In this holy place, you've come to forgive? My treasure! All these years of waiting for it! All these years of misery . . . all these years of longing . . . How many? Eighteen! But all's forgiven now . . . at last, at last!"

Careless of the raging ointment, Bostock drew his hands out of the font as the old man tottered by, mumbling and gabbling as he went.

For the old man did pass him by, his face quite transfigured by yearning and relief. He went out into the tumbledown churchyard, clucking over the neglected graves like an ancient gardener, revisiting an overgrown garden he'd once tended well . . .

Absorbed beyond measure, the luminous Bostock followed – straining to catch the drift of the old man's broken words.

There was no doubt now, the ghost had been that of the foundling boy who'd long ago drummed for the smugglers. Likewise, there was no doubt that the sexton had brought him to his death.

"I never knew you was ailing, my dear. I never knew the paint was a-poisoning you. I swear I'd never have made you go out when the mists was gone if I'd known! Ask the others – if you're situated to do so. They'll tell you I never knew. Thought you was pretending for more of the haul. Thought your cries and moans were play-acting. Never, never thought you'd die, my dear!"

Thus he mumbled and muttered – half over his shoulder – to what he fancied was the ghost he hoped had forgiven him at last.

For it turned out that this ancient sexton had been of the smugglers himself; and had most cunningly escaped hanging with the rest.

"There, my dear. There's your grave. See – I've tended it all these years . . ."

He paused by a patch of ground where the grass had been newly cut.

"But my treasure . . . now I can go fetch my treasure. Now I can live once more . . . now I can leave this accursed place! A – a house in London, maybe . . . a coach and pair . . . Just for my last years . . . my treasure will make up for all!"

Hastening now, he fumbled among the altar-tombs, heaving at the slabs till at last he came upon the one he sought.

"It's here! It's here!"

With a loud grinding, the slab of stone slid sideways and

fell upon the ground. The old man reached within and fumbled for the hoard that had waited in the earth for eighteen years.

Bostock moved nearer. He strained to see. He sniffed the heavy air. His heart contracted in grief for the luckless sexton.

From the smugglers' hiding place, came forth only the dismal smell of rotting tea and mouldered tobacco leaf. All had crumbled away.

The old man had begun to sob. A ruinous sound.

Quite consumed with pity, Bostock laid a hand on the sexton's wasted shoulder and muttered:

"I'm sorry . . . truly sorry, sir . . ."

Whereupon the old man whirled round upon him in a sudden access of amazement and fist-shaking rage.

The hand on his shoulder, the voice in his ear had been no ghost's, but those of a mortal boy.

He beheld the fantastic Bostock. An undersized, somewhat timid grenadier whose protruding ears alone prevented his mansize cap from quite extinguishing him.

Was it to this small, mocking villain he'd opened his heart and betrayed it?

He stared – but saw no laughter in Bostock's face. Rather did he see a startled compassion that came in a gentle flood from Bostock's heart and filled up Bostock's eyes – making them to shine softly – and from thence, ran resistless down Bostock's cheeks. The boy was crying for him. The boy had partly understood, and was grieving for the wastage of his poor life, for his heart that had turned to dust – by reason of the haunting of his soul.

"What – what are you doing here, boy?"

Bostock shook his head; made to wipe his eyes, then stared, frightened, at his luminous hand and hid it behind his back.

The sexton went grey with horror – on the memory of an old, old occasion. He gave some four or five harsh, constricted cries – for all the world as if the organ that produced them was stirring after long disuse. Then he partly screamed and partly shouted:

"What have you done with your hands? What – have – you – done? Oh God, you'll die! You'll die again! He died of it! A doctor! Quick – quick! This time, I'll save you! Please God, let me save you this time!"

He reached out and seized the terrified Bostock by a cuff. Now he began to drag him, as fast as his hobble would permit, out of the churchyard and toward Brighthelmstone. And all the while, he panted: "Let me save him – let me save him!"

Tremendous sight . . . remarked on for years afterward by startled tavern-leavers who'd glimpsed the bounding, limping old man and the phosphorescent boy.

A sight never to be forgotten – least of all by Dr Harris at whose door the sexton banged and kicked till it was opened.

Before he could be gainsaid, he'd dragged the wretched Bostock in and begged the doctor try to save him.

"What's amiss? What's amiss, then?"

"He'll die – he'll die!" wept the sexton. "Just like the other one!"

Then out tumbled the sexton's grim secret while the doctor's household listened in judgement and in pity. For though the old man had been a murderer, – had done for the foundling by his eager greed – it was plain to all he'd paid a high price for his crime.

"This boy will be saved," muttered Dr Harris, as he began treating those hands inflamed by the evil ointment. "But may God forgive you for that other one."

Now it seemed to Bostock as he sat, with wise old night-gowned Harris come down to be by his side, that the night was grown suddenly warmer. The fire burned bright – as if an obstruction had been lifted off the chimney . . .

He was not alone in noticing this. It was remarked on by the doctor, who diagnosed a sudden, beneficial draught. Likewise, it was observed by the sexton – the confessed murderer – who peered at it, then glanced toward the window as if the cause was passing down the street. For he nodded . . .

And though Bostock, who followed his gaze, saw nothing but darkness, he knew that the usurping phantom had at last slipped away, its purpose achieved, its office at full term.

So did the phantom drummer boy haunt the churchyard no more? Did it never stalk on misty Saturday nights? And was its drum heard never again to echo across the tumbled tombs? Yes: but only once more – and that not so long after.

D'you remember when they buried the old sexton at Hove? The old sexton who from that night on had seemed to give up interest in life let alone bedevilling the young boys who came inside his domain. It was late on a Saturday night, and the sea mists were coming up.

D'you remember the sound of drumming that accompanied his coffin? And the gentle beating as it was lowered into its grave? It had a strangely forgiving sound . . . They say it was a retreat that was being beaten; but to Bostock and Harris it sounded more like a welcome.

A Pair of Hands

Sir Arthur Quiller-Couch

"Yes," said Miss Le Petyt, gazing into the deep fireplace and letting her hands and her knitting lie idle for the moment in her lap. "Oh, yes, I have seen a ghost. In fact, I have lived in a house with one for quite a long time."

"How could you?" began one of my host's daughters; and "You, Aunt Emily?" cried the other at the same moment.

Miss Le Petyt, gentle soul, withdrew her eyes from the fireplace and protested with a gay little smile. "Well, my dears, I am not quite the coward you take me for. And, as it happens, mine was the most harmless ghost in the world. In fact" – and here she looked at the fire again – "I was quite sorry to lose her."

"It was a woman, then? Now, I think," said Miss Blanche, "that female ghosts are the horridest of all. They wear little shoes with high red heels, and go tap, tap, wringing their hands."

"This one wrung her hands, certainly. But I don't know about the high red heels, for I never saw her feet. Perhaps she was like the Queen of Spain, and hadn't any. And as for the hands, it all depends how you wring them. There's an elderly shopwalker at Knightsbridge, for instance."

"Don't be prosy, dear, when you know that we're just dying to hear the story."

Miss Le Petyt turned to me with a small deprecating laugh. "It's such a little one."

"The story or the ghost?"

"Both."

And this was Miss Le Petyt's story:

"It happened when I lived down in Cornwall, at Tresillack,

on the south coast. Tresillack was the name of the house, which stood quite alone at the head of a coombe, within sound of the sea but without a sight of it; for though the coombe led down to a wide open beach it wound and twisted half a dozen times on its way, and its overlapping sides closed the view from the house, which was advertised as 'secluded'. I was very poor in those days. Your father and all of us were poor then, as I trust, my dears, you will never be; but I was young enough to be romantic and wise enough to like independence, and this word 'secluded' took my fancy.

"The misfortune was that it had taken the fancy, or just suited the requirements, of several previous tenants. You know, I dare say, the kind of person who rents a secluded house in the country? Well, yes, there are several kinds; but they seem to agree in being odious. No one knows where they come from, though they soon remove all doubt about where they're 'going to', as the children say. 'Shady' is the word, is it not? Well, the previous tenants of Tresillack (from first to last a bewildering series) had been shady with a vengeance.

"I knew nothing of this when I first made application to the landlord, a solid yeoman inhabiting a farm at the foot of the coombe, on a cliff overlooking the beach.

"To him I presented myself fearlessly as a spinster of decent family and small but assured income, intending a rural life of combined seemliness and economy. He met my advances politely enough, but with an air of suspicion which offended me. I began by disliking him for it; afterwards I set it down as an unpleasant feature in the local character. I was doubly mistaken. Farmer Hosking was slow-witted, but as honest a man as ever stood up against hard times; and a more open and hospitable race than the people on that coast I never wish to meet. It was the caution of a child who had burnt his fingers, not once but many times. Had I known what I afterwards learned of Farmer Hosking's tribulations as landlord of a 'secluded country residence', I should have approached him with the bashfulness proper to my suit and faltered as I undertook to prove the bright exception in a long line of painful experiences. He had bought the Tresillack estate twenty years before – on mortgage, I fancy – because the land adjoined his own and would pay him for tillage. But the house was a nuisance, an incubus; and had been so from the beginning.

" 'Well, miss,' he said, 'you're welcome to look over it; a pretty enough place, inside and out. There's no trouble about keys, because I've put in a housekeeper, a widow-woman, and she'll show you round. With your leave I'll step up the coombe so far with you, and put you in your way.' As I thanked him he paused and rubbed his chin. 'There's one thing I must tell you, though. Whoever takes the house must take Mrs Carkeek along with it.'

" 'Mrs Carkeek?' I echoed dolefully. 'Is that the housekeeper?'

" 'Yes; she was wife to my late hand. I'm sorry, miss,' he added, my face telling him no doubt what sort of woman I expected Mrs Carkeek to be; 'but I had to make it a rule after – after some things had happened. And I dare say you won't find her so bad. Mary Carkeek's a sensible, comfortable woman, and knows the place. She was in service there to Squire Kendall when he sold up and went; her first place it was.'

" 'I may as well see the house, anyhow,' said I dejectedly. So we started to walk up the coombe. The path, which ran beside a little chattering stream, was narrow for the most part, and Farmer Hosking, with an apology, strode on ahead to beat aside the brambles. But whenever its width allowed us to walk side by side I caught him from time to time stealing a shy inquisitive glance under his rough eyebrows. Courteously though he bore himself, it was clear that he could not sum me up to his satisfaction or bring me square with his notion of a tenant of his 'secluded country residence'.

"I don't know what foolish fancy prompted it, but about half-way up the coombe I stopped short and asked:

" 'There are no ghosts, I suppose?'

"It struck me, a moment after I had uttered it, as a supremely silly question; but he took it quite seriously. 'No: I never

heard tell of any ghosts.' He laid a queer sort of stress on the word. 'There's always been trouble with servants, and maids' tongues will be runnin'. But Mary Carkeek lives up there alone, and she seems comfortable enough.'

"We walked on. By and by he pointed with his stick. 'It don't look like a place for ghosts, now, do it?'

"Certainly it did not. Above an untrimmed orchard rose a terrace of turf scattered with thorn bushes, and above this a terrace of stone, upon which stood the prettiest cottage I had ever seen. It was long and low and thatched; a deep verandah ran from end to end. Clematis, banksia roses and honeysuckle climbed the posts of this verandah, and big blooms of Maréchal Niel were clustered along its roof, beneath the lattices of the bedroom windows. The house was small enough to be called a cottage, and rare enough in features and in situation to confer distinction on any tenant. It suggested what in those days we should have called 'elegant' living. And I could have clapped my hands for joy.

"My spirits mounted still higher when Mrs Carkeek opened the door to us. I had looked for a Mrs Gummidge, and I found a healthy middle-aged woman with a thoughtful, but contented face, and a smile which, without a trace of obsequiousness, quite bore out the farmer's description of her. She was a comfortable woman; and while we walked through the rooms together (for Mr Hosking waited outside) I 'took to' Mrs Carkeek. Her speech was direct and practical; the rooms, in spite of their faded furniture, were bright and exquisitely clean; and somehow the very atmosphere of the house gave me a sense of well-being, of feeling at home and cared for; yes, of being loved. Don't laugh, my dears; for when I've done you may not think this fancy altogether foolish.

"I stepped out into the verandah, and Farmer Hosking pocketed the pruning-knife which he had been using on a bush of jasmine.

" 'This is better than anything I had dreamed of,' said I.

" 'Well, miss, that's not a wise way of beginning a bargain, if you'll excuse me.'

"He took no advantage, however, of my admission; and we struck the bargain as we returned down the coombe to his farm, where the hired chaise waited to convey me back to the market town. I had meant to engage a maid of my own, but now it occurred to me that I might do very well with Mrs Carkeek. This, too, was settled in the course of the next day or two, and within the week I had moved into my new home.

"I can hardly describe to you the happiness of my first month at Tresillack, because (as I now believe) if I take the reasons which I had for being happy, one by one, there remains over something which I cannot account for. I was moderately young, entirely healthy; I felt myself independent and adventurous; the season was high summer, the weather glorious, the garden in all the pomp of June, yet sufficiently unkempt to keep me busy, give me a sharp appetite for meals, and send me to bed in that drowsy stupor which comes of the odours of earth. I spent the most of my time out of doors, winding up the day's work as a rule with a walk down the cool valley, along the beach and back.

"I soon found that all housework could be safely left to Mrs Carkeek. She did not talk much; indeed, her only fault (a rare one in housekeepers) was that she talked too little, and even when I addressed her seemed at times unable to give me her attention. It was as though her mind strayed off to some small job she had forgotten, and her eyes wore a listening look, as though she waited for the neglected task to speak and remind her. But, as a matter of fact, she forgot nothing. Indeed, my dears, I was never so well attended to in my life.

"Well, that is what I'm coming to. That, so to say, is just it. The woman not only had the rooms swept and dusted and my meals prepared to the moment.

"In a hundred odd little ways this orderliness, these preparations, seemed to read my desires. Did I wish the roses renewed in a bowl upon the dining-table, sure enough at the next meal they would be replaced by fresh ones. Mrs Carkeek (I told myself) must have surprised and interpreted a glance of mine. And yet I could not remember having glanced at the bowl in her presence. And how on earth had she guessed the very roses, the very shapes and colours I had lightly wished for? This is only an instance, you understand? Every day, and from morning to night, I happened on others, each slight enough, but all together bearing witness to a ministering intelligence as subtle as it was untiring.

"I am a light sleeper, as you know, with an uncomfortable knack of waking with the sun and roaming early. No matter how early I rose at Tresillack, Mrs Carkeek seemed to have preceded me. Finally I had to conclude that she arose and dusted and tidied as soon as she judged me safely a-bed. For once, finding the drawing-room (where I had been sitting late) 'redded up' at four in the morning, and no trace of a plate of raspberries which I had carried thither after dinner and left overnight, I determined to test her, and walked through to the kitchen, calling her by name.

"I found the kitchen as clean as a pin, and the fire laid, but no trace of Mrs Carkeek. I walked upstairs and knocked at her door. At the second knock, a sleepy voice cried out, and presently the good woman stood before me in her nightgown, looking (I thought) very badly scared.

" 'No,' I said, 'it's not a burglar. But I've found out what I wanted, that you do your morning's work overnight. But you mustn't wait for me when I choose to sit up. And now go back to your bed like a good soul, whilst I take a run down to the beach.'

"She stood blinking in the dawn. Her face was still white.

" 'O, miss,' she gasped, 'I made sure you must have seen something!'

" 'And so I have,' I answered, 'but it was neither burglars nor ghosts.'

" 'Thank God!' I heard her say as she turned her back to me in her grey bedroom – which faced the north. And I took this for a carelessly pious expression and ran downstairs thinking no more of it.

"A few days later I began to understand.

"The plan of Tresillack house (I must explain) was simplicity itself. To the left of the hall as you entered was the dining-room; to the right the drawing-room, with a boudoir beyond. The foot of the stairs faced the front door, and beside it, passing a glazed inner door, you found two others right and left, the left opening on the kitchen, the right on a passage which ran by a store cupboard under the bend of the stairs to a neat pantry with the usual shelves and linen-press, and under the window (which faced north) a porcelain basin and brass tap. On the first morning of my tenancy I had visited this pantry and turned the tap, but no water ran. I supposed this to be accidental. Mrs Carkeek had to wash up glassware and crockery, and no doubt Mrs Carkeek would complain of any failure in the water supply.

"But the day after my surprise visit (as I called it) I had picked a basketful of roses, and carried them into the pantry as a handy place to arrange them in. I chose a china bowl and went to fill it at the tap. Again the water would not run.

"I called Mrs Carkeek. 'What is wrong with this tap?' I asked. 'The rest of the house is well enough supplied.'

" 'I don't know, miss, I never use it.'

" 'But there must be a reason; and you must find it a great nuisance washing up the plates and glasses in the kitchen. Come around to the back with me, and we'll have a look at the cisterns.'

" 'The cisterns'll be all right, miss. I assure you I don't find it a trouble.'

"But I was not to be put off. The back of the house stood but ten feet from a wall which was really but a stone face built against the cliff cut away by the architect. Above the cliff rose the kitchen garden, and from its lower path we looked over the wall's parapet upon the cisterns. There were two – a very large one, supplying the kitchen and the bathroom above the kitchen; and a small one, obviously fed by the other, and as obviously leading by a pipe which I could trace, to the pantry. Now the big cistern stood almost full, and yet the small one, though on a lower level was empty.

" 'It's as plain as daylight,' said I. 'The pipe between the two is choked,' And I clambered on to the parapet.

" 'I wouldn't, miss. The pantry tap is only cold water, and no use to me. From the kitchen boiler I get it hot, you see,'

" 'But I want the pantry water for my flowers.' I bent over and groped. 'I thought as much!' said I, as I wrenched out a thick plug of cork, and immediately the water began to flow. I turned triumphantly on Mrs Carkeek, who had grown suddenly red in the face. Her eyes were fixed on the cork in my hand. To keep it more firmly wedged in its place, somebody had wrapped it round with a rag of calico print; and, discoloured though the rag was, I seemed to recall the pattern (a lilac sprig). Then, as our eyes met, it occurred to me that only two mornings before Mrs Carkeek had worn a print gown of that same sprigged pattern.

"I had the presence of mind to hide this very small discovery, sliding over it some quite trivial remark; and presently Mrs Carkeek regained her composure. But I own I felt disappointed in her. It seemed such a paltry thing to be disingenuous over. She had deliberately acted a fib before me; and why? Merely because she preferred the kitchen to the pantry tap. It was childish. 'But servants are all the same,' I told myself. 'I must take Mrs Carkeek as she is; and, after all, she is a treasure.'

"On the second night after this, and between eleven and twelve o'clock, I was lying in bed and reading myself sleepy over a novel of Lord Lytton's, when a small sound disturbed me. I listened. The sound was clearly that of water trickling, and I set it down to rain. A shower (I told myself) had filled the water-pipes which drained the roof. Somehow I could not fix the sound. There was a water pipe against the wall just outside my window. I rose and drew up the blind.

"To my astonishment no rain was falling; no rain had fallen. I felt the slate window-sill; some dew had gathered there – no more. There was no wind, no cloud; only a still moon high over the eastern slope of the coombe, the distant splash of waves, and the fragrance of many roses. I went back to bed and listened again. Yes, the trickling sound continued, quite distinct in the silence of the house, not to be confused for a moment with the dull murmur of the beach. After a while it began to grate on my nerves. I caught up my candle, flung my dressing-gown about me, and stole softly downstairs.

"Then it was simple. I traced the sound to the pantry. 'Mrs Carkeek has left the tap running,' said I: and, sure enough, I found it so – a thin trickle steadily running to waste in the porcelain basin. I turned off the tap, went contentedly back to my bed, and slept . . .

" . . . for some hours. I opened my eyes in darkness and at once knew what had awakened me. The tap was running again. Now, it had shut easily in my hand, but not so easily that I could believe it had slipped open again of its own accord. 'This is Mrs Carkeek's doing,' said I; and I am afraid I added, 'Drat Mrs Carkeek!'

"Well there was no help for it: so I struck a light, looked at my watch, saw that the hour was just three o'clock, and I descended the stairs again. At the pantry door I paused. I was not afraid – not one little bit. In fact the notion that anything might be wrong had never crossed my mind. But I remember thinking with my hand on the door, that if Mrs Carkeek were in the pantry I might happen to give her a severe fright.

"I pushed the door open briskly. Mrs Carkeek was not there. But something was there, by the porcelain basin – something which might have sent me scurrying upstairs two steps at a time, but which as a matter of fact held me to the spot. My heart seemed to stand still – so still! And in the stillness I remember setting down the brass candlestick on a tall nest of drawers beside me.

"Over the porcelain basin and beneath the water trickling from the tap I saw two hands.

"That was all – two small hands, a child's hands. I cannot tell how they ended.

"No; they were not cut off. I saw them quite distinctly; just a pair of small hands and the wrists, and after that –

nothing. They were moving briskly – washing themselves clean. I saw the water trickle and splash over them – not through them – but just as it would on real hands. They were the hands of a little girl, too. Oh, yes, I was sure of that at once. Boys and girls wash their hands differently. I can't just tell you what the difference is, but it's unmistakable.

"I saw all this before my candle slipped and fell with a crash. I had set it down without looking – for my eyes were fixed on the basin – and had balanced it on the edge of the nest of drawers. After the crash, in the darkness there, with the water running, I suffered some bad moments.

"Oddly enough, the thought uppermost with me was that I must shut off that tap before escaping. I had to. And after a while I picked up all my courage, so to say, between my teeth, and with a little sob thrust out my hand and did it. Then I fled.

"The dawn was close upon me: and as soon as the sky reddened I took my bath, dressed and went downstairs. And there at the pantry door I found Mrs Carkeek, also dressed, with my candlestick in her hand.

" 'Ah,' said I, 'you picked it up.'

"Our eyes met. Clearly Mrs Carkeek wished me to begin, and I determined at once to have it out with her.

" 'And you knew all about it. That's what accounts for your plugging up the cistern.'

" 'You saw . . .?' she began.

" 'Yes, yes. And you must tell me all about it – never mind how bad. Is – is it – murder?'

" 'Law bless you, miss, whatever put such horrors in your head?'

" 'She was washing her hands.'

" 'Ah, so she does, poor dear! But – murder! And dear little Miss Margaret, that wouldn't go to hurt a fly!'

" 'Miss Margaret?'

" 'Eh, she died at seven year. Squire Kendall's only daughter; and that's over twenty years ago. I was her nurse, miss, and I know – diphtheria it was; she took it down in the village.'

" 'But how do you know it is Margaret?'

" 'Those hands – why, how could I mistake, that used to be her nurse?'

" 'But why does she wash them?'

" 'Well, miss, being always a dainty child – and the housework, you see . . .'

"I took a long breath. 'Do you mean to tell me that all this tidying and dusting . . .' I broke off. 'Is it she who has been taking this care of me?'

"Mrs Carkeek met my look steadily.

" 'Who else, miss?'

" 'Poor little soul!'

" 'Well, now' – Mrs Carkeek rubbed my candlestick with the edge of her apron – 'I'm so glad you take it like this. For there isn't really nothing to be afraid of – is there?' She eyed me wistfully. 'It's my belief she loves you, miss. But only to think what a time she must have had with the others!'

" 'Were they bad?'

" 'They was awful. Didn't Farmer Hosking tell you? They carried on fearful – one after another, and each one worse than the last.'

" 'What was the matter with them? Drink?'

" 'Drink, miss, with some of 'em. There was the Major – he used to go mad with it, and run about the coombe in his nightshirt. Oh, scandalous! And his wife drank too – that is, if she ever was his wife. Just think of that tender child washing up after their nasty doings.'

" 'But that wasn't the worst, miss – not by a long way. There was a pair here – from the colonies, or so they gave out – with two children, a boy and gel, the eldest scarce six. Poor mites.'

" 'They beat those children, miss – your blood would boil! And starved, and tortured 'em, it's my belief. You could hear their screams, I've been told, away back in the high-road, and that's the best part of half a mile.

" 'Sometimes they was locked up without food for days together. But it's my belief that little Miss Margaret managed to feed them somehow. Oh, I can see her creeping to the door and comforting!'

" 'But perhaps she never showed herself when these awful people were here, but took to flight until they left.'

" 'You didn't never know her, miss. That brave she was! She'd have stood up to lions. She've been here all the while: and only to think what her innocent eyes and ears must have took in! There was another couple . . .' Mrs Carkeek sunk her voice.

" 'Oh, hush!' said I, 'if I'm to have any peace of mind in this house!'

" 'But you won't go, miss? She loves you, I know she do. And think what you might be leaving her to – what sort of tenant might come next. For she can't go. She've been here ever since her father sold the place. He died soon after. You mustn't go!'

"Now I had resolved to go, but all of a sudden I felt how mean this resolution was.

" 'After all,' said I, 'there's nothing to be afraid of.'

" 'That's it, miss; nothing at all. I don't even believe it's so very uncommon. Why, I've heard my mother tell of farm-houses where the rooms were swept every night as regular as clockwork, and the floors sanded, and the pots and pans scoured, and all while the maids slept. They put it down to the piskies; but we know better, miss, and now we've got the secret between us we can lie easy in our beds, and if we hear anything, say, "God bless the child!" and go to sleep.'

"I spent three years at Tresillack, and all that while Mrs Carkeek lived with me and shared the secret. Few women, I dare to say, were ever so completely wrapped around with love as we were during those five years.

"It ran through my waking life like a song: it smoothed my pillow, touched and made my table comely, in summer lifted the heads of the flowers as I passed, and in winter watched the fire with me and kept it bright.

" 'Why did I ever leave Tresillack?' Because one day, at the end of five years, Farmer Hosking brought me word that he had sold the house – or was about to sell it; I forget which. There was no avoiding it, at any rate; the purchaser being a Colonel Kendall, a brother of the old Squire.

" 'A married man?' I asked.

" 'Yes, miss; with a family of eight. As pretty children as ever you see, and the mother a good lady. It's the old home to Colonel Kendall.'

" 'I see. And that is why you feel bound to sell.'

" 'It's a good price, too, that he offers. You mustn't think but I'm sorry enough . . .'

" 'To turn me out? I thank you, Mr Hosking; but you are doing the right thing.'

" 'She – Margaret – will be happy,' I said; 'with her cousins, you know.'

" 'Oh, yes, miss, she will be happy, sure enough,' Mrs Carkeek agreed.

"So when the time came I packed up my boxes and tried to be cheerful. But on the last morning, when they stood corded in the hall, I sent Mrs Carkeek upstairs upon some poor excuse, and stepped alone into the pantry.

" 'Margaret!' I whispered.

"There was no answer at all. I had scarcely dared to hope for one. Yet I tried again, and, shutting my eyes this time, stretched out both hands and whispered:

" 'Margaret!'

"And I will swear to my dying day that two little hands stole and rested – for a moment only – in mine."

Feet Foremost

L. P. Hartley

The house warming at Low Threshold Hall was not an event that affected many people. The local newspaper, however, had half a column about it, and one or two daily papers supplemented the usual August dearth of topics with pictures of the house. They were all taken from the same angle, and showed a long, low building in the Queen Anne style flowing away from a square tower on the left which was castellated and obviously of much earlier date, the whole structure giving somewhat the impression to a casual glance of a domesticated church, or even of a small railway train that had stopped dead on finding itself in a park. Beneath the photograph was written something like "Suffolk Manor House re-occupied after a hundred and fifty years", and, in one instance, "Inset (L.) Mr Charles Ampleforth, owner of Low Threshold Hall; (R.) Sir George Willings, the architect responsible for the restoration of this interesting medieval relic." Mr Ampleforth's handsome, slightly Disraelian head, nearly spiked on his own flagpole, smiled congratulations at the grey hair and rounded features of Sir George Willings who, suspended like a bubble above the Queen Anne wing, discreetly smiled back.

To judge from the photograph, time had dealt gently with Low Threshold Hall. Only a trained observer could have told how much of the original fabric had been renewed. The tower looked particularly convincing. While as for the gardens sloping down to the stream which bounded the foreground of the picture – they had that old-world air which gardens so quickly acquire. To see those lush lawns and borders as a meadow, that mellow brickwork under scaffolding, needed a strong effort of the imagination.

But the guests assembled in Mr Ampleforth's drawing room after dinner and listening to their host as, not for the first time, he enlarged upon the obstacles faced and overcome in the work of restoration, found it just as hard to believe that the house was old. Most of them had been taken to see it, at one time or another, in process of reconstruction; yet even within a few days of its completion, how unfinished a house looks! Its habitability seems determined in the last few hours. Magdalen Winthrop, whose beautiful, expressive face still (to her hostess's sentimental eye) bore traces of the slight disappointment she had suffered earlier in the evening, felt as if she were in an Aladdin's palace. Her glance wandered appreciatively from the Samarcand rugs to the pale green walls, and dwelt with pleasure on the high shallow arch, flanked by slender columns, the delicate lines of which were emphasised by the darkness of the hall behind them. It all seemed so perfect and so new; not only every sign of decay but the very sense of age had been banished. How absurd not to be able to find a single grey hair, so to speak, in a house that had stood empty for a hundred and fifty years! Her eyes, still puzzled, came to rest on the company, ranged in an irregular circle round the fireplace.

"What's the matter, Maggie?" said a man at her side, obviously glad to turn the conversation away from bricks and mortar. "Looking for something?"

Mrs Ampleforth, whose still lovely skin under the abundant white hair made her face look like a rose in snow, bent forward over the cream-coloured satin bedspread she was embroidering and smiled. "I was only thinking," said Maggie, turning to her host whose recital had paused but not died upon his lips, "how surprised the owls and bats would be if they could come in and see the change in their old home."

"Oh, I do hope they won't," cried a high female voice from the depths of a chair whose generous proportions obscured the speaker.

"Don't be such a baby, Eileen," said Maggie's neighbour in tones that only a husband could have used. "Wait till you see the family ghost."

"Ronald, please! Have pity on my poor nerves!" The upper half of a tiny, childish, imploring face peered like a crescent moon over the rim of the chair.

"If there is a ghost," said Maggie, afraid that the original remark might be construed as a criticism, "I envy him his beautiful surroundings. I would willingly take his place."

"Hear, hear," agreed Ronald. "A very happy hunting-ground. Is there a ghost, Charles?"

There was a pause. They all looked at their host.

"Well," said Mr Ampleforth, who rarely spoke except after a pause and never without a slight impressiveness of manner, "there is and there isn't."

The silence grew even more respectful.

"The ghost of Low Threshold Hall," Mr Ampleforth continued, "is no ordinary ghost."

"It wouldn't be," muttered Ronald in an aside Maggie feared might be audible.

"It is for one thing," Mr Ampleforth pursued, "exceedingly considerate."

"Oh, how?" exclaimed two or three voices.

"It only comes by invitation."

"Can anyone invite it?"

"Yes, anyone."

There was nothing Mr Ampleforth liked better than answering questions; he was evidently enjoying himself now.

"How is the invitation delivered?" Ronald asked. "Does one telephone, or does one send a card: 'Mrs Ampleforth requests the pleasure of Mr Ghost's company on – well – what is tomorrow? – the eighteenth August, Moaning and Groaning and Chain Rattling, R.S.V.P.'?"

"That would be a sad solecism," said Mr Ampleforth. "The ghost of Low Threshold Hall is a lady."

"Oh," cried Eileen's affected little voice, "I'm so thankful, I should be much less frightened of a female phantom."

"She hasn't attained years of discretion," Mr Ampleforth said. "She was only sixteen when –"

"Then she's not 'out'?"

"Not in the sense you mean. I hope she's not 'out' in any sense," said Mr Ampleforth, with grim facetiousness.

There was a general shudder.

"Well, I'm glad we can't ask her to an evening party," observed Ronald, "A ghost at tea-time is much less alarming. Is she what is called a 'popular' girl?"

"I'm afraid not."

"Then why do people invite her?"

"They don't realise what they're doing."

"A kind of pig in a poke business, what? But you haven't told us yet how we're to get hold of the little lady."

"That's quite simple," said Mr Ampleforth readily. "She comes to the door."

The drawing-room clock began to strike eleven, and no one spoke till it had finished.

"She comes to the door," said Ronald with an air of deliberation, "and then – don't interrupt, Eileen, I'm in charge of the cross-examination – she – she hangs about –"

"She waits to be asked inside."

"I suppose there is a time-honoured formula of invitation: 'Sweet Ermyntrude, in the name of the master of the house, I bid thee welcome to Low Threshold Hall. There's no step, so you can walk straight in.' Charles, much as I admire your house, I do think it's incomplete without a doorstep. A ghost could just sail in."

"There you make a mistake," said Mr Ampleforth impressively. "Our ghost cannot enter the house unless she is lifted across the threshold."

"Like a bride," exclaimed Magdalen.

"Yes," said Mr Ampleforth. "Because she came as a bride." He looked round at his guests with an enigmatic smile.

They did not disappoint him. "Now, Charlie, don't be so mysterious! Do tell us! Tell us the whole story."

Mr Ampleforth settled himself into his chair. "There's very

little to tell," he said, with the reassuring manner of someone who intends to tell a great deal, "but this is the tale. In the time of the Wars of the Roses the owner of Low Threshold Hall (I need not tell you his name was not Ampleforth) married 'en troisièmes noces' the daughter of a neighbouring baron much less powerful than he. Lady Elinor Stortford was sixteen when she came and did not live to see her seventeenth birthday. Her husband was a bad hat (I'm sorry to have to say so of a predecessor of mine), a very bad hat. He ill-treated her, drove her mad with terror, and finally killed her."

The narrator paused dramatically, but the guests felt slightly disappointed. They had heard so many stories of the kind.

"Poor thing," said Magdalen, feeling that some comment was necessary, however flat. "So now she haunts the place. I suppose it's the nature of ghosts to linger where they've suffered, but it seems illogical to me. I should want to go somewhere else."

"The Lady Elinor would agree with you. The first thing she does when she gets into the house is make plans for getting out. Her visits, as far as I can gather, have generally been brief."

"Then why does she come?" asked Eileen.

"She comes for vengeance." Mr Ampleforth's voice dropped at the word. "And apparently she gets it. Within a short time of her appearance, someone in the house always dies."

"Nasty spiteful little girl," said Ronald, concealing a yawn. "Then how long is she in residence?"

"Until her object is accomplished."

"Does she make a dramatic departure – in a thunderstorm or something?"

"No, she is just carried out."

"Who carries her this time?"

"The undertaker's men. She goes out with the corpse. Though some say –"

"Oh, Charlie, do stop!" Mrs Ampleforth interrupted,

bending down to gather up the corners of her bedspread. "Eileen will never sleep. Let's go to bed."

"No! No!" shouted Ronald. "He can't leave off like that. I must hear the rest. My flesh was just beginning to creep."

Mr Ampleforth looked at his wife. "I've had my orders."

"Well, well," said Ronald, resigned, "Anyhow, remember what I said. A decent fall of rain, and you'll have a foot of water under the tower there, unless you put in a door-step."

Mr Ampleforth looked grave. "Oh no, I couldn't do that. That would be to invite er – er – trouble. The absence of a step was a precaution. That's how the house got its name."

"A precaution against what?"

"Against Lady Elinor."

"But how? I should have thought a drawbridge would have been more effective?"

"Lord Deadham's immediate heirs thought the same. According to the story they put every material obstacle they could to bar the lady's path. You can still see in the tower the grooves which contained the portcullis. And there was a flight of stairs so steep and dangerous they couldn't be used without risk to life and limb. But that only made it easier for Lady Elinor."

"How did it?"

"Why, don't you see, everyone who came to the house, friends and strangers alike, had to be helped over the threshold! There was no way of distinguishing between them. At last when so many members of the family had been killed off that it was threatened with extinction, someone conceived a brilliant idea. Can you guess what it was, Maggie?"

"They removed all the barriers and levelled the threshold, so that any stranger who came to the door and asked to be helped into the house was refused admittance."

"Exactly, and the plan seems to have worked remarkably well."

"But the family did die out in the end," observed Maggie.

"Yes," said Mr Ampleforth, "soon after the middle of the

eighteenth century. The best human plans are fallible, and Lady Elinor was very persistent."

He held the company with his glittering raconteur's eye.

But Mrs Ampleforth was standing up. "Now, now," she said, "I gave you twenty minutes' grace. It will soon be midnight. Come along, Maggie, you must be tired after your journey. Let me light you a candle." She took the girl's arm and piloted her into the comparative darkness of the hall. "I think they must be on this table," she said, her fingers groping; "I don't know the house myself yet. We ought to have had a light put here. But it's one of Charlie's little economies to have as few lights as possible. I'll tell him about it. But it takes so long to get anything done in this out-of-the-way spot. My dear, nearly three miles to the nearest clergyman, four to the nearest doctor! Ah, here we are, I'll light some for the others. Charlie is still holding forth about Lady Elinor. You didn't mind that long recital?" she added, as, accompanied by their shadows, they walked up the stairs. "Charlie does so love an audience. And you don't feel uncomfortable or anything? I am always so sorry for Lady Elinor, poor soul, if she ever existed. Oh, and I wanted to say we were so disappointed about Antony. I feel we got you down today on false pretences. Something at the office kept him. But he's coming tomorrow. When is the wedding to be, dearest?"

"In the middle of September."

"Quite soon, now. I can't tell you how excited I am about it. I think he's such a dear. You both are. Now which is your way, left, right or middle? I'm ashamed to say I've forgotten."

Maggie considered. "I remember; it's to the left."

"In that black abyss? Oh, darling, I forgot; do you feel equal to going on the picnic tomorrow? We shan't get back till five. It'll be a long day; I'll stay at home with you if you like – I'm tired of ruins."

"I'd love to go."

"Goodnight, then."

"Goodnight."

In the space of ten minutes the two men, left to themselves, had succeeded in transforming the elegant Queen Mary drawing-room into something that looked and smelt like a bar-parlour.

"Well," observed Ronald who, more than his host, had been responsible for the room's deterioration, "time to turn in. I have a rendezvous with Lady Elinor. By the way, Charles," he went on, "have you given the servants instructions in anti-Elinor technique – told them only to admit visitors who can enter the house under their own steam, so to speak?"

"Mildred thought it wisest, and I agree with her," said Mr Ampleforth, "to tell the servants nothing at all. It might unsettle them, and we shall have hard work to keep them as it is."

"Perhaps you're right," said Ronald. "Anyhow it's no part of their duty to show the poor lady out. Charles, what were you going to say that wasn't fit for ears polite when Mildred stopped you?"

Mr Ampleforth reflected, "I wasn't aware . . ."

"Oh, yes, she nipped your smoking-room story in the bud. I asked, 'Who carried Lady Elinor out?' and you said, 'The undertaker's men, she goes out with the corpse', and you were going to say something else when you were called to order."

"Oh, I remember," said Mr Ampleforth. "It was such a small point, I couldn't imagine why Mildred objected. According to one story, she doesn't go out *with* the corpse, she goes out *in* it."

Ronald pondered. "Don't see much difference, do you?"

"I can't honestly say I do."

"Women are odd creatures," Ronald said. "So long."

*

The cat stood by the library door, miaowing. Its intention was perfectly plain. First it had wanted to go out; then it strolled up and down outside the window, demanding to come in; now it wanted to go out again. For the third time in half an hour Antony Fairfield rose from his comfortable chair to do its bidding. He opened the door gently – all his movements were gentle; but the cat scuttled ignominiously out, as though he had kicked it. Antony looked round. How could he defend himself from disturbance without curtailing the cat's liberty of movement? He might leave the window and the door open, to give the animal freedom of exit and entrance; though he hated sitting in a room with the door open, he was prepared to make the sacrifice. But he couldn't leave the window open because the rain would come in and spoil Mrs Ampleforth's beautiful silk cushions. Heavens, how it rained! Too bad for the farmers, thought Antony, whose mind was always busying itself with other people's misfortunes. The crops had been looking so well as he drove in the sunshine from the station, and now this sudden storm would beat everything down. He arranged his chair so that he could see the window and not keep the cat waiting if she felt like paying him another visit. The pattering of the rain soothed him. Half an hour and they would be back – Maggie would be back. He tried to visualise their faces, all so well known to him; but the experiment was not successful. Maggie's image kept ousting the others; it even appeared, somewhat grotesquely, on the top of Ronald's well-tailored shoulders. They mustn't find me asleep, thought Antony; I should look too middle-aged. So he picked up the newspaper from the floor and turned to the cross-word puzzle. "Nine points of the law" in nine-ten letters. That was a very easy one: "Possession." Possession, thought Antony; I must put that down. But as he had no pencil and was too sleepy to get one, he repeated the word over and over again: Possession, Possession. It worked like a charm. He fell asleep and dreamed.

In his dream he was still in the library, but it was night and somehow his chair had got turned around so that he no longer faced the window, but he knew that the cat was there, asking to come in; only someone – Maggie – was trying to persuade him not to let it in. "It's not a cat at all," she kept saying; "it's a Possession. I can see its nine points and they're very sharp." But he knew that she was mistaken, and really meant nine lives, which all cats have: so he thrust her aside and ran to the window and opened it. It was too dark to see, so he put out his hand where he thought the cat's body would be, expecting to feel the warm fur; but what met his hand was not warm, nor was it fur . . . He woke with a start to see the butler standing in front of him. The room was flooded with sunshine.

"Oh, Rundle," he cried, "I was asleep. Are they back?"

The butler smiled.

"No, sir, but I expect them every minute now."

"But you wanted me?"

"Well, sir, there's a young lady called, and I said the master was out, but she said could she speak to the gentleman in the library? She must have seen you, sir, as she passed the window."

"How very odd. Does she know me?"

"That was what she said, sir. She talks rather funny."

"All right. I'll come."

Antony followed the butler down the long corridor. When they reached the tower their footsteps ran on the paved floor. A considerable pool of water, the result of the recent heavy shower, had formed on the flagstones near the doorway. The door stood open, letting in a flood of light, but of the caller there was no sign.

"She was here a moment ago," the butler said.

"Ah, I see her," cried Antony. "At least, isn't that her reflected in the water? She must be leaning against the door-post."

"That's right," said Rundle. "Mind the puddle, sir. Let me give you a hand. I'll have all this cleared up before they come back."

Five minutes later two cars, closely following each other, pulled up at the door, and the picnic party tumbled out.

"Dear me, how wet!" cried Mrs Ampleforth, standing in the doorway. "What has happened, Rundle? Has there been a flood?"

"It was much worse before you arrived, madam," said the

butler, disappointed that his exertions with mop, floor-cloth, scrubbing-brush and pail were being so scantily recognised. "You could have sailed a boat on it. Mr Antony, he . . ."

"Oh, has he arrived? Antony's here, isn't that splendid?"

"Antony!" they all shouted. "Come out! Come down! Where are you?"

"I bet he's asleep, the lazy devil," remarked Ronald.

"No, sir," said the butler, at last able to make himself heard. "Mr Antony's in the drawing-room with a lady."

Mrs Ampleforth's voice broke the silence that succeeded this announcement.

"With a lady, Rundle? Are you sure?"

"Well, madam, she's hardly more than a girl."

"I always thought Antony was that sort of man," observed Ronald. "Maggie, you'd better . . ."

"It's too odd," interposed Mrs Ampleforth hastily, "who in the world can she be?"

"I don't see there's anything odd in someone calling on us," said Mr Ampleforth. "What's her name, Rundle?"

"She didn't give a name, sir,"

"That is rather extraordinary. Antony is so impulsive and kind-hearted. I hope – ah, here he is."

Antony came towards them along the passage, smiling and waving his hands. When the welcoming and handshaking were over:

"We were told you had a visitor," said Mrs Ampleforth.

"Yes," said Ronald. "I'm afraid we arrived at the wrong moment."

Antony laughed and then looked puzzled. "Believe me, you didn't," he said. "You almost saved my life. She speaks such a queer dialect when she speaks at all, and I had reached the end of my small talk. But she's rather interesting. Do come along and see her: I left her in the library." They followed Antony down the passage. When they reached the door he said to Mrs Ampleforth:

"Shall I go in first? She may be shy at meeting so many people."

He went in. A moment later they heard his voice raised in excitement.

"Mildred! I can't find her! She's gone!"

*

Tea had been cleared away, but Antony's strange visitor was still the topic of conversation. "I can't understand it," he was saying, not for the first time. "The windows were shut, and if she'd gone by the door we must have seen her."

"Now, Antony," said Ronald severely, "let's hear the whole story again. Remember, you are accused of smuggling into the house a female of doubtful reputation. Furthermore the prosecution alleges that when you heard us call (we were shouting ourselves hoarse, but he didn't come at once, you remember) you popped her out of that window and came out to meet us, smiling sheepishly, and feebly gesticulating. What do you say?"

"I've told you everything," said Antony. "I went to the door and found her leaning against the stonework. Her eyes were shut. She didn't move and I thought she must be ill. So I said, 'Is anything the matter?' and she looked up and said, 'My leg hurts'. Then I saw by the way she was standing that her hip must have been broken once and never properly set. I asked her where she lived, and she didn't seem to understand me; so I changed the form of the question, as one does on the telephone, and asked where she came from, and she said, 'A little further down', meaning down the hill, I suppose."

"Probably from one of the men's cottages," said Mrs Ampleforth.

"I asked if it was far, and she said 'No', which was obvious, otherwise her clothes would have been wet and they weren't, only a little muddy. She even had some mud on her medieval bridesmaid's head-dress (I can't describe her clothes again, Mildred; you know how bad I am at that). So I asked if she'd had a fall, and she said, 'No, I got dirty coming up,' or so I understood her. It wasn't easy to understand her; I suppose she talked the dialect of these parts. I concluded (you all say you would have known long before) that she was a little mad, but I didn't like to leave her looking so rotten, so I said, 'Won't you come in and rest a minute?' Then I wished I hadn't."

"Because she looked so pleased?"

"Oh, much more than pleased. And she said, 'I hope you won't live to regret it', rather as though she hoped I should. And then I only meant just to take her hand, because of the water, you know, and she was lame . . ."

"And instead she flung herself into the poor fellow's arms . . ."

"Well, it amounted to that. I had no option! So I carried her across and put her down and she followed me here, walking better than I expected. A minute later you arrived; I asked her to wait and she didn't. That's all."

"I should like to have seen Antony doing the St Christopher act!" said Ronald. "Was she heavy, old boy?"

Antony shifted his chair. "Oh, no," he said, "not at all. Not at all heavy." Unconsciously he stretched his arms out in front of him, as though testing an imaginary weight. "I see my hands are grubby," he said with an expression of distaste. "I must go and wash them. I won't be a moment, Maggie."

*

That night, after dinner, there was some animated conversation in the servants' hall.

"Did you hear any more, Mr Rundle?" asked a housemaid of the butler, who had returned from performing his final office at the dinner-table.

"I did," said Rundle, "but I don't know that I ought to tell you."

"It won't make any difference, Mr Rundle, whether you do or don't. I'm going to give in my notice tomorrow. I won't stay in a haunted house. We've been lured here. We ought to have been warned."

"They certainly meant to keep it from us," said Rundle. "I myself had put two and two together after seeing Lady

Elinor; what Wilkins said when he came in for his tea only confirmed my suspicions. No gardener can ever keep a still tongue in his head. It's a pity."

"Wouldn't you have told us yourself, Mr Rundle?" asked the cook.

"I should have used my discretion," the butler replied. "When I informed Mr Ampleforth that I was no longer in ignorance, he said, 'I rely on you, Rundle, not to say anything which might alarm the staff'."

"Mean, I call it," exclaimed the kitchen-maid indignantly. "They want to have all the fun and leave us to die like rats in a trap."

Rundle ignored the interruption.

"I told Mr Ampleforth that Wilkins had been tale-bearing and would he excuse it in an outdoor servant, but unfortunately we were now in possession of the facts."

"That's why they talked about it at dinner," said the maid who helped Rundle to wait.

"They didn't really throw the mask off till after you'd gone, Lizzie," said the butler. "Then I began to take part in the conversation."

He paused for a moment.

"Mr Ampleforth asked me whether anything was missing from the house, and I was able to reply, 'No, everything was in order'."

"What else did you say?" inquired the cook.

"I made the remark that the library window wasn't fastened, as they thought, but only closed, and Mrs Turnbull laughed and said, 'Perhaps it's only a thief, after all', but the others didn't think she could have got through the window anyhow, unless her lameness was all put on. And then I told them what the police had said about looking out for a suspicious character."

"Did they seem frightened?" asked the cook.

"Not noticeably," replied the butler. "Mrs Turnbull said she hoped the gentlemen wouldn't stay long over their port. Mr Ampleforth said, 'No, they have had a full day, and would be glad to go to bed'. Mrs Ampleforth asked Miss Winthrop if she wanted to change her bedroom, but she said she didn't. Then Mr Fairfield asked if he could have some iodine for his hand, and Miss Winthrop said she would fetch him some. She wanted to bring it after dinner, but he said, 'Oh, tomorrow morning will do, darling'. He seemed rather quiet."

"What's he done to his hand?"

"I saw the mark when he took his coffee. It was like a burn."

"They didn't say they were going to shut the house up, or anything?"

"Oh, Lord, no. There's going to be a party next week. They'll all have to stay for that."

"I never knew such people," said the kitchen-maid. "They'd rather die, and us too, than miss their pleasures. I wouldn't stay another day if I wasn't forced. When you think she may be here in this very room, listening to us!" She shuddered.

"Don't you worry, my girl," said Rundle, rising from his chair with a gesture of dismissal. "She won't waste her time listening to you."

"We really might be described as a set of crocks," said Mr Ampleforth to Maggie, after luncheon the following day. "You, poor dear, with your headache; Eileen with her nerves; I with – well – a touch of rheumatism; Antony with his bad arm."

Maggie looked troubled.

"My headache is nothing, but I'm afraid Antony isn't very well."

"He's gone to lie down, hasn't he?"

"Yes."

"The best thing. I telephoned for the doctor to come this evening. He can have a look at all of us, ha! ha! Meanwhile, where will you spend the afternoon? I think the library's the coolest place on a stuffy day like this and I did want you to see my collection of books about Low Threshold – my Thresholdiana I call them."

Maggie followed him into the library.

"Here they are. Most of them are nineteenth-century books, publications of the Society of Antiquaries, and so on; but some are older. I got a little man in Charing Cross Road to hunt them out for me; I haven't had time to read them all myself."

Maggie took a book at random from the shelves.

"Now I'll leave you," said her host. "And later in the afternoon I know that Eileen would appreciate a little visit. Ronald says it's nothing, just a little nervous upset, stomach trouble. Between ourselves, I fear Lady Elinor is to blame."

Maggie opened the book. It was called *An Enquiry into the Recent Tragicall Happennings at Low Threshold Hall in the County of Suffolk, with some Animadversions on the Barbarous Customs of our Ancestors*. It opened with a rather tedious account of the semi-mythical origins of the Deadham family. Maggie longed to skip this, but she might have to discuss the book with Mr Ampleforth, so she ploughed on. Her persistence was rewarded by a highly coloured picture of Lady Elinor's husband and an account of the cruelties he practised on her. The story would have been too painful to read had not the author (Maggie felt) so obviously drawn upon a very vivid imagination. But suddenly her eyes narrowed. What was this?

*

– Once in a Drunken Fitt he so mishandled her that her thigh was broken near the hip, and her screams were so loud they were heard by the servants through three closed doores; and yet he would not summon a Chirurgeon, for (quoth he) . . .

– Lord Deadham's reason was coarse in the extreme; Maggie hastened on.

And in consequence of these Barbarities, her nature, which was soft and yielding at the first, was greatly changed, and those who sawe her now (but Pitie seal'd their lips) would have said she had a Bad Hearte.

No wonder, thought Maggie, reading with a new and painful interest how the murdered woman avenged herself on various descendants, direct and collateral, of her persecutor.

And it had been generally supposed by the vulgar that her vengeance was directed only against members of that family from which she had taken so many Causeless Hurtes; and the depraved, defective, counterfeit records of those times have lent colour to this Opinion. Whereas the truth is as I now state it, having had access to those deathbed and testamentary depositions which, preserved in ink, however faint, do greater service to verity than the relations of Pot-House Historians, enlarged by Memory and confused by Ale. Yet it is on such Testimonies that rash and sceptical Heads rely when they assert that the Lady Elinor had no hand in the later Horrid Occurrence at Low Threshold Hall, which I shall presently describe, thinking that a meer visitor and no blood relation could not be the object of her vengeance, notwithstanding the evidence of two serving-maids one at the door and one craning her neck from an upper casement, who saw him beare her in: The truth being that she maketh no distinction between persons, but whoso admits her, on him doth her vengeance fall. Seven times she hath brought death to Low Threshold Hall; Three, it is true, being members of the family, but the remaining four indifferent Persons and not connected with them, having in common only this piece of folie, that they, likewise, let her in. And in each case she hath used the same manner of attack, as those who have beheld her first a room's length, then no further than a Lover's Embrace, from her victim have 'in articulo mortis' delivered. And the moment when she is no longer seen, which to the watchers seems the Clarion and Reveille of their hopes, is in reality the knell; for she hath not withdrawn further, but approached nearer, she hath not gone out but entered in: and from her dreadful Citadel within the body rejoyces, doubtless, to see the tears and hear the groanes, of those who with Comfortable Faces (albeit with sinking Hearts), would soothe the passage of the parting Soul. Their lacrimatory effusions are balm to her wicked Minde; the sad gale and ventilation of their sighs a pleasing Zephyr to her vindictive spirit.

Maggie put down the book for a moment and stared in front of her. Then she began again to read.

*

Once only hath she been cheated of her Prey, and it happened thus. His Bodie was already swollen with the malignant Humours she had stirred up in him and his life despaired of when a kitchen-wench was taken with an Imposthume that bled inwardly. She being of small account and but lately arrived they did only lay her in the Strawe, charging the Physician (and he nothing loth, expecting no Glory or Profitt from attendance on such a wretched creature) not to divide his Efforts but use all his skill to save their Cousin (afterwards the twelfth Lord). Notwithstanding which precaution he did hourly get worse until sodainely a change came and he began to amend. Whereat was such rejoycing (including an Ox roasted whole) that the night was spent before they heard that the serving-maid was dead. In their Revels they gave small heed to this Event, not realising that they owed His life to Hers; for a fellow-servant who tended the maid (out of charity) declared that her death and the cousin's recovery followed as quickly as a clock striking Two. And the Physician said it was well, for she would have died in any case.

Whereby we must conclude that the Lady Elinor, like other Apparitions, is subject to certain Lawes. One, to abandon her Victim and seeking another tenement to transfer her vengeance, should its path be crossed by a

Body yet nearer Dissolution; and another is, she cannot possess or haunt the corpse after it hath received Christian Buriall. As witness the fact that the day after the interment of the tenth Lord she again appeared at the Doore and being recognised by her inability to make the Transit was turned away and pelted. And another thing I myself believe but have no proof of is: That her power is circumscribed by the walls of the House; those victims of her Malignitie could have been saved but for the dreadful swiftness of the disease and the doctors unwillingness to move a Sicke man; otherwise how could the Termes of her Curse that she pronounced be fulfilled: "They shall be carried out Feet Foremost"?

*

Maggie read no more. She walked out of the library with the book under her arm. Before going to see how Antony was, she would put it in her bedroom where no one could find it. Troubled and oppressed, she paused at the head of the stairs. Her way lay straight ahead, but her glance automatically travelled to the right where, at the far end of the passage, Antony's bedroom lay. She looked again; the door which she could only just see, was shut now. But she could swear it had closed upon a woman. There was nothing odd in that; Mildred might have gone in, or Muriel, or a servant. But all the same she could not rest. Hurriedly she changed her dress and went to Antony's room. Pausing at the door she listened and distinctly heard his voice, speaking rapidly and in a low tone; but no one seemed to reply. She got no answer to her knock, so, mustering her courage, she walked in.

The blind was down and the room half dark, and the talking continued, which increased her uneasiness. Then, as her eyes got used to the darkness, she realised, with a sense of relief, that he was talking in his sleep. She pulled up the blind a little, so that she might see his hand. The brown mark had spread, she thought, and looked rather puffy as though coffee had been injected under the skin. She felt concerned for him.

He would never have gone properly to bed like that, in his pyjamas, if he hadn't felt ill, and he tossed about restlessly. Maggie bent over him. Perhaps he had been eating a biscuit; there was some gritty stuff on the pillow. She tried to scoop it up but it eluded her. She could make no sense of his mutterings, but the word "light" came in a good deal. Perhaps he was only half asleep and wanted the blind down. At last her ears caught the sentence which was running on his lips: "She was so light." Light? A light woman? Browning. The words conveyed nothing to her, and not wishing to wake him she tiptoed from the room.

"The doctor doesn't seem to think seriously of any of us, Maggie, you'll be glad to hear," said Mr Ampleforth, coming into the drawing-room about six o'clock. "Eileen's coming down to dinner. I am to drink less port – I didn't need a doctor, alas! to tell me that. Antony's the only casualty; he's got a slight temperature, and had better stay where he is until tomorrow. The doctor thinks it is one of those damnable horseflies; his arm is a bit swollen, that's all."

"Has he gone?" asked Maggie quickly.

"Who, Antony?"

"No, no, the doctor."

"Oh, I'd forgotten your poor head. No, you'll just catch him. His car's on the terrace."

The doctor, a kindly, harassed, middle-aged man, listened patiently to Maggie's questions.

"The brown mark? Oh, that's partly the inflammation, partly the iodine – he's been applying it pretty liberally, you know; amateur physicians are all alike; feel they can't have too much of a good thing."

"You don't think the water here's responsible? I wondered if he ought to go away."

"The water? Oh, no. No, it's a bite all right, though I confess I can't see the place where the devil got his beak in. I'll come tomorrow, if you like, but there's really no need."

The next morning, returning from his bath, Ronald

marched into Antony's room. The blind went up with a whizz and a smack, and Antony opened his eyes.

"Good morning, old man," said Ronald cheerfully, "Thought I'd look in and see you. How goes the blood-poisoning? Better?"

Antony drew up his sleeve and hastily replaced it. The arm beneath was chocolate-coloured to the elbow.

"I feel pretty rotten," he said.

"I say, that's bad luck. What's this?" added Ronald, coming nearer, "Have you been sleeping in both beds?"

"Not to my knowledge," murmured Antony.

"You have, though," said Ronald. "If this bed hasn't been slept in, it's been slept on, or lain on. That I can swear. Only a head, my boy, could have put that dent in the pillow, and only a pair of muddy – hullo! The pillow's got it, too."

"Got what?" asked Antony drowsily.

"Well, if you ask me, it's common garden mould."

"I'm not surprised. I feel pretty mouldy too."

"Well, Antony; to save your good name with the servants, I'll remove the traces."

With characteristic vigour Ronald swept and smoothed the bed.

"Now you'll be able to look Rundle in the face."

There was a knock at the door.

"If this is Maggie," said Ronald, "I'm going."

It was, and he suited the action to the word.

"You needn't trouble to tell me, dearest," she said, "that you are feeling much better, because I can see that you aren't."

Antony moved his head uneasily on the pillow.

"I don't feel very flourishing, to tell you the honest truth."

"Listen" – Maggie tried to make her voice sound casual – "I don't believe this is a very healthy place. Don't laugh, Antony; we're all of us more or less under the weather. I think you ought to go away."

"My dear, don't be hysterical. One often feels rotten when one wakes up. I shall be all right in a day or two."

"Of course you will. But all the same if you were in Sussex Square you could call in Fosbrook – and, well, I should be more comfortable."

"But you'd be here!"

"I could stay at Pamela's."

"But, darling, that would break up the party. I couldn't do it; and it wouldn't be fair to Mildred."

"My angel, you're no good to the party, lying here in bed. And as long as you're here, let me warn you they won't see much of me."

A look of irritation Maggie had never noticed before came into his face as he said, almost spitefully:

"Supposing the doctor won't allow you to come in? It may be catching, you know."

Maggie concealed the hurt she felt.

"All the more reason for you to be out of the house."

He pulled up the bedclothes with a gesture of annoyance and turned away.

"Oh, Maggie, don't keep nagging at me. You ought to be called Naggie, not Maggie."

This was an allusion to an incident in Maggie's childhood. Her too great solicitude for a younger brother's safety had provoked the gibe. It had always wounded her, but never so much as coming from Antony's lips. She rose to go.

"Do put the bed straight," said Antony, still with face averted. "Otherwise they'll think you've been sleeping here."

"What?"

"Well, Ronald said something about it."

Maggie closed the door softly behind her. Antony was ill, of course, she must remember that. But he had been ill before, and was always an angelic patient. She went down to breakfast feeling miserable.

After breakfast, at which everyone else had been unusually cheerful, she thought of a plan. It did not prove so easy of execution as she hoped.

"But, dearest Maggie," said Mildred, "the village is nearly three miles away. And there's nothing to see there."

"I love country post-offices," said Maggie, "They always have such amusing things."

"There is a post-office," admitted Mildred. "But are you sure it isn't something we could do from here? Telephone, telegraph?"

"Perhaps there'd be a picture-postcard of the house," said Maggie feebly.

"Oh, but Charlie has such nice ones," Mildred protested. "He's so house-proud, you could trust him for that. Don't leave us for two hours just to get postcards. We shall miss you so much, and think of poor Antony left alone all the morning."

Maggie had been thinking of him.

"He'll get on all right without me," she said lightly.

"Well, wait till the afternoon when the chauffeur or Ronald can run you over in a car. He and Charlie have gone into Norwich and won't be back till lunch."

"I think I'll walk," said Maggie. "It'll do me good."

"I managed that very clumsily," she thought, "so how shall I persuade Antony to tell me the address of his firm?"

To her surprise his room was empty. He must have gone away in the middle of writing a letter, for there were sheets lying about on the writing table and, what luck! an envelope addressed to Higgins & Stukeley, 312 Paternoster Row. A glance was all she really needed to memorise the address; but her eyes wandered to the litter on the table. What a mess! There were several pages of notepapers covered with figures. Antony had been making calculations and, as was his habit, decorating them with marginal illustrations. He was good at drawing faces, and he had a gift for catching a likeness. Maggie had often seen, and been gratified to see, slips of paper embellished with portraits of herself – full-face, side-face, three-quarter-face. But this face that looked out from among the figures and seemed to avoid her glance, was not hers. It was the face of a woman she had never seen before but whom she felt she would recognise anywhere, so consistent and vivid were the likenesses. Scattered among the loose leaves were the contents of Antony's pocket-book. She knew he always carried her photograph. Where was it? Seized by an impulse, she began to rummage among the papers. Ah, here it was. But it was no longer hers! With a few strokes, Antony had transformed her oval face, unlined and soft of feature, into a totally different one, a pinched face with high cheekbones, hollow cheeks, and bright hard eyes from whose corners a sheaf of fine wrinkles spread like a fan: a face with which she was already too familiar.

Unable to look at it, she turned away and saw Antony standing behind her. He seemed to have come from the bath for he carried a towel and was wearing his dressing-gown.

"Well," he said. "Do you think it's an improvement?"

She could not answer him, but walked over to the washstand, and took up the thermometer that was lying on it.

"Ought you to be walking about like that," she said at last, "with a temperature of a hundred?"

"Perhaps not," he replied, making two or three goat-like skips towards the bed. "But I feel rather full of beans this morning."

Maggie edged away from his smile towards the door.

"There isn't anything I can do for you?"

"Not today, my darling."

The term of endearment struck her like a blow.

*

Maggie sent off her telegram and turned into the village street. The fact of being able to do something had relieved her mind: already in imagination she saw Antony being packed into the Ampleforths' Daimler with rugs and hot-water bottles, and herself, perhaps, seated by the driver. They were endlessly kind and would make no bones about motoring him to London. But, though her spirits were rising her body felt tired; the day was sultry, and she had hurried. Another bad night like last night, she thought, and I shall be a wreck. There was a chemist's shop over the way, and she walked in.

"Can I have some sal volatile?"

"Certainly, madam."

She drank it and felt better.

"Oh, and have you anything in the way of a sleeping draught?"

"We have some allodanol tablets, madam."

"I'll take them."

"Have you a doctor's prescription?"

"No."

"Then I'm afraid you'll have to sign the poison book. Just a matter of form."

Maggie recorded her name, idly wondering what J. Bates, her predecessor on the list, meant to do with his cyanide of potassium.

*

"We must try not to worry," said Mrs Ampleforth handing Maggie her tea, "but I must say I'm glad the doctor has come. It relieves one of responsibility, doesn't it? Not that I feel disturbed about Antony – he was quite bright when I went to see him just before lunch. And he's been sleeping since. But I quite see what Maggie means. He doesn't seem himself. Perhaps it would be a good plan, as she suggests, to send him to London. He would have better advice there."

Rundle came in.

"A telegram for Mr Fairfield, madam."

"It's been telephoned: 'Your presence urgently required Tuesday morning – Higgins & Stukeley.' Tuesday, that's tomorrow. Everything seems to point to his going, doesn't it, Charles?"

Maggie was delighted, but a little surprised, that Mrs Ampleforth had fallen in so quickly with the plan of sending Antony home.

"Could he go today?" she asked.

"Tomorrow would be too late, wouldn't it?" said Mr Ampleforth drily. "The car's at his disposal; he can go whenever he likes."

Through her relief Maggie felt a little stab of pain that they were both so ready to see the last of Antony. He was generally such a popular guest.

"I could go with him," she said.

Instantly they were up in arms. Ronald the most vehement of all. "I'm sure Antony wouldn't want you to; you know what I mean, Maggie, it's such a long drive, in a closed car on a stuffy evening. Charlie says he'll send a man, if necessary."

Mr Ampleforth nodded.

"But if he were ill!" cried Maggie.

The entrance of the doctor cut her short. He looked rather grave.

"I wish I could say I was satisfied with Mr Fairfield's progress," he said, "but I can't. The inflammation has spread up the arm as far as the shoulder, and there's some fever. His manner is odd, too, excitable and apathetic by turns." He paused. "I should like a second opinion."

Mr Ampleforth glanced at his wife.

"In that case wouldn't it be better to send him to London? As a matter of fact, his firm had telegraphed for him. He could go quite comfortably in the car."

The doctor answered immediately:

"I wouldn't advise such a course. I think it would be most unwise to move him. His firm – you must excuse me – will have to do without him for a day or two."

"Perhaps," suggested Maggie trembling, "it's a matter that could be arranged at his house. They could send over someone from the office. I know they make a fuss about having him on the spot," she concluded lamely.

"Or, doctor," said Mr Ampleforth, "could you do us a very great kindness and go with him? We could telephone to his doctor to meet you, and the car would get you home by midnight."

The doctor squared his shoulders: he was clearly one of those men whose resolution stiffens under opposition.

"I consider it would be the height of folly," he said, "to move him out of the house. I dare not do it on my responsibility. I will get a colleague over from Ipswich tomorrow morning. In the meantime, with your permission, I will arrange for a trained nurse to be sent tonight."

Amid a subdued murmur of final instructions, the doctor left.

As Maggie, rather late, was walking upstairs to dress for dinner, she met Rundle. He looked anxious.

"Excuse me, miss," he said, "but have you seen Mr Fairfield? I've asked everyone else, and they haven't. I took up his supper half an hour ago, and he wasn't in his room. He'd got his dress clothes out, but they were all on the bed except the stiff shirt.

"Have you been to look since?" asked Maggie.

"No, miss."

"I'll go and see."

She tiptoed along the passage to Antony's door. A medley of sounds, footsteps, drawers being opened and shut, met her ears.

She walked back to Rundle. "He's in there all right," she said. "Now I must make haste and dress."

A few minutes later a bell rang in the kitchen.

"Who's that?"

"Miss Winthrop's room," said the cook. "Hurry up, Lettice, or you'll have Rundle on your track – he'll be back in a minute."

"I don't want to go," said Lettice. "I tell you I feel that nervous –"

"Nonsense, child," said the cook. "Run along with you."

No sooner had the maid gone than Rundle appeared.

"I've had a bit of trouble with Master Antony," he said. "He's got it into his head that he wants to come down to dinner. 'Rundle,' he said to me, confidentially, 'do you think it would matter us being seven? I want them to meet my new friend.' 'What friend, Mr Fairfield?' I said. 'Oh,' he said, 'haven't you seen her? She's always about with me now'. Poor chap, he used to be the pick of the bunch, and now I'm afraid he's going potty."

"Do you really think he'll come down to dinner?" asked

the cook, but before Rundle could answer Lettice rushed into the room.

"Oh," she cried, "I knew it would be something horrid! I knew it would be! And now she wants a floor cloth and pail! She says they mustn't know anything about it! But I won't go again – I won't bring it down. I won't even touch it."

"What won't you touch?"

"That waste-paper basket."

"Why, what's the matter with it?"

"It's . . . it's all bloody!"

When the word was out she grew calmer, and even seemed anxious to relate her experience.

"I went upstairs directly she rang" ("That's an untruth to start with," said the cook) "and she opened the door a little way and said, 'Oh, Lettice, I've been so scared!' And I said, 'What's the matter, miss?' and she said (deceitful-like, as it turned out), ' There's a cat in here.' Well, I didn't think that was much to be frightened of, so I said, 'Shall I come in and catch him, miss?' and she said, 'I should be so grateful.' Then I went in, but I couldn't see the cat anywhere, so I said, 'Where is he?' At which she pointed to the waste-paper basket away by the dressing-table and said, 'In that waste-paper basket.' I said, 'Why, that makes it easier, miss, if he'll stay there.' She said, 'Oh, he'll stay there all right.' Of course I took her meaning in a moment, because I know cats do choose queer, out-of-the-way places to die in, so I said, 'You mean the poor creature's dead, miss?' and I was just going across to get him because ordinarily I don't mind the body of an animal, when she said (I will do her that justice), 'Stop a minute, Lettice, he isn't dead; he's been murdered.' I saw she was all trembling, and that made me tremble, too. And when I looked in the basket – well –"

She paused, partly perhaps to enjoy the dramatic effect of her announcement. "Well, if it wasn't our Thomas! Only you couldn't have recognised him, poor beast, his head was bashed in that cruel."

"Thomas!" said the cook. "Why, he was here only an hour ago."

"That's what I said to Miss Winthrop, 'Why, he was in the kitchen only an hour ago,' and then I came over funny, and when she asked me to help her clean the mess up I couldn't, not if my life depended on it. But I don't feel like that now," she ended inconsequently. "I'll go back and do it!" She collected her traps and departed.

"Thomas!" muttered Rundle. "Who could have wished the poor beast any harm? Now I remember, Mr Fairfield did ask me to get him out a clean shirt . . . I'd better go up and ask him."

He found Antony in evening dress seated at the writing-table. He had stripped it of writing materials and the light from two candles gleamed on its polished surface. Opposite to him on the other side of the table was an empty chair. He was sitting with his back to the room; his face, when he turned it at Rundle's entrance, was blotchy and looked terribly tired.

"I decided to dine here after all, Rundle," he said. Rundle saw that the Bovril was still untouched in his cup.

"Why, your supper'll get cold, Mr Fairfield," he said.

"Mind your own business," said Antony, "I'm waiting."

*

The Empire clock on the drawing-room chimney-piece began to strike, breaking into a conversation which neither at dinner nor afterwards had been more than desultory.

"Eleven," said Mr Ampleforth. "The nurse will be here any time now. She ought to be grateful to you, Ronald, for getting him into bed."

"I didn't enjoy treating Antony like that," said Ronald.

There was a silence.

"What was that?" asked Maggie suddenly.

"It sounded like the motor."

"Might have been," said Mr Ampleforth. "You can't tell from here."

They strained their ears, but the rushing sound had already died away. "Eileen's gone to bed, Maggie," said Mrs Ampleforth. "Why don't you? We'll wait up for the nurse, and tell you when she comes."

Rather reluctantly, Maggie agreed to go.

She had been in her bedroom about ten minutes, and was feeling too tired to take her clothes off, when there came a knock at the door. It was Eileen.

"Maggie," she said, "the nurse has arrived. I thought you'd like to know."

"Oh, how kind of you," said Maggie. "They were going to tell me, but I expect they forgot. Where is she?"

"In Antony's room. I was coming from the bath and his door was open."

"Did she look nice?"

"I only saw her back."

"I think I'll go along and speak to her," said Maggie.

"Yes, do. I don't think I'll go with you."

As she walked along the passage, Maggie wondered what she would say to the nurse. She didn't mean to offer her professional advice. But even nurses are human, and Maggie didn't want this stranger to imagine that Antony was, well, always like that – the spoilt, tiresome, unreasonable creature of the last few hours. She could find no harsher epithets for him, even after all his deliberate unkindness. The woman would probably have heard that Maggie was his fiancée; Maggie would try to show her that she was proud of the relationship and felt it an honour.

The door was still open, so she knocked and walked in. But the figure that uncoiled itself from Antony's pillow and darted at her a look of malevolent triumph was not a nurse, nor was her face strange to Maggie; Maggie could see, so intense was her vision at that moment, just what strokes Antony had used to transform her own portrait into Lady Elinor's. She was terrified, but she could not bear to see Antony's rather long hair nearly touching the floor nor the creature's thin hand on his labouring throat. She advanced, resolved at whatever cost to break up this dreadful tableau. She approached near enough to realise that what seemed a stranglehold was probably a caress, when Antony's eyes rolled up at her and words, frothy and toneless like a chain of bursting bubbles, came popping from the corner of his swollen mouth: "Get out, damn you!" At the same moment she heard the stir of presences behind her and a voice saying, "Here is the patient, nurse; I'm afraid he's half out of bed, and here's Maggie, too. What *have* you been doing to him, Maggie?" Dazed, she turned about. "Can't you see?" she cried; but she might have asked the question of herself, for when she looked back she could only see the tumbled bed, the vacant pillow, and Antony's hair trailing the floor.

*

The nurse was a sensible woman. Fortified by tea, she soon bundled everybody out of the room. A deeper quiet than night ordinarily brings invaded the house. The reign of illness had begun.

A special embargo was laid on Maggie's visits. The nurse said she had noticed that Miss Winthrop's presence agitated the patient. But Maggie extracted a promise that she should be called if Antony got worse. She was too tired and worried to sleep, even if she had tried to, so she sat up fully dressed in a chair, every now and then trying to allay her anxiety by furtive visits to Antony's bedroom door.

The hours passed on leaden feet. She tried to distract herself by reading the light literature with which her hostess had provided her. Though she could not keep her attention on the books, she continued to turn their pages, for only so could she keep at bay the conviction that had long been forming at the back of her mind and that now threatened to engulf her whole consciousness: the conviction that the legend about Low Threshold was true. She was neither hysterical nor superstitious, and for a moment she had managed to persuade herself that what she had seen in Antony's room was an hallucination. The passing hours robbed her of that solace.

Antony was the victim of Lady Elinor's vengeance. Everything pointed to it; the circumstances of her appearance, the nature of Antony's illness, the horrible deterioration in his character – to say nothing of the drawings, and the cat.

There were only two ways of saving him. One was to get him out of the house; she had tried that and failed; if she tried again she would fail more signally than before. But there remained the other way.

The old book about "The Tragicall Happennings at Low Threshold Hall" still reposed in a drawer; for the sake of her peace of mind Maggie had vowed not to take it out, and till now she had kept her vow. But as the sky began to pale with the promise of dawn and her conviction of Antony's mortal danger grew apace, her resolution broke down.

> "Whereby we must conclude," she read, "that the Lady Elinor like other Apparitions, is subject to certain Lawes. One, to abandon her Victim and seeking another tenement enter into it and transfer her vengeance, should its path be crossed by a Body yet nearer Dissolution . . ."

A knock, that had been twice repeated, startled her out of her reverie.

"Come in!"

"Miss Winthrop," said the nurse, "I'm sorry to tell you the patient is weaker. I think the doctor had better be telephoned for."

"I'll go and get someone," said Maggie. "Is he much worse?"

"Very much, I'm afraid."

Maggie had no difficulty in finding Rundle; he was already up.

"What time is it, Rundle?" she asked. "I've lost count."

"Half-past four, miss." He looked very sorry for her.

"When will the doctor be here?"

"In about an hour, miss, not more."

Suddenly she had an idea. "I'm so tired, Rundle, I think I

shall try to get some sleep. Tell them not to call me unless . . . unless . . ."

"Yes, miss," said Rundle, "You look altogether done up."

About an hour! So she had plenty of time. She took up the book again ". . . transfer her vengeance . . . seeking another tenement . . . a Body nearer Dissolution . . ." Her idle thoughts turned with compassion to the poor servant girl whose death had spelt recovery to Lord Deadham's cousin but had been so little regarded: "the night was spent" before they heard that she was dead. Well, this night was spent already. Maggie shivered. "I shall die in my sleep," she thought. "But shall I feel her come?" Her tired body sickened with nausea at the idea of such a loathsome violation. But the thought still nagged at her. "Shall I realise even for a moment that I'm changing into . . . into?" Her mind refused to frame the possibility. "Should I have time to do anyone an injury?" she wondered. "I could tie my feet together with a handkerchief; that would prevent me from walking." Walking . . . walking . . . The word let loose on her mind a new flood of terrors. She could not do it! She could not lay herself open for ever to this horrible contemplation! Her tormented imagination began to busy itself with the details of her funeral; she saw mourners following her coffin into the church. But Antony was not amongst them; he was better, but too ill to be there. He could not understand why she had killed herself, for the note she had left gave no hint of the real reason, referred only to continual sleeplessness and nervous depression. So she would not have his company when her body was committed to the ground. But that was a mistake; it would not be her body, it would belong to that other woman and be hers to return to by the right of possession.

All at once the screen which had recorded such vivid images to her mind's eye went blank; and her physical eye, released, roamed wildly about the room. It rested on the book she was still holding. "She cannot possess or haunt the corpse," she read, "after it hath received Christian Buriall."

Here was a ray of comfort. But (her fears warned her) being a suicide she might not be allowed Christian burial. How then? Instead of the churchyard she saw a cross-roads, with a slanting signpost on which the words could no longer be read; only two or three people were there; they kept looking furtively about them, and the grave-digger had thrown his spade aside and was holding a stake . . .

She pulled herself together with a jerk. "These are all fancies," she thought. "It wasn't fancy when I signed the poison book." She took up the little glass cylinder; there were eighteen tablets and the dose was one or two. Daylight was broadening apace; she must hurry. She took some note-paper and wrote for five minutes. She had reached the words "No one is to blame" when suddenly her ears were assailed by a tremendous tearing, whirring sound; it grew louder and louder until the whole room vibrated. In the midst of the deafening din something flashed past the window, for a fraction of a second blotting out the daylight. Then there was a crash such as she had never heard in her life.

All else forgotten, Maggie ran to the window. An indescribable scene of wreckage met her eyes. The aeroplane had been travelling at a terrific pace; it was smashed to atoms. To right and left the lawn was littered with fragments, some of which had made great gashes in the grass, exposing the earth. The pilot had been flung clear, she could just see his legs sticking out from a flower-bed under the wall of the house. They did not move and she thought he must be dead.

While she was wondering what to do she heard voices underneath the window.

"We don't seem to be very lucky here just now, Rundle," said Mr Ampleforth.

"No, sir."

There was a pause. Then Mr Ampleforth spoke again.

"He's still breathing, I think."

"Yes, sir, he is, just."

"You take his head and I'll take his feet, and we'll get him into the house."

Something began to stir in Maggie's mind. Rundle replied:

"If you'll pardon me saying so, sir, I don't think we ought to move him. I was told once by a doctor that if a man's had a fall or anything it's best to leave him lying."

"I don't think it'll matter if we're careful."

"Really, sir, if you'll take my advice –"

There was a note of obstinacy in Rundle's voice. Maggie, almost beside herself with agitation, longed to fling open the window and cry, "Bring him in! Bring him in!" But her hand seemed paralysed and her throat could not form the words.

Presently Mr Ampleforth said:

"You know, we can't let him stay here. It's beginning to rain."

(Bring him in! Bring him in!)

"Well, sir, it's your responsibility . . ."

Maggie's heart almost stopped beating.

"Naturally I don't want to do anything to hurt the poor chap."

(Oh, bring him in! Bring him in!)

The rain began to patter on the pane.

"Look here, Rundle, we must get him under cover."

"I'll fetch that bit of wing, sir, and put it over him."

(Bring him in! Bring him in!)

Maggie heard Rundle pulling something that grated on the gravel path. The sound ceased and Mr Ampleforth said:

"The very thing for a stretcher, Rundle! The earth's so soft we can slide it under him. Careful, careful!" Both men were breathing hard. "Have you got your end? Right." Their heavy, measured footfalls grew fainter and fainter.

The next thing Maggie heard was the car returning with the doctor. Not daring to go out and unable to sit down, she stood, how long she did not know, holding her bedroom door ajar.

At last she saw the nurse coming towards her.

"The patient's a little better, Miss Winthrop. The doctor thinks he'll pull through now."

"Which patient?"

"Oh, there was never any hope for the other poor fellow."

Maggie closed her eyes.

"Can I see Antony?" she said at last.

"Well, you may just peep at him."

Antony smiled at her feebly from the bed.

The Bus Conductor

E. F. Benson

My friend, Hugh Grainger, and I had just returned from a two days' visit in the country, where we had been staying in a house of sinister repute which was supposed to be haunted by ghosts of a peculiarly fearsome and truculent sort. The house itself was all that such a house should be. Jacobean and oak-panelled, with long dark passages and high vaulted rooms. It stood also, very remote, and was encompassed by a wood of sombre pines that muttered and whispered in the dark, and all the time that we were there a south-westerly gale with torrents of scalding rain had prevailed, so that by day and night weird noises moaned and fluted in the chimneys, a company of uneasy spirits held colloquy among the trees, and sudden tattoos and tappings beckoned from the window panes. But in spite of these surroundings, which were sufficient in themselves, one would almost say, to spontaneously generate occult phenomena, nothing of any description had occurred. I am bound to add, also, that my own state of mind was peculiarly well adapted to receive or even to invent the sights and sounds we had gone to seek, for I was, I confess, during the whole time that we were there, in a state of abject apprehension, and lay awake both nights through hours of terrified unrest, afraid of the dark, yet more afraid of what a lighted candle might show me.

Hugh Grainger, on the evening after our return to town, had dined with me, and after dinner our conversation, as was natural, soon came back to these entrancing topics.

"But why you go ghost-seeking, I cannot imagine," he said, "because your teeth were chattering and your eyes starting out of your head all the time you were there, from sheer fright. Or do you like being frightened?"

Hugh, though generally intelligent is dense in certain ways; this is one of them.

"Why, of course, I like being frightened," I said. "I want to be made to creep and creep and creep. Fear is the most absorbing and luxurious of emotions. One forgets all else if one is afraid."

"Well, the fact that neither of us saw anything," he said, "confirms what I have always believed."

"And what have you always believed?"

"That these phenomena are purely objective, not subjective, and that one's state of mind has nothing to do with the perception that perceives them, nor have circumstances or surroundings anything to do with them either. Look at Osburton. It has the reputation of being a haunted house for years, and it certainly has all the accessories of one. Look at yourself, too, with all your nerves on edge, afraid to look round or light a candle for fear of seeing something! Surely there was the right man in the right place then, if ghosts are subjective."

He got up and lit a cigarette, and looking at him – Hugh is about six feet high, and as broad as he is long – I felt a retort on my lips, for I could not help my mind going back to a certain period in his life, when, from some cause which, as far as I knew, he had never told anybody, he had become a mere quivering mass of disordered nerves. Oddly enough, at the same moment and for the first time, he began to speak of it himself.

"You may reply that it was not worth my while to go either," he said, "because I was so clearly the wrong man in the wrong place. But I wasn't. You for all your apprehensions and expectancy have never seen a ghost. But I have, though I am the last person in the world you would have thought likely to do so, and, though my nerves are steady enough now, it knocked me all to bits."

He sat down again in his chair.

"No doubt you remember my going to bits," he said, "and

since I believe that I am sound again now, I should rather like to tell you about it. But before I couldn't; I couldn't speak of it at all to anybody. Yet there ought to have been nothing frightening about it; what I saw was certainly a most useful and friendly ghost. But it came from the shaded side of things; it looked suddenly out of the night and the mystery with which life is surrounded.

"I want first to tell you quite shortly my theory about ghost-seeking," he continued, "and I can explain it best by a simile, an image. Imagine then that you and I and everybody in the world are like people whose eye is directly opposite a little tiny hole in a sheet of cardboard which is continually shifting and revolving and moving about. Back to back with that sheet of cardboard is another, which also, by laws of its own, is in perpetual but independent motion. In it, too, there is another hole, and when fortuitously it would seem, these two holes, the one through which we are always looking, and the other in the spiritual plane, come opposite one another, we see through, and then only do the sights and sounds of the spiritual world become visible or audible to us. With most people these holes never come opposite each other during their life. But at the hour of death they do, and then they remain stationary. That, I fancy, is how we 'pass over'.

"Now, in some natures, these holes are comparatively large, and are constantly coming into opposition. Clairvoyants, mediums, are like that. But, as far as I knew, I had no clairvoyant or mediumistic powers at all. I therefore am the sort of person who long ago made up his mind that he never would see a ghost. It was, so to speak, an incalculable chance that my minute spy-hole should come into opposition with the other. But it did: and it knocked me out of time."

I had heard some such theory before, and though Hugh put it rather picturesquely, there was nothing in the least convincing or practical about it. It might be so, or again it might not.

"I hope your ghost was more original than your theory," said I, in order to bring him to the point.

"Yes, I think it was. You shall judge."

I put on more coal and poked up the fire. Hugh has got, so I have always considered, a great talent for telling stories, and that sense of drama which is so necessary for the narrator. Indeed before now, I have suggested to him that he should take this up as a profession, sit by the fountain in Piccadilly Circus, when times are, as usual, bad, and tell stories to the passers-by in the street, Arabian fashion, for reward. The most part of mankind, I am aware, do not like long stories, but to the few, among whom I number myself, who really like to listen to lengthy accounts of experiences, Hugh is an ideal narrator. I do not care for his theories, or for his similes, but when it comes to facts, to things that happened, I like him to be lengthy.

"Go on, please, and slowly," I said. "Brevity may be the soul of wit, but it is the ruin of story-telling. I want to hear when and where and how it all was, and what you had for lunch and where you had dined and what – "

Hugh began:

"It was the 24th of June, just eighteen months ago," he said. "I had let my flat, you may remember, and came up from the country to stay with you for a week. We had dined alone here –"

I could not help interrupting.

"Did you see the ghost here?" I asked. "In this square little box of a house in a modern street?"

"I was in the house when I saw it."

I hugged myself in silence.

"We had dined alone here in Graeme Street," he said, "and after dinner I went out to some party, and you stopped at home. At dinner your man did not wait, and when I asked where he was, you told me he was ill, and, I thought, changed the subject rather abruptly. You gave me your latch-key when I went out, and on coming back, I found you had gone to bed. There were, however, several letters for me, which required answers. I wrote them there and then, and posted them at the pillar-box opposite. So I suppose it was rather late when I went upstairs.

"You had put me in the front room, on the third floor, overlooking the street, a room which I thought you generally occupied yourself. It was a very hot night, and though there had been a moon when I started to my party, on my return the whole sky was cloud-covered, and it both looked and felt as if we might have a thunderstorm before morning. I was feeling very sleepy and heavy, and it was not till after I had got into bed that I noticed by the shadows of the window-frames on the blind that only one of the windows was open. But it did not seem worth while to get out of bed in order to open it, though I felt rather airless and uncomfortable, and I went to sleep.

"What time it was when I awoke I do not know, but it was certainly not yet dawn, and I never remembered being conscious of such extraordinary stillness as prevailed. There was no sound either of foot-passengers or wheeled traffic; the music of life appeared to be absolutely mute. But now, instead of being sleepy and heavy, I felt, though I must have slept an hour or two at most, since it was not yet dawn, perfectly fresh and wide-awake, and the effort which had seemed not worth making before, that of getting out of bed and opening the other window, was quite easy now, and I pulled up the blind, threw it wide open, and leaned out, for somehow I parched and pined for air. Even outside the oppression was very noticeable, and though, as you know, I am not easily given to feel the mental effects of climate, I was aware of an awful creepiness coming over me. I tried to analyse it away, but without success; the past day had been pleasant, I looked forward to another pleasant day tomorrow, and yet I was full of some nameless apprehension. I felt, too, dreadfully lonely in this stillness before the dawn.

"Then I heard suddenly and not very far away the sound of some approaching vehicle; I could distinguish the tread of two horses walking at a slow foot's pace. They were, though, yet invisible, coming up the street, and yet this indication of life did not abate that dreadful sense of loneliness which I have spoken of. Also in some dim unformulated way that which was coming seemed to me to have something to do with the cause of my oppression.

"Then the vehicle came into sight. At first I could not distinguish what it was. Then I saw that the horses were black and had long tails, and that what they dragged was made of glass, but had a black frame. It was a hearse. Empty.

"It was moving up this side of the street. It stopped at your door.

"Then the obvious solution struck me. You had said at dinner that your man was ill, and you were, I thought, unwilling to speak more about his illness. No doubt, so I imagined now, he was dead, and for some reason, perhaps because you did not want me to know anything about it, you were having the body removed at night. This, I must tell you, passed through my mind quite instantaneously, and it did not occur to me how unlikely it really was, before the next thing happened.

"I was still leaning out of the window, and I remember also wondering, yet only momentarily, how odd it was that I saw things – or rather the one thing I was looking at – so very distinctly. Of course, there was a moon behind the clouds, but it was curious how every detail of the hearse and the horses was visible. There was only one man, the driver, with it and the street was otherwise absolutely empty. It was at him I was looking now. I could see every detail of his clothes, but from where I was, so high above him, I could not see his face. He had on grey trousers, brown boots, a black coat buttoned all the way up, and a straw hat. Over his shoulder there was a strap, which seemed to support some sort of little bag. He looked exactly like – well, from my description what did he look exactly like?"

"Why – a bus-conductor," I said instantly.

"So I thought, and even while I was thinking this, he looked up at me. He had a rather long thin face, and on his left cheek there was a mole with a growth of dark hair on it. All this was as distinct as if it had been noonday, and as if I was within a yard of him. But – so instantaneous was all that takes so long in the telling – I had not time to think it strange that the driver of a hearse should be so unfunereally dressed.

"Then he touched his hat to me, and jerked his thumb over his shoulder.

" 'Just room for one inside, sir,' he said.

"There was something so odious, so coarse, so unfeeling about this that I instantly drew my head in, pulled the blind down again, and then, for what reason I do not know, turned on the electric light in order to see what time it was. The hands of my watch pointed to half past eleven.

"It was then for the first time, I think, that a doubt crossed my mind as the nature of what I had just seen. But I put out the light again, got into bed, and began to think. We had dined; I had gone to a party, I had come back and written

letters, had gone to bed and slept, so how could it be half past eleven? . . . Or – *what* half past eleven was it?

"Then another easy solution struck me; my watch must have stopped. But it had not; I could hear it ticking.

"There was stillness and silence again. I expected every moment to hear muffled footsteps on the stairs, footsteps moving slowly and smally under the weight of a heavy burden, but from inside the house there was no sound whatever. Outside, too, there was the same dead silence, while the hearse waited at the door. And the minutes ticked on and ticked on, and at length I began to see a difference in the light in the room, and knew that the dawn was beginning to break outside. But how had it happened then that if the corpse was to be removed at night it had not gone, and that the hearse still waited, when morning was already coming?

"Presently I got out of bed again, and with the sense of strong physical shrinking, I went to the window, and pulled back the blind. The dawn was coming fast, the whole street was lit by that silver hueless light of morning; but there was no hearse there.

"Once again I looked at my watch. It was just a quarter past four. But I would swear that not half an hour had passed since it had told me that it was half past eleven.

"Then a curious double sense, as if I was living in the present and at the same moment had been living in some other time, came over me. It was dawn on June 25th, and the street, as natural, was empty. But a little while ago, the driver of a hearse, had spoken to me, and it was half past eleven. What was that driver, to what plane did he belong? And again *what* half past eleven was it that I had seen recorded on the dial of my watch?

"And then I told myself that the whole thing had been a dream. But if you asked me whether I believed what I told myself, I must confess that I did not.

"Your man did not appear at breakfast next morning, nor did I see him again before I left that afternoon; I think if I had, I should have told you about all this, but it was still possible, you see, that what I had seen was a real hearse, driven by a real driver, for all the ghastly gaiety of the face that had looked up to mine and the levity of his pointing hand. I might possibly have fallen asleep soon after seeing him, and slumbered through the removal of the body and the departure of the hearse. So I did not speak of it to you."

*

There was something wonderfully straightforward and prosaic in all this; here were no Jacobean houses oak-panelled and surrounded by weeping pine-trees, and somehow the very absence of suitable surroundings made the story more impressive. But for a moment a doubt assailed me.

"Don't tell me it was all a dream," I said.

"I don't know whether it was or not. I can only say that I believe myself to have been wide awake. In any case the rest of the story is – odd.

"I went out of town again that afternoon," he continued, "and I may say that I don't think that even for a moment did I get the haunting sense of what I had seen or dreamed that night out of my mind. It was present to me always as some vision unfulfilled. It was as if some clock had struck the four quarters, and I was still waiting to hear what the hour would be.

"Exactly a month afterwards I was in London again, but only for the day. I arrived at Victoria about eleven, and took the underground to Sloane Square in order to see if you were in town and would give me lunch. It was a baking hot morning, and I intended to take a bus from the King's Road as far as Graeme Street. There was one standing at the corner just as I came out of the station, but I saw that the top was full, and the inside appeared to be full also. Just as I came up to it the conductor who, I suppose, had been inside, collecting fares or what not, came out on to the step within a few feet of me. He wore grey trousers, brown boots, a black coat buttoned, a straw hat, and over his shoulder was a strap on which hung his little machine for punching tickets. I saw his face, too; it was the face of the driver of the hearse, with a mole on the left cheek. Then he spoke to me, jerking his thumb over his shoulder.

"'Just room for one inside, sir,'" he said.

"At that a sort of panic-terror took possession of me, and I knew I gesticulated wildly with my arms, and cried, 'No, no!' But at that moment I was living not in the hour that was then passing, but in that hour which had passed a month ago, when I leaned from the window of your bedroom here just before the dawn broke. At this moment, too, I knew that my spy-hole had been opposite the spy-hole into the spiritual world. What I had seen there had some significance, now being fulfilled, beyond the significance of the trivial happenings of today and tomorrow. The Powers of which we know so little were visibly working before me. And I stood there on the pavement shaking and trembling.

"I was opposite the post-office at the corner, and just as the bus started my eye fell on the clock in the window there. I need not tell you what time it was.

"Perhaps I need not tell you the rest, for you probably conjecture it, since you will not have forgotten what happened at the corner of Sloane Square at the end of July, the summer before last. The bus pulled out from the pavement into the street in order to get round a van that was standing in front of it. At that moment there came down the King's Road a big motor going at a hideously dangerous pace. It crashed full into the bus, burrowing into it as a gimlet burrows into a board."

He paused.

"And that's my story," he said.

August Heat

W. F. Harvey

PENISTONE ROAD, CLAPHAM,
August 20th, 190–

I have had what I believe to be the most remarkable day in my life, and while the events are still fresh in my mind, I wish to put them down on paper as clearly as possible.

Let me say at the outset that my name is James Clarence Withencroft.

I am forty years old, in perfect health, never having known a day's illness.

By profession I am an artist, not a very successful one, but I earn enough money by my black-and-white work to satisfy my necessary wants.

My only relative, a sister, died five years ago, so that I am independent.

I breakfasted this morning at nine, and after glancing through the morning paper I lighted my pipe and proceeded to let my mind wander in the hope that I might chance upon some subject for my pencil.

The room, though door and windows were open, was oppressively hot, and I had just made up my mind that the coolest and most comfortable place in the neighbourhood would be the deep end of the public swimming bath, when the idea came.

I began to draw. So intent was I on my work that I left my lunch untouched, only stopping work when the clock of St Jude's struck four.

The final result, for a hurried sketch, was, I felt sure, the best thing I had done.

It showed a criminal in the dock immediately after the judge had pronounced sentence, The man was fat – enormously fat. The flesh hung in rolls about his chin; it creased his huge stumpy neck. He was clean shaven (perhaps I should say a few days before he must have been clean shaven) and almost bald. He stood in the dock, his short, clumsy fingers clasping the rail, looking straight in front of him. The feeling that his expression conveyed was not so much one of horror as of utter, absolute collapse.

There seemed nothing in the man strong enough to sustain that mountain of flesh.

I rolled up the sketch, and without quite knowing why, placed it in my pocket. Then with the rare sense of happiness which the knowledge of a good thing well done gives, I left the house.

I believe that I set out with the idea of calling upon Trenton, for I remember walking along Lytton Street and turning to the right along Gilchrist Road at the bottom of the hill where the men were at work on the new tram lines.

From there onwards I have only the vaguest recollection of where I went. The one thing of which I was fully conscious was the awful heat, that came up from the dusty asphalt pavement as an almost palpable wave. I longed for the thunder promised by the great banks of copper-coloured cloud that hung low over the western sky.

I must have walked five or six miles, when a small boy roused me from my reverie by asking the time.

It was twenty minutes to seven.

When he left me I began to take stock of my bearings. I found myself standing before a gate that led into a yard bordered by a strip of thirsty earth, where there were flowers, purple stock and scarlet geranium. Above the entrance was a board with the inscription –

CHS. ATKINSON. MONUMENTAL MASON.
WORKER IN ENGLISH AND ITALIAN MARBLES

From the yard itself came a cheery whistle, the noise of

hammer blows, and the cold sound of steel meeting stone.

A sudden impulse made me enter.

A man was sitting with his back towards me, busy at work on a slab of curiously veined marble. He turned round as he heard my steps and I stopped short.

It was the man I had been drawing, whose portrait lay in my pocket.

He sat there, huge and elephantine, the sweat pouring from his scalp, which he wiped with a red silk handkerchief. But though the face was the same, the expression was absolutely different.

He greeted me smiling, as if we were old friends, and shook my hand.

I apologised for my intrusion.

"Everything is hot and glary outside," I said. "This seems an oasis in the wilderness."

"I don't know about the oasis," he replied, "but it certainly is hot, as hot as hell. Take a seat, sir!"

He pointed to the end of the gravestone on which he was at work, and I sat down.

"That's a beautiful piece of stone you've got hold of," I said.

He shook his head. "In a way it is," he answered, "the surface here is as fine as anything you could wish, but there's a big flaw at the back, though I don't expect you'd ever notice it. I could never make a really good job of a bit of marble like that. It would be all right in a summer like this; it wouldn't mind the blasted heat. But wait till the winter comes. There's nothing quite like frost to find out the weak points in stone."

"Then what's it for?" I asked.

The man burst out laughing.

"You'd hardly believe me if I was to tell you it's for an exhibition, but it's the truth. Artists have exhibitions: so do grocers and butchers; we have them too. All the latest little things in headstones, you know."

He went on to talk of marbles, which sort best withstood wind and rain, and which were easiest to work; then of his garden and a new sort of carnation he had bought. At the end of every other minute he would drop his tools, wipe his shining head, and curse the heat.

I said little, for I felt uneasy. There was something unnatural, uncanny, in meeting this man.

I tried to persuade myself that I had seen him before, that

his face, unknown to me, had found a place in some out-of-the-way corner of my memory, but I knew that I was practising little more than a plausible piece of self-deception.

Mr Atkinson finished his work, spat on the ground, and got up with a sigh of relief.

"There! What do you think of that?" he said with an air of evident pride.

The inscription which I read for the first time was this:

SACRED TO THE MEMORY
OF
JAMES CLARENCE WITHENCROFT
BORN JAN. 18TH, 1860
HE PASSED AWAY VERY SUDDENLY
ON AUGUST 20TH, 190–
"*In the midst of life we are in death*"

For some time I sat in silence. Then a cold shudder ran down my spine. I asked him where he had seen the name.

"Oh, I didn't see it anywhere," replied Mr Atkinson, "I wanted some name, and I put down the first that came into my head. Why do you want to know?"

"It's a strange coincidence, but it happens to be mine."

He gave a long, low whistle.

"And the dates?"

"I can only answer for one of them and that's correct."

"It's a rum go!" he said.

But he knew less than I did. I told him of my morning's work. I took the sketch from my pocket and showed it to him. As he looked, the expression on his face altered until it became more and more like that of the man I had drawn.

"And it was only the day before yesterday," he said, "that I told Maria there were no such things as ghosts!"

Neither of us had seen a ghost, but I knew what he meant.

"You probably heard my name," I said.

"And you must have seen me somewhere and have forgotten it! Were you at Clacton-on-Sea last July?"

I had never been to Clacton in my life. We were silent for some time. We were both looking at the same thing, the two dates on the gravestone, and one was right.

"Come inside and have some supper," said Mr Atkinson.

His wife is a cheerful little woman, with the flaky red cheeks of the country-bred. Her husband introduced me as a friend of his who was an artist. The result was unfortunate, for after the sardines and watercress had been removed, she brought out a Doré Bible, and I had to sit and express my admiration for nearly an hour.

I went outside, and found Atkinson sitting on the gravestone, smoking.

We resumed the conversation at the point we had left off.

"You must excuse me asking," I said, "but do you know of anything you've done for which you could be put on trial?"

He shook his head.

"I'm not a bankrupt, the business is prosperous enough. Three years ago I gave turkeys to some of the guardians at Christmas, but that's all I can think of. And they were small ones, too," he added as an afterthought.

He got up, fetched a can from the porch, and began to water the flowers. "Twice a day regular in the hot weather," he said, "and then the heat sometimes gets the better of the delicate ones. And ferns, good Lord! They could never stand it. Where do you live?"

I told him my address. It would take an hour's quick walk to get back home.

"It's like this," he said. "We'll look at the matter straight. If you go back home tonight, you take your chance of accidents. A cart may run over you, and there's always banana skins and orange peel, to say nothing of falling ladders."

He spoke of the improbable with an intense seriousness that would have been laughable six hours before. But I did not laugh.

"The best thing we can do," he continued, "is for you to stay here till twelve o'clock. We'll go upstairs and smoke, it may be cooler inside."

To my surprise I agreed.

*

We are sitting now in a long, low room beneath the eaves. Atkinson has sent his wife to bed. He himself is busy sharpening some tools at a little oilstone, smoking one of my cigars the while.

The air seems charged with thunder. I am writing this at a shaky table before the open window. The leg is cracked, and Atkinson, who seems a handy man with his tools, is going to mend it as soon as he has finished putting an edge on his chisel.

It is after eleven now. I shall be gone in less than an hour.

But the heat is stifling.

It is enough to send a man mad.

Coincidence

A. J. Alan

This is the story of a coincidence. At any rate I call it a coincidence.

The road where I live is very long and very straight. It's paved with wood and well lighted after dark. The result is that cars and taxis going by during the night . . . often go quite fast. I don't blame 'em. They hardly ever wake me unless they stop near the house.

However, about two months ago one did.

I mean he did wake me. He jammed on his brakes for all he was worth just opposite my window and pulled up dead. You know what a row that makes. Then after quite a short pause he drove on again. That was nothing, of course, and it didn't make much impression on me at the moment. I was only just not asleep. But about two minutes later the same thing happened again. This time it was a taxi – at least it sounded like a taxi. Just about the same place the driver shoved on his brakes with a regular scream and *he* stopped. Then I think he backed a few yards, but I don't know. At all events he did a bit of shunting and in a minute or two *he* cleared off. As you can imagine this second . . . business . . . made more of an impression, and when still a third car went through the same . . . programme – I really did quite try to address my mind to the problem. You know how utterly vague one can be at three o'clock in the morning. I said, "Oh, yes. I know what it is – it's the same as last February."

In February, or was it January? – anyway whenever it was – the water main bust – and a hole became in the middle of the road. They fenced it off with poles and red lamps, and put a watchman and brazier and sentry box inside.

That was all right, of course, but during the night a thickish fog came on, and cars came whizzing along, banking on a clear road, and didn't see the lights until they were nearly on top of them, and had to pull up in a hurry. Can't you see the watchman striking out for the shore – after the first two or three? mit brazier.

At all events I thought, "That's what's happened again." But then I said, "Hang it all it's *August* – there can't be a fog – so it isn't that. This must be looked into." So I got out of bed and went and hung out of the window. Presently a large touring car came buzzing along and just opposite me on went the brakes and it tried to loop the loop like the others had. I couldn't quite see where it had pulled up because there are rather a lot of trees on each side of my window, but I heard people get out and there was a general air of excitement for about a minute. Then they climbed in again and the door banged and away they went. You can quite imagine how intriguing it all was. I said, "This cannot be borne for another moment. I simply must go and see what it's all about." So I put on some slippers and my dressing gown (pale blue, and much admired about the house) and went downstairs and out into the road.

Beautiful warm night and no end of a moon. I looked up and down but there wasn't a thing in sight, and apparently nothing whatever wrong with the road. So I crossed over to where the marks of skidding began. There were great shining scrawks all over the shop – and then I saw the cause of all the trouble. The moonlight was pretty bright, and about fifteen yards up the road was a patch of deep shadow thrown by a tree. In this shadow there was a man lying. His back was towards me and his feet were about a yard from the pavement. He seemed to be dressed in light brown clothes – not exactly a check pattern but ruled off in squares, so to speak. You often see girls with cloaks made of that kind of stuff.

Well, of course, I started walking up the road towards him, but when I got within five or six yards an extraordinary thing happened. He disappeared. At least he didn't exactly disappear, but I suddenly saw what he really was. He was a rough patch in the road – er . . . don't misjudge me. I'd spent an absolutely blameless evening. No – something had evidently gone wrong with the water main during the afternoon. They'd come and mended the pipe, but hadn't had time to make good the paving. They'd just shoved the wood blocks back loose, bashed them down with a – basher – and brushed some sand over the whole thing. Anyway, it produced a perfectly astounding optical illusion. And as if it wasn't realistic enough already, there was a small piece of paper stuck on the road, and it gave a gleam of white just where the collar would be.

Well, as I was walking backwards and forwards across the critical point – that is – the point where the optical illusion ceased to opp, as it were – and you've no idea how startling it was – it's a little difficult to describe.

I don't know whether any of you have ever been to a cinema, but the time I went one of the scenes showed a beautiful maiden sitting on a stone seat by the side of a lake with water lilies and swans and so on, really very fine, and then, before you could say knife, the whole thing sort of dissolved and you found yourself in a low-down eating house in New York, watching a repulsive looking individual eating spaghetti.

Well that's what it was like and while I was coquetting with this effect – round the corner came a policeman, very surprised to see me playing, "Here we go gathering nuts in May" – er – so early in the morning. He probably said – "Here's a gink in a dressing gown. I'll arrest him – he must be cracked, and I shall get promoted."

He came up to me with a certain amount of – hesitation – but I reassured him and said, "Now you stand just here and look at that man lying there." And he looked and said, "Well I'm – something or other," and started off up the road – evidently meaning to pick him up. But in three or four yards he got to the place where the mirage melted – and then it really was as good as a play. He looked – and rubbed his

eyes – and looked again. Then he walked to the patch in the road and examined that. And as soon as he'd decided it wasn't my fault, I explained to him how dangerous it was, that all the cars and taxis were shying at it, and one of them might easily come to grief. *And* they were waking me up every two minutes. So I said, "If you'll stop here and warn things, I'll go across and see Sir William Horwood in the morning and get him to make you a sergeant." And he said, "I am a sergeant." So I said, "Never mind – perhaps he'll make you another." And I went back to bed.

At about four o'cock there were noises in the road, so I got up and looked out and there was my sergeant and an inspector doing a sort of foxtrot backwards and forwards – having a great time. No, it wasn't a foxtrot – it was more of a pavane, which has been described as a slow and stately dance – the sort of thing they used to dance in armour. I think they went on playing till it got light.

Well the next day men came and made a proper job of the patch in the road – with concrete and tar and so on – and there it was.

That was in August. Now comes the peculiar part. Exactly a fortnight ago – at about one in the morning – there was the same old noise of a car pulling up in a violent hurry. I was sort of half asleep – and I said; "There – the same thing's going to go on happening all night and I shan't get a wink of sleep." However, this car didn't drive on as it ought to have done. There were voices and footsteps and the sound of the car being backed. General excitement. After a few minutes of this I got curious – and again went out – in my blue dressing gown. The car was pulled up just at the same old place. But there wasn't any optical illusion about it this time. They'd run over a man and he was very dead. They said he'd walked off the pavement right into them. And now comes the coincidence. He was wearing light brown clothes – not exactly a check pattern, but ruled off into squares, so to speak. You often see girls with cloaks made of that kind of stuff.

School for the Unspeakable

Manly Wade Wellman

Bart Setwick dropped off the train at Carrington and stood for a moment on the station platform, an honest-faced, well-knit lad in tweeds. This little town and its famous school would be his home for the next eight months; but which way to the school? The sun had set, and he could barely see the shop signs across Carrington's modest main street. He hesitated, and a soft voice spoke at his very elbow.

"Are you for the school?"

Startled, Bart Setwick wheeled. In the grey twilight stood another youth, smiling thinly and waiting as if for an answer. The stranger was all of nineteen years old – that meant maturity to young Setwick, who was fifteen – and his pale face had shrewd lines to it. His tall, shambling body was clad in high-necked jersey and unfashionably tight trousers. Bart Setwick skimmed him with the quick, appraising eye of young America.

"I just got here," he replied. "My name's Setwick."

"Mine's Hoag." Out came a slender hand. Setwick took it and found it froggy-cold, with a suggestion of steel-wire muscles. "Glad to meet you. I came down on the chance someone would drop off the train. Let me give you a lift to the school."

Hoag turned away, felinely light for all his ungainliness, and led his new acquaintance around the corner of the little wooden railway station. Behind the structure, half hidden in its shadow, stood a shabby buggy with a lean bay horse in the shafts.

"Get in," invited Hoag, but Bart Setwick paused for a moment. His generation was not used to such vehicles. Hoag chuckled and said, "Oh, this is only a school wrinkle. We run to funny customs. Get in."

Setwick obeyed. "How about my trunk?"

"Leave it." The taller youth swung himself in beside Setwick and took the reins. "You'll not need it tonight."

He snapped his tongue and the bay horse stirred, drew them around and off down a bush-lined road. Its hoofbeats were oddly muffled.

They turned a corner, another, and came into open country. The lights of Carrington, newly kindled against the night, hung behind like a constellation settled down to Earth. Setwick felt a hint of chill that did not seem to fit the September evening.

"How far is the school from town?" he asked.

"Four or five miles," Hoag replied in his hushed voice. "That was deliberate on the part of the founders – they wanted to make it hard for the students to get to town for larks. It forced us to dig up our own amusements." The pale face creased in a faint smile, as if this were a pleasantry. "There's just a few of the right sort on hand tonight. By the way, what did you get sent out for?"

Setwick frowned his mystification. "Why, to go to school. Dad sent me."

"But what for? Don't you know that this is a high-class prison prep? Half of us are lunkheads that need poking along, the other half are fellows who got in scandals somewhere else. Like me." Again Hoag smiled.

Setwick began to dislike his companion. They rolled a mile or so in silence before Hoag again asked a question:

"Do you go to church, Setwick?"

The new boy was afraid to appear priggish, and made a careless show with, "Not very often."

"Can you recite anything from the Bible?" Hoag's soft voice took on an anxious tinge.

"Not that I know of."

"Good," was the almost hearty response. "As I was

saying, there's only a few of us at the school tonight – only three, to be exact. And we don't like Bible-quoters."

Setwick laughed, trying to appear sage and cynical. "Isn't Satan reputed to quote the Bible to his own . . ."

"What do you know about Satan?" interrupted Hoag. He turned full on Setwick, studying him with intent, dark eyes. Then, as if answering his own question: "Little enough, I'll bet. Would you like to know about him?"

"Sure I would," replied Setwick, wondering what the joke would be.

"I'll teach you after a while," Hoag promised cryptically, and silence fell again.

*

Half a moon was well up as they came in sight of a dark jumble of buildings.

"Here we are," anounced Hoag, and then, throwing back his head, he emitted a wild, wordless howl that made Setwick almost jump out of the buggy. "That's to let the others know we're coming," he explained. "Listen!"

Back came a seeming echo of the howl, shrill, faint and eerie. The horse wavered in its muffled trot, and Hoag clucked it back into step. They turned in at a driveway well grown up in weeds, and two minutes more brought them up to the rear of the closest building. It was dim grey in the wash of moonbeams, with blank inky rectangles for windows. Nowhere was there a light, but as the buggy came to a halt Setwick saw a young head pop out of a window on the lower floor.

"Here already, Hoag?" came a high, reedy voice.

"Yes," answered the youth at the reins, "and I've brought a new man with me."

Thrilling a bit to hear himself called a man, Setwick alighted.

"His name's Setwick," went on Hoag. "Meet Andoff, Setwick. A great friend of mine."

Andoff flourished a hand in greeting and scrambled out over the window-sill. He was chubby and squat and even paler than

Hoag, with a low forehead beneath lank, wet-looking hair, and black eyes set wide apart in a fat, stupid-looking face. His shabby jacket was too tight for him, and beneath worn knickers his legs and feet were bare. He might have been an overgrown thirteen or an undeveloped eighteen.

"Felcher ought to be along in half a second," he volunteered.

"Entertain Setwick while I put up the buggy," Hoag directed him.

Andoff nodded, and Hoag gathered the lines in his hands, but paused for a final word.

"No funny business yet, Andoff," he cautioned seriously. "Setwick, don't let this lard-bladder rag you or tell you wild stories until I come back."

Andoff laughed shrilly. "No, no wild stories," he promised. "You'll do the talking, Hoag."

The buggy trundled away, and Andoff swung his fat, grinning face to the new arrival.

"Here comes Felcher," he announced. "Felcher, meet Setwick."

Another boy had bobbed up, it seemed, from nowhere. Setwick had not seen him come around the corner of the building, or slip out of a door or window. He was probably as old as Hoag, or older, but so small as to be almost a dwarf, and frail to boot. His most notable characteristic was his hairiness. A great mop covered his head, brushed over his neck and ears, and hung unkemptly to his bright, deepset eyes. His lips and cheeks were spread with a rank down, and a curly thatch peeped through the unbuttoned collar of his soiled white shirt. The hand he offered Setwick was almost simian in its shagginess and in the hardness of its palm. Too, it was cold and damp. Setwick remembered the same thing of Hoag's handclasp.

"We're the only ones here so far," Felcher remarked. His voice, surprisingly deep and strong for so small a creature, rang like a great bell.

"Isn't even the headmaster here?" inquired Setwick, and

at that the other two began to laugh uproariously, Andoff's fife-squeal rendering an obbligato to Felcher's bell-boom. Hoag, returning, asked what the fun was.

"Setwick asks," groaned Felcher, "why the headmaster isn't here to welcome him."

More fife-laughter and bell-laughter.

"I doubt if Setwick would think the answer was funny," Hoag commented, and then chuckled softly himself.

Setwick, who had been well brought up, began to grow nettled.

"Tell me about it," he urged, in what he hoped was a bleak tone, "and I'll join your chorus of mirth."

Felcher and Andoff gazed at him with eyes strangely eager and learning. Then they faced Hoag.

"Let's tell him," they both said at once, but Hoag shook his head.

"Not yet. One thing at a time. Let's have the song first."

They began to sing. The first verse of their offering was obscene, with no pretence of humour to redeem it. Setwick had never been squeamish, but he found himself definitely repelled. The second verse seemed less objectionable, but it hardly made sense:

> All they tried to teach here
> Now goes untaught.
> Ready, steady, each here,
> Knowledge we sought.
> What they called disaster
> Killed us not, O master!
> Rule us, we beseech here,
> Eye, hand and thought.

It was something like a hymn, Setwick decided, but before what altar would such hymns be sung? Hoag must have read that question in his mind.

"You mentioned Satan in the buggy on the way out," he recalled, his knowing face hanging like a mask in the half-dimness close to Setwick. "Well, that was a Satanist song."

"It was? Who made it?"

"I did," Hoag informed him. "How do you like it?"

Setwick made no answer. He tried to sense mockery in Hoag's voice, but could not find it. "What," he asked finally, "does all this Satanist singing have to do with the headmaster?"

"A lot," came back Felcher deeply, and "a lot," squealed Andoff.

Hoag gazed from one of his friends to the other, and for the first time he smiled broadly. It gave him a toothy look.

"I believe," he ventured quietly, but weightily, "that we might as well let Setwick in on the secret of our little circle."

Here it would begin, the new boy decided – the school hazing of which he had heard and read so much. He had anticipated such things with something of excitement, even eagerness, but now he wanted none of them. He did not like his three companions, and he did not like the way they approached whatever it was they intended to do. He moved backward a pace or two, as if to retreat.

Swift as darting birds, Hoag and Andoff closed in at either elbow. Their chill hands clutched him and suddenly he felt light-headed and sick. Things that had been clear in the moonlight went hazy and distorted.

"Come on and sit down, Setwick," invited Hoag, as though from a great distance. His voice did not grow loud or harsh, but it embodied real menace. "Sit on that window-sill. Or would you like us to carry you?"

At the moment Setwick wanted only to be free of their touch, and so he walked unresistingly to the sill and scrambled up on it. Behind him was the blackness of an unknown chamber, and at his knees gathered the three who seemed so eager to tell him their private joke.

"The headmaster was a proper churchgoer," began Hoag, as though he were the spokesman for the group. "He didn't have any use for devils or devil-worship. Went on record against them when he addressed us in chapel. That was what started us."

"Right," nodded Andoff, turning up his fat, larval face. "Anything he outlawed, we wanted to do. Isn't that logic?"

"Logic and reason," wound up Felcher. His hairy right hand twiddled on the sill near Setwick's thigh. In the moonlight it looked like a big, nervous spider.

Hoag resumed, "I don't know of any prohibition of his it was easier or more fun to break."

Setwick found that his mouth had gone dry. His tongue could barely moisten his lips. "You mean," he said, "that you began to worship devils?"

Hoag nodded happily, like a teacher at an apt pupil. "One vacation I got a book on the cult. The three of us studied it, then began ceremonies. We learned the charms and spells, forward and backward . . ."

"They're twice as good backward," put in Felcher, and Andoff giggled.

"Have you any idea, Setwick," Hoag almost cooed, "what it was that appeared in our study the first time we burned wine and sulphur, with the proper words spoken over them?"

Setwick did not want to know. He clenched his teeth. "If you're trying to scare me," he managed to growl out, "it certainly isn't going to work."

All three laughed once more, and began to chatter out their protestations of good faith.

"I swear that we're telling the truth, Setwick," Hoag assured him. "Do you want to hear it, or don't you?"

Setwick had very little choice in the matter, and he realised it. "Oh, go ahead," he capitulated, wondering how it would do to crawl backward from the sill into the darkness of the room.

Hoag, leaned toward him, with the air as of one confiding. "The headmaster caught us. Caught us red-handed."

"Book open, fire burning," chanted Felcher.

"He had something very fine to say about the vengeance of heaven," Hoag went on. "We got to laughing at him. He worked up a frenzy. Finally he tried to take heaven's vengeance into his own hands – tried to visit it on us, in a very primitive way. But it didn't work."

Andoff was laughing immoderately, his fat arms across his bent belly.

"He thought it worked," he supplemented between high gurgles, "but it didn't."

"Nobody could kill us," Felcher added. "Not after the oaths we'd taken, and the promises that had been made us."

"What promises?" demanded Setwick, who was struggling hard not to believe. "Who made you any promises?"

"Those we worshipped," Felcher told him. If he was simulating earnestness, it was a supreme bit of acting. Setwick, realising this, was more daunted that he cared to show.

"When did all these things happen?" was his next question.

"When?" echoed Hoag. "Oh, years and years ago."

"Years and years ago," repeated Andoff.

"Long before you were born," Felcher assured him.

They were standing close together, their backs to the moon that shone in Setwick's face. He could not see their expressions clearly. But their three voices – Hoag's soft, Felcher's deep and vibrant, Andoff's high and squeaky – were absolutely serious.

"I know what you're arguing within yourself," Hoag announced somewhat smugly. "How can we, who talk about those many past years, seem so young? That calls for an explanation, I'll admit." He paused, as if choosing words. "Time – for us – stands still. It came to a halt on that very night, Setwick; the night our headmaster tried to put an end to our worship."

"And to us," smirked the gross-bodied Andoff, with his usual air of self-congratulation at capping one of Hoag's statements.

"The worship goes on," pronounced Felcher, in the same chanting manner that he had affected once before. "The worship goes on, and we go on, too."

"Which brings us to the point," Hoag came in briskly. "Do you want to throw in with us, Setwick? – make the fourth of this lively little party?"

"No, I don't," snapped Setwick vehemently.

They fell silent, and gave back a little – a trio of bizarre silhouettes against the pale moonglow. Setwick could see the flash of their staring eyes among the shadows of their faces. He knew that he was afraid, but hid his fear. Pluckily he dropped from the sill to the ground. Dew from the grass spattered his sock-clad ankles between oxfords and trouser-cuffs.

"I guess it's my turn to talk," he told them levelly. "I'll make it short. I don't like you, nor anything you've said. And I'm getting out of here."

"We won't let you," said Hoag, hushed but emphatic.

"We won't let you," murmured Andoff and Felcher together, as though they had rehearsed it a thousand times.

Setwick clenched his fists. His father had taught him to box. He took a quick, smooth stride toward Hoag and hit him hard in the face. Next moment all three had flung themselves upon him. They did not seem to strike or grapple or tug, but he went down under their assault. The shoulders of his tweed coat wallowed in sand, and he smelled crushed weeds. Hoag, on top of him, pinioned his arms with a knee on each bicep. Felcher and Andoff were stooping close.

Glaring up in helpless rage, Setwick knew once and for all that this was no schoolboy prank. Never did practical jokers gather around their victim with such staring, green-gleaming eyes, such drawn jowls, such quivering lips.

Hoag bared white fangs. His pointed tongue quested once over them.

"Knife!" he muttered, and Felcher fumbled in a pocket, then passed him something that sparkled in the moonlight.

Hoag's lean hand reached for it, then whipped back. Hoag had lifted his eyes to something beyond the huddle. He choked and whimpered inarticulately, sprang up from Setwick's labouring chest, and fell back in awkward haste. The others followed his shocked stare, then as suddenly cowered and retreated in turn.

"It's the master!" wailed Andoff.

"Yes," roared a gruff new voice. "Your old headmaster – and I've come back to master you!"

Rising upon one elbow, the prostrate Setwick saw what they had seen – a tall, thick-bodied figure in a long dark coat, topped with a square, distorted face and a tousle of white locks. Its eyes glittered with their own pale, hard light. As it advanced slowly and heavily it emitted a snigger of murderous joy. Even at first glance Setwick was aware that it cast no shadow.

"I am in time," mouthed the newcomer. "You were going to kill this poor boy."

Hoag had recovered and made a stand. "Kill him?" he quavered, seeming to fawn before the threatening presence. "No. We'd have given him life –"

"You call it life!" trumpeted the long-coated one. "You'd have sucked out his blood to teem your own dead veins, damned him to your filthy condition. But I'm here to prevent you!"

A finger pointed, huge and knuckly, and then came a torrent of language. To the nerve-stunned Setwick it sounded like a bit from the New Testament, or perhaps from the Book of Common Prayer. All at once he remembered Hoag's avowed dislike for such quotations.

His three erstwhile assailants reeled as if before a high wind that chilled or scorched. "No, no! Don't!" they begged wretchedly.

The square old face gaped open and spewed merciless laughter. The knuckly finger traced a cross in the air, and the trio wailed in chorus as though the sign had been drawn upon their flesh with a tongue of flame.

Hoag dropped to his knees. "Don't!" he sobbed.

"I have power," mocked their tormentor. "During years shut up I won it, and now I'll use it." Again a triumphant burst of mirth. "I know you're damned and can't be killed, but you can be tortured! I'll make you crawl like worms before I'm done with you!"

Setwick gained his shaky feet. The long coat and the blocky head leaned toward him.

"Run, you!" dinned a rough roar in his ears. "Get out of here – and thank God for the chance!"

Setwick ran, staggering. He blundered through the weeds of the driveway, gained the road beyond. In the distance gleamed the lights of Carrington. As he turned his face toward them and quickened his pace he began to weep, chokingly, hysterically, exhaustingly.

He did not stop running until he reached the platform in front of the station. A clock across the street struck ten, in a deep voice not unlike Felcher's. Setwick breathed deeply, fished out his handkerchief and mopped his face. His hand was quivering like a grass stalk in a breeze.

"Beg pardon!" came a cheery hail. "You must be Setwick."

As once before on this same platform, he whirled around with startled speed. Within touch of him stood a broad-shouldered man of thirty or so, with horn-rimmed spectacles. He wore a neat Norfolk jacket and flannels. A short briar pipe was clamped in a good-humoured mouth.

"I'm Collins, one of the masters at the school," he introduced himself. "If you're Setwick, you've had us worried. We expected you on that seven o'clock train, you know. I dropped down to see if I couldn't trace you."

Setwick found a little of his lost wind. "But I've – been to the school," he mumbled protestingly. His hand, still trembling, gestured vaguely along the way he had come.

Collins threw back his head and laughed, then apologised. "Sorry," he said. "It's no joke if you really had all that walk for nothing. Why, that old place is deserted – used to be a catch-all for incorrigible rich boys. They closed it about fifty years ago, when the headmaster went mad and killed three of his pupils. As a matter of coincidence, the master himself died just this afternoon, in the state hospital for the insane."

Ghost Riders of the Sioux

Kenneth Ulyatt

I suppose I saw the ghost riders afore anyone else in the valley.

It was the time between supper and bed. Ma had told me to sit and read. She was always on about schooling but I'd no sooner picked up my reading book and settled against the back wall of the house to get the last of the sun afore it went behind the hills when Dave come by. He had a gun and his dog, Jim, and it was that dog and ours that started us off up the valley. They don't agree; never did and they was fighting and snarling and kicking up an awful ruckus so that soon Ma hollered out of the kitchen to get them tarnation animals parted and clear off so folks could have some peace after eating.

Reckon she forgot about schooling!

Dave and I didn't want no pushing. I tied our Sam up in the barn and we lit out up the valley, his dog, Jim, bouncing ahead and snuffing at the scrub and pretending he'd smelled a cottontail while I asked Dave if I could carry the gun. Of course, he wouldn't let me.

"It's loaded."

"I won't touch the trigger, honest."

"There ain't no safety catch. It's busted."

"I'll be careful, Dave. Pa's taught me how to handle our new gun."

"What new gun? I never knowed you got a new gun."

"It's a Winchester. It can fire . . . twenty shots a minute." I was guessing, of course, to put on a show. Dave was two year older'n me. He knew most things, like where the railroad ran after Potter's Point and how far it was to Oregon and how many steers there was in the whole of our valley . . . and he had this gun.

"Let me carry it, Dave."

"When we get up the valley."

I shut up then. I knew that meant not never. When we got up the valley, he'd say: "We ain't far enough up yet," and so it would go on until we turned back and then there'd be some other reason so that I wouldn't get to carry the gun at all. I didn't care. It was a rotten old gun, anyway.

But to get back to the ghost riders.

We scouted along the stream, Dave making a great play of seeing beaver and levelling the gun. But he never fired it and I began to reckon that there weren't no bullets in it, anyway.

The sun had gone down by this time and it was sort of half light, with deep shadows beneath the trees so that you didn't rightly want to go too far into the scrub. We'd just decided to turn back when Jim started to growl.

Now that dog had been growling and snuffling ever since we left the house. If there was a stone in the path or a tuft of hair hanging on a bush where some steer had passed he'd raise a barking like it was a cottontail pulling a long nose at him. But he'd been quiet by the stream and when we reached the glade about two miles from the house he'd got to padding along at our heels while Dave decided that it wasn't the right night for a hunt after all and we turned back to look down the valley.

Ma had put a lamp in the window and it glowed yellow all that way off. From across the valley you could hear the bellow of some stray calf looking for its mother.

"C'mon, Jim."

Dave looked back at the dog. "What's got into him?"

I turned to look, too. The creature was at the top of a steep slope that made the lip of the glade we was standing in. He leaned forward, his tail stiff behind him and his muzzle pointing direct at the dark trees beyond.

"Here, boy." Dave put on a gruff, commanding voice but the dog didn't move.

The shadows seemed to creep closer while we waited.

Then Jim gave a sort of whine. His tail dropped lower until it crept, trembling, between his back legs. The hair all along his back was bristling up and his whole body was shaking.

"It's a bear. Pa said there was bears in the hills."

"Ain't no bear," said Dave. "If it was a bear we'd have smelled it." But he was worried just the same and he levelled the old gun and made to move up the slope.

We inched forward as the dog went down on its belly. A coldness had come into the air as if it was night already.

At the top of the slope there was nothing, just the shadows of the trees up there and the white trunks of the birches shining. And then one of them moved!

Dave jumped back so quick he cannoned into me and we both fell on the grass. The dog, disturbed by the clatter, sprang to its feet and leaped forward with a barking you could've heard a mile off. For where we was sprawling on the ground you couldn't see him, but you could hear him plenty.

Then suddenly that barking changed to a shriek of pain. I'd seen a dog get caught once in a harrow that some dirt farmer had on the other side of the valley and it sounded like that. He came over the top of the slope still yowling but it was one long moaning cry now and he blundered into us as we scrambled for the gun.

He was wet, but whether from slavering so much or what I didn't know then. All I knew was Dave shaking my arm and pointing up the glade. He didn't speak.

They stood there, white against the blackness that was coming down fast. They swayed together and moaned and the trees seemed to go from side to side with them.

We got to hell outa there, as one of the hired hands said. Although Ma reckoned I shouldn't use such words that's just what we did. Later, the old gun roared out. Dave said he fired when he first saw them but I reckon he tripped when we run and it went off. It didn't have no safety catch anyhow.

We got clear of the trees and pounded down the path to that welcoming light. A mile farther on I stumbled over something and fell.

It was Jim. He was lying stretched on the dirt, his head pointed to the house and his legs drawn back under him like he was still trying to run when he dropped. There was blood all over his side and he was dead.

We carried him back to the house and we was pretty bloody by the time Ma opened the door, exclaiming about where we had been and what sense was there in firing off a gun at that time of night. Then she saw the blood and Dave was crying now because Jim was dead and I guess I cried too, 'cause we was safe back home and they hadn't caught us.

"Who didn't catch you?" Pa was impatient. He stooped down and peered into my face and asked again but I couldn't say any more and the tears came up inside.

"Leave the boy alone, Mark," said Ma. "Can't you see he's frightened out of his wits, and the dog dead, too."

She dragged us near the fire and sat us down. There was a smell of meat coming from the pot on the range and pretty soon we was both more hungry than scared. When Mr Hannery, Dave's Pa, come in we was drinking the last of our bowls of soup and only the dead dog by the back door told him that something was amiss.

"I shot at him, Pa, but he kept comin'." Dave still pushed the story about shooting at what we had seen up the valley and I didn't let on that I thought the gun had gone off by accident. When it come for me to tell my part I just let them think we had stopped to fire back at what was chasing us.

"But who was after you?" Pa asked again, waving Ma back now that she had had her say and we was sitting there all warm with a good soup inside us even if it was tomorrow's dinner.

"They was all white, Pa. Come out of the trees an' killed th' dog an' would've killed us too if we hadn't run." Dave told most of the story again and they listened to him more; after all, he was older'n me and he worked for his Pa on their ranch like any other man – or so he said.

To me, thinking back, it was just something white that had moved among the birch trunks. I wasn't sure that anybody'd really come after us 'though I'd been plenty scared and hadn't stopped long enough to look, after that first glimpse.

But the dog was killed, wasn't he. Deader'n a stick, I heard someone say.

"It's a knife." Mr Hannery's voice drifted through the door. "Now, who'd 've killed a dog, like that?"

"Perhaps we'd better go and look, Tom," I heard my Pa answer and presently they rode off, taking our hound with them and two of the hands from the bunkhouse.

But they never found nothing beyond a few hoofprints across the top of the valley. Unshod, they was. Could've been wild ponies – even Indians, though it was ten year since the Sioux come this far south. Mr Hannery picked up a small pellet of red stuff – "ochre", he said it was but it looked like dirt to me and nobody thought much of it. They was all too busy looking for some drifter who could've killed the dog.

But I know now that they was ghost riders. And the white shirts they was wearing was the first sign of the troubles that was to come.

*

That was the summer the chinook come on real hot.

There was always a warm wind up the valley, on and off through the summer months, but this was different. It just kept on coming; off the badlands, south of the Black Hills, Pa said. The little garden Ma growed behind the house just curled up and died and the farmers in the valley lost their oats and wheat and vegetables.

Even the range grass burned up in the heat.

Dave said that in Nebraska the homesteaders were packing up and going back east; leaving the farms they'd come west to get 'cause nothing would grow there that year.

It was bad for us, too. Pa lost a lot of stock. They just dropped dead out on the range when the water ran out. I used to lie on the bed on top of the covers and listen to the shutters banging and the old house creaking in the wind. And all the time the old windmill that Pa had made squeaked and groaned and turned and sucked up water from deep down. Hundreds of feet deep that well was. An old Indian well. And it was this old well that saved us, I guess.

The river stopped running and was just a mess of pot-hole ponds with stag-edy water and scum on the top that even the cattle wouldn't touch – at first. And skeeters in clouds, 'though they died off, too, as the summer and the hot wind went on and on.

I think it was because things was so bad that Dave and I got to make the trip north with Takawa. We would never have gone on our own if everyone hadn't been so busy fighting the drought. We went to see some folks of Dave's just south of the Cheyenne fork, about two days' ride from our own White River.

"You ain't letting them go off alone and the hills all burnt up like this?" Ma asked, in a sort of high voice that was not at all like her usual tone.

Dave had come over with the ponies and a message from Mr Hannery and he stood in the sun, trailing the reins and looking from her to Pa who was standing by him. Ma had a ladle in one hand, the other was on her hip. And when she stood like that she usually got her own way. I was just thinking that I wouldn't get to go on the trip when Pa spoke out, sharp like. "Boy's got to learn to stand on his own feet, Sarah. He'll be all right. They know the road an' they'll stop over at the Colbys' for th' night. It's all been arranged."

"Yeah. Pa says he's sending 'Kawa with us so we can bring back the ponies Uncle Jack's givin' us. An' *he* won't get lost." Dave put his bit in, like it was carefully thought out and I guess it was, really. Mr Hannery and Pa wouldn't have let us go off if there'd been any likelihood of trouble.

Though, of course, they didn't know about the ghost riders then.

Maybe it was the hot day, maybe it was because things had begun to get on top of her, but Ma give in. First time I knowed her to do it.

"All right. You know what I think. But all right. Go ahead." And she waved the ladle in the air and went back into the kitchen.

"Yippee!"

I let out a scream and lit off for the barn where old Sam was lying in the shade and just for devilment I rolled him over and scattered straw over him so that he sneezed with the dust like I knowed he would.

Dave helped me saddle the pony and waited while I begged Ma pack me a bed roll and something to eat. We left, waving back all the while until the house was small and shimmering in the distance and only the windmill stuck up sharp in the haze.

Takawa was already at the Hannerys' when we got there. He was about the only Indian I'd ever knowed except his folks, of course, who lived on the far side of the valley where the ground was poor and they scratched a living.

Takawa's father was a breed who worked for Dave's Pa. His wife was a full-blood Sioux and there was a tribe of kids, younger'n me, except for Takawa, who was about the same age as Dave.

Takawa never came near the house except sometimes when Pa had told the breed he could take this or that from the ranch; usually something we had finished with or didn't want. Then Takawa and his old man would come with their mule and hitch the stores or whatever it was up on the old aparejo pack and that's the last we'd see of them round the house.

He was a straight, willowy boy, dark brown. But then so were we with the sun. Except when we took our clothes off and went swimming you could see he wasn't the same, he was dark all over.

We left about noon, going north up the valley. Soon you

could see the tops of the Black Hills away to our left as the ground flattened out and began to give way to the plains proper.

I'd never been out on the range before on my own. I'd been to Cheyenne and Pierre and, once even, to Custer City, but that was with Pa. It was a funny feeling, being all alone in all that space; just rolling grass as far as you could see, bending and swaying in the hot wind.

Takawa rode ahead and didn't speak much. Dave and I followed, riding side by side and making out we was pioneers crossing the country for the first time and that there was Indians watching us. Pretty soon I got to half believing that there really was Indians out on the plains with us but Dave said that the agents kept them north on the reservations and that they daren't come out now 'cause of the soldiers.

The ride was tame, really. The trail was marked with stones and afore long we could see the country dipping down to the big river and the tops of the trees by the Colby place where we was to spend the night.

*

Dave's uncle lived at Plum Creek, just where the Cheyenne turned east. Towards the Missouri, Dave said, waving an arm at the cottonwoods and aspens that trailed along the river.

"Over there's Standing Rock," says Dave's Uncle Jack, who'd just come up at that moment. "Pierre first, then, where there's a sort of blue haze, that's Standing Rock Reservation where old Sitting Bull's been kept since he come back from Canada."

"When did he go to Canada, and why?" asked Dave.

"Just after you was born, lad," answered Uncle Jack. "The Sioux had killed Custer and half his regiment and the soldiers chased them right up to the border. Old Sitting Bull stayed in Canada best part of four year afore he reckoned it was safe to come back. Now they keep him pinned down on the reservation at Standing Rock."

He waved a hand over our heads, making a big curve.

"Ten year ago this was all Sioux country. Then th' Gov'n-ment bought th' Black Hills and opened it up for settlement. We're right in the middle of the reservations here. Standing Rock to the north; Brulé to the east and Pine Ridge, south there, behind your home range, Davy."

Takawa was standing a little way off, looking to the blue hills in the north.

"Do th' Injuns ever come here, Uncle Jack?"

"They ain't allowed to travel off th' reservation without permission, though they do. Party came by here early this summer. Bin all th' way down to Nevada, I hear. Injuns ride th' rail-roads, too; whole parties go off on a trip to see relatives, just like you come up to see us."

The evening light was beginning to come down by this time and as we went back to the ranch I was minded of the time we'd seen the ghost riders up the valley.

We were going back the next day, so we went to bed early. All the same it was a good evening, with a big supper Dave's Aunt Betty had specially got for us and a fiddler and folks riding over to visit. After we got to bed we lay there for some time with the music still ringing in our heads.

"You seen many Injuns, Dave?"

" 'Course I have. Went over to Pine Ridge once with Pa and 'Kawa's old man, didn't we, 'Kawa?"

The Indian boy had a bed at the end of the room. Dave's aunt had give him a hard look when we come but then, I suppose seeing we'd come to no harm so far, made him up a bed in the room with us. He lay with his hands behind his head, looking through the window at the stars and he grunted in answer to Dave's question.

We talked for a while and then, one by one, we went to sleep. In the morning we said our "goodbyes" and set off, driving the ponies before us. We played at being on a cattle drive for most of the morning until we got tired of it. Then we just pushed silently on and it got hotter and hotter.

We passed several pot-hole ponds, all dried up and the ducks and marsh birds gone and the mud cracked so you could ride across the bottom like it was a road. The river was away to our right and when we stopped to eat the pie that Dave's aunt had given us we watched the ponies snuffing at the burnt grass and pointing their heads at the trees in the distance as though they could smell water.

"I reckon we won't make Colbys' tonight," said Dave, suddenly. "Look at 'em. We'd better camp by the river where they can get freshed up. What do you say, 'Kawa?"

"Your father said we were not to camp – that we should stay at Captain Colby's both nights," said the Indian boy, gravely.

"Yeah, I know, but we'll be all right." Dave looked at me. "No good bringing in half-dead ponies. Why they might jest drop afore we could get 'em home if we don't stop for water."

It was late afternoon and certainly hot. The sun beat in our faces and when the chinook let up, as it did from time to time, flies buzzed black on the remains of the pie. Far off, across the trees, there was a dust cloud where someone was probably moving cattle down to the river for the night.

It seemed the right thing to do 'though I knowed what Pa would have said. Still, Pa wasn't there, so we headed for the river and after we'd watered the ponies we moved back to some high ground where the trees reached out on to the edge of the plain. It was a funny grey light now that the sun had gone and I was mighty glad when Takawa lit a fire and we huddled round it on our blankets.

The wind, instead of dying like it usually does in the evening, just kept on, rocking the branches above our heads.

Out there on the plains with no one around for hundreds of miles – or so Dave said, though I hadn't reckoned we'd come more than forty mile from home myself – it took a long time to get to sleep. And when I did it seemed only a minute afore I was awake again. Not drowsy-awake, like you are first time you open your eyes in the morning. But wide awake and sitting up and clutching my blanket round my middle.

And scared.

I could see the others were awake too. Though it seemed we'd only just bedded down it must have been near dawn. It was dark; that thick darkness that comes just afore the sun comes up.

And right away I knew that it was the same darkness that had surrounded us in the glade when the ghost riders had killed Dave's dog.

The tree trunks stood out dimly against the blackness and the branches rustled slightly above our heads. But the wind had dropped and in its place was what had awakened us all.

It was a sort of moaning noise that went up and down and didn't stop and it made the hair on the back of my neck stand up and my skin sort of creep. The ponies were restless and pulling at their tethers.

And the ground, when I leaned on it with my elbow, trembled.

"What is it?"

Dave's voice was hoarse and he had to swallow afore he could speak.

"I dunno. I just waked up."

He was fumbling for the gun under the blankets.

" 'Kawa! 'Kawa! You awake?"

The Indian boy looked at us from across the dead fire. I could see the whites of his eyes, rolling. He didn't answer or stir from his blankets.

"C'mon!"

Dave shuffled up, dragging on his jacket and tugging at his belt. He rested the gun against his knee and I knew, as he looked round, that the ghosts of the valley was in his mind, too.

We scrambled to our feet and stood undecided. We could see nothing, but the awful moaning noise went on and on, rising higher now and then lulling off.

"C'mon, 'Kawa. Git up."

Dave pulled the blankets from the Indian boy and, kneeling down, shook him violently, all the while looking over his shoulder this way and that as if he half expected the ghost riders to come sweeping down on the camp.

Takawa was plenty scared, too. I could see that he just wanted to bury his head under the blankets and shut that moaning out of his ears. I guess I wanted to, as well, but Dave wouldn't have any. I'll give him credit. There was danger, we all knew, and Dave wanted us to be ready to meet it. I reckon Mr Hannery would've been proud of him.

But our thoughts was a long way from home, that cosy, safe place that we'd kicked against so often. The ghost riders was mighty near and, suddenly, a long shriek tore through the blackness and brought Takawa to his feet with a great jump. He stood shaking so much that I could feel it, though I weren't within arm's length of him.

"Take this, and come on."

Dave had whirled round at the shrieking to face the gloomy trees. The fire was out. The sky was dark. Nothing moved, but beyond the slope, beyond the fringe of cottonwoods the whole night seemed to be shuddering.

Takawa clutched at the knife that Dave was holding out and then we went scrambling up the slope beyond the ponies. I had the rifle Pa had given me for the trip – the old breechloader that he'd let me use since we got the Winchester and I hugged it close. It was a comfort, 'though I forgot it weren't loaded and that the cartridges was down there in the saddlebag by the fire!

At the top of the slope Dave sprawled down and crawled under some bushes. Out away from the open space round the fire, it didn't seem so bad.

"What is it? What're we goin' to do?"

"I dunno. It's them ghost riders again, I know it is."

Dave jerked in the dark as another shriek rang out. It seemed to come from over the rise. We huddled down closer. Below, the ponies bunched and turned and pulled at the ropes.

While we lay there, undecided, there come a glimmer of light from beyond the ridge, as if someone had stirred a fire to flame, then doused it again. The moaning stopped. Then a voice wailed and all the moaning swept up in answer. And a drumming started and the trembling feeling in the earth seemed to be coming right up underneath us.

All this time Dave had been making up his mind. He'd been plenty scared that night back in the valley when we'd run and ashamed, afterwards, I guess. Now he was going to make up for it and 'though I was scared and Takawa weren't much help I was with him.

"There ain't no such thing as ghosts." Dave was saying what my Pa and Mr Hannery had told us, his voice tight and sort of high. "I'm goin' t'see."

Left to me, I would have high-tailed it out of the place but Dave gave me no time to argue and rather than be left alone with a frightened Indian boy I scrambled up the slope after him, dragging my empty gun.

Of course, Takawa followed. I knew he was following for I could feel his breath on my legs when we stopped crawling to get over a tree stump and I could see his wide eyes when I looked back, very close to me. Pretty soon, I bumped into Dave's feet. We were near the top of the ridge and it had got lighter and I crawled round Dave and lay down beside him. Dave's hand gripped my shoulder so hard I nearly cried out. Then I looked down the dark slope where the ground was clear and the earth moved.

And I froze stiff.

I can't never forget that moment. Even now, when it's all over and I know what it was, I still wake up sweating some nights and see the drifting smoke and the ghosts swarming up out of the hole beyond the buffalo skull. The light had begun to creep over the hills and the first thing I saw was a tall, leaning pole and hanging at the top, a bunch of arms that moved slowly in time to the drumming and shaking.

There was a white mist that spread all before us, curling and twisting out of some great heap on the ground. A heap which moved and cried and hissed. And below the pole was a great gathering of ghosts, all white and shining like we had seen in the valley. And they seemed to be sinking down and then rising up and all the time crying out in the most horrible tones I ever heard.

I couldn't move after I saw them; I just lay there holding my gun and trembling. My mouth was dry and I tried to shut my eyes to keep out the sight but I couldn't. Takawa's body was shaking against mine and even Dave's mouth hung open and his fingers was letting the rifle slip.

So there *was* ghosts and Pa and Mr Hannery was *wrong*!

How long we lay there I don't know, but it got lighter and the smoke or mist kept billowing up out of the hole and every so often another ghost would come out and join the rest and dance horribly.

As the noise got wilder we sank lower and lower into the bushes. Then a great shout went up, followed by a quiet so still I could hear my heart beating and the others', too. We scrambled back a bit, Dave shuffling alongside me, and it was only afterwards that I realised we'd left Takawa on the ridge, alone.

The shrieking burst out afresh and a terrible thing happened. The ghosts began to run in all directions, crying out and falling and rolling and heaving on the ground. And we could see plainer now, 'though we didn't want to, and other ghosts with horrible, swirling faces and white bodies moving with the signs of birds and animals all mixed up and butting the trees and laying stiff or kicking on the ground with other ghosts bending over them doing heaven knows what.

Quite sudden, as I knew it must afore long, one loomed out of the mist above us. Maybe it was 'cause I was lying on the ground but it was taller than ever I saw, with white and red on its face and eyes that seemed to bulge. It stood over Takawa and its arm was raised as though it was going to beat him into the ground. It couldn't see us, for we had rolled into the bushes. And it screamed at Takawa and the Indian boy got slowly up and faced it.

He had guts, Dave said, afterwards. Me, I would have laid

there and covered my ears and eyes but Takawa, who was the most frightened of us all, rose up to face whatever it was that had come out of the mist to find us.

For a moment they stood against the reddening sky. Then the ghost screeched again and was gone and Takawa, half-running, half-sliding, came down the slope and made for the camp. We followed and when we got there the Indian boy was grabbing the blankets and packing the gear.

The moaning had stopped and it was light and because we could see the ponies and the packs and was getting ready to go, it all felt better.

We went out on to the plain, anywhere, away from the cottonwoods, leading the ponies, flying along, not caring much whether we lost them or not. We left the cooking pot and the plates but we didn't think of this 'till we was a long ways out and the sun was up.

It was a breathless ride. I didn't know where we was or where we was heading. All I knowed was that we'd got away from the ghost dancers. But Takawa led the way. Somehow he was different. Not frightened any more. Yet he'd been closer than anyone.

When we got near to the Colbys' we reined in and talked about what we'd tell them. Dave was for keeping it quiet and Takawa just sat silent, not looking at us and not joining in the talk. But I knew that we should have been back at the Colbys' place for the night and that there'd be questions. And I guess I knew that the sight of the ghost riders would still be on our faces.

So we told them. Everything we could remember and Captain Colby looked at us for a long time after we'd finished but said nothing. I didn't know whether he believed us or not.

Then he collected some of the hands and sent a messenger towards Custer City and rode back the way we had come himself, while Mrs Colby cooked us breakfast and Takawa sat outside in the shade of the house and wouldn't talk He wouldn't even talk to Captain Colby when the Captain asked him to describe the ghost he'd seen close up. Not anything.

Well, they didn't find much. They brought back a long pole with tattered strips of rag hanging from it. They'd found a buffalo skull looking into the hole in the mound where the smoke had come from. And some pellets of red ochre near the ashes of a fire. I heard them say there was a big circle where the ground had been flattened by stamping but I didn't think ghosts weighed heavy and said so.

Captain Colby smiled and said what my Pa had said, that there weren't such things as ghosts.

But he sent two riders back with us and they come right into the valley and talked long with Pa. Ma made a fuss of me and went on at Pa for letting us go. But we was back home and safe, 'though I still didn't know what it was all about.

*

"Shirts that stop bullets? There ain't no such thing."

"That's what he says."

Dave stubbed his stick into the ground. I knowed he didn't like it when I went against him, but this story was nonsense. I didn't say any more and presently he began to trace the outline of a man in the dust. Then he dug the point of his stick into it just where the heart would have been and said: "The shirts have got some sort of power woven into 'em. They turn the bullets aside. That's what Takawa says."

"Has he got one of these shirts?" I asked Dave.

It was almost two weeks since we got back from the trip to Dave's uncle. Takawa had gone off that same night and we hadn't seen him again till Dave come over this afternoon I'm telling about now.

"He says they weren't ghosts we saw, they was Injuns and that they had these magic shirts on that made 'em look like ghosts. I knew they weren't ghosts," he added, scuffling the stick in the dirt.

That wasn't what he had told Captain Colby, but I didn't say so. We went off up the creek and found Takawa sitting by one of the pools and staring down into the water. He was throwing a stick into it from time to time and at first he wouldn't talk but after a while he looked at us and began a sort of speech.

All the time he was talking he was different. I don't know what it was about him but he had a calm, strong – yes, that was it, a *strong* look. Before, he'd always been just an Indian boy who nobody in the valley thought much about and who lived there just because we let him. Now he had changed and he told us a strange story about what was going to happen and who the ghost riders really were.

Long ago, all the land had belonged to the Indians, began Takawa. There had been no white people at all and the tribes had hunted and followed the buffalo; so many buffalo that they spread like black clouds over the prairie. And this old life was a good life with no sickness or disease and everyone was happy.

Takawa paused and looked into the pool for so long that I thought he wasn't going to tell us no more. Then he went on: the Whites came from the east and killed off the buffalo and took the land. They put the Indians into shacks on reservations, which was just land that nothing would grow on and was no good to them, anyway.

A new land was coming for the Indian, he said. It was already on its way from the west and would reach our valley about next year. And when it came there would be a signal. The ground would tremble.

Dave and I looked at each other, startled.

At this signal, Takawa went on, the Indians would fix sacred eagle's feathers into their hair and rise up above while the new land rolled east and pushed the Whites back into the sea from where they'd come. After this, the Indians would let themselves down on the new land and there they would find all the Indians who had ever lived before. Friends and relations long dead and who were now alive again. And they would all be happy leading the old life.

"All the nations of the Indian coming home," Takawa almost sang it and swayed from side to side as he did so. On every hand there would be herds of deer and antelope and the buffalo would once more blacken the prairie.

"And the ghost riders and the shirts," cried Dave. "Go on, tell about them."

The Indian boy looked straight at me and although it was near noon I shivered.

"The ghost riders come from Wovoka, who is a great shaman and who will lead us to the new land. He is the son of god who the white men killed and nailed to a cross."

"Jesus?" I said. "You mean Jesus, in the Bible?"

"He has the marks on his hands and feet," replied Takawa, "and he can work great magic. He has caused rain to fall in the dry season and ice to appear in the river in summer.

"And he has given the Sioux ghost shirts that will turn away the soldiers' bullets."

"How do you know all this, 'Kawa?"

"Many chiefs went from the reservation to see. He gave them the magic paint for the signs on the shirts and he taught them the ghost dance by which the Indian can see this new land before it comes and help to bring it about."

Well, that was Takawa's story. And Dave and I talked it over and I reckoned we'd better ask Pa. I didn't think he'd believe us or even want to listen but he took it mighty serious and spoke like I'd never heard him speak before to me. Straight out, as if I was a man.

"You must speak up, Ben, tell everything you know. Not just to me but to Captain Colby and everyone else."

"Captain Colby ain't here."

"No, but he will be tonight, and so will many others."

That night, when Dave and I got back from some chore round the meadows, Ma called us in. There was more horses tied up outside the house than I'd seen for a long whiles and the big room was full of men. Some I knowed, like Mr Hannery and Captain Colby. But there were others I didn't, and more than one blue uniform.

We had to tell everything, standing there by the table. About the ghost riders we'd seen up the valley in the spring and about the ghost dancers that we'd stumbled on on that summer trip to Dave's Uncle Jack. Every little detail, right down to the paintings on the ghosts and the sort of noise they made.

After we'd finished there was a long silence.

"That first bunch must have been Big Foot and his party,

comin' back from Nevada," said a voice from the corner where I couldn't see.

"When they first brought stories of this Wovoka to th' reservations," added someone else.

Captain Colby nodded. "They went down two months before with the agent's permission. It was when they returned that it all started."

" 'Kawa told us about Wovoka," I blurted out. "Said he was like Jesus."

I looked round, a bit scared, but no one, not even Pa told me to hold my tongue.

"Wovoka is a Paiute sheep-herder down in Nevada, Ben," said Captain Colby quietly. "He has dreams of a new world coming for the Indians and he teaches them a dance to make these dreams come true."

"But the ghosts? We saw the ghosts in the smoke."

An old man leaned forward and spoke gently.

"They weren't ghosts, Ben, they was Injuns. And it was steam, not smoke. They heat stones and put them in a big hut covered tight with leaves and then they throw water over the stones and sit in the steam to purify themselves. It's an old custom. Then they put on the white shirts and paint themselves with red ochre."

"And then they dance and sing this song about the coming of the Indian nations," said another voice. "They dance 'till they go into a trance and see a vision of the new land that they think is coming."

There was more general talking now but I wasn't listening. I was thinking of the ghost dancers and the way they had rolled on the ground and butted the trees. And the terrible shrieking.

". . . what I cannot understand," it was Captain Colby speaking and he brought my mind back to the crowded room, ". . . what I cannot understand is the thought *behind* this teaching. It goes against all the Indians hold dear. They've always rated success in war as a man's highest achievement. This sheep-herder's preaching peace. All the Indians have to do is to follow the ten commandments and the old life will return a hundred times better."

He paused and cleared his throat. Somebody put in from the back of the room in a big booming voice: "Then it's a better religion he's offering the tribes than all our teachings have accomplished in a hundred years."

That was Mr Farley who preached on the Sabbath and if he was getting into it there was going to be more long words and stuff I wouldn't understand. But there was one more thing I did hear before Ma took me out.

It was Captain Colby speaking and his voice was hard.

"If the Sioux have got hold of it it won't mean peace. It'll be twisted to mean war, and war on the Whites. It's been a hard, dry summer. Food's scarce on the reservations and the hunting's poor. The Sioux have been down a long time – they're ready to clutch at anything."

And as I went out of the door, with Ma sweeping through all those men and them, for once, not even noticing her and standing aside like they usually do, I heard another voice shouting:

"Then we want soldiers in all the towns round the reservations – and an end to these ghost dances!"

We sat in the kitchen 'till the meeting broke up and Mr Hannery come in for Dave. I stood on the porch and watched the horses move off up the road, all white in the moonlight.

Like ghosts themselves, they were.

*

Next thing that happened was the soldiers coming through the valley. It must have been two-three month after the meeting 'cause the drought had broken and I remember the creek was running so they came splashing over the ford and turned south, down the trail.

I'd ridden like fury to fetch Dave, soon as I knew they was coming. I liked to be the first to tell, sometimes, and he was sure keen to see them. We sat on our ponies on the ridge and watched. And we waved and some of the soldiers waved back.

It was a good sight: the sun flashed on the bridles and the harness jingled. There must have been three hundred or more, I reckon.

"Look," cried Dave. "Lookit that gun on wheels."

It rolled behind the column, just before the wagon train, pulled by a black team and flashing its brass bands and long thin barrel.

We sat there 'till they was out of sight and then turned towards home.

"Goin' to Pine Ridge, I shouldn't wonder," said Dave.

There was an Army horse at the house when I got back and Ma was in a tizzy, shouting at me to ride off and get Pa who was over the other side of the hill, branding the new steers which had been shared out in the big valley round-up. When we got back Ma was making a big show like she does when a stranger comes. There was china on the table and the big, old tea-pot with flowers on it that she'd brought from her home when she was first married. We didn't see that often.

The man rose to greet Pa and they shook hands. He was an officer, I guess, with gold braid on his shoulders and a trimming to his hat which was lying on the table.

"It's been a long time," said Pa.

"Four years," answered the officer, smiling. "Your boy's grown."

Ma beamed and Pa nodded, rubbing my hair like he does sometimes. I stepped away and then Ma said: "Get along, Ben. Men want to talk."

That was always the way when strangers come. They'd want to talk and I'd want to listen. And usually I got sent away. When I grow up and get me a son I'll never send him away when strangers come.

I hung around the house but couldn't hear anything and I was swinging on the gate when the soldier stepped out and mounted up. He had a hand-gun strapped to his belt and it thumped as he swung into the saddle. He had a rifle in the scabbard on his horse but then so did most riders in the valley, these days. It was the hand-gun and holster that I'd not seen close up.

He looked at me hanging on the gate.

"Ever seen real wild Indians, Ben?" he asked.

"No."

"No, *sir*," said Ma.

"No, sir."

"Know what year it is, Ben?"

"1889, sir,"

"What year were you born?"

I didn't answer.

"Well, how old are you now?"

"Eleven, sir."

The officer looked at Pa and then back at me. "Custer was long dead an' the war finished before you came here. No wonder the boy knows nothing of Indians." He raised a hand. "Well, good-bye, Ben." I saluted back. He took off his hat to Ma. "Remember, Ma'am. Keep close to the house." He pointed at me. "Him, too."

"We'll see he stays in the valley," said Pa.

"Within sound of the iron," added Ma, grimly, striking the triangle that hung from a beam of the porch roof and was used to call the hands to eat. Old Sam came out of the barn, wagging his tail.

The officer waved and rode off, not the way he had come but north, for the Hannery place.

I followed Ma into the house. "What is it, Ma? Why can't I go out of the valley?"

"Because there may be trouble, that's why. Now go and get on with your chores and leave me to work."

I went out to Pa. "What's the trouble, Pa? Who was he? You knowed him, didn't you?"

Pa was saddling the mare and he didn't answer right away. He pulled the cinch tight, putting his knee into the horse's side so she couldn't blow out and leave the saddle loose when he mounted. She was an old cunning.

"That was Major Morgan, son, and the column was part of

Custer's old regiment, the Seventh." He straightened up and put a hand on the saddle horn. "Yes, I knew him several years back when he was at Laramie."

"What's up, Pa? What's the troubles he talked of?"

"Ain't nothing to worry about, Ben. You jest keep close to home and look after things. I'm going over to Captain Colby's with the Volunteers."

And he mounted and rode off.

Pretty soon, Dave came trailing up the road. He had another dog now and he carried the old gun. Only I seen that the safety catch was mended. He was bursting with news and called out before he reached me: "Major o' th' cavalry come. There's Injun trouble."

"He was here before," I said, "and his name's Major Morgan." That quieted him for a bit but when we'd settled in the barn and his dog and our Sam was sniffing for rats, he burst out again.

"It's the Sioux at Pine Ridge. They're dancin' th' ghost dance an' wearin' th' ghost shirts that Takawa told us about. The agent can't stop them so they've sent for the soldiers."

"Pa's gone to Captain Colby's," I said. "Something about the Volunteers."

David whistled and slipped the safety catch of the old gun back and forth. "Then they must be expecting trouble. Wonder where 'Kawa is?"

But we couldn't find the Indian boy and presently Dave went back to help guard the house, so he said, and I went indoors and looked at the gun rack on the wall and went to ask Ma about the cartridges.

*

Well, that's about all of it, except what the soldiers done to the Indians. It wasn't till Christmas that it happened at a place called Wounded Knee Creek.

The snow come early that winter. We'd gone all through the hot summer praying for rain and then it came cold, sudden like. Afore you knowed it the leaves, which was burned brown anyway, fell off the trees and it was blowing down from the north and freezing. Snow begun to fall and I helped Pa stack up a wagon with straw and drive over to Takawa's so they could spread the straw in their tepee and keep warm. They had the animals in with them and Takawa looked cold and thin and Dave, who'd come with us, took him on one side and asked him what the ghost dancers were going to do now the soldiers had come but he didn't reply or say much at all.

Ma had put food in the wagon for the children. "They got to eat, Injuns or no," she had said and Pa had nodded. We drove back along the same tracks that the wagon had made through the snow coming out.

There'd been a lot of coming and going all fall and then one day, near Christmas, when the whole valley was white, Captain Colby and Mr Hannery and a lot of men come riding by and went off south after speaking to Pa. They were the Volunteers from all the ranches and homesteads round about, got together to protect the valley. They was all grim and quiet.

Pa stayed back to ride round the valley, calling on all the women in turn to see they was all right. Ma kept going out on to the porch all the time he was away, never minding the cold and watching the trail for him to come galloping back. And every time I slipped off from the house she would shout at me to come in.

Christmas was over when Captain Colby and the Volunteers came back. A mighty poor Christmas it was, with the men gone from the valley and no fun or visiting. We usually decorated the schoolhouse and had a play about the baby Jesus and the wise men but it wasn't like that this year I'm telling you about.

Kind of funny, really, when all the time the Indians was saying *their* Messiah had come.

When the men got back they was all excited and telling about fighting the Sioux and how the tribes were finished now once and for all and that there'd be no more ghost dances.

"You saw them first, Ben," said Captain Colby, putting a hand on my head and smiling, 'though it was a hard sort of smile. "You won't see ghosts in this valley any more."

After that, no one took much notice of me, and Ma was too busy to head me off, what with getting them all things to eat and drink and so I just hung around and listened to the talk.

It seems the soldiers got all the dancers together for a council at Wounded Knee. Old Big Foot, and Kicking Bear and Yellow Bird and many others, though I didn't hear no mention of Sitting Bull. Mr Hannery said later that he guessed he was too cunning to come. They told the Indians that the ghost dances must stop, but, of course, the Sioux wouldn't agree.

Well, they argued for two days and the Indians kept coming and going and the soldiers cursed the cold and got impatient.

Then they rolled the gun to the top of a hill, looking down on all the Indians. It was a Hotchkiss gun, I heard someone say and that the battery commander would get a medal for his part in what happened.

They said that the Indians had guns under their blankets and told them to give them up.

"But there were women and children there, too, weren't there?" I heard Pa ask.

The men argued a bit and some of them thought that there was. But they all agreed that they had guns hidden, even the squaws.

Finally, one old Indian got up and threw down his blanket and waved a gun at the soldiers who had been searching the tepees and the braves themselves, looking for rifles.

The men weren't at all clear about what happened then. They were someways off behind the soldiers and near some buildings. But anyway, that gun went off.

And Yellow Bird, this old chief, rose up and threw a handful of dirt in the air like it was a signal. And before the dust hit the ground some young braves leaped up and begun shooting at the soldiers.

Then the Hotchkiss gun, that gun with wheels and the long barrel that we'd been so excited to see rolling through our valley, started to fire and send shells screaming down into the Indian camp. They burst among the tepees and knocked some of them down so that all the women and children ran away and hid in a ditch.

Some of the braves lined up and tried to protect them, but all the time the other Indians worked their rifles on the soldiers. Captain Colby said he'd never seen repeating rifles used so quickly or so smart.

Our men by the buildings couldn't do much on account of the soldiers and the Indians on the council square being all mixed up, fighting. But the team with the Hotchkiss gun fired at the Indian village all the time and I guess that's what won the battle in the end and why they're going to get a medal.

Only it don't seem right that they was firing at the squaws and their children, does it? Why, it might have been Takawa there.

After the battle the snow came and covered the ground and the dead so that when Mr Hannery and some men from our valley went back two-three days after there was nothing to see except just humps on the snow, hundreds of them. And the bodies were frozen stiff, so they said.

The men went among them turning them over to see if anyone was still alive and picking up ghost shirts for souvenirs.

Ma cried out when she heard that they found three babies all alive and an old woman. They took them back to the town where there was an Indian doctor to look after them.

But most of the Indians was killed. Old Yellow Bird and Big Foot, too, who had been with the ghost riders when we first saw them that evening up near the creek.

I seen a picture of him in a newspaper; it's still around somewheres. He's sitting up in the snow, looking at the sky as if he expected Wovoka to come down with the snowflakes and save him. He's even got his arm stretched out. Only he's froze stiff with cold and he sat there for three days, with the wind blowing his black hair over his face, 'till they come and pulled him out and put him in a pit they dug.

Then the men who had done the burying all lined up and had *their* picture took standing round the big grave, full of dead ghost dancers and the painted shirts that didn't stop no bullets.

The Sioux rode for the last time at Wounded Knee and the dance they danced there was the dance of death.

I heard Mr Hannery tell Pa they got two dollars for every Indian they buried. I didn't know what to think about it all, at the end. Takawa went away into the hills and he didn't come back for nigh on three days.

I reckon he didn't want Dave and me to see him crying.

Feel Free

Alan Garner

The line of sight from Tosh's den to Brian went under the Giant Panda's belly, between the gilded coffin of Bak-en-Mut and the town stocks, through the Taj Mahal and over Lady Henrietta Maria's dyed bodice. The first morning when Brian had started his drawing the Taj Mahal had blocked Tosh's view, but when Brian came back from his dinner three doors had been opened to give a clear run through, and whenever he looked Tosh's eye was on him.

Tosh kept to his den, where he brewed tea and filled in his coupon, unless he was on patrol. He patrolled every hour, on the hour, up one side, across the back and down the other side, which meant that he came upon Brian from behind. He said nothing the first day, but stood at ease, lifting his heels and lowering them; click; click; click; and he sucked his teeth. Then he patrolled back to his den. There were no visitors to the museum all day, all week.

"What are you on?" said Tosh half-way through the second afternoon.

"Eh up," said Brian. "It talks."

"None of your lip," said Tosh. His medal ribbons bristled.

But on the third day Tosh patrolled with a mug of hot brown water thickened with condensed milk. "Cuppertea," he said.

Brian put down his drawing board. "Thanks, Tosh."

"Yer welcome."

"How's trade?" said Brian.

"Average," said Tosh. "For the season."

"Been pretty quiet here, hasn't it?" said Brian. "Since they built the Holiday Camp, I mean. The old park just can't compete, can it?"

"We have our regulars," said Tosh. "And our aberlutions is still second to none."

"It's Open Day up the Camp," said Brian. "Anyone can go, free."

"It's all kidology," said Tosh. "There's nowt free in this world, lad."

"There is today," said Brian. "I'm going, anyroad."

"What are you on here?" said Tosh.

"It's my Project for school," said Brian. "Last term it was Compost: this term it's Pottery."

The next time round Tosh said, "What you got to do with this malarky?"

"I'm trying to draw that Ancient Greek dish from all sides and see if I can copy it."

"What for?"

"Greek pottery's supposed to be the best, so I thought I'd start at the top."

"Fancy it, do you?"

"Yes," said Brian. "It's funny, is that. I seem to be quite knacky with it, though I've only just started. I may go on and do evening classes."

"I'm partial to a bit of art, meself," said Tosh. "Sign-writing: but painting's favourite. Not yon modern stuff, though: more traditional – dogs and flowers and that. It makes you realise how much work they put in, them fellers. Same as him there." Tosh pointed to the Egyptian coffin. "Yon Back-in-a-Minute. The gold leaf and stuff, all them little pictures – that wasn't done on piece work. Eh? Not on piece work."

"Nor this dish, neither," said Brian. "That's why I'm having such a sweat over the drawing. Every line's perfect."

"Ah," said Tosh. "They had time in them days. They had all the time there is. All the time in the world."

The dish stood alone in its case, a typed label on the glass: "Attic Krater, 5th Century BC, Artist Unknown. The scene depicts Charon, ferryman of the dead, conveying a soul across the river Acheron in the Underworld."

At first Brian had thought the design was too wooden and formal. The old boatman Charon crouched with bent knees, and the dead man was as blank as any traveller. The waves curled in solid, regular spirals and the rest of the design was geometry – squares, crosses, leaf patterns without life. But as he worked Brian found a balance and a rhythm in the dish. Nothing was there without a reason, and its place in the design was so accurately fixed that to move it was like playing a wrong note. And all this Brian had found in two days from a red and black dish in a glass case.

"Have you done, then?" said Tosh an hour later.

Brian sat with his hands in his pockets, glaring at the dish.

"No. Eh, Tosh: let's have the case open. I want to cop hold of that dish."

"Not likely," said Tosh. "It's more than my job's worth. Can't you see all you want from here?"

"Seeing's not enough. That's why these drawings don't work. They're on the flat, and the dish is curved. Pattern and shape are all part of it – you can't have one without the other. My drawing's like sucking sweets with the wrapper on."

"What if you bust it, though?" said Tosh.

"It'd mend. It's been bust before. Come on, Tosh, be a pal."

Tosh went to his den and came back with a key. "I know nowt about this," he said.

Brian moved his fingers along the surfaces of the dish. "That's it," he kept saying. "That's it. Yes. That's it. Eh, Tosh, the man as made this was a blooming marvel. It's perfect. It's like I don't know what, it's like – it's – heck, it's like flying."

"Ay, well, one thing's for sure," said Tosh. "The feller as made yon: his head doesn't ache. How old is it?"

"A good two thousand year," said Brian. "Two thousand year. He sat and worked this out, these curves and lines and colours and patterns, and then he made it. Two thousand year. Heck. And it's come all that way. To me. So as I know what he was thinking. Two thousand . . ."

"Ay, his head doesn't ache any more, right enough," said Tosh.

Brian turned the cup over to examine the base.

"It'd do for a cake stand, would that," said Tosh. "For Sundays."

"Tosh, look!" Brian nearly dropped the dish. On the base was a clear thumb print fired hard as the rest of the clay.

"There he is," whispered Brian.

The change from the case to the outside air had put a mist on the surface of the dish, and Brian set his own fingers against the other hand.

"Two thousand year, Tosh. That's nothing. Who was he?"

"No, he'll not have a headache."

Brian stared at his own print and the fossilled clay. "Tosh," he said, "they're the same. That thumb print and mine. What do you make of it?"

"They're not," said Tosh. "No two people ever has the same tabs."

"These are."

"They can't be," said Tosh. "I went on courses down London when I was a constable."

"These are the same."

"You might think so, but you'd be wrong. It's been proved as how every man woman and child is born with different finger prints from anyone else."

"How's it been proved?" said Brian.

"Because the same prints have never turned up twice. Why, men have been hanged on the strength of that, and where would be the sense if it wasn't true?"

"Look for yourself," said Brian.

Tosh put on his glasses. For a while he said nothing, then, "Ah. Very good. Very close, I'll allow, but see at yon line across the other feller's thumb. That's a scar. You haven't got one."

"But a scar's something that happens," said Brian. "It's nothing to do with what you're born like. If he hadn't gashed his thumb, they'd be the same."

"But they're not, are they?" said Tosh. "And it was a long time ago, so what's the odds?"

Brian finished his drawings early. He was taking Sandra to the Open Day at the Camp, and he wanted to have a shave. They met at the bus stop.

"There's that Beryl Fletcher," said Sandra.

"What about her?" said Brian.

"She only left school last week, and she's cracking on she's dead sophisticated."

"Give over," said Brian. "You're jealous."

Two buses came and went.

"Do you like me dress?" said Sandra.

"Yes."

"Just 'yes'?"

"It's all right," said Brian. "Smashing."

"You never noticed," said Sandra.

"I did. It's nice – better than Beryl Fletcher's."

Sandra laughed. "You'd never notice, you great cloth-head. What's up? You've not had two words to say for yourself."

"Sorry," said Brian. "I was thinking about that dish I've been working on all week at the museum."

"What's her name?"

"I don't know her name, but she's very mature."

"How old is she?" said Sandra.

"Two-and-a-bit thousand year."

A bus came and they got on.

"You know Tosh, the head Parky, him as looks after the museum?" said Brian.

"Yes. He's our kid's wife's uncle."

"Was he ever a bobby?"

"He used to be a sergeant," said Sandra.

Three stops later Sandra said, "You're quiet."

"Am I? Sorry."

"What's to do, love? What's wrong?"

"Have you ever hidden something to chance it being found again years and years later – perhaps long after you're dead?"

"No," said Sandra.

"I have," said Brian. "I was a great one for filling screw-top bottles with junk and then burying them. I put notes inside, and pieces out of the newspaper. You're talking to somebody you'll never meet, never know: but if they find the bottle they'll know you. There's bits of you in the bottle, waiting all this time, see, in the dark, and as soon as the bottle's opened – time's nothing – and – and –"

"Eh up," said Sandra, "people are looking. You do get some ideas, Brian Walton!"

"It's that dish at the museum," said Brian. "I thought it was a crummy old pot, but when I started to sort it out I found what was inside it."

"What? A message?" said Sandra.

"No. Better than that. This fellow as made it over two thousand year ago – he knew nothing about me, but he worked out how to fit the picture and the shape together. When you look at it you don't see how clever he was, but when you touch it, and try to copy it, you're suddenly with him, – same as if you're watching over his shoulder and he's talking to you, showing you. So when I do a pot next, he'll be helping. It'll be his pot. And he's been dead two thousand year! What about that, eh?"

"Fancy," said Sandra.

The bus had arrived at the camp. Sandra was about to step down from the platform when she tipped forward at the waist. Her eyes widened and she clutched at the rail.

"What's the matter?" said Brian.

"It's me shoe!" she hissed. "It's fast!" The stiletto heel had jammed between the ridges of the platform, and Sandra had to take her shoe off to get it free. "Oh, it's scratched!" she said. "First time out, and all."

"Come on," said Brian. "If you will be sophisticated . . ."

"Hello! Hello! Hello!" said the loudspeakers. "This is Open Day, friends, and it's free, free, free! Walk in! Have fun!"

"Where do you want to start?" said Brian.

"I don't know," said Sandra. "Let's see what there is."

"Hello! Hello! Hello! This is Your Day and Your Camp. The Camp with a Difference, friends and neighbours, Where Only You Matter. This is the Camp with Only One Rule – Feel Free! Feel free, friends!"

Brian and Sandra danced to two of the five resident tape recordings, drove a motor boat on the Marine Lake, spun their own candy floss. . . .

"Hello! Hello! Hello! Feel free, friends! This is the Lay-Say-Fair Holiday Camp, a totally new concept in Family Camping, adding a new dimension to leisure, where folk come to stay, play, make hay, or relax in the laze-away-days that you find only at the Lay-Say-Fair Holiday Camp. Yes! And it's all free, friends. Thanks to the All-in L.S.F. Tariff, which you pay when you reserve your chalet. There are no hidden extras: this once-and-for-all payment is your passport to delight. Yes! Remember! L.S.F. saves L.S.D.! Now!"

"Me feet are killing me," said Sandra.

They sat on a bench in the Willow Pattern Garden. Brian stroked the head of a Chinese bronze dragon, from which the Camp's music tinkled. The sun was low, the day at its best after the heat.

"Isn't it dreamy?" said Sandra. "Better than the old park. These banks and banks of flowers and rock gardens: and the bees buzzing."

"It's hard luck on the bees," said Brian. "They'll be dead by morning."

"You're proper cheerful today, you are," said Sandra. "Why will they be dead?"

"Selective weedkiller," said Brian. "You couldn't keep the soil as clean as that, else. They spray it on, and nobody bothers to tell the bees."

"How do you know?"

"I read quite a lot about it last term," said Brian, "When I was doing Compost. There's a lot in soil; you may not think it, but there is."

"We're off," said Sandra.

"No. Look," said Brian, and leant backwards to gather a handful of earth from a rockery flower bed. "Soil isn't muck, it's . . . well, I'll be . . . Sandra? This here soil's plastic!"

Smooth, clean granules rolled between his fingers.

"The whole blooming lot's plastic – grass, flowers, and all!"

"Now that's what I call sensible. It helps to keep the cost down," said Sandra. "And it doesn't kill bees."

"Ay," said Brian. "Bees. Surely they're not that daft."

He climbed up the rockery, and he soon found the bees.

They were each mounted on a quivering hair spring, the buzzer plugged in to a time switch.

"Hello! Hello! Hello!" said the bronze dragon. "Lay-Say-Fair, The Camp with a Difference. Have you visited the Pleasureteria yet, friends? The L.S.F. Pleasureteria is the only Do-it-Yourself Fun-Drome in existence: all the fun of the fair for free! Free! Now!"

"We'll have a stab at that, shall we?" said Brian.

They rode on the Big Wheel, the Dodgems, the Roller Coaster, the Dive Bomber, the Octopus. The equipment was automatically controlled. Lights winked, recorded voices gave instructions, bells rang.

In the Pally-Palais Sandra battled with sudden air jets from the floor, and clung to Brian on the Cake Walk. It was late dusk when they came out of the Palais. They laughed a lot.

"Well, something's made you buck up at last," said Sandra. "I thought I was landed with pottery and compost for the night."

"What shall we go on now?" said Brian.

"There's the Tunnel of Love, if you're feeling romantic," said Sandra.

"You never know till you try, do you?" said Brian.

They walked on to the stage by the water channel. There was a gate across the channel with a notice saying: "Passengers wait here. Pull illuminated handle for boat. Do not board boat until boat has stopped. Do not stand up in boat. Passengers must be seated when bell rings. No smoking."

" 'Feel free, friends'," said Brian.

Beyond the gate was a grotto of plaster stalactites and stalagmites, and the channel rushed among them to a black tunnel.

"Queer green light there, isn't it?" said Sandra. "Ever so eerie."

"Special paint," said Brian. "It shows up luminous in ultra-violet light. Remember that Bottom of the Sea Spectacular in 'Goldilocks on Ice' at the Opera House last year? Same thing in this grotto."

Brian pulled the lever and a boat came out of the darkness upstream. Its prow was shaped to fit in a recess in the gate, which kept it firm.

"Passengers board now," said a recorded voice. "Take your seats immediately. Passengers board now. Take your seats immediately. Do not stand."

Brian climbed into the boat and turned to help Sandra. She put one foot on the seat, then twisted awkwardly.

"Hurry up," said Brian.

"It's me heel again. It's caught in something. On the stage."

They began to laugh. Brian tried to lift Sandra into the boat but had nothing to brace himself against.

"Kick your shoe off."

"I can't."

They pushed and pulled. A bell rang. "All passengers sit. Stand clear. Do not try to board. Stand clear."

The bell rang again, and the gate flew open.

Sandra was still laughing, but Brian felt the water take the boat, and he knew he could not hold it. Already he was being dragged off balance.

"Get back," he said. "You'll fall in. Get back."

"I can't, I'm stuck."

"I'm going to shove you," said Brian. "Shove you. Ready? On three. One. Two. Three. . . . !"

He pushed Sandra as hard as he could, and she fell back on to the stage. He lurched in the boat and grabbed at the stern to save himself. For a moment the boat hung level with Sandra, who was three feet away, but dry, as she scrambled up, still laughing.

"Enjoy yourself!" she shouted. The boat bobbed away on the race, and Brian stood watching. Now he was in the grotto, and Sandra was distant in another light.

"Sit down, Brian! Coo-ee! Have a nice trip, love, and if you can't be good be careful! Shall I see you next time round? Coo-ee!"

She was swinging away from him, a tiny figure lost among stalactites. He stood, looking, looking, and slowly lifted his hand off the nail that had worked loose at the edge of the stern. He had not felt its sharpness, but now the gash throbbed across the ball of his thumb. The boat danced towards the tunnel.

Minuke

Nigel Kneale

The estate agent kept an uncomfortable silence until we had reached his car. "Frankly, I wish you hadn't got wind of that," he said. "Don't know how you did: I thought I had the whole thing carefully disposed of. Oh, please get in."

He pulled his door shut and frowned. "It puts me in a rather awkward spot. I suppose I'd better tell you all I know about that case, or you'd be suspecting me of heaven-knows-what kinds of chicanery in your own."

As we set off to see the property I was interested in, he shifted the cigarette to the side of his mouth.

"It's quite a distance, so I can tell you on the way there," he said. "We'll pass the very spot, as a matter of fact, and you can see it for yourself. Such as there is to see."

*

It was away back before the war (said the estate agent). At the height of the building boom. You remember how it was: ribbon development in full blast everywhere; speculative builders sticking things up almost overnight. Though at least you could get a house when you wanted it in those days.

I've always been careful in what I handle – I want you to understand that. Then one day I was handed a packet of coast-road bungalows, for letting. Put up by one of these gone tomorrow firms, and bought by a local man. I can't say I exactly jumped for joy, but for once the things looked all right, and – business is inclined to be business.

The desirable residence you heard about stood at the end of the row. Actually, it seemed to have the best site. On a sort of natural platform, as it were, raised above road level and looking straight out over the sea. Like all the rest, it had a simple two-bedroom, lounge, living-room, kitchen, bathroom layout. Red-tiled roof, roughcast walls. Ornamental portico, garden strip all round. Sufficiently far from town, but with all conveniences.

It was taken by a man named Pritchard. Cinema projectionist, I think he was. Wife, a boy of ten or so, and a rather younger daughter. Oh – and dog, one of those black, lop-eared animals. They christened the place "Minuke", M-I-N-U-K-E. My Nook. Yes, that's what I said too. And not even the miserable excuse of its being phonetically correct. Still, hardly worse than most.

Well, at the start everything seemed quite jolly. The Pritchards settled in and busied themselves with rearing a privet hedge and shoving flowers in. They'd paid the first quarter in advance, and as far as I was concerned, were out of the picture for a bit.

Then, about a fortnight after they'd moved in, I had a telephone call from Mrs P to say there was something odd about the kitchen tap. Apparently the thing had happened twice. The first time was when her sister was visiting them, and tried to fill the kettle: no water would come through for a long time, then suddenly squirted violently and almost soaked the woman. I gather the Pritchards hadn't really believed this – thought she was trying to find fault with their little nest – it had never happened before, and she couldn't make it happen again. Then, about a week later, it did: with Mrs. Pritchard this time. After her husband had examined the tap and could find nothing wrong with it, he decided that the water supply must be faulty; so they got on to me.

I went round personally, as it was the first complaint from any of these bungalows. The tap seemed normal, and I remember asking if the schoolboy son could have been experimenting with their main stop, when Mrs Pritchard, who had been fiddling with the tap, suddenly said, "Quick, look at this! It's off now!" They were quite cocky about its happening when I was there.

It really was odd. I turned the tap to the limit, but – not a drop! Not even the sort of gasping gurgle you hear when the supply is turned off at the main. After a couple of minutes, though, it came on. Water shot out, I should say, with about ten times' normal force, as if it had been held under pressure. Then gradually it died down and ran steadily.

Both children were in the room with us until we all dodged out of the door to escape a soaking – it had splashed all over the ceiling – so they couldn't have been up to any tricks. I promised the Pritchards to have the pipes checked. Before returning to town, I called at the next two bungalows in the row: neither of the tenants had had any trouble at all with the water. I thought, well, that localised it at least.

When I reached my office there was a telephone message waiting from Pritchard. I rang him back and he was obviously annoyed. "Look here," he said, "Not ten minutes after you left, we've had something else happen! The wall of the large bedroom's cracked from top to bottom. Big pieces of plaster fell, and the bed's in a terrible mess." And then he said, "You wouldn't have got me in a jerry-built place like this if I'd known!"

I had plasterers on the job next morning, and the whole water supply to "Minuke" under examination. For about three days there was peace. The tap behaved itself, and absolutely nothing was found to be wrong. I was annoyed at what seemed to have been unnecessary expenditure. It looked as if the Pritchards were going to be difficult – and I've had my share of that type: fault-finding cranks occasionally carry eccentricity to the extent of a little private destruction, to prove their points. I was on the watch from now on.

Then it came again.

Pritchard rang me at my home, before nine in the morning. His voice sounded a bit off. Shaky.

"For God's sake can you come round here right away," he said. "Tell you about it when you get here." And then he said, almost fiercely, but quietly and close to the mouthpiece, "There's something damned queer about this place!" Dramatising is a typical feature of all cranks, I thought, but particularly the little mousy kind, like Pritchard.

I went to "Minuke" and found that Mrs Pritchard was in bed, in a state of collapse. The doctor had given her a sleeping dose.

Pritchard told me a tale that was chiefly remarkable for the expression on his face as he told it.

I don't know if you're familiar with the layout of that type of bungalow? The living-room is in the front of the house, with the kitchen behind it. To get from one to the other you have to use the little hallway, through two doors. But for convenience at meal-times, there's a serving hatch in the wall between these rooms. A small wooden door slides up and down over the hatch-opening.

"The wife was just passing a big plate of bacon and eggs through from the kitchen," Pritchard told me, "when the hatch door came down on her wrists. I saw it and I heard her yell. I thought the cord must've snapped, so I said, 'All right, all right!' and went to pull it up because it's only a light wooden frame."

Pritchard was a funny colour and as far as I could judge, it was genuine.

"Do you know, it wouldn't come! I got my fingers under it and heaved, but it might have weighed two hundredweight. Once it gave an inch or so, and then pressed harder. I said, 'Hold on!' and nipped round through the hall. When I got into the kitchen she was on the floor, fainted. And the hatch-door was hitched up as right as ninepence. That gave me a turn!" He sat down, quite deflated; it didn't appear to be put on. Still, ordinary neurotics can be almost as troublesome as out-and-out cranks.

I tested the hatch, gingerly; and, of course, the cords were sound and it ran easily.

"Possibly a bit stiff at times, being new," I said. "They're apt to jam if you're rough with them." And then, "By the way, just what were you hinting on the phone?"

He looked at me. It was warm sunlight outside, with a bus

passing. Normal enough to take the mike out of Frankenstein's monster. "Never mind," he said, and gave a sheepish half-grin. "Bit of – well, funny construction in this house, though, eh?"

I'm afraid I was rather outspoken with him.

Let alone any twaddle about a month-old bungalow being haunted, I was determined to clamp down on this "jerry-building" talk. Perhaps I was beginning to have doubts myself.

I wrote straight off to the building company when I'd managed to trace them, busy developing an arterial road about three counties away. I dare say my letter was on the insinuating side: I think I asked if they had any record of difficulties in the construction of this bungalow. At any rate I got a sniffy reply by return, stating that the matter was out of their hands; in addition, their records were not available for discussion. Blind alley.

In the meantime, things at "Minuke" had worsened to a really frightening degree. I dreaded the phone ringing. One morning the two Pritchards senior awoke to find that nearly all the furniture in their bedroom had been moved about, including the bed they had been sleeping in: they had felt absolutely nothing. Food became suddenly and revoltingly decomposed. All the chimney pots had come down, not just into the garden, but to the far side of the high road, except one which appeared, pulverised, on the living-room floor. The obvious attempts of the Pritchards to keep a rational outlook had put paid to most of my suspicions by this time.

I managed to locate a local man who had been employed during the erection of the bungalows, as an extra hand. He had worked only on the foundations of "Minuke", but what he had to say was interesting.

They had found the going slow because of striking a layer of enormous flat stones, apparently trimmed slate, but as the site was otherwise excellent, they pressed on, using the stone as foundation where it fitted in with the plan, and laying down rubble where it didn't. The concrete skin over the rubble – my ears burned when I heard about that, I can tell you – this wretched so-called concrete had cracked, or shattered, several times. Which wasn't entirely surprising, if it had been laid as he described. The flat stones, he said had not been seriously disturbed. A workmate had referred to them as a "giant's grave", so it was possibly an old burial mound. Norse, perhaps – those are fairly common along this coast – or even very much older.

Apart from this – I'm no diehard sceptic, I may as well confess – I was beginning to admit modest theories about a poltergeist, in spite of a lack of corroborative knockings and ornament-throwing. There were two young children in the house, and the lore has it that kids are often unconsciously connected with phenomena of that sort, though usually adolescents. Still, in the real-estate profession you have to be careful, and if I could see the Pritchards safely off the premises without airing these possibilities, it might be kindest to the bungalow's future.

I went to "Minuke" the same afternoon.

It was certainly turning out an odd nook. I found a departing policeman on the doorstep. That morning the back door had been burst in by a hundredweight or so of soil, and Mrs Pritchard was trying to convince herself that a practical joker had it in for them. The policeman had taken some notes, and was giving vague advice about "civil action" which showed that he was out of his depth.

Pritchard looked very tired, almost ill. "I've got leave from my job, to look after them," he said, when we were alone. I thought he was wise. He had given his wife's illness as the reason, and I was glad of that.

"I don't believe in – unnatural happenings," he said.

I agreed with him, non-committally.

"But I'm afraid of what ideas the kids might get. They're both at impressionable ages, y'know."

I recognised the symptoms without disappointment. "You mean, you'd rather move elsewhere," I said.

He nodded. "I like the district, mind you. But what I –"

There was a report like a gun in the very room.

I found myself with both arms up to cover my face. There were tiny splinters everywhere, and a dust of fibre in the air. The door had exploded. Literally.

To hark back to constructional details, it was one of those light, hollow frame-and-plywood jobs. As you'll know, it takes considerable force to splinter plywood: well this was in tiny fragments. And the oddest thing was that we had felt no blast effect.

In the next room I heard their dog howling. Pritchard was as stiff as a poker.

"I felt it!" he said. "I felt this lot coming. I've got to knowing when something's likely to happen. It's all round!" Of course I began to imagine I'd sensed something too, but I doubt if I had really; my shock came with the crash. Mrs Pritchard was in the doorway by this time with the kids behind her. He motioned them out and grabbed my arm.

"The thing is," he whispered, "that I can still feel it! Stronger than ever, by God! Look, will you stay at home tonight, in case I need – well, in case things get worse? I can phone you."

On my way back I called at the town library and managed to get hold of a volume on supernatural possession and whatnot. Yes, I was committed now. But the library didn't specialise in that line, and when I opened the book at home, I found it was very little help. "Vampires of south-eastern Europe" type of stuff. I came across references to something the jargon called an "elemental" which I took to be a good deal more vicious and destructive than any poltergeist. A thoroughly nasty form of manifestation, if it existed. Those Norse gravestones were fitting into the picture uncomfortably well; it was fashionable in those days to be buried with all the trimmings, human sacrifice and even more unmentionable attractions.

But I read on. After half a chapter on zombies and Rumanian were-wolves, the whole thing began to seem so fantastic that I turned seriously to working out methods of exploding somebody's door as a practical joke. Even a totally certifiable joker would be likelier than vampires. In no time I'd settled down with a whisky, doodling wiring diagrams and only occasionally – like twinges of conscience – speculating on contacting the psychic investigation people.

When the phone rang I was hardly prepared for it.

It was a confused, distant voice, gabbling desperately, but I recognised it as Pritchard. "For God's sake, don't lose a second! Get here – it's all hell on earth! Can't you hear it? My God, I'm going crazy!" And in the background I thought I was able to hear something. A sort of bubbling, shushing "wah-wah" noise. Indescribable. But you hear some odd sounds on telephones at any time.

"Yes," I said, "I'll come immediately. Why don't you all leave –" But the line had gone dead.

Probably I've never moved faster. I scrambled out to the car with untied shoes flopping, though I remembered to grab a heavy stick in the hall – whatever use it was to be. I drove like fury, heart belting, straight to "Minuke" expecting to see heaven knows what.

But everything looked still and normal there. The moon was up and I could see the whole place clearly. Curtained lights in the windows. Not a sound.

I rang. After a moment Pritchard opened the door. He was quiet and seemed almost surprised to see me.

I pushed inside. "Well?" I said. "What's happened?"

"Not a thing, so far," he said. "That's why I didn't expect –"

I felt suddenly angry. "Look here," I said, "what are you playing at? Seems to me that any hoaxing round here begins a lot nearer home than you'd have me believe!" Then the penny dropped. I saw by the fright in his face that he knew something had gone wrong. That was the most horrible, sickening moment of the whole affair for me.

"Didn't you ring?" I said.

And he shook his head.

I've been in some tight spots. But there was always some concrete actual business in hand to screw the mind safely down to. I suppose panic is when the subconscious breaks loose and everything in your head dashes screaming out. It was only just in time that I found a touch of the concrete and actual. A kiddie's paintbox on the floor, very watery.

"The children," I said. "Where are they?"

"Wife's just putting the little 'un to bed. She's been restless tonight; just wouldn't go, crying and difficult. Arthur's in the bathroom. Look here, what's happened?"

I told him, making it as short and matter-of-fact as I could. He turned ghastly.

"Better get them dressed and out of here right away," I said. "Make some excuse, not to alarm them."

He'd gone before I finished speaking.

I smoked hard, trying to build up the idea of "Hoax! Hoax!" in my mind. After all, it could have been. But I knew it wasn't.

Everything looked cosy and normal. Clock ticking. Fire red and mellow. Half-empty cocoa mug on the table. The sound of the sea from beyond the road. I went through to the kitchen. The dog was there, looking up from its sleeping-basket under the sink. "Good dog," I said, and it wriggled its tail.

Pritchard came in from the hall. He jumped when he saw me.

"Getting nervy!" he said. "They won't be long. I don't know where we can go if we – well, if we have to – to leave tonight –"

"My car's outside," I told him. "I'll fix you up. Look here, did you ever 'hear things'? Odd noises?" I hadn't told him that part of the telephone call.

He looked at me so oddly, I thought he was going to collapse.

"I don't know," he said. "Can you?"

"At this moment?"

I listened.

"No," I said. "The clock on the shelf. The sea. Nothing else. No."

"The sea," he said, barely whispering. "But you can't hear the sea in this kitchen!"

He was close to me in an instant. Absolutely terrified. "Yes, I have heard this before! I think we all have. I said it was the sea: so as not to frighten them. But it isn't! And I recognised it when I came in here just now. That's what made me start. It's getting louder: it does that."

He was right. Like slow breathing. It seemed to emanate from inside the walls, not at a particular spot, but everywhere. We went into the hall, then the front room; it was the same there. Mixed with it now was a sort of thin crying.

"That's Nellie," Pritchard said. "The dog: she always whimpers when it's on – too scared to howl. My God. I've never heard it as loud as this before."

"Hurry them up, will you!" I almost shouted. He went.

The "breathing" was ghastly. Slobbering. Stertorous, I think the term is. And faster. Oh, yes, I recognised it. The background music to the phone message. My skin was pure ice.

"Come along!" I yelled. I switched on the little radio to drown the noise. The old National Programme, as it was in those days, for late dance music. Believe it or not, what came through that loud-speaker was the same vile sighing noise, at double the volume. And when I tried to switch it off, it stayed the same.

The whole bungalow was trembling. The Pritchards came running in, she carrying the little girl. "Get them into the car," I shouted. We heard glass smashing somewhere.

Above our heads there was an almighty thump. Plaster showered down.

Half-way out of the door the little girl screamed, "Nellie! Where's Nellie? Nellie, Nellie!"

"The dog," Pritchard moaned. "Oh, curse it!" He dragged them outside. I dived for the kitchen, where I'd seen the animal, feeling a lunatic for doing it. Plaster was springing out of the walls in painful showers.

In the kitchen I found water everywhere. One tap was

squirting like a fire-hose. The other was missing, water belching across the window from a torn end of pipe.

"Nellie!" I called.

Then I saw the dog. It was lying near the oven, quite stiff. Round its neck was twisted a piece of painted piping with the other tap on the end.

Sheer funk got me then. The ground was moving under me. I bolted down the hall, nearly bumped into Pritchard. I yelled and shoved. I could actually feel the house at my back.

We got outside. The noise was like a dreadful snoring, with rumbles and crashes thrown in. One of the lights went out. "Nellie's run away," I said, and we all got in the car, the kids bawling. I started up. People were coming out of the other bungalows – they're pretty far apart and the din was just beginning to make itself felt. Pritchard grumbled, "We can stop now. Think it'd be safe to go back and grab some of the furniture?" As if he was at a fire; but I don't think he knew what he was doing.

"Daddy – look!" screeched the boy.

We saw it. The chimney of "Minuke" was going up in a horrible way. In the moonlight it seemed to grow quite slowly, to about sixty feet, like a giant crooked finger. And then – burst. I heard bricks thumping down. Somewhere somebody screamed.

There was a glare like an ungodly great lightning flash. It lasted for a second or so.

Of course, we were dazzled, but I thought I saw the whole of "Minuke" fall suddenly and instantaneously flat, like a swatted fly. I probably did, because that's what happened, anyway.

There isn't much more to tell.

Nobody was really hurt, and we were able to put down the whole thing to a serious electrical fault. Main fuses had blown throughout the whole district, which helped this theory out. Perhaps it was unfortunate in another respect, because a lot of people changed over to gas.

There wasn't much recognisably left of "Minuke". But some

of the bits were rather unusual. Knots in pipes for instance – I buried what was left of the dog myself. Wood and brick cleanly sliced. Small quantities of completely powdered metal. The bath had been squashed flat, like tinfoil. In fact, Pritchard was lucky to land the insurance money for his furniture.

My professional problem, of course, remained. The plot where the wretched place had stood. I managed to persuade the owner it wasn't ideal for building on. Incidentally, lifting those stones might reveal something to somebody some day – but not to me, thank you!

I think my eventual solution showed a touch of wit: I let it very cheaply as a scrap-metal dump.

Well? I know I've never been able to make any sense out of it. I hate telling you all this stuff, because it must make me seem either a simpleton or a charlatan. In so far as there's any circumstantial evidence in looking at the place, you can see it in a moment or two. Here's the coast road –

*

The car pulled up at a bare spot beyond a sparse line of bungalows. The space was marked by a straggling, tufty square of privet bushes. Inside I could see a tangle of rusting iron; springs, a car chassis, oil drums.

"The hedge keeps it from being too unsightly," said the estate agent, as we crossed to it. "See – the remains of the gate."

A few half-rotten slats dangled from an upright. One still bore part of a chrome-plated name. "MI – – – –" and, a little farther on, "K".

"Nothing worth seeing now," he said. I peered inside. "Not that there ever was much – Look out!" I felt a violent push. In the same instant something zipped past my head and crashed against the car behind. "My God!"

"Went right at you!" gasped the agent.

It had shattered a window of the car and gone through the open door opposite. We found it in the road beyond, sizzling on the tarmac. A heavy steel nut, white-hot.

"I don't know about you," the estate agent said, "but I'm rather in favour of getting out of here."

And we did. Quickly.

The Witch's Bone

William Croft Dickinson

Michael Elliott M.A., LL.D., F.S.A.(Scot.) frowned at the letter which had come from the Honorary Curator of the local museum. It was quite a short letter and quite a simple one; merely asking him if he would allow the Museum to borrow his "Witch's Bone" for a special exhibition covering Folk Beliefs and Customs. But Michael Elliott found the letter far from welcome. Short and simple as it was, it revived and increased all the fearful troubles of his mind. More than that, dare he now let the "Bone" pass out of his own keeping – even if only for a little while?

Every day, for the last week, that witch's bone had preoccupied his mind to the exclusion of all else. The witch's bone that brought to an end all his quarrels with Mackenzie Grant. The witch's bone that had possibly given him a revenge far more terrible than anything he had sought or expected. In a fit of anger he had thought only of testing its efficacy, never really believing it would work. And now he knew that the bone had worked only too well. Or had it? Had he indeed compassed Grant's death? All he knew was that Grant had died and that now he found it hard to recover his peace of mind.

Of course, he had only himself to blame. He had shown the bone at the last meeting of their local Antiquarian Society, just after he had acquired it; and, pleased with himself, he had expatiated upon its awful power. Mackenzie Grant had contradicted him – as usual. Grant had always treated his theories with contempt. There was his paper on lake-dwellings, and, after that, his paper on the iron-age forts in the Central

Highlands. Upon both occasions Grant had stood up and pooh-poohed everything he had said. At meetings of the Council, too, the man could be relied upon to speak against everything he proposed. But all that was past history. Grant had poured scorn upon his story of the bone. And now Grant was dead. Yet how unbounded would be the relief to his tortured mind if Grant had been right, and if the story of the bone were "stuff and nonsense" and nothing more. The very night that Grant had ridiculed his story he had put the bone to the test, directing its malevolent powers against Mackenzie Grant. And Grant had died a horrible death a few hours later. But could it not have been a ghastly coincidence in which the bone had played no part at all?

It was only a short piece of bone – probably sheep-bone – about six inches long, with a narrow ring of black bog-oak tightly encircling it near its centre. He had acquired it during his recent holiday in Sutherland. An old woman had died in a remote glen, and, because she had been reputed to be a witch, and had been feared as such, no one would bear her to burial. The local minister had called upon him, beseeching his help. "The poor body was no witch at all," the minister had said. "She was just old and ill-favoured. I have had a coffin made of about the right size – at any rate it will be large enough – and if you could just drive me to the old body's hut, with the coffin in the rear of your estate-wagon, maybe we could manage to coffin her, and give her a Christian burial."

A strange request to make of any man! But the minister had won him over, and his reward had been the witch's bone.

They had found it on a shelf in the old woman's hut. The minister had seen it first, and had prodded it gently with his finger. "So," he had said softly, "the witch's bone. I have been told of it. There are those of my people who say that she would utter her curse upon some man or woman, and then would make a wax figure and stick a pin into it. Then they say that if this bone rattled on its shelf, she knew that her curse had taken effect and that the person portrayed in the wax would be seized with pains in that part of the body which corresponded with the place of the pin in the wax. Some have even said that she could kill by sticking her pin in the heart or the head. For the power is in the bone. It can wound or kill any who are cursed by its possessor. And never are they spared."

He had listened and looked with astonishment until, suddenly, the minister's face had changed and he had cried out: "But what am I saying to you? There is no Witch of Endor in Sutherland. Indeed there is not. No such devilry is possible. I am not believing one word of it." And the minister had boldly picked up the bone and had offered it to him. "Take it with you," he had said. "It may interest some of your friends in the south." And, wondering, he had taken it.

Yes, it had interested some of his friends. But Mackenzie Grant had laughed at him. "A witch's bone!" he had said, contemptuously. "Stuff and nonsense. Anyone can see by just looking at it that it's a handle, and nothing more. That ring round its centre simply means that, when it is grasped, two fingers go on one side of the ring, and two fingers on the other. Any boy, flying a kite, grasps a piece of wood in exactly the same way at the end of his string. A witch's bone, indeed. I believe, Elliott, I could persuade you that a handkerchief with a hole in it is a witch's veil to be worn at meetings of her coven. And the hole, of course, would be symbolic, indicative of her lapse from the Christian faith." And so the man had gone on. Laughing at him before his friends.

He had kept down the anger which had surged within him; but, when he had returned home, and had taken the bone from his pocket, all his pent-up feelings had broken their bounds. He had marched straight into his study and, placing the bone upon a bookshelf near the fireplace, had resolved to prove its power to hurt. Aloud and deliberately he had cursed Mackenzie Grant; but, searching for sealing-wax, could find none. Then he had recalled the photograph of Mackenzie Grant in a recent volume of the Transactions of their Society.

He had recalled, too, his aversion to destroying any photograph. To tear up a photograph had always seemed to him to be akin to tearing the living flesh and bones. So much the better. Mackenzie Grant should be torn asunder with a vengeance.

He had ripped the full-page photograph from the book and had deliberately torn it to pieces. In the fury of his task he had, for the moment, forgotten the bone. But, as the torn pieces had multiplied between his hands, suddenly there had come a rattling sound from the nearby shelf. And, at that, his heart had turned to ice. Fearfully he had looked at the bone; but it lay exactly where he had placed it, and it lay inert and still. He remembered assuring himself that he had simply imagined that rattle. He was overwrought. Yes, it was imagination and nothing more.

Yet, the next morning, when reading the *Scotsman* at breakfast-time, again a chill had struck his heart and his whole body had numbed with fear. For the paper announced with regret that a distinguished antiquary, Mr Mackenzie Grant, had been killed in a road accident. According to the announcement, Mr Grant, when driving home about midnight, after having dined with a friend, had unaccountably run head-on into a heavy lorry that had stopped for some minor adjustment on the opposite side of the road. It was a bad accident. Grant's car has been completely telescoped. But, in the opinion of the doctors, he must have been killed instantaneously, for their examination showed that he had suffered multiple injuries and that practically every bone in his body was broken.

No wonder his mind was ill at ease. He had striven to persuade himself that it was pure coincidence. That those multiple injuries had naught to do with a photograph torn into many shreds. He had laboured to free himself from a haunting burden of guilt. Yet the torturing thought was still there. Had the bone indeed the power of killing those who were cursed by its possessor?

Since then he had locked it up in his coin-cabinet. He had even been afraid to open the cabinet to make certain it was still there. And now the Museum had asked to be allowed to borrow it, to put it on display. To say that he had lost it, or had destroyed it, would be childish. Yet dare he lend it? Dare he allow it to pass out of his own keeping?

These were but some of the thoughts that troubled the mind of Dr Michael Elliott as he sat with a letter that lay before him on his desk.

*

About nine o'clock in the evening of the same day, when Sir Stephen Rowandson C.I.E. the Honorary Curator of the Museum, was deep in a detective story, his housekeeper knocked on his study door and announced: "Dr Michael Elliott."

Somewhat surprised, Rowandson put down his book and rose to greet his visitor.

"Come in, Elliott. Come in. This is an unexpected pleasure."

Michael Elliott entered the room slowly and hesitantly.

"Man, but you do look tired," continued Rowandson, as Elliott came into the light. "It's these cold nights. Take that chair by the fire and warm yourself. I'll get you a whisky."

Elliott took the proffered chair and sank down in it. If, indeed, he was looking tired, he knew full well that it was not due to the coldness of the night.

"I've called about your letter, asking for the loan of my witch's bone," he said, turning to his host and gratefully accepting the whisky which had been poured out for him. "I thought I'd sooner bring it to you personally at your home, rather than give it to you, or leave it for you, at the Museum."

"Why, certainly," replied Rowandson, concealing his surprise. "You think I might possibly leave it lying about in the Museum, and it might fall into the wrong hands?"

Rowandson spoke with a smile. But Elliott coloured slightly.

"You have guessed correctly. It may be more dangerous than we know."

Rowandson looked more closely at his visitor. Did Elliott really believe that this bit of bone could exert occult force? He had been one of those standing by when Mackenzie Grant had poured scorn upon it; and although he had not heard Elliott's account of its supposed malignant power, he knew full well that the man was apt to be too credulous. But perhaps he had better humour him.

"You are right," he conceded, gravely. "I have seen some strange things myself in India. We must be careful. Would it make you happier if I promised that when I do put it on display I will put it in a locked case?"

Elliott's relief was too apparent to be disguised.

"I was hoping for something like that," he said, taking the bone from his breast pocket. "It is good of you to go to so much trouble; but I should feel reassured if it was under lock and key."

"You can rely on me," returned Rowandson, "I will keep it safely here, in the house, until I have a locked case ready for it. And I will tell no one it is here."

Once more Elliott's relief was so obvious that Rowandson, taking the bone from him, ostentatiously looked around his study for a safe keeping-place. Not finding one, he placed the bone on his desk. "I'll find a safe place for it later," he assured Elliott. "You can rely on me. And I will certainly keep it here until I take it personally to the Museum and myself place it in a display case that can be securely locked."

Thereafter for some ten minutes or so, Sir Stephen Rowandson strove in vain to find some topic of conversation which would interest his visitor. But Elliott answered only in monosyllables, while his eyes constantly strayed to the witch's bone lying on the Curator's desk, and his only thought was whether he should warn Rowandson of its dangerous power, or whether that would merely make him look foolish and at the same time make Rowandson less responsive and also more careless.

"Well," said Rowandson, as he wearied of his task, "I

mustn't keep you too late. And don't worry about your bone. It will be quite safe."

Elliott rose heavily to his feet. "Thank you," he said. "I am sorry to be so fussy, but, you know, I do believe it may be a witch's bone and not, as . . . as . . . Mackenzie Grant maintained, simply a handle of some kind."

The last words had come out with difficulty, and Rowandson thought he understood.

"Yes, poor fellow. We shall miss his sceptical comments. We were all his victims at one time or another."

Elliott winced. Again his eyes strayed to the witch's bone.

"You won't leave it there, will you?" he asked.

"No, no," replied Rowandson, quickly, "I'll find a safe place for it all right."

Seemingly reassured, Elliott moved towards the door of the room. Rowandson opened it and, conducting his visitor through the hall, let him out of the house. For a minute or two he watched the retreating figure. "There goes one of the most distinguished classical scholars in Europe," he said to himself, "and yet with more antiquarian bees in his bonnet than any man I know. A witch's bone, indeed. It may be. But, even so, what harm can it do to anyone?"

He returned to his study and, picking up the bone from his desk, examined it under the reading lamp. But his examination made him no wiser.

"Well, well. Old Elliott was certainly mighty concerned about it, and I'd better do what I said. But where shall I put the wretched thing? I haven't a safe, and there isn't a drawer in the whole house that would defeat a ten-year-old."

Moving about the room with the bone in his hand, Rowandson finally stopped in front of an old-fashioned knick-knack stand which bore on its shelves a medley of flints, cylindrical seals, Roman nails, and other small archaeological objects of varying periods and kinds. "The very place," he muttered. "Not so much Poe's idea in 'The Purloined Letter' as Chesterton's idea of hiding a leaf in a forest."

By moving some of the specimens closer to one another he

cleared a small space on one of the shelves and placed the bone there. Stepping back, he surveyed the result and found it good.

*

Two days later, as Sir Stephen Rowandson entered his study after a frugal breakfast, he was feeling thoroughly disgruntled. His housekeeper, summoned yesterday afternoon to nurse a sister who had suddenly been taken ill, had left him to fend for himself; and Sir Stephen Rowandson was not accustomed to domestic work. He had managed to prepare his coffee, toast and marmalade for breakfast; but now the dead ashes in his study fire-place mocked him. He would have to take out those ashes and lay the fire himself. Unwillingly he began his task. As he busied himself with paper and firewood, his mind turned to the Museum and to his forthcoming exhibition. And his thoughts made him more disgruntled still. Why should everything go wrong at one and the same time? For, yesterday morning, when one or two members of the Society had come to the Museum to help with the final preparations, and when, in accordance with his promise, he had arranged for a place in one of the two locked cases to be reserved for Michael Elliott's witch's bone, the interfering and officious Colonel Hogan had actually presumed to give contrary orders, even asserting that the bone wasn't worth a place in the exhibition anywhere. He had had trouble with the Colonel before. The man seemed to think he was in command of everything. But this time there had followed an unseemly wrangle in which he had completely lost his temper. More than that, in defending his promise to Elliott, he had hotly argued that the bone might be more dangerous than any of them realised. That heated altercation had made him look foolish; and he remembered, to his annoyance, the glances that had been exchanged. The word would now go round that he was becoming as credulous as Elliott himself. But if Elliott hadn't been so fussy, the argument would never have started at all.

"I could curse the old fool," he muttered angrily, as he

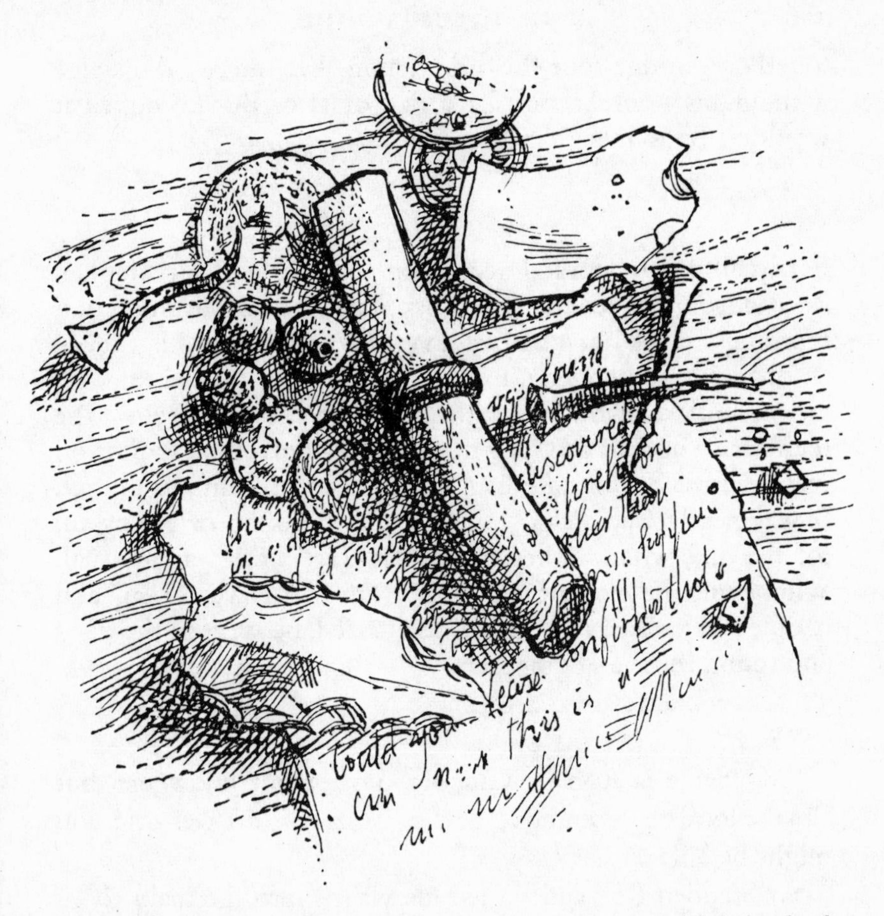

thrust the sticks of firewood among the paper which he had crushed up and laid in the hearth. "Damn Michael Elliott, and damn his bone."

He finished laying the fire and rose up from his task when, as he did so, he heard a strange rattle which seemed to come from somewhere within the room. Startled, he looked round. But nothing had fallen; nothing seemed to be out of place. "Probably a bird fluttered against the window," he said dubiously. "But it didn't sound like it. It was a queer sound. Never heard anything like it before."

Well, what now? He could go to the Museum and work there, then he could lunch at his Club; back to the Museum again; dinner at the Club; and perhaps he could even collect together a bridge-four for the evening. Yes, he could manage without his housekeeper for a day or two. But he hoped it wouldn't be longer than that.

*

Everything had worked according to plan, and Sir Stephen Rowandson was feeling much happier. He had put in a good morning's work; he had had an excellent lunch at his Club – and had even arranged a bridge-four; he had carried on with his exhibition in the afternoon; and, to his great relief, the members who had dropped in to help had given no indication that yesterday's wrangle had affected them in any way at all. It was nearly five o'clock, and he was thinking of giving up for the day, when he heard the bell ring. That was unusual. Who could be ringing the bell? The door was open, and people just walked in. Somewhat puzzled, he went to the door and found there a young man.

"Sir Stephen Rowandson?"

"Yes."

"My name is Robert Reid, sir. You won't know me, but I'm the local representative of the *Scotsman* and I was told you might be able to help me."

Sir Stephen Rowandson led his visitor into the main room of the Museum.

"And what can I do to help you?" he asked.

"I'm anxious to trace a photograph of Dr Michael Elliott. The paper wishes to carry one tomorrow. I do not like to call at his house, and it was suggested to me that probably you would have one here since, or so I gather, Dr Elliott was a prominent member of your Society."

"But why can't you call at his house?"

The young man looked up quickly.

"But, of course, how stupid of me. You cannot have heard." Then in a slightly lower voice, he continued: "I'm very sorry to tell you, sir, that Dr Michael Elliott is dead. He was killed in a bad accident in Edinburgh, about half-past eleven this morning. And, as you will understand, we must carry a fairly long obituary notice. We would also like a photograph, if possible."

"Michael Elliott dead," repeated Rowandson, dully.

"Yes, sir. Apparently he was walking along the pavement by a site where a new building is going up when, for some unknown reason, a steel girder that was being lifted by a crane slipped from the chains which were holding it. Hitting the side of the building, it slewed round and, by sheer bad luck, fell on Dr Elliott and crushed him to death."

"How horrible!"

"Yes, sir. But we are told that death must have been instantaneous. For not only was Dr Elliott badly crushed but also the girder, in falling, broke down a wooden screen which was shielding the site, and, according to the doctors, drove a wedge of broken wood from the screen straight through Dr Elliott's heart."

For a brief space, Sir Stephen Rowandson remained silent.

"It comes to all of us, sooner or later," he said at last. "But I wish it could have come in a way different from this. A photograph? Yes, I think I can help. There was a photograph of Dr Elliott in our local paper, the *Standard*, only the other day. Come up to my house and I'll show it to you. Then, if you think it suitable, I'm sure the *Standard* people will be only too glad to lend you the block."

*

Sir Stephen Rowandson led the newspaper-man into his study, where, almost at once, he apologised for the coldness of the room.

"I'm sorry to offer you such a chilly reception," he said. "But my housekeeper is away and I am looking after myself. However, we'll soon have a fire, and then I'll hunt for that photograph."

Although the young man held out a restraining hand, Rowandson struck a match, and lit the fire. Then, crossing to a pile of newspapers on a small table by his desk, he began to turn over the papers one by one. But the *Standard* which he wanted was not there.

"Queer," he said, "I could have sworn it was in this pile. But warm yourself at what fire there is while I have a look in the dining-room. I sometimes leave the paper there."

He went out of the room, and the young man looked ruefully at the fire. The edges of the paper had burned, but nothing more. As one last wisp of smoke curled up towards the chimney, the fire was out.

"I can't find it anywhere," growled Rowandson, coming back into the room. Once more he went through the pile of papers on the table, and still without success. Then he saw the dead hearth.

"Oh, I am sorry," he cried. "The fire has gone out. I must have packed it too tightly. Stupid of me. But it's years since I laid a fire."

Then a new thought came to him.

"And I'm willing to bet that the *Standard* I'm looking for is there, at the bottom of my wretched fire. I just took the first paper that came to hand. I really am sorry. But look! If you go to the offices of the *Standard*, in the High Street, they'll willingly show you the issue, and then you can ask about the block. Say I sent you. Really, I should have taken you there in the first place."

With many apologies for troubling the Honorary Curator of the Museum, the young newspaper-man left. Sir Stephen Rowandson returned to his study and there looked balefully at the dead fire.

"I suppose I shall have to re-lay the damned thing," he muttered to himself. "I'd better do it now, and have done with it."

Kneeling down in front of the hearth, he removed the coal, then the firewood, and finally the paper. Yes, he had packed it too tightly. But he had learned his lesson. Straightening out a piece of the crushed-up paper, he saw it was the *Standard* for which he had been looking. He might have guessed he would use the one newspaper that was wanted. Ah! here was the page that bore poor Elliott's photograph. He straightened the page. It was still a good likeness, even though the photograph was badly crushed, and a splinter from the rough firewood had pierced it in the very heart.

But all that held no significance for Sir Stephen Rowandson. He re-laid the fire, went to his bathroom, and there – washed his hands.

Lucky's Grove

H. R. Wakefield

Mr Braxton strolled with his land-agent, Curtis, into the Great Barn.

"There you are," said Curtis in a satisfied tone, "the finest little larch I ever saw, and the kiddies will never set eyes on a lovelier Christmas tree."

Mr Braxton examined it; it stood twenty feet from huge green pot to crisp, straight peak, and was exquisitely sturdy, fresh and symmetrical.

"Yes, it's a beauty," he agreed, "Where did you find it?"

"In that odd little spinney they call Lucky's Grove in the long meadow near the river boundary."

"Oh!" remarked Mr Braxton uncertainly. To himself he was saying vaguely, "He shouldn't have got it from there, of course he wouldn't realise it, but he shouldn't have got it from there."

"Of course we'll replant it," said Curtis, noticing his employer's diminished enthusiasm. "It's a curious thing, but it isn't a young tree; it's apparently full-grown. Must be a dwarf variety, but I don't know as much about trees as I should like."

Mr Braxton was surprised to find there was one branch of country lore on which Curtis was not an expert; for he was about the best-known man at his job in the British Isles. Pigs, bees, chickens, cattle, crops, running a shoot, he had mastered them one and all. He paid him two thousand a year with house and car. He was worth treble.

"I expect it's all right," said Mr Braxton, "it's just that Lucky's Grove is – is – well, 'sacred' is perhaps too strong a word. Maybe I should have told you, but I expect it's all right."

"That accounts for it then," laughed Curtis. "I thought there seemed some reluctance on the part of the men while we were yanking it up and getting it on the lorry. They handled it a bit gingerly; on the part of the older men, I mean; the youngsters didn't worry."

"Yes, there would be," said Mr Braxton. "But never mind, it'll be back in a few days and it's a superb little tree. I'll bring Mrs Braxton along to see it after lunch," and he strolled back into Abingdale Hall.

Fifty-five years ago Mr Braxton's father had been a labourer on this very estate, and in that year young Percy, aged eight, had got an errand boy's job in Oxford. Twenty years later he'd owned one small shop. Twenty-five years after that fifty big shops. Now, though he had finally retired, he owned two hundred and eighty vast shops and was a millionaire whichever way you added it up. How had this happened? No one can quite answer such questions. Certainly he'd worked like a brigade of Trojans, but midnight oil has to burn in Aladdin's Lamp before it can transform ninepence into one million pounds. It was just that he asked no quarter from the unforgiving minute, but squeezed from it the fruit of others' many hours. Those like Mr Braxton seem to have their own time-scale; they just say the word and up springs a fine castle of commerce, but the knowledge of that word cannot be imported; it is as mysterious as the Logos. But all through his great labours he had been moved by one fixed resolve – to avenge his father – that fettered spirit – for he had been an able, intelligent man who had had no earthly chance of revealing the fact to the world. Always the categorical determination had blazed in his son's brain, "I will own Abingdale Hall, and, where my father sweated, I will rule and be lord," And of course it had happened. Fate accepts the dictates of such men as Mr Braxton, shrugs its shoulders, and leaves its revenge to Death. The Hall had come on the market just when he was about to retire, and with an odd delight, an obscure sense of home-coming, the native returned, and his riding-boots, shooting-boots, golf shoes, and all the many glittering guineas' worth, stamped in and obliterated the prints of his father's hob-nails.

That was the picture he often re-visualised, the way it amused him to "put it to himself," as he roamed his broad acres and surveyed the many glowing triumphs of his model husbandry.

Some credit was due to buxom, blithe and debonair Mrs Braxton, kindly, competent and innately adaptable. She was awaiting him in the morning room and they went in solitary state, to luncheon. But it was the last peaceful lunch they would have for a spell – the "Families" were pouring in on the morrow.

As a footman was helping them to *Sole Meunière*, Mr Braxton said, "Curtis has found a very fine Christmas tree. It's in the barn. You must come and look at it after lunch."

"That *is* good," replied his wife. "Where did he get it from?"

Mr Braxton hesitated for a moment.

"From Lucky's Grove."

Mrs Braxton looked up sharply.

"From the grove!" she said, surprised.

"Yes, of course he didn't realise – anyway it'll be all right, it's all rather ridiculous, and it'll be replanted before the New Year."

"Oh, yes," agreed Mrs Braxton. "After all it's only just a clump of trees."

"Quite. And it's just the right height for the ballroom. It'll be taken in there tomorrow morning and the electricians will work on it in the afternoon."

"I heard from Lady Pounser just now," said Mrs Braxton. "She's bringing six over, that'll make seventy-four; only two refusals. The presents are arriving this afternoon."

They discussed the party discursively over the cutlets and Peach Melba and soon after lunch walked across to the barn. Mr Braxton waved to Curtis, who was examining a new tractor in the garage fifty yards away, and he came over.

Mrs Braxton looked the tree over and was graciously

delighted with it, but remarked that the pot could have done with another coat of paint. She pointed to several streaks, rust-coloured, running through the green. "Of course it won't show when it's wrapped, but they didn't do a very good job."

Curtis leant down. "They certainly didn't," he answered irritably. "I'll see to it. I think it's spilled over from the soil: that copse is on a curious patch of red sand – there are some at Frilford too. When we pulled it up I noticed that the roots were stained a dark crimson." He put his hand down and scraped at the stains with his thumb. He seemed a shade puzzled.

"It shall have another coat at once," he said. "What did you think of Lampson and Collett's scheme for the barn?"

"Quite good," replied Mrs Braxton, "but the sketches for the chains are too fancy."

"I agree," said Curtis, who usually did so in the case of un-essentials, reserving his tactful vetoes for the others.

The Great Barn was by far the most aesthetically satisfying, as it was the oldest feature of the Hall buildings; it was vast, exquisitely proportioned, and mellow. That could hardly be said of the house itself, which the 4th Baron of Abingdale had rebuilt on the cinders of its predecessor in 1752.

This nobleman had travelled abroad extensively and returned with most enthusiastic, grandiose and indigestible ideas of architecture. The result was a gargantuan piece of rococo-jocoso which only an entirely humourless pedant could condemn. It contained forty-two bedrooms and eighteen reception rooms – so Mrs Braxton had made it at the last recount. But Mr Braxton had not repeated with the interior the errors of the 4th Baron. He'd briefed the greatest expert in Europe with the result that the interior was quite tasteful and sublimely comfortable.

"Ugh!" he exclaimed, as they stepped out into the air, "It *is* getting nippy!"

"Yes," said Curtis, "there's a nor'-easter blowing up – may be snow for Christmas."

On getting back to the house Mrs Braxton went into a

huddle with butler and housekeeper, and Mr Braxton retired to his study for a doze. But instead his mind settled on Lucky's Grove. When he'd first seen it again after buying the estate, it seemed as if fifty years had rolled away, and he realised that Abingdale was far more summed up to him in the little copse than in the gigantic barracks two miles away. At once he felt at home again. Yet, just as when he'd been a small boy, the emotion the Grove had aroused in him had been sharply tinged with awe, so it had been now, half a century later. He still had a sneaking dread of it. How precisely he could see it, glowing darkly in the womb of the fire before him, standing starkly there in the centre of the big, fallow field, a perfect circle; and first, a ring of holm-oaks and, facing east, a breach therein to the larches and past them on the west a gap to the yews. It had always required a tug at his courage – not always forthcoming – to pass through them and face the mighty Scotch fir, rearing up its great bole from the grass mound. And when he stood before it, he'd always known an odd longing to fling himself down and – well, worship – it was the only word – the towering tree. His father had told him his forebears had done that very thing, but always when alone and at certain seasons of the year; and that no bird or beast was ever seen there. A lot of traditional nonsense, no doubt, but he himself had absorbed the spirit of the place and knew it would always be so.

One afternoon in late November, a few weeks after they had moved in, he'd gone off alone in the drowsing misty dusk; and when he'd reached the holm-oak bastion and seen the great tree surrounded by its sentinels, he'd known again that quick turmoil of confused emotions. As he'd walked slowly towards it, it had seemed to quicken and be aware of his coming. As he passed the shallow grassy fosse and entered the oak ring he felt there was something he ought to say, some greeting, password or prayer. It was the most aloof, silent little place under the sun, and oh, so old. He'd tiptoed past the larches and faced the barrier of yews. He'd stood there for a long musing minute, tingling with the sensation that he was

being watched and regarded. At length he stepped forward and stood before the God – that mighty word came abruptly and unforeseen – and he felt a wild desire to fling himself down on the mound and do obeisance. And then he'd hurried home. As he recalled all this most vividly and minutely, he was seized with a sudden gust of uncontrollable anger at the thought of the desecration of the grove. He knew now that if he'd had the slightest idea of Curtis's purpose he'd have resisted and opposed it. It was too late now. He realised he'd "worked himself up" rather absurdly. What could it matter! He was still a superstitious bumpkin at heart. Anyway it was no fault of Curtis. It was the finest Christmas tree anyone could hope for, and the whole thing was too nonsensical for words. The general tone of these cadentic conclusions did not quite accurately represent his thoughts – a very rare failing with Mr Braxton.

About dinner-time the blizzard set furiously in, and the snow was lying.

"Chains on the cars tomorrow," Mrs Braxton told the head chauffeur.

"Boar's Hill'll be a beggar," thought that person.

Mr and Mrs Braxton dined early, casually examined the presents and went to bed. Mr Braxton was asleep at once as usual, but was awakened by the beating of a blind which had slipped its moorings. Reluctantly he got out of bed and went to fix it. As he was doing so he became conscious of the frenzied hysterical barking of a dog. The sound, muffled by the gale, came, he judged, from the barn. He believed the underkeeper kept his whippet there. Scared by the storm, he supposed, and returned to bed.

The morning was brilliantly fine and cold, but the snowfall had been heavy.

"I heard a dog howling in the night, Perkins," said Mr Braxton to the butler at breakfast; "Drake's I imagine. What's the matter with it?"

"I will ascertain, sir," said Perkins.

"It *was* Drake's dog," he announced a little later. "Apparently something alarmed the animal, for when Drake went to let it out this morning, it appeared to be extremely frightened. When the barn door was opened, it took to its heels and, although Drake pursued it, it jumped into the river and Drake fears it was drowned."

"Um," said Mr Braxton, "must have been the storm; whippets are nervous dogs."

"So I understand, sir."

"Drake was so fond of it," said Mrs Braxton, "though it always looked so naked and shivering to me."

"Yes, madam," agreed Perkins, "it had that appearance."

Soon after, Mr Braxton sauntered out into the blinding glitter. Curtis came over from the garage. He was heavily muffled up.

"They've got chains on all the cars," he said, "Very seasonable and all that, but farmers have another word for it." His voice was thick and hoarse.

"Yes," said Mr Braxton. "You're not looking very fit."

"Not feeling it. Had to get up in the night. Thought I heard someone trying to break into the house: thought I saw him too."

"Indeed," said Mr Braxton. "Did you see what he was like?"

"No," replied Curtis uncertainly. "It was snowing like the devil. Anyway, I got properly chilled to the marrow, skipping around in my nightie."

"You'd better get to bed," said Mr Braxton solicitously. He had affection and a great respect for Curtis.

"I'll stick it out today and see how I feel tomorrow. We're going to get the tree across in a few minutes. Can I borrow the two footmen? I want another couple of pullers and haulers."

Mr Braxton consented, and went off on his favourite little stroll across the sparkling meadows to the river and the pool where the big trout set their running noses to the stream.

Half an hour later Curtis had mobilised his scratch team of sleeve-rolled assistants and, with Perkins steering and himself braking, they got to grips with the tree and bore it like a camouflaged battering-ram towards the ballroom, which occupied the left centre of the frenetic frontage on the ground floor. There was a good deal of bumping and boring and genial blasphemy before the tree was manoeuvred into the middle of the room and levered by rope and muscle into position. As it came up its pinnacle just cleared the ceiling. Sam, a cow-man, whose ginger mop had been buried in the foliage for some time, exclaimed tartly as he slapped the trunk, "There ye are, ye old sod! Thanks for the scratches on me mug, ye old –!"

The next minute he was lying on his back, a livid weal across his right cheek.

This caused general merriment and even Perkins permitted himself a spectral smile. There was more astonishment than pain on the face of Sam. He stared at the tree in a humble way for a moment, like a chastised and guilty dog, and then slunk from the room. The merriment of the others died away.

"More spring in these branches than you'd think," said Curtis to Perkins.

"No doubt, sir, that is due to the abrupt release of the tension," replied Perkins scientifically.

The "Families" met at Paddington and travelled down together, so at five o'clock three car-loads drew up at the Hall. There were Jack and Mary with Paddy aged eight, Walter and Pamela with Jane and Peter, seven and five respectively, and George and Gloria with Gregory and Phyllis, ten and eight.

Jack and Walter were sons of the house. They were much of a muchness, burly, handsome and as dominating as their sire; a fine pair of commercial kings, entirely capable rulers, but just lacking that something which founds dynasties. Their wives conformed equally to the social type to which they belonged, good-lookers, smart dressers, excellent wives and mothers; but rather coolly colourless, spiritually. Their offspring were "charming children," flawless products of the English matrix, though Paddy showed signs of some obstreperous originality. "George" was the Honourable George Calvin Roderick etcetera Penables, and Gloria was Mr and Mrs Braxton's only daughter. George had inherited half a million and had started off at twenty-four to be something big in the City. In a sense he achieved his ambition, for two years later he was generally reckoned the biggest "something" in the City, from which he then withdrew, desperately clutching his last hundred thousand and vowing lachrymose repentance. He had kept his word and his wad, hunted and shot six days a week in winter, and spent most of the summer wrestling with the two dozen devils in his golf bag. According to current jargon he was the complete extrovert, but what a relief are such, in spite of the pitying shrugs of those who for ever are peering into the septic recesses of their souls.

Gloria had inherited some of her father's force. She was rather overwhelmingly primed with energy and pep for her opportunities of releasing it. So she was always rather pent up and explosive, though maternity had kept the pressure down. She was dispassionately fond of George who had presented her with a nice little title and aristocratic background and two "charming children." Phyllis gave promise of such extreme beauty that, beyond being the cynosure of every press-camera's eye, and making a resounding match, no more was to be expected of her. Gregory, however, on the strength of some artistic precocity and a violent temper was already somewhat prematurely marked down as a genius to be.

Such were the "Families."

During the afternoon four engineers arrived from one of the Braxton factories to fix up the lighting of the tree. The fairy lamps for this had been specially designed and executed for the occasion. Disney figures had been grafted upon them and made to revolve by an ingenious mechanism; the effect being to give the tree, when illuminated, an aspect of whirling life meant to be very cheerful and pleasing.

Mr Braxton happened to see these electricians departing in their lorry and noticed one of them had a bandaged arm and a rather white face. He asked Perkins what had happened.

"A slight accident, sir. A bulb burst and burnt him in some manner. But the injury is, I understand, not of a very serious nature."

"He looked a bit white."

"Apparently, sir, he got a fright, a shock of some kind, when the bulb exploded."

After dinner the grown-ups went to the ballroom. Mr Braxton switched on the mechanism and great enthusiasm was shown. "Won't the kiddies love it," said George, grinning at the kaleidoscope. "Look at the Big Bad Wolf. He looks so darn realistic I'm not sure I'd give him a 'U' certificate."

"It's almost frightening," said Pamela, "they look incredibly real. Daddy, you really are rather bright, darling."

It was arranged that the work of decoration should be tackled on the morrow and finished on Christmas Eve.

"All the presents have arrived," said Mrs Braxton, "and are being unpacked. But I'll explain about them tomorrow."

They went back to the drawing-room. Presently Gloria puffed and remarked: "Papa, aren't you keeping the house rather too hot?"

"I noticed the same thing," said Mrs Braxton.

Mr Braxton walked over to a thermometer on the wall. "You're right," he remarked, "seventy." He rang the bell.

"Perkins," he asked, "who's on the furnace?"

"Churchill, sir."

"Well, he's overdoing it. It's seventy. Tell him to get it back to fifty-seven."

Perkins departed and returned shortly after.

"Churchill informs me he has damped down and cannot account for the increasing warmth, sir."

"Tell him to get it back to fifty-seven at once," rapped Mr Braxton.

"Very good, sir."

"Open a window," said Mrs Braxton.

"It is snowing again, madam."

"Never mind."

"My God!" exclaimed Mary, when she and Jack went up to

bed. "That furnace-man is certainly stepping on it. Open all the windows."

A wild flurry of snow beat against the curtains.

Mr Braxton did what he very seldom did, woke up in the early hours. He awoke sweating from a furtive and demoralising dream. It had seemed to him that he had been crouching down in the fosse round Lucky's Grove, and peering beneath the holm-oaks and that there had been activity of a sort vaguely to be discerned therein, some quick shadowy business. He knew a very tight terror at the thought of being detected at this spying, but he could not wrench himself away. That was all, and he awoke still trembling and troubled. No wonder he'd had such a nightmare, the room seemed like a stokehold. He went to the windows and flung another open, and as he did so glanced out. His room looked over the rock garden and down the path to the maze. Something moving just outside it caught his eye. He thought he knew what it was, that big Alsatian which had been sheep-worrying in the neighbourhood. What an enormous brute! Or was it just because it was outlined against the snow? It vanished suddenly, apparently into the maze. He'd organise a hunt for it after Christmas; if the snow lay, it should be easy to track.

The first thing he did after breakfast was to send for Churchill, severely reprimand him and threaten him with dismissal from his ship. That person was almost tearfully insistent that he had obeyed orders and kept his jets low. "I can't make it out, sir. It's got no right to be as 'ot as what it is."

"That's nonsense!" said Mr Braxton. "The system has been perfected and cannot take charge, as you suggest. See to it. You don't want me to get an engineer down, do you?"

"No, sir."

"That's enough. Get it to fifty-seven and keep it there."

Shortly after, Mrs Curtis rang up to say her husband was quite ill with a temperature and that the doctor was coming. Mr Braxton asked her to ring him again after he'd been.

During the morning the children played in the snow. After

a pitched battle in which the girls lost their tempers, Gregory organised the erection of a snowman. He designed, the others fetched the material. He knew he had a reputation for brilliance to maintain and he produced something Epsteinish, huge and squat. The other children regarded it with little enthusiasm, but, being Gregory, they supposed it must be admired. When it was finished, Gregory wandered off by himself while the others went in to dry. He came in a little late for lunch, during which he was silent and pre-occupied. Afterwards the grown-ups sallied forth.

"Let's see your snowman, Greg," said Gloria, in a mother-of-genius tone.

"It isn't all his, we helped," said Phyllis, voicing a point of view which was to have many echoes in the coming years.

"Why, he's changed it!" exclaimed a chorus two minutes later.

"What an ugly thing!" exclaimed Mary, rather pleased at being able to say so with conviction.

Gregory had certainly given his imagination its head, for now the squat, inert trunk was topped by a big wolf's head with open jaw and ears snarlingly laid back, surprisingly well modelled. Trailing behind it was a coiled, serpentine tail.

"Whatever gave you the idea for that?" asked Jack.

Usually Gregory was facile and eloquent in explaining his inspiration, but this time he refused to be drawn, bit his lip and turned away.

There was a moment's silence and then Gloria said with convincing emphasis, "I think it's wonderful, Greg!"

And then they all strolled off to examine the pigs and the poultry and the Suffolk Punches.

They had just got back for tea when the telephone rang in Mr Braxton's study. It was Mrs Curtis. The patient was no better and Doctor Knowles had seemed rather worried, and so on. So Mr Braxton rang up the doctor.

"I haven't diagnosed his trouble, yet," he said. "And I'm going to watch him carefully and take a blood-test if he's not better tomorrow. He has a temperature of a hundred and two, but no other superficial symptoms, which is rather peculiar. By the way, one of your cow-men, Sam Colley, got a nasty wound on the face yesterday and shows signs of blood poisoning. I'm considering sending him to hospital. Some of your other men have been in to see me – quite a little outbreak of illness since Tuesday. However, I hope we'll have a clean bill again soon. I'll keep you informed about Curtis."

Mr Braxton was one of those incredible people who never have a day's illness – till their first and last. Consequently his conception of disease was unimaginative and mechanical. If one of his more essential human machines was running unsatisfactorily, there was a machine-mender called a doctor whose business it was to ensure that all the plug leads were attached firmly and that the manifold drain-pipe was not blocked. But he found himself beginning to worry about Curtis, and this little epidemic amongst his henchmen affected him disagreeably – there was something disturbing to his spirit about it. But just what and why, he couldn't analyse and decide.

After dinner, with the children out of the way, the business of decorating the tree was begun. The general scheme had been sketched out and coloured by one of the Braxton display experts and the company consulted this as they worked, which they did rather silently; possibly, Mr Braxton's palpable anxiety somewhat affected them.

Pamela stayed behind after the others had left the ballroom to put some finishing touches to her section of the tree. When she rejoined the others she was looking rather white and tight-lipped. She said good-night a shade abruptly and went to her room. Walter, a very, very good husband, quickly joined her.

"Anything the matter, old girl?" he asked anxiously.

"Yes," replied Pamela, "I'm frightened."

"Frightened! What d'you mean?"

"You'll think it's all rot, but I'll tell you. When you'd all left the ballroom, I suddenly felt very uneasy – you know the sort of feeling when one keeps on looking round and can't concentrate. However, I stuck at it. I was a little way up the steps when I heard a sharp hiss from above me in the tree. I jumped back to the floor and looked up; now, of course you won't believe me, but the trunk of the tree was moving – it was like the coils of a snake writhing upwards, and there was something at the top of the tree, horrid-looking, peering at me. I know you won't believe me."

Walter didn't, but he also didn't know what to make of it. "I know what happened!" he improvised lightly. "You'd been staring in at that trunk for nearly two hours and you got dizzy – like staring at the sun on the sea; and that snow dazzle this afternoon helped it. You've heard of snow-blindness – something like that, it still echoes from the retina or whatever . . ."

"You think it might have been that?"

"I'm sure of it."

"And that horrible head?"

"Well, as George put it rather brightly, I don't think some of those figures on the lamps should get a 'U' certificate. There's the wolf to which he referred, and the witch."

"Which witch?" laughed Pamela a little hysterically. "I didn't notice one."

"I did. I was working just near it, at least, I suppose it's meant to be a witch. A figure in black squinting from behind a tree. As a matter of fact fairies never seemed all fun and frolic to me, there's often something diabolical about them – or rather casually cruel. Disney knows that."

"Yes, there is," agreed Pamela. "So you think that's all there was to it?"

"I'm certain. One's eyes can play tricks on one."

"Yes," said Pamela. "I know what you mean, as if they saw what one knew wasn't there or was different. Though who would 'one' be then?"

"Oh, don't ask me that sort of question!" laughed Walter. "Probably Master Gregory will be able to tell you in a year or two."

"He's a nice little boy, really," protested Pamela. "Gloria just spoils him and it's natural."

"I know he is, it's not his fault, but they will *force* him. Look at that snow-man – and staying behind to do it. A foul looking thing!"

"Perhaps his eyes played funny tricks with him," said Pamela.

"What d'you mean by that?"

"I don't know why I said it," said Pamela frowning, "sort of echo, I suppose. Let's go to bed."

Walter kissed her gently, but fervently, as he loved her. He was a one-lady's-man and had felt a bit nervous about her for a moment or two.

Was the house a little cooler? wondered Mr Braxton, as he was undressing, or was it that he was getting more used to it? He was now convinced that there was something wrong with the installation; he'd get an expert down. Meanwhile they must stick it. He yawned, wondered how Curtis was, and switched off the light.

Soon all the occupants were at rest and the great house swinging silently against the stars. Should have been at rest, rather, for one and all recalled that night with reluctance and dread. Their dreams were harsh and unhallowed, yet oddly related, being concerned with dim, uncertain and yet somehow urgent happenings in and around the house, as though some thing or things were stirring while they slept and communicated their motions to their dreaming consciousness. They awoke tired with a sense of unaccountable malaise.

Mrs Curtis rang up during breakfast and her voice revealed her distress. Timothy was delirious and much worse. The doctor was coming at 10.30.

Mr and Mrs Braxton decided to go over there, and sent for the car. Knowles was waiting just outside the house when they arrived.

"He's very bad," he said quietly. "I've sent for two nurses and Sir Arthur Galley; I want another opinion. Has he had some trouble with a tree?"

"Trouble with a tree!" said Mr Braxton his nerves giving a flick.

"Yes, it's probably just a haphazard, irrational idea of delirium, but he continually fusses about some tree."

"How bad is he?" asked Mrs Braxton.

The doctor frowned. "I wish I knew. I'm fairly out of my depth. He's keeping up his strength fairly well, but he can't go on like this."

"As bad as that!" exclaimed Mr Braxton.

"I'm very much afraid so. I'm anxiously awaiting Sir Arthur's verdict. By the way, that cow-man is very ill indeed; I'm sending him into hospital."

"What happened to him?" asked Mr Braxton, absently, his mind on Curtis.

"Apparently a branch of your Christmas tree snapped back at him and struck his face. Blood-poisoning set in almost at once."

Mr Braxton felt that tremor again, but merely nodded.

"I was just wondering if there might be some connection between the two, that Curtis is blaming himself for the accident. Seems an absurd idea, but judging from his ravings he appears to think he is lashed to some tree and that the great heat he feels comes from it."

They went into the house and did their best to comfort and reassure Mrs Curtis, instructed Knowles to ring up as soon as Sir Arthur's verdict was known, and then drove home.

The children had just come in from playing in the snow.

"Grandpa, the snow-man's melted," said Paddy. "Did it thaw in the night?"

"Must have done," replied Mr Braxton, forcing a smile.

"Come and look, Grandpa," persisted Paddy, "there's nothing left of it."

"Grandpa doesn't want to be bothered," said May, noticing his troubled face.

"I'll come," said Mr Braxton. When he reached the site of the snow-man his thoughts were still elsewhere, but his mind quickly re-focused itself, for he was faced with something a little strange. Not a vestige of the statue remained, though the snow was frozen crisp and crunched hard beneath their feet; and yet the snow-man was completely obliterated and where it had stood was a circle of bare, brown grass.

"It must have thawed in the night and then frozen again," he said uncertainly.

"Then why –" began Paddy.

"Don't bother Grandpa," said Mary sharply. "He's told you what happened."

They wandered off towards the heavy, hurrying river.

"Are those dog-paw marks?" asked Phyllis.

That reminded Mr Braxton. He peered down. "Yes," he replied. "And I bet they're those of that brute of an Alsatian; it must be a colossal beast."

"And it must have paws like a young bear," laughed Mary. "They're funny dogs, sort of Jekyll-and-Hydes. I rather adore them."

"You wouldn't adore this devil. He's all Hyde." (I'm in the wrong mood for these festivities, he thought irritably.)

During the afternoon George and Walter took the kids to cinema in Oxford; the others finished the decoration of the tree.

The presents, labelled with the names of their recipients, were arranged on tables round the room and the huge cracker, ten feet long and forty inches in circumference, was placed on its gaily decorated trestle near the tree. Just as the job was finished, Mary did a three-quarters faint, but was quickly revived with brandy.

"It's the simply ghastly heat in the house!" exclaimed Gloria, who was not looking too grand herself. "The installation must be completely diseased. Ours always works perfectly." Mary had her dinner in bed and Jack came up to her immediately he had finished his.

"How are you feeling, darling?" he asked.

"Oh, I'm all right."

"It *was* the heat, of course?"

"Oh, yes," replied Mary with rather forced emphasis.

"Scared you a bit, going off like that?" suggested Jack, regarding her rather sharply.

"I'm quite all right, thank you," said Mary in the tone she always adopted when she'd had enough of a subject. "I'd like to rest. Switch off the light."

But when Jack had gone, she didn't close her eyes, but lay on her back staring up at the faint outline of the ceiling. She frowned and lightly chewed the little finger of her left hand, a habit of hers when unpleasantly puzzled. Mary, like most people of strong character and limited imagination, hated to be puzzled. Everything, she considered, ought to have a simple explanation if one tried hard enough to find it. But how could one explain this odd thing that had happened to her? Besides the grandiose gifts on the tables which bore a number, as well as the recipient's name, a small present for everyone was hung on the tree. This also bore a number, the same one as the lordly gift, so easing the Braxtons' task of handing these out to the right people. Mary had just fixed Curtis's label to a cigarette lighter and tied it on the tree when it swung on its silk thread, so that the back of the card was visible; and on it was this inscription: "Died, December 25th, 1938". It spun away again and back and the inscription was no longer there.

Now Mary came of a family which rather prided itself on being unimaginative. Her father had confined his flights of fancy to the Annual Meeting of his shareholders, while, to her mother, imagination and mendacity were at least first cousins. So Mary could hardly credit the explanation that, being remotely worried about Mr Curtis, she had subconsciously concocted that sinister sentence. On the other hand she knew poor Mr Curtis was very ill and, therefore, perhaps if her brain had played that malign little trick on her, it might have done so in "tombstone writing."

This was a considerable logical exercise for Mary, the effort tired her, the impression began to fade and she started wondering how much longer Jack was going to sit up. She dozed off and there, as if flashed on the screen "inside her head" was "Died, December 25th, 1938". This, oddly enough, completely reassured her. There was "nothing there" this time. There had been nothing that other time. She'd been very weak and imaginative even to think otherwise.

While she was deciding this, Dr Knowles rang up. "Sir Arthur has just been," he said. "And I'm sorry to say he's pessimistic. He says Curtis is very weak."

"But what's the matter with him?" asked Mr Braxton urgently.

"He doesn't know. He calls it P.U.O. which really means nothing."

"But what's it stand for?"

"Pyrexia unknown origin. There are some fevers which cannot be described more precisely."

"How ill is he really?"

"All I can say is, we must hope for the best."

"My God!" exclaimed Mr Braxton. "When's Sir Arthur coming again?"

"At eleven tomorrow. I'll ring you up after he's been."

Mr Braxton excused himself and went to his room. Like many men of his dominating, sometimes ruthless type, he was capable of an intensity of feeling, anger, resolution, desire for revenge, but also affection and sympathy, unknown to more superficially Christian and kindly souls. He was genuinely attached to Curtis and his wife and was very harshly and poignantly moved by this news which, he realised, could hardly have been worse. He would have to exercise all his will-power if he was to sleep.

If on the preceding night the rest of the sleepers had been broken by influences which had insinuated themselves into their dreams, that which caused the night of that Christmas Eve to be unforgettable was the demoniacal violence of the elements. The north-easter had been waxing steadily all the evening and by midnight reached hurricane force, driving before it an almost impenetrable wall of snow. Not only so, but continually all through the night the wall was enflamed, and the roar of the hurricane silenced, by fearful flashes of lightning and rafales of thunder. The combination was almost intolerably menacing. As the great house shook from the gale and trembled at the blasts and the windows blazed with strange polychromatic balls of flame, all were tense and troubled. The children fought or succumbed to their terror according to their natures; their parents soothed and reassured them.

Mr Braxton was convinced the lightning conductors were struck three times within five minutes, and he could imagine them recoiling from the mighty impacts and seething from the terrific charges. Not till a dilatory, chaotic dawn staggered up the sky did the storm temporarily lull. For a time the sky cleared and the frost came hard. It was a yawning and haggard company which assembled at breakfast. But determined efforts were made to engender a communal cheerfulness. Mr Braxton did his best to contribute his quota of seasonable bonhomie, but his mind was plagued by thoughts of Curtis. Before the meal was finished the vicar rang up to say the church tower had been struck and almost demolished, so there could be no services. It rang again to say that Brent's farmhouse had been burnt to the ground.

While the others went off to inspect the church, Mr Braxton remained in the study. Presently Knowles rang to say Sir Arthur had been and pronounced Curtis weaker, but his condition was not quite hopeless. One of the most ominous symptoms was the violence of the delirium. Curtis appeared to be in great terror and sedatives had no effect.

"How's that cow-man?" asked Mr Braxton.

"He died in the night, I'm sorry to say."

Whereupon Mr Braxton broke one of his strictest rules by drinking a very stiff whisky with very little soda.

Christmas dinner was tolerably hilarious, and after it, the children, bulging and incipiently bilious, slept some of it off, while their elders put the final touches to the preparations for the party.

In spite of the weather, not a single "cry-off" was telephoned. There was a good reason for this; Mr Braxton's entertainments were justly famous.

So from four-thirty onwards the "Cream of North Berkshire Society" came ploughing through the snow to the Hall; Lady Pounser and party bringing up the rear in her heirloom Rolls which was dribbling steam from its ancient and aristocratic beak. A tea of teas, not merely a high-tea, an Everest tea, towering, sky-scraping, was then attacked by the already stuffed juveniles who, by the end of it, were almost livid with repletion, finding even the efforts of cracker-pulling almost beyond them.

They were then propelled into the library where rows of chairs had been provided for them. There was a screen at one end of the room, a projector at the other. Mr Braxton had provided one of his famous surprises! The room was darkened and on the screen was flashed the sentence: "The North Berks News Reel".

During the last few weeks Mr Braxton had had a sharp-witted and discreetly furtive camera-man at work shooting some of the guests while busy about their more or less lawful occasions.

For example, there was a sentence from a speech by Lord Gallen, the Socialist Peer: "It is a damnable and calculated lie for our opponents to suggest we aim at a preposterous and essentially *inequitable* equalisation on income –" And then there was His Lordship just entering his limousine, and an obsequious footman, rug in hand, holding the door open for him.

His Lordship's laughter was raucous and vehement, though he *would* have liked to have said a few words in rebuttal.

And there was Lady Pounser's Rolls, locally known as "the hippograffe" stuck in a snow-drift and enveloped in steam, with the caption, "Oh, Mr Mercury, *do* give me a start!" And other kindly, slightly sardonic japes at the expense of the North Berks Cream.

The last scene was meant as an appropriate prelude to the climax of the festivities. It showed Curtis and his crew digging up the tree from Lucky's Grove. Out they came from the holm oaks straining under their load, but close observers noticed there was one who remained behind, standing menacing and motionless, a very tall, dark, brooding figure. There came a blinding lightning flash which seemed to blaze sparking round the room, and a fearsome metallic bang. The storm had returned with rasping and imperious salute.

The lights immediately came on and the children were marshalled to the ballroom. As they entered and saw the high tree shining there and the little people so lively upon its branches a prolonged "O – h!" of astonishment was exhorted from the blasé brats. But there was another wave of flame against the windows which rattled wildly at the ensuing roar, and the cries of delight were tinged with terror. And, indeed, the hard, blue glare flung a sinister glow on the tree and its whirling throng.

The grown-ups hastened to restore equanimity and, forming rings of children, circled the tree.

Presently Mrs Braxton exclaimed: "Now then, look for your names on the cards and see what Father Christmas has brought you."

Though hardly one of the disillusioned infants retained any belief in that superannuated Deliverer of Goods, the response was immediate. For they had sharp ears which had eagerly absorbed the tales of Braxton munificence. At the same time it was noticeable that some approached the tree with diffidence, almost reluctance, and started back as a livid flare broke against the window-blinds and the dread peals shook the streaming snow from the eaves.

Mary had just picked up little Angela Rayner so that she could reach her card, when the child screamed and pulled away her hand.

"The worm," she cried, and a thick, black-grey squirming maggot fell from her fingers to the floor and writhed away. George, who was near, put his shoe on it with a squish.

One of the Pounser tribe, whose card was just below the Big Bad Wolf, refused to approach it. No wonder, thought Walter, for it looked horribly hunting and alive. There were other mischances too. The witch behind the sombre tree seemed to pounce out at Clarissa Balder, so she tearfully complained, and Gloria had to pull off her card for her. Of course Gregory was temperamental, seeming to stare at a spot just below the taut peak of the tree, as if mazed and entranced. But the presents were wonderful and more than worth the small ordeal of finding one's card and pretending not to be frightened when the whole room seemed full of fiery hands and the thunder cracked against one's ear-drums and shook one's teeth. Easy to be afraid!

At length the last present had been bestowed and it was time for the pièce de résistance, the pulling of the great cracker. Long, silken cords streamed from each end with room among them for fifty chubby fists, and a great surprise inside, for sure. The languid, uneasy troop were lined up at each end and took a grip on the silken cords.

At that moment a footman came in and told Mr Braxton he was wanted on the telephone.

Filled with foreboding he went to his study. He heard the voice of Knowles –

"I'm afraid I have very bad news for you . . ."

*

The chubby fists gripped the silken cords.

"Now pull!" cried Mrs Braxton.

The opposing teams took the strain.

A leaping flash and a blasting roar. The children were hurled, writhing and screaming over each other.

Up from the middle of the cracker leapt a rosy shaft of flame which, as it reached the ceiling, seemed to flatten its peak so that it resembled a great snake of fire which turned and hurled itself against the tree in a blinding embrace. There was a fierce sustained "Hiss," the tree flamed like a torch, and all the fairy globes upon it burst and splintered. And then the roaring torch cast itself down amongst the screaming chaos. For a moment the great pot, swathed in green, was a carmine cauldron and its paint streamed like blood upon the floor. Then the big room was a dream of fire and those within it driven wildly from its heat.

*

Phil Tangler, whose farmhouse, on the early slopes of Missen Rise, overlooked both Lucky's Grove and the Hall, solemnly declared that at 7.30 on Christmas Day, 1938, he was watching from a window and marvelling at the dense and boiling race of snow, the bitter gale, and the wicked flame and fury of the storm, when he saw a huge fist of fire form a rift in the cloud-rack, a fist with two huge blazing fingers, one of which speared down on the Hall, another touched and kindled the towering fir in Lucky's Grove, as though saluting it. Five minutes later he was racing through the hurricane to join in a vain night-long fight to save the Hall, already blazing from stem to stern.

The Moon Bog

H. P. Lovecraft

Somewhere, to what remote and fearsome region I know not, Denys Barry has gone. I was with him the last night he lived among men, and heard his screams when the thing came to him; but all the peasants and police in County Meath could never find him, or the others, though they searched long and far. And now I shudder when I hear the frogs piping in swamps, or see the moon in lonely places.

I had known Denys Barry well in America, where he had grown rich, and had congratulated him when he bought back the old castle by the bog at sleepy Kilderry. It was from Kilderry that his father had come, and it was there that he wished to enjoy his wealth among ancestral scenes. Men of his blood had once ruled over Kilderry and built and dwelt in the castle, but those days were very remote, so that for generations the castle had been empty and decaying. After he went to Ireland Barry wrote to me often, and told me how under his care the grey castle was rising tower by tower to its ancient splendour, how the ivy was climbing slowly over the restored walls as it had climbed so many centuries ago, and how the peasants blessed him for bringing back the old days with his gold from over the sea. But in time there came troubles, and the peasants ceased to bless him, and fled away instead as from a doom. And then he sent a letter and asked me to visit him, for he was lonely in the castle with no one to speak to save the new servants and labourers he had brought from the North.

The bog was the cause of all these troubles, as Barry told me the night I came to the castle. I had reached Kilderry in the summer sunset, as the gold of the sky lighted the green of the hills and groves and the blue of the bog, where on a far islet a strange olden ruin glistened spectrally. The sunset was very beautiful, but the peasants at Ballylough had warned me against it and said that Kilderry had become accursed, so that I almost shuddered to see the high turrets of the castle gilded with fire. Barry's motor had met me at the Ballylough station, for Kilderry is off the railway. The villagers had shunned the car and the driver from the North, but had whispered to me with pale faces when they saw I was going to Kilderry. And that night, after our reunion, Barry told me why.

The peasants had gone from Kilderry because Denys Barry was to drain the great bog. For all his love of Ireland, America had not left him untouched, and he hated the beautiful wasted space where peat might be cut and land opened up. The legends and superstitions of Kilderry did not move him, and he laughed when the peasants first refused to help, and then cursed him and went away to Ballylough with their few belongings as they saw his determination. In their place he sent for labourers from the North, and when the servants left he replaced them likewise. But it was lonely among strangers, so Barry had asked me to come.

When I heard the fears which had driven the people from Kilderry I laughed as loudly as my friend had laughed, for these fears were of the vaguest, wildest, and most absurd character. They had to do with some preposterous legend of the bog, and of a grim guardian spirit that dwelt in the strange olden ruin on the far islet I had seen in the sunset. There were tales of dancing lights in the dark of the moon, and of chill winds when the night was warm; of wraiths in white hovering over the waters, and of an imagined city of stone deep down below the swampy surface. But foremost among the weird fancies, and alone in its absolute unanimity, was that of the curse awaiting him who should dare to touch or drain the vast reddish morass. There were secrets, said the peasants, which must not be uncovered; secrets that had lain hidden since the plague came to the children of Partholan in the fabulous years beyond history. In the *Book of Invaders* it is told that these sons of the Greeks were all buried at Tallaght, but old men in Kilderry said that one city was overlooked save by its patron moon-goddess; so that only the wooded hills buried it when the men of Nemed swept down from Scythia in their thirty ships.

Such were the idle tales which had made the villagers leave Kilderry, and when I heard them I did not wonder that Denys Barry had refused to listen. He had, however, a great interest in antiquities, and proposed to explore the bog thoroughly when it was drained. The white ruins on the islet he had often visited, but though their age was plainly great, and their contour very little like that of most ruins in Ireland, they were too dilapidated to tell the days of their glory. Now the work of drainage was ready to begin, and the labourers from the North were soon to strip the forbidden bog of its green moss and red heather, and kill the tiny shell-paved streamlets and quiet blue pools fringed with rushes.

After Barry had told me these things I was very drowsy, for the travels of the day had been wearying and my host had talked late into the night. A man-servant showed me to my room, which was in a remote tower overlooking the village, and the plain at the edge of the bog, and the bog itself; so that I could see from my windows in the moonlight the silent roofs from which the peasants had fled and which now sheltered the labourers from the North, and too, the parish church with its antique spire, and far out across the brooding bog the remote olden ruin on the islet gleaming white and spectral. Just as I dropped to sleep I fancied I heard faint sounds from the distance; sounds that were wild and half musical, and stirred me with a weird excitement which coloured my dreams. But when I awakened next morning I felt it had all been a dream, for the visions I had seen were more wonderful than any sound of wild pipes in the night. Influenced by the legends that Barry had related, my mind had in slumber hovered around a stately city in a green valley, where marble streets and statues, villas and temples, carvings and inscriptions, all spoke in certain tones the glory that was Greece. When I told this dream to Barry we both laughed; but I laughed the louder, because he was perplexed about his labourers from the North. For the sixth time they had all overslept, waking very slowly and dazedly, and acting as if they had not rested, although they were known to have gone early to bed the night before.

That morning and afternoon I wandered alone through the sun-gilded village and talked now and then with idle labourers, for Barry was busy with the final plans for beginning his work of drainage. The labourers were not as happy as they might have been, for most of them seemed uneasy over some dream which they had had, yet which they tried in vain to remember. I told them of my dream, but they were not interested till I spoke of the weird sounds I thought I had heard. Then they looked oddly at me, and said that they seemed to remember weird sounds, too.

In the evening Barry dined with me and announced that he would begin the drainage in two days. I was glad, for although I disliked to see the moss and the heather and the little streams and lakes depart, I had a growing wish to discern the ancient secrets the deep-matted peat might hide. And that night my dreams of piping flutes and marble peristyle came to a sudden and disquieting end; for upon the city in the valley I saw a pestilence descend, and then a frightful avalanche of wooded slopes that covered the dead bodies in the streets and left unburied only the temple of Artemis on the high peak, where the aged moon-priestess Cleis lay cold and silent with a crown of ivory on her silver head.

I have said that I awakened suddenly and in alarm. For some time I could not tell whether I was waking or sleeping, for the sound of flutes still rang shrilly in my ears; but when I saw on the floor the icy moonbeams and the outlines of a latticed Gothic window I decided I must be awake and in the castle of Kilderry. Then I heard a clock from some remote landing below strike the hour of two, and knew I was awake. Yet still there came that monotonous piping from afar; wild, weird airs that made me think of some dance of fauns on distant Maenalus. It would not let me sleep, and in impatience I sprang up and paced the floor. Only by chance did I go to the north window and look out upon the silent village and the plain at the edge of the bog. I had no wish to gaze abroad, for I wanted to sleep; but the flutes tormented me, and I had to do or see something. How could I have suspected the thing I was to behold?

There in the moonlight that flooded the spacious plain was a spectacle which no mortal, having seen it, could ever forget. To the sound of reedy pipes that echoed over the bog there glided silently and eerily a mixed throng of swaying figures, reeling through such a revel as the Sicilians may have danced to Demeter in the old days under the harvest moon beside the Cyane. The wide plain, the golden moonlight, the shadowy moving forms, and above all the shrill monotonous piping, produced an effect which almost paralysed me; yet I noted amidst my fear that half of these tireless, mechanical dancers were the labourers whom I had thought asleep, whilst the other half were strange airy beings in white, half-indeterminate in nature, but suggesting pale wistful naiads from the haunted fountains of the bog. I do not know how long I gazed at this sight from the lonely turret window before I dropped suddenly in a dreamless swoon, out of which the high sun of morning aroused me.

My first impulse on awaking was to communicate all my fears and observations to Denys Barry, but as I saw the sunlight glowing through the latticed east window I became sure that there was no reality in what I thought I had seen. I am given to strange fantasms, yet am never weak enough to believe in them; so on this occasion contented myself with questioning the labourers, who slept very late and recalled nothing of the previous night save misty dreams of shrill sounds. This matter of the spectral piping harassed me greatly, and I wondered if the crickets of autumn had come before their time to vex the night and haunt the visions of men. Later in the day I watched Barry in the library poring over his plans for the great work which was to begin on the morrow, and for the first time felt a touch of the same kind of fear that had driven the peasants away. For some unknown reason I dreaded the thought of disturbing the ancient bog and its sunless secrets, and pictured terrible sights lying black under the unmeasured depth of age-old peat. That these secrets should be brought to light seemed injudicious, and I began to wish for an excuse to leave the castle and the village. I went so far as to talk casually to Barry on the subject, but did not dare continue after he gave his resounding laugh. So I was silent when the sun set fulgently over the far hills, and Kilderry blazed all red and gold in a flame that seemed a portent.

Whether the events of that night were reality or illusion I shall never ascertain. Certainly they transcend anything we dream of in nature and the universe; yet in no normal fashion can I explain those disappearances which were known to all men after it was over. I retired early and full of dread, and for a long time could not sleep in the uncanny silence of the tower. It was very dark, for although the sky was clear the moon was now well on the wane, and would not rise till the small hours. I thought as I lay there of Denys Barry, and of what would befall that bog when the day came, and found myself almost frantic with an impulse to rush out into the night, take Barry's car, and drive madly to Ballylough out of the menaced lands. But before my fears could crystallise into action I had fallen asleep, and gazed in dreams upon the city in the valley, cold and dead under a shroud of hideous shadow.

Probably it was the shrill piping that awaked me, yet that piping was not what I noticed first when I opened my eyes. I was lying with my back to the east window overlooking the bog, where the waning moon would rise, and therefore expected to see light cast on the opposite wall before me; but I had not looked for such a sight as now appeared. Light indeed glowed on the panels ahead, but it was not any light that the moon gives. Terrible and piercing was the shaft of ruddy refulgence that streamed through the Gothic window, and the whole chamber was brilliant with a splendour intense and unearthly. My immediate actions were peculiar for such a situation, but it is only in tales that a man does the dramatic and foreseen thing. Instead of looking out across the bog, toward the source of the new light, I kept my eyes from the window in panic fear, and clumsily drew on my clothing with some dazed idea of escape. I remember seizing my revolver and hat, but before it was over I had lost them both without firing the one or donning the other. After a time the fascination of the red radiance overcame my fright, and I crept to the east window and looked out whilst the maddening, incessant piping whined and reverberated through the castle and over all the village.

Over the bog was a deluge of flaring light, scarlet and sinister, and pouring from the strange olden ruin on the far islet. The aspect of that ruin I cannot describe – I must have been mad, for it seemed to rise majestic and undecayed, splendid and column-cinctured, the flame-reflecting marble of its entablature piercing the sky like the apex of a temple on a mountain-top. Flutes shrieked and drums began to beat, and as I watched in awe and terror I thought I saw dark saltant forms silhouetted grotesquely against the vision of marble and effulgence. The effect was titanic – altogether unthinkable – and I might have stared indefinitely had not the sound of the piping seemed to grow stronger at my left. Trembling with a terror oddly mixed with ecstasy I crossed the circular room to the north window from which I could see the village and the plain at the edge of the bog. There my eyes dilated again with a wild wonder as great as if I had not just turned from a scene beyond the pale of nature, for on the ghastly red-lit plain was moving a procession of beings in such a manner as none ever saw before save in nightmares.

Half gliding, half floating in the air, the white-clad bog-wraiths were slowly retreating toward the still waters and the island ruin in fantastic formations suggesting some ancient and solemn ceremonial dance. Their waving translucent arms, guided by the detestable piping of those unseen flutes, beckoned in uncanny rhythm to a throng of lurching labourers who followed doglike with blind, brainless, floundering steps as if dragged by a clumsy but resistless demon-will. As the naiads neared the bog, without altering their course, a new line of stumbling stragglers zigzagged drunkenly out of the castle from some door far below my window, groped sightlessly across the courtyard and through the intervening bit of village, and joined the floundering column of labourers on the plain. Despite their distance below me I at once knew they were the servants brought from the North, for I recognised the ugly and unwieldy form of the cook, whose very absurdness had now become unutterably tragic. The flutes piped horribly, and again I heard the beating of the drums from the direction of the island ruin. Then silently and gracefully the naiads reached the water and melted one by one into the ancient bog; while the line of followers, never checking their speed, splashed awkwardly after them and vanished amidst a tiny vortex of unwholesome bubbles which I could barely see in the scarlet light. And as the last pathetic straggler, the fat cook, sank heavily out of sight in that sullen pool, the flutes and the drums grew silent, and the blinding red rays from the ruins snapped instantaneously out, leaving the village of doom lone and desolate in the wan beams of a new-risen moon.

My condition was now one of indescribable chaos. Not knowing whether I was mad or sane, sleeping or waking, I was saved only by a merciful numbness. I believe I did ridiculous things such as offering prayers to Artemis, Latona, Demeter, Persephone and Plouton. All that I recalled of a classical youth came to my lips as the horrors of the situation roused my deepest superstitions. I felt that I had witnessed the death of a whole village, and knew I was alone in the castle with Denys Barry, whose boldness had brought down a doom. As I thought of him new terrors convulsed

me, and I fell to the floor, not fainting, but physically helpless. Then I felt the icy blast from the east window where the moon had risen, and began to hear the shrieks in the castle far below me. Soon these shrieks had attained a magnitude and quality which cannot be written of, and which make me faint as I think of them. All I can say is that they came from something I had known as a friend.

At some time during this shocking period the cold wind and the screaming must have roused me, for my next impression is of racing madly through inky rooms and corridors and out across the courtyard into the hideous night. They found me

at dawn wandering mindless near Ballylough, but what unhinged me utterly was not any of the horrors I had seen or heard before. What I muttered about as I came slowly out of the shadows was a pair of fantastic incidents which occurred in my flight: incidents of no significance, yet which haunt me unceasingly when I am alone in certain marshy places or in the moonlight.

As I fled from that accursed castle along the bog's edge I heard a new sound: common, yet unlike any I had heard before at Kilderry. The stagnant waters, lately quite devoid of animal life, now teemed with a horde of slimy enormous frogs which piped shrilly and incessantly in tones strangely out of keeping with their size. They glistened bloated and green in the moonbeams, and seemed to gaze up at the fount of light. I followed the gaze of one very fat and ugly frog, and saw the second of the things which drove my senses away.

Stretching directly from the strange olden ruin on the far islet to the waning moon, my eyes seemed to trace a beam of faint quivering radiance having no reflection in the waters of the bog. And upward along that pallid path my fevered fancy pictured a thin shadow slowly writhing, a vague contorted shadow struggling as if drawn by unseen demons. Crazed as I was, I saw in that awful shadow a monstrous resemblance – a nauseous, unbelievable caricature – a blasphemous effigy of him who had been Denys Barry.

The White Cat of Drumgunniol

J. S. LeFanu

There is a famous story of a white cat, with which we all become acquainted in the nursery. I am going to tell a story of a white cat very different from the amiable and enchanted princess who took that disguise for a season. The white cat of which I speak was a more sinister animal.

The traveller from Limerick towards Dublin, after passing the hills of Killaloe upon the left, as Keeper Mountain raises high in view, finds himself gradually hemmed in, up the right, by a range of lower hills. An undulating plain that dips gradually to a lower level than that of the road interposes, and some scattered hedgerows relieve its somewhat wild and melancholy character.

One of the few human habitations that send up their films of turf-smoke from that lonely plain, is the loosely-thatched, earth-built dwelling of a "strong farmer", as the more prosperous of the tenant-farming classes are termed in Munster. It stands in a clump of trees near the edge of a wandering stream, about half-way between the mountains and the Dublin road, and had been for generations tenanted by people named Donovan.

In a distant place, desirous of studying some Irish records which had fallen into my hands, and inquiring for a teacher capable of instructing me in the Irish language, a Mr Donovan, dreamy, harmless and learned, was recommended to me for the purpose.

I found that he had been educated as a Sizar in Trinity College, Dublin. He now supported himself by teaching, and the special direction of my studies, I suppose, flattered his national partialities, for he unbosomed himself of much of his long-reserved thoughts, and recollections about his country and his early days. It was he who told me this story, and I mean to repeat it, as nearly as I can, in his own words.

I have myself seen the old farm-house, with its orchard of huge mossgrown apple trees. I have looked round on the peculiar landscape; the roofless, ivied tower, that two hundred years before had afforded a refuge from raid and rapparee, and which still occupies its old place in the angle of the haggard; the bush-grown "liss", that scarcely a hundred and fifty steps away records the labours of a bygone race; the dark and towering outline of old Keeper in the background; and the lonely range of furze and heath-clad hills that form a nearer barrier, with many a line of grey rock and clump of dwarf oak or birch. The pervading sense of loneliness made it a scene not unsuited for a wild and unearthly story. And I could quite fancy how, seen in the grey of a wintry morning, shrouded far and wide in snow, or in the melancholy glory of an autumnal sunset, or in the chill splendour of a moonlight night, it might have helped to tone a dreamy mind like honest Dan Donovan's to superstition and a proneness to the illusions of fancy. It is certain, however, that I never anywhere met with a more simple-minded creature, or one on whose good faith I could more entirely rely.

When I was a boy, said he, living at home at Drumgunniol, I used to take my Goldsmith's *Roman History* in my hand and go down to my favourite seat, the flat stone, sheltered by a hawthorn tree beside the little lough, a large and deep pool, such as I have heard called a tarn in England. It lay in the gentle hollow of a field that is overhung toward the north by the old orchard, and being a deserted place was favourable to my studious quietude.

One day reading here, as usual, I wearied at last, and began to look about me, thinking of the heroic scenes I had just been reading of. I was as wide awake as I am at this moment, and I saw a woman appear at the corner of the orchard and walk down the slope. She wore a long, light grey dress, so long that it seemed to sweep the grass behind her, and so singular was her appearance in a part of the world where female attire is so inflexibly fixed by custom, that I could not take my eyes off her. Her course lay diagonally from corner to corner of the field, which was a large one, and she pursued it without swerving.

When she came near I could see that her feet were bare, and that she seemed to be looking steadfastly upon some remote object for guidance. Her route would have crossed me – had the tarn not interposed – about ten or twelve yards below the point at which I was sitting. But instead of arresting her course at the margin of the lough, as I had expected, she went on without seeming conscious of its existence, and I saw her, as plainly as I see you, sir, walk across the surface of the water, and pass, without seeming to see me, at about the distance I had calculated.

I was ready to faint from sheer terror. I was only thirteen years old then, and I remember every particular as if it had happened this hour.

The figure passed through the gap at the far corner of the field, and there I lost sight of it. I had hardly strength to walk home, and was so nervous, and ultimately so ill, that for three weeks I was confined to the house, and could not bear to be alone for a moment. I never entered that field again, such was the horror with which from that moment every object in it was clothed. Even at this distance of time I should not like to pass through it.

This apparition I connected with a mysterious event; and, also, with a singular liability, that has for nearly eighty years distinguished, or rather afflicted, our family. It is no fancy. Everybody in that part of the country knows all about it. Everybody connected what I had seen with it.

I will tell it all to you as well as I can.

When I was about fourteen years old – that is about a year after the sight I had seen in the lough field – we were one night expecting my father home from the fair of Killaloe. My mother sat up to welcome him home and I with her, for I liked nothing better than such a vigil. My brothers and sisters, and the farm servants, except the men who were driving home the cattle from the fair, were asleep in their beds. My mother and I were sitting in the chimney corner chatting together, and watching my father's supper, which was kept hot over the fire. We knew that he would return before the men who were driving home the cattle, for he was riding, and told us that he would only wait to see them fairly on the road, and then push homeward.

At length we heard his voice and the knocking of his loaded whip at the door, and my mother let him in. I don't think I ever saw my father drunk, which is more than most men of my age, from the same part of the country, could say of theirs. But he could drink his glass of whisky as well as another, and he usually came home from fair or market a little merry and mellow, and with a jolly flush in his cheeks.

Tonight he looked sunken, pale and sad. He entered with the saddle and bridle in his hand, and he dropped them against the wall, near the door, and put his arms round his wife's neck, and kissed her kindly.

"Welcome home, Meehal," said she, kissing him heartily.

"God bless you, mavourneen," he answered.

And hugging her again, he turned to me, who was plucking him by the hand, jealous of his notice. I was little, and light of my age, and he lifted me up in his arms and kissed me, and my arms being about his neck, he said to my mother:

"Draw the bolt, acuishla."

She did so, and setting me down very dejectedly, he walked to the fire and sat down on a stool, and stretched his feet toward the glowing turf, leaning with his hands on his knees.

"Rouse up, Mick, darlin'," said my mother, who was growing anxious, "and tell me how did the cattle sell, and did everything go lucky at the fair, or is there anything wrong with the landlord, or what in the world is it that ails you, Mick, jewel?"

"Nothin,' Molly. The cows sould well, thank God, and there's nothin' fell out between me an' the landlord, an' everything's the same way. There's no fault to find anywhere."

"Well, then, Mickey, since so it is, turn round to your hot supper, and ate it, and tell us is there anything new."

"I got my supper, Molly, on the way, and I can't ate a bit," he answered.

"Got your supper on the way, an' you knowin' 'twas waiting for you at home, an' your wife sitting up an' all!" cried my mother reproachfully.

"You're takin' a wrong meanin' out of what I say," said my father. "There's something happened that leaves me that

I can't ate a mouthful, and I'll not be dark with you, Molly, for, maybe it ain't very long I have to be here, an' I'll tell you what it was. It's what I've seen, the white cat."

"The Lord between us and harm!" exclaimed my mother, in a moment as pale and as chap-fallen as my father; and then, trying to rally, with a laugh, she said: "Ha! 'tis only funnin' me you are. Sure a white rabbit was snared a Sunday last, in Grady's wood; an' Teigue seen a big white rat in the haggard yesterday."

" 'Twas neither rat nor rabbit was in it. Don't ye think but I'd know a rat or a rabbit from a big white cat, with green eyes as big as halfpennies, and its back riz up like a bridge, trottin' on and across me, and ready, if I dar' stop, to rub its sides against my shins, and maybe to make a jump and seize my throat, if that it's a cat, at all, an' not something worse?"

As he ended his description in a low tone, looking straight at the fire, my father drew his big hand across his forehead once or twice, his face being damp and shining with the moisture of fear, and he sighed, or rather groaned, heavily.

My mother had relapsed into panic, and was praying again in her fear. I, too, was terribly frightened, and on the point of crying, for I knew all about the white cat.

Clapping my father on the shoulder, by way of encouragement, my mother leaned over him, kissing him, and at last began to cry. He was wringing her hands in his, and seemed in great trouble.

"There was nothin' came into the house with me?" he asked, in a very low tone, turning to me.

"There was nothin,' father," I said, "but the saddle and bridle that was in your hand."

"Nothin' white kem in at the doore wid me?" he repeated.

"Nothin' at all," I answered.

"So be it," said my father, and making the sign of the cross, he began mumbling to himself, and I knew he was saying his prayers.

Waiting for a while, to give him time for this exercise, my mother asked him where he first saw it.

"When I was riding up the bohereen," – the Irish term meaning a little road, such as leads up to a farm-house – "I bethought myself that the men was on the road with the cattle, and no one to look to the horse barrin' myself, so I thought I might as well leave him in the crooked field below, an' I tuck him there, he bein' cool, and not a hair turned, for I rode him aisy all the way. It was when I turned, after lettin' him go – the saddle and bridle bein' in my hand – that I saw it, pushin' out o' the long grass at the side o' the path, an' it walked across it, in front of me, an' then back again, before me, the same way, an' sometimes at one side, an' then at the other, lookin' at me wid them shinin' eyes; and I consayted I heard it growlin' as it kep' beside me – as close as ever you see – till I kem up to the doore, here, an' knocked an' called, as ye heerd me."

Now, what was it, in so simple an incident, that agitated my father, my mother, myself, and finally, every member of this rustic household, with a terrible foreboding? It was this that we, one and all, believed that my father had received, in thus encountering the white cat, a warning of his approaching death.

The omen had never failed hitherto. It did not fail now. In a week after my father took the fever that was going, and before a month he was dead.

My honest friend, Dan Donovan, paused here; I could perceive that he was praying, for his lips were busy, and I concluded that it was for the repose of that departed soul.

In a little while he resumed.

It is eighty years now since that omen first attached to my family. Eighty years? Ay, is it? Ninety is nearer the mark. And I have spoken to many old people, in those earlier times, who had a distinct recollection of everything connected with it.

It happened in this way.

My grand-uncle, Connor Donovan, had the old farm of Drumgunniol in his day. He was richer than ever my father was, or my father's father either, for he took a short lease of

Balraghan, and made money of it. But money won't soften a hard heart, and I'm afraid my grand-uncle was a cruel man – a profligate man he was, surely, and that is mostly a cruel man at heart. He drank his share, too, and cursed and swore, when he was vexed, more than was good for his soul, I'm afraid.

At that time there was a beautiful girl of the Colemans, up in the mountains, not far from Capper Cullen. I'm told that there are no Colemans there now at all, and that family has passed away. The famine years made great changes.

Ellen Coleman was her name. The Colemans were not rich. But, being such a beauty, she might have made a good match. Worse than she did for herself, poor thing, she could not.

Con Donovan – my grand-uncle, God forgive him! – sometimes in his rambles saw her at fairs or patterns, and he fell in love with her, as who might not?

He used her ill. He promised her marriage, and persuaded her to come away with him; and, after all, he broke his word. It was just the old story. He tired of her, and he wanted to push himself in the world; and he married a girl of the Collopys, that had a great fortune – twenty-four cows, seventy sheep, and a hundred and twenty goats.

He married this Mary Collopy, and grew richer than before; and Ellen Coleman died broken-hearted. But that did not trouble the strong farmer much.

He would have liked to have children, but he had none, and this was the only cross he had to bear, for everything else went much as he wished.

One night he was returning from the fair of Nenagh. A shallow stream at that time crossed the road – they have thrown a bridge over it, I am told, some time since – and its channel was often dry in summer weather. When it was so, as it passes close by the old farm-house of Drumgunniol, without a great deal of winding, it makes a sort of road, which people then used as a short cut to reach the house by. Into this dry channel, as there was plenty of light from the moon, my grand-uncle turned his horse, and when he had reached the two ash-trees at the meeting of the farm he turned his horse short into the river-field, intending to ride through the gap at the other end, under the oak-tree, and so he would have been within a few hundred yards of his door.

As he approached the "gap" he saw, or thought he saw, with a slow motion, gliding along the ground towards the same point, and now and then with a soft bound, a white object, which he described as being no bigger than his hat, but what it was he could not see, as it moved along the hedge and disappeared at the point to which he himself was tending.

When he reached the gap the horse stopped short. He urged and coaxed it in vain. He got down to lead it through, but it recoiled, snorted and fell into a wild trembling fit. He mounted it again. But its terror continued, and it obstinately resisted his caresses and his whip. It was bright moonlight, and my grand-uncle was chafed by the horse's resistance and, seeing nothing to account for it, and being so near home, what little patience he possessed forsook him, and, plying his whip and spur in earnest, he broke into oaths, and curses.

All of a sudden the horse sprang through, and Con Donovan, as he passed under the broad branch of the oak, saw clearly a woman standing on the bank beside him, her arm extended, with the hand of which, as he flew by, she struck him a blow upon the shoulders. It threw him forward upon the neck of the horse, which, in wild terror, reached the door at a gallop, and stood there quivering and steaming all over.

Less alive than dead, my grand-uncle got in. He told his story, at least, so much as he chose. His wife did not quite know what to think. But that something very bad had happened she could not doubt. He was very faint and ill, and begged the the priest should be sent for forthwith. When they were getting him to his bed they saw distinctly the marks of five fingerpoints on the flesh of his shoulder, where the spectral blow had fallen. These singular marks – which they said resembled in tint the hue of a body struck by lightning – remained imprinted on his flesh, and were buried with him.

When he had recovered sufficiently to talk with the people

about him – speaking, like a man at his last hour, from a burdened heart, and troubled conscience – he repeated his story, but said he did not see, or, at all events, know, the face of the figure that stood in the gap. No one believed him. He told more about it to the priest than to others. He certainly had a secret to tell. He might as well have divulged it frankly, for the neighbours all knew well enough that it was the face of dead Ellen Coleman that he had seen.

From that moment my grand-uncle never raised his head. He was a scared, silent, broken-spirited man. It was early summer then, and at the fall of the leaf in the same year he died.

Of course there was a wake, such as beseemed a strong farmer so rich as he. For some reason the arrangements of this ceremonial were a little different from the usual routine.

The usual practice is to place the body in the great room, or kitchen, as it is called, of the house. In this particular case there was, as I told you, for some reason, an unusual arrangement. The body was placed in a small room that opened upon the greater one. The door of this, during the wake, stood open. There were candles about the bed, and pipes and tobacco on the table, and stools for such guests as chose to enter, the door standing open for their reception.

The body, having been laid out, was left alone, in this smaller room, during the preparation for the wake. After nightfall one of the women, approaching the bed to get a chair which she had left near it, rushed from the room with a scream, and, having recovered her speech at the further end of the "kitchen", and surrounded by a gaping audience, she said, at last:

"May I never sin, if his face bain't riz up again the back o' the bed, and he starin' down to the doore, wid eyes as big as pewter plates, that id be shinin' in the moon!"

"Arra, woman! Is it cracked you are?" said one of the farm boys as they are termed, being men of any age you please.

"Agh, Molly, don't be talkin', woman! 'Tis what ye consayted it, goin' into the dark room, out o' the light. Why didn't ye take a candle in your fingers, ye aumadhaun?" said one of her female companions.

"Candle, or no candle, I seen it," insisted Molly. "An' what's more, I could a'most tak' my oath I seen his arum, too, stretchin' out o' the bed along the flure, three times as long as it should be, to take hould o' me be the fut."

"Nansinse, ye fool, what id he want o' yer fut?" exclaimed one scornfully.

"Gi' me the candle, some o' yez – in the name o' God," said old Sal Doolan, that was straight and lean, and a woman that could pray like a priest almost.

"Give her a candle," agreed all.

But whatever they might say, there wasn't one among them that did not look pale and stern enough as they followed Mrs Doolan, who was praying as fast as her lips could patter, and leading the van with a tallow candle, held like a taper, in her fingers.

The door was half open, as the panic-stricken girl had left it; and holding the candle on high the better to examine the room, she made a step or so into it.

If my grand-uncle's hand had been stretched along the floor, in the unnatural way described, he had drawn it back again under the sheet that covered him. And tall Mrs Doolan was in no danger of tripping over his arm as she entered. But she had not gone more than a step or two with her candle aloft, when, with a drowning face, she suddenly stopped short, staring at the bed which was now fully in view.

"Lord, bless us, Mrs Doolan, ma'am, come back," said the woman next her, who had fast hold of her dress, or her "coat" as they call it, and drawing her backwards with a frightened pluck, while a general recoil among her followers betokened the alarm which her hesitation had inspired.

"Whisht, will yez?" said the leader, peremptorily, "I can't hear my own ears wid the noise ye're making, an' which iv yez let the cat in here, an' whose cat is it?" she asked peering suspiciously at a white cat that was sitting on the breast of the corpse.

"Put it away, will yez?" she resumed, with horror at the profanation. "Many a corpse as I sthretched and crossed in the bed the likes o' that I never seen yet. The man o' the house, wid a brute baste like that mounted on him, like a phooka, Lord forgi' me for namin' the like in this room. Dhrive it away, some o' yez! Out o' that, this minute, I tell ye."

Each repeated the order, but no one seemed inclined to execute it. They were crossing themselves, and whispering their conjectures and misgivings as to the nature of the beast, which was no cat of that house, nor one that they had ever seen before. On a sudden, the white cat placed itself on the pillow over the head of the body, and having from that place glared for a time at them over the features of the corpse, it crept softly along the body towards them, growling low and fiercely as it drew near.

Out of the room they bounced, in dreadful confusion, shutting the door fast after them, and not for a good while did the hardiest venture to peep in again.

The white cat was sitting in its old place, on the dead man's breast, but this time it crept quietly down the side of the bed, and disappeared under it, the sheet which was spread like a coverlet, and hung down nearly to the floor, concealing it from view.

Praying, crossing themselves, and not forgetting a sprinkling of holy water, they peeped, and finally searched, poking spades, "wattles", pitchforks and such implements under the bed. But the cat was not to be found, and they concluded that it had made its escape among their feet as they stood near the threshold. So they secured the door carefully, with hasp and padlock.

But when the door was opened next morning they found the white cat sitting, as if it had never been disturbed, upon the breast of the dead man.

Again occurred very nearly the same scene with a like result, only that some said they saw the cat afterwards lurking under a big box in a corner of the outer-room, where my grand-uncle kept his leases and papers, and his prayer-book and beads.

Mrs Doolan heard it growling at her heels wherever she went; and although she could not see it, she could hear it spring on the back of her chair when she sat down, and growl in her ear, so that she would bounce up with a scream and a prayer, fancying that it was on the point of taking her by the throat.

And the priest's boy, looking round the corner, under the branches of the old orchard, saw a white cat sitting under the little window of the room where my grand-uncle was laid out and looking up at the four small panes of glass as a cat will watch a bird.

The end of it was that the cat was found on the corpse again, when the room was visited, and do what they might, whenever the body was left alone, the cat was found again in the same ill-omened contiguity with the dead man. And this continued, to the scandal and fear of the neighbourhood, until the door was opened finally for the wake.

My grand-uncle being dead, and, with all due solemnities, buried, I have done with him. But not quite yet with the white cat. No banshee ever yet was more inalienably attached to a family than this ominous apparition is to mine. But there is this difference. The banshee seems to be animated with an affectionate sympathy with the bereaved family to whom it is hereditarily attached, whereas this thing has about it a suspicion of malice. It is the messenger simply of death. And its taking the shape of a cat – the coldest, and they say, the most vindictive of brutes – is indicative of the spirit of its visit.

When my grandfather's death was near, although he seemed quite well at the time, it appeared not exactly, but very nearly in the same way in which I told you it showed itself to my father.

The day before my Uncle Teigue was killed by the bursting of his gun, it appeared to him in the evening, at twilight, by the lough, in the field where I saw the woman who walked across the water, as I told you. My uncle was washing the barrel of his gun in the lough. The grass is short there, and there is no cover near it. He did not know how it approached but the first he saw of it, the white cat was walking close round his feet, in the twilight, with an angry twist of its tail, and a green glare in its eyes, and do what he would, it continued walking round and round him, in larger or smaller circles, till he reached the orchard, and there he lost it.

My poor Aunt Peg – she married one of the O'Brians, near Oolah – came to Drumgunniol to go to the funeral of a cousin who died about a mile away. She died herself, poor woman, only a month after.

Coming from the wake, at two or three o'clock in the morning, as she got over the stile into the farm of Drumgunniol, she saw the white cat at her side, and it kept close beside her, she ready to faint all the time, till she reached the door of the house, where it made a spring up into the whitethorn tree that grows close by, and so it parted from her. And my little brother Jim saw it also, just three weeks before he died. Every member of our family who dies, or takes his death-sickness at Drumgunniol, is sure to see the white cat, and no one of us who sees it need hope for long life after.

The Bottle Imp

R. L. Stevenson

There was a man of the island of Hawaii, whom I shall call Keawe; for the truth is, he still lives, and his name must be kept secret; but the place of his birth was not far from Honaunau, where the bones of Keawe the Great lie hidden in a cave. This man was poor, brave, and active; he could read and write like a schoolmaster; he was a first-rate mariner besides, sailed for some time in the island steamers, and steered a whale-boat on the Hamakua coast. At length it came in Keawe's mind to have a sight of the great world and foreign cities, and he shipped on a vessel bound to San Francisco.

This is a fine town, with a fine harbour, and rich people uncountable; and, in particular, there is one hill which is covered with palaces. Upon this hill Keawe was one day taking a walk, with his pocket full of money, viewing the great houses upon either hand with pleasure. "What fine houses there are!" he was thinking, "and how happy must these people be who dwell in them, and take no care for the morrow!" The thought was in his mind when he came abreast of a house that was smaller than some others, but all finished and beautiful like a toy; the steps of that house shone like silver, and the borders of the garden bloomed like garlands, and the windows were bright like diamonds; and Keawe stopped and wondered at the excellence of all he saw. So stopping, he was aware of a man that looked forth upon him through a window, so clear that Keawe could see him as you see a fish in a pool upon the reef. The man was elderly, with a bald head and a black beard; and his face was heavy with sorrow, and he bitterly sighed. And the truth of it is, that as

Keawe looked in upon the man, and the man looked out upon Keawe, each envied the other.

All of a sudden the man smiled and nodded, and beckoned Keawe to enter, and met him at the door of the house.

"This is a fine house of mine," said the man, and bitterly sighed. "Would you not care to view the chambers?"

So he led Keawe all over it, from the cellar to the roof, and there was nothing there that was not perfect of its kind, and Keawe was astonished.

"Truly," said Keawe, "this is a beautiful house; if I lived in the like of it, I should be laughing all day long. How comes it, then, that you should be sighing?"

"There is no reason," said the man, "why you should not have a house in all points similar to this, and finer, if you wish. You have some money, I suppose?"

"I have fifty dollars," said Keawe; "but a house like this will cost more than fifty dollars."

The man made a computation. "I am sorry you have no more," said he, "for it may raise you trouble in the future; but it shall be yours at fifty dollars."

"The house?" asked Keawe.

"No, not the house," replied the man; "but the bottle. For I must tell you, although I appear to you so rich and fortunate, all my fortune, and this house itself and its garden, came out of a bottle not much bigger than a pint. This is it."

And he opened a lockfast place, and took out a round-bellied bottle with a long neck; the glass of it was white like milk, with changing rainbow colours in the grain. Withinsides something obscurely moved, like a shadow and a fire.

"This is the bottle," said the man; and, when Keawe laughed, "You do not believe me?" he added. "Try, then, for yourself. See if you can break it."

So Keawe took the bottle up and dashed it on the floor till he was weary; but it jumped on the floor like a child's ball, and was not injured.

"This is a strange thing," said Keawe. "For by the touch of it, as well as by the look, the bottle should be of glass."

"Of glass it is," replied the man, sighing more heavily than ever; "but the glass of it was tempered in the flames of hell. An imp lives in it, and that is the shadow we behold there moving; or, so I suppose. If any man buy this bottle the imp is at his command; all that he desires – love, fame, money, houses like this house, aye, or a city like this city – all are his at the word uttered. Napoleon had this bottle, and by it he grew to be the king of the world; but he sold it at the last and fell. Captain Cook had this bottle, and by it he found his way to so many islands; but he too sold it, and was slain upon Hawaii. For, once it is sold, the power goes and the protection; and unless a man remain content with what he has, ill will befall him."

"And yet you talk of selling it yourself?" Keawe said.

"I have all I wish, and I am growing elderly," replied the man. "There is one thing the imp cannot do – he cannot prolong life; and it would not be fair to conceal from you there is a drawback to the bottle; for if a man die before he sells it, he must burn in hell for ever."

"To be sure, that is a drawback and no mistake," cried Keawe. "I would not meddle with the thing. I can do without a house, thank God; but there is one thing I could not be doing with one particle, and that is to be damned."

"Dear me, you must not run away with things," returned the man. "All you have to do is to use the power of the imp in moderation, and then sell it to someone else, as I do to you, and finish your life in comfort."

"Well, I observe two things," said Keawe. "All the time you keep sighing like a maid in love – that is one; and for the other, you sell this bottle very cheap."

"I have told you already why I sigh," said the man. "It is because I fear my health is breaking up; and, as you said yourself, to die and go to the devil is a pity for any one. As for why I sell so cheap, I must explain to you there is a peculiarity about the bottle. Long ago, when the devil brought it first upon earth, it was extremely expensive, and was sold first of all to Prester John for many millions of dollars; but it cannot be sold at all, unless sold at a loss. If you sell it for as much as you paid for it, back it comes to you again like a homing pigeon. It follows that the price has kept falling in these centuries, and the bottle is now remarkably cheap. I bought it myself from one of my great neighbours on this hill, and the price I paid was only ninety dollars. I could sell it for as high as eighty-nine dollars and ninety-nine cents, but not a penny dearer, or back the thing must come to me. Now, about this there are two bothers. First, when you offer a bottle so singular for eighty-odd dollars, people suppose you to be jesting. And second – but there is no hurry about that – and I need not go into it. Only remember it must be coined money that you sell it for."

"How am I to know that this is all true?" asked Keawe.

"Some of it you can try at once," replied the man. "Give me your fifty dollars, take the bottle, and wish your fifty dollars back into your pocket. If that does not happen, I pledge you my honour I will cry off the bargain and restore your money."

"You are not deceiving me?" said Keawe.

The man bound himself with a great oath.

"Well, I will risk that much," said Keawe, "for that can do no harm," and he paid over his money to the man, and the man handed him the bottle.

"Imp of the bottle," said Keawe, "I want my fifty dollars back." And sure enough, he had scarce said the word before his pocket was as heavy as ever.

"To be sure this is a wonderful bottle," said Keawe.

"And now good-morning to you, my fine fellow, and the devil go with you for me," said the man.

"Hold on," said Keawe, "I don't want any more of this fun. Here, take your bottle back."

"You have bought it for less than I paid for it," replied the man, rubbing his hands. "It is yours now; and, for my part, I am only concerned to see the back of you." And with that he rang for his Chinese servant, and had Keawe shown out of the house.

Now, when Keawe was in the street, with the bottle under his arm, he began to think. "If all is true about this bottle, I may have made a losing bargain," thinks he. "But perhaps the man was only fooling me." The first thing he did was to count his money; the sum was exact – forty-nine dollars, American money, and one Chili piece. "That looks like the truth," said Keawe. "Now I will try another part."

The streets in that part of the city were as clean as a ship's decks, and though it was noon, there were no passengers. Keawe set the bottle in the gutter and walked away. Twice he looked back, and there was the milky, round-bellied bottle where he left it. A third time he looked back and turned a corner; but he had scarce done so, when something knocked upon his elbow, and behold! it was the long neck sticking up; and as for the round belly, it was jammed into the pocket of his pilot-coat.

"And that looks like the truth," said Keawe.

The next thing he did was to buy a corkscrew in a shop, and go apart into a secret place in the fields. And there he tried to draw the cork, but as often as he put the screw in, out it came again, and the cork was as whole as ever.

"This is some new sort of cork," said Keawe, and all at once he began to shake and sweat, for he was afraid of that bottle.

On his way back to the port-side he saw a shop where a man sold shells and clubs from the wild islands, old heathen deities, old coined money, pictures from China and Japan, and all manner of things that sailors bring in their sea-chests. And here he had an idea. So he went in and offered the bottle for a hundred dollars. The man of the shop laughed at him at first, and offered him five; but, indeed, it was a curious bottle, such glass was never blown in any human glass-works, so prettily the colours shone under the milky white, and so strangely the shadow hovered in the midst; so, after he had disputed a while after the manner of his kind, the shopman gave Keawe sixty silver dollars for the thing and set it on a shelf in the midst of his window.

"Now," said Keawe, "I have sold that for sixty which I bought for fifty – or, to say truth, a little less, because one of my dollars was from Chili. Now I shall know the truth upon another point."

So he went back on board his ship, and when he opened his chest, there was the bottle, which had come more quickly than himself. Now Keawe had a mate on board whose name was Lopaka.

"What ails you," said Lopaka, "that you stare in your chest?"

They were alone in the ship's forecastle, and Keawe bound him to secrecy, and told all.

"This is a very strange affair," said Lopaka; "and I fear you will be in trouble about this bottle. But there is one point very clear – that you are sure of the trouble, and you had better have the profit in the bargain. Make up your mind what you want with it; give the order, and if it is done as you desire, I will buy the bottle myself; for I have an idea of my own to get a schooner, and go trading through the islands."

"That is not my idea," said Keawe; "but to have a beautiful house and garden on the Kona coast, where I was born, the sun shining in at the door, flowers in the garden, glass in the windows, pictures on the walls, and toys and fine carpets on the tables, for all the world like the house I was in this day – only a storey higher, and with balconies all about like the king's palace; and to live there without care and make merry with my friends and relatives."

"Well," said Lopaka, "let us carry it back with us to Hawaii; and if all comes true as you suppose, I will buy the bottle, as I said, and ask a schooner."

Upon that they were agreed, and it was not long before the ship returned to Honolulu, carrying Keawe and Lopaka, and the bottle. They were scarce come ashore when they met a friend upon the beach, who began at once to condole with Keawe.

"I do not know what I am to be condoled about," said Keawe.

"Is it possible you have not heard," said the friend, "your

uncle – that good old man – is dead, and your cousin – that beautiful boy – was drowned at sea?"

Keawe was filled with sorrow, and, beginning to weep and to lament, he forgot about the bottle. But Lopaka was thinking to himself, and presently, when Keawe's grief was a little abated, "I have been thinking," said Lopaka, "had not your uncle lands in Hawaii, in the district of Kaü?"

"No," said Keawe, "not in Kaü: they are on the mountain-side – a little be-south Hookena."

"These lands will now be yours?" asked Lopaka.

"And so they will," says Keawe, and began again to lament for his relatives.

"No," said Lopaka, "do not lament at present. I have a thought in my mind. How if this should be the doing of the bottle? For here is the place ready for your house."

"If this be so," cried Keawe, "it is a very ill way to serve me by killing my relatives. But it may be, indeed; for it was in just a station that I saw the house with my mind's eye."

"The house, however, is not yet built," said Lopaka.

"No, nor like to be!" said Keawe; "for though my uncle has some coffee and ava and bananas, it will not be more than will keep me in comfort; and the rest of that land is the black lava."

"Let us go to the lawyer," said Lopaka; "I have still this idea in my mind."

Now, when they came to the lawyer's, it appeared Keawe's uncle had grown monstrous rich in the last days, and there was a fund of money.

"And here is the money for the house!" cried Lopaka.

"If you are thinking of a new house," said the lawyer, "here is the card of a new architect of whom they tell me great things."

"Better and better!" cried Lopaka. "Here is all made plain for us. Let us continue to obey orders."

So they went to the architect, and he had drawings of houses on his table.

"You want something out of the way," said the architect.

"How do you like this?" and he handed a drawing to Keawe.

Now, when Keawe set eyes on the drawing, he cried out aloud, for it was the picture of his thought exactly drawn.

"I am in for this house," thought he. "Little as I like the way it comes to me, I am in for it now, and I may as well take the good along with the evil."

So he told the architect all that he wished, and how he would have that house furnished, and about the pictures on the walls and the knick-knacks on the tables; and he asked the man plainly for how much he would undertake the whole affair.

The architect put many questions, and took his pen and made a computation; and when he had done he named the very sum that Keawe had inherited.

Lopaka and Keawe looked at one another and nodded.

"It is quite clear," thought Keawe, "that I am to have this house, whether or no. It comes from the devil, and I fear I will get little good by that; and of one thing I am sure, I will make no more wishes as long as I have this bottle. But with the house I am saddled, and I may as well take the good along with the evil."

So he made his terms with the architect, and they signed a paper; and Keawe and Lopaka took ship again and sailed to Australia; for it was concluded between them they should not interfere at all, but leave the architect and the bottle imp to build and to adorn the house at their own pleasure.

The voyage was a good voyage, only all the time Keawe was holding in his breath, for he had sworn he would utter no more wishes, and take no more favours from the devil. The time was up when they got back. The architect told them that the house was ready, and Keawe and Lopaka took a passage in the *Hall*, and went down Kona way to view the house, and see if all had been done fitly according to the thought that was in Keawe's mind.

Now, the house stood on the mountain-side, visible to ships. Above, the forest ran up into the clouds of rain: below, the black lava fell in cliffs, where the kings of old lay buried. A garden bloomed about the house with every hue of flowers;

and there was an orchard of papaia on the one hand and an orchard of bread-fruit on the other, and right in front, towards the sea, a ship's mast had been rigged up and bore a flag. As for the house, it was three storeys high, with great chambers and broad balconies on each. The windows were of glass, so excellent that it was as clear as water and as bright as day. All manner of furniture adorned the chambers. Pictures hung upon the wall in golden frames – pictures of ships, and men fighting, and of the most beautiful women, and of singular places; nowhere in the world are there pictures of so bright a colour as those Keawe found hanging in his house. As for the knick-knacks, they were extraordinarily fine: chiming clocks and musical boxes, little men with nodding heads, books filled with pictures, weapons of price from all quarters of the world, and the most elegant puzzles to entertain the leisure of a solitary man. And as no one would care to live in such chambers, only to walk through and view them, the balconies were made so broad that a whole town might have lived upon them in delight; and Keawe knew not which to prefer, whether the back porch, where you get the land breeze and looked upon the orchards and the flowers, or the front balcony, where you could drink the wind of the sea, and look down the steep wall of the mountain and see the *Hall* going by once a week or so between Hookena and the hills of Pele, or the schooners plying up the coast for wood and ava and bananas.

When they had viewed all, Keawe and Lopaka sat on the porch.

"Well," asked Lopaka, "is it all as you designed?"

"Words cannot utter it," said Keawe. "It is better than I dreamed, and I am sick with satisfaction."

"There is but one thing to consider," said Lopaka; "all this may be quite natural, and the bottle imp have nothing whatever to say to it. If I were to buy the bottle, and got no schooner after all, I should have put my hand in the fire for nothing. I gave you my word, I know; but yet I think you would not grudge me one more proof."

"I have sworn I would take no more favours," said Keawe. "I have gone already deep enough."

"This is no favour I am thinking of," replied Lopaka. "It is only to see the imp himself. There is nothing to be gained by that, and so nothing to be ashamed of, and yet, if I once saw him, I should be sure of the whole matter. So indulge me so far, and let me see the imp; and, after that, here is the money in my hand, and I will buy it."

"There is only one thing I am afraid of," said Keawe. "The imp may be very ugly to view, and if you once set eyes upon him you might be very undesirous of the bottle."

"I am a man of my word," said Lopaka. "And here is the money betwixt us."

"Very well," replied Keawe, "I have a curiosity myself. So come, let us have one look at you, Mr Imp."

Now as soon as that was said, the imp looked out of the bottle, and in again, swift as a lizard; and there saw Keawe and Lopaka turned to stone. The night had quite come, before either found a thought to say or voice to say it with; and then Lopaka pushed the money over and took the bottle.

"I am a man of my word," said he, "and had need to be so, or I would not touch this bottle with my foot. Well, I shall get my schooner and a dollar or two for my pocket; and then I will be rid of this devil as fast as I can. For to tell you the plain truth, the look of him has cast me down."

"Lopaka," said Keawe, "do not you think any worse of me than you can help; I know it is night, and the roads bad, and the pass by the tombs an ill place to go by so late, but I declare since I have seen that little face, I cannot eat or sleep or pray till it is gone from me. I will give you a lantern, and a basket to put the bottle in, and any picture or fine thing in all my house that takes your fancy; and be gone at once, and go sleep at Hookena with Nahinu."

"Keawe," said Lopaka, "many a man would take this ill; above all, when I am doing you a turn so friendly, as to keep my word and buy the bottle; and for that matter, the night and the dark, and the way by the tombs, must be all tenfold more dangerous to a man with such a sin upon his conscience and such a bottle under his arm. But for my part, I am so extremely terrified myself, I have not the heart to blame you. Here I go, then; and I pray God you may be happy in your house, and I fortunate with my schooner, and both get to heaven in the end in spite of the devil and his bottle."

So Lopaka went down the mountain; and Keawe stood in his front balcony, and listened to the clink of the horses' shoes, and watched the lantern go shining down the path, and along the cliff of caves where the old dead are buried; and all the time he trembled and clasped his hands, and prayed for his friend, and gave glory to God that he himself was escaped out of that trouble.

But the next day came very brightly, and that new house of his was so delightful to behold that he forgot his terrors. One day followed another, and Keawe dwelt there in perpetual joy. He had his place on the back porch; it was there he ate and lived, and read the stories in the Honolulu newspapers; but when any one came by they would go in and view the chambers and the pictures. And the fame of the house went far and wide; it was called *Ka-Hale Nui* – the Great House – in all Kona; and sometimes the Bright House, for Keawe kept a Chinaman, who was all day dusting and furbishing; and the glass, and the gilt, and the fine stuffs, and the pictures, shone as bright as the morning. As for Keawe himself, he could not walk in the chambers without singing, his heart was so enlarged; and when ships sailed by upon the sea, he would fly his colours on the mast.

So time went by, until one day Keawe went upon a visit as far as Kailua to certain of his friends. There he was well feasted; and left as soon as he could the next morning, and rode hard, for he was impatient to behold his beautiful house; and, besides, the night then coming on was the night in which the dead old days go abroad in the sides of Kona; and having already meddled with the devil, he was the more chary of meeting with the dead. A little beyond Honaunau, looking far ahead, he was aware of a woman bathing in the edges of the sea; and she seemed a well-grown girl, but he thought no more of it. Then he saw her white shift flutter as she put it on, and then her red holoku; and by the time he came abreast of her she was done with her toilet, and had come up from the sea, and stood by the trackside in her red holoku, and she was all freshened with the bath, and her eyes shone and were kind. Now Keawe no sooner beheld her than he drew rein.

"I thought I knew every one in this country," said he. "How comes it that I do not know you?"

"I am Kokua, daughter of Kiano," said the girl, "and I have just returned from Oahu. Who are you?"

"I will tell you who I am in a little," said Keawe, dismounting from his horse, "but not now. For I have a thought in my mind, and if you knew who I was, you might have heard of me, and would not give me a true answer. But tell me, first of all, one thing: are you married?"

At this Kokua laughed out aloud. "It is you who ask questions," she said. "Are you married yourself?"

"Indeed, Kokua, I am not," replied Keawe, "and never thought to be until this hour. But here is the plain truth. I have met you here at the roadside, and I saw your eyes, which are like the stars, and my heart went to you as swift as a bird. And so now, if you want none of me, say so and I will go on to my own place; but if you think me no worse than any other young man, say so, too, and I will turn aside to your father's for the night, and tomorrow I will talk with the good man."

Kokua said never a word, but she looked at the sea and laughed.

"Kokua," said Keawe, "if you say nothing, I will take that for the good answer; so let us be stepping to your father's door."

She went on ahead of him, still without speech; only sometimes she glanced back and glanced away again, and she kept the strings of her hat in her mouth.

Now, when they had come to the door, Kiano came out on his veranda, and cried out and welcomed Keawe by name. At that the girl looked over, for the fame of the great house had come to her ears; and, to be sure, it was a great temptation. All that evening, they were very merry together; and the girl was as bold as brass under the eyes of her parents, and made a mark of Keawe, for she had a quick wit. The next day he had a word with Kiano, and found the girl alone.

"Kokua," said he, "you made a mark of me all the evening; and it is still time to bid me go. I would not tell you who I was, because I have so fine a house, and I feared you would think too much of that house and too little of the man that loves you. Now you know all, and if you wish to have seen the last of me, say so at once."

"No," said Kokua, but this time she did not laugh, nor did Keawe ask for more.

This was the wooing of Keawe; things had gone quickly; but so an arrow goes, and the ball of a rifle swifter still, and yet both may strike the target. Things had gone fast, but they had gone far also, and the thought of Keawe rang in the maiden's head; she heard his voice in the breach of the surf upon the lava, and for this young man that she had seen but twice she would have left father and mother and her native islands. As for Keawe himself, his horse flew up the path of the mountain under the cliff of tombs, and the sound of the hoofs, and the sound of Keawe singing to himself for pleasure, echoed in the caverns of the dead. He came to the Bright House, and still he was singing. He sat and ate in the broad balcony, and the Chinaman wondered at his master, to hear how he sang between the mouthfuls. The sun went down into the sea, and the night came; and Keawe walked the balconies by lamplight, high on the mountains, and the voice of his singing started men on ships.

"Here am I now upon my high place," he said to himself. "Life may be no better; this is the mountain top; and all shelves about me towards the worse. For the first time I will light up the chambers, and bathe in my fine bath with the hot water and the cold, and sleep above in the bed of my bridal chamber."

So the Chinaman had word, and he must rise from sleep and

light the furnaces; and as he walked below, beside the boilers, he heard his master singing and rejoicing above him in the lighted chambers. When the water began to be hot the Chinaman cried to his master: and Keawe went into the bathroom; and the Chinaman heard him sing as he filled the marble basin; and heard him sing, and the singing broken, as he undressed; until of a sudden, the song ceased. The Chinaman listened, and listened; he called up the house to Keawe to ask if all were well, and Keawe answered him "Yes", and bade him go to bed; but there was no more singing in the Bright House; and all night long the Chinaman heard his master's feet go round and round the balconies without repose.

Now, the truth of it was this: as Keawe undressed for his bath, he spied upon his flesh a patch like a patch of lichen on a rock, and it was then that he stopped singing. For he knew the likeness of that patch, and knew that he was fallen in the Chinese Evil.*

Now, it is a sad thing for any man to fall into this sickness. And it would be a sad thing for any one to leave a house so beautiful and so commodious; and depart from all his friends to the north coast of Molokai, between the mighty cliff and the sea-breakers. But what was that to the case of the man Keawe, he who had met his love but yesterday and won her but that morning, and now saw all his hopes break, in a moment, like a piece of glass?

A while he sat upon the edge of the bath, then sprang, with a cry, and ran outside; and to and fro, to and fro, along the balcony, like one despairing.

"Very willingly could I leave Hawaii, the home of my fathers," Keawe was thinking. "Very lightly could I leave my house, the high-placed, the many-windowed, here upon the mountains. Very bravely could I go to Molokai, to Kalaupapa by the cliffs, to live with the smitten and to sleep there, far from my fathers. But what wrong have I done, what sin lies upon my soul, that I should have encountered Kokua coming cool from the sea-water in the evening? Kokua, the

*Leprosy

soul-en-snarer! Kokua, the light of my life! Her may I never wed, her may I look upon no longer, her may I no more handle with my loving hand; and it is for this, it is for you, O Kokua! that I pour my lamentations!"

Now you are to observe what sort of a man Keawe was, for he might have dwelt there in the Bright House for years, and no one been the wiser of his sickness; but he reckoned nothing of that, if he must lose Kokua. And again he might have wed Kokua even as he was; and so many would have done, because they have the souls of pigs; but Keawe loved the maiden manfully, and he would do her no hurt and bring her in no danger.

A little beyond the midst of the night, there came in his mind the recollection of that bottle. He went round to the back porch, and called to memory the day when the devil had looked forth; and at the thought ice ran in his veins.

"A dreadful thing is the bottle," thought Keawe, "and dreadful is the imp, and it is a dreadful thing to risk the flames of hell. But what other hope have I to cure my sickness or to wed Kokua! What!" he thought, "would I beard the devil once, only to get me a house, and not face him again to win Kokua?"

Thereupon he called to mind it was the next day the *Hall* went by on her return to Honolulu. "There must I go first," he thought, "and see Lopaka. For the best hope that I have now is to find that same bottle I was so pleased to be rid of."

Never a wink could he sleep; the food stuck in his throat; but he sent a letter to Kiano, and about the time when the steamer would be coming, rode down beside the cliff of the tombs. It rained; his horse went heavily; he looked up at the black mouths of the caves, and he envied the dead that slept there and were done with trouble; and called to mind how he had galloped by the day before, and was astonished. So he came down to Hookena, and there was all the country gathered for the steamer as usual. In the shed before the store they sat and jested and passed the news; but there was no matter of speech in Keawe's bosom, and he sat in their midst and looked without on the rain falling on the houses, and the surf beating among the rocks, and the sighs arose in his throat.

"Keawe of the Bright House is out of spirits," said one to another. Indeed, and so he was, and little wonder.

Then the *Hall* came, and the whale-boat carried him on board. The after-part of the ship was full of Haoles* – who had been to visit the volcano, as their custom is; and the midst was crowned with Kanakas, and the forepart with wild bulls from Hilo and horses from Kaü; but Keawe sat apart from all in his sorrow, and watched for the house of Kiano. There it sat low upon the shore in the black rocks, and shaded by the cocoa-palms, and there by the door was a red holoku, no greater than a fly, and going to and fro with a fly's busyness. "Ah, queen of my heart," he cried, "I'll venture my dear soul to win you!"

Soon after darkness fell and the cabins were lit up, and the Haoles sat and played at the cards and drank whisky as their custom is; but Keawe walked the deck all night; and all the next day, as they steamed under the lee of Maui or of Molokai, he was still pacing to and fro like a wild animal in a menagerie.

Towards evening they passed Diamond Head, and came to the pier of Honolulu. Keawe stepped out among the crowd and began to ask for Lopaka. It seemed he had become the owner of a schooner – none better in the islands – and was gone upon an adventure as far as Pola-Pola or Kahiki; so there was no help to be looked for from Lopaka. Keawe called to mind a friend of his, a lawyer in the town (I must not tell his name), and inquired of him. They said he was grown suddenly rich, and had a fine new house upon Waikiki shore; and this put a thought in Keawe's head, and he called a hack and drove to the lawyer's house.

The house was all brand new, and the trees in the garden

*Whites

no greater than walking-sticks, and the lawyer, when he came, had the air of a man well pleased.

"What can I do to serve you?" said the lawyer.

"You are a friend of Lopaka's," replied Keawe, "and Lopaka purchased from me a certain piece of goods that I thought you might enable me to trace."

The lawyer's face became very dark. "I do not profess to misunderstand you, Mr Keawe," said he, "though this is an ugly business to be stirring in. You may be sure I know nothing, but yet I have a guess, and if you would apply in a certain quarter I think you might have news."

And he named the name of a man, which, again, I had better not repeat. So it was for days, and Keawe went from one to another, finding everywhere new clothes and carriages, and fine new houses, and men everywhere in great contentment, although, to be sure, when he hinted at his business their faces would cloud over.

"No doubt I am upon the track," thought Keawe. "These new clothes and carriages are all the gifts of the little imp, and these glad faces are the faces of men who have taken their profit and got rid of the accursed thing in safety. When I see pale cheeks and hear sighing, I shall know that I am near the bottle."

So it befell at last he was recommended to a Haole in Beritania Street. When he came to the door, about the hour of the evening meal, there were the usual marks of the new house, and the young garden, and the electric light shining in the windows; but when the owner came, a shock of hope and fear ran through Keawe; for here was a young man, white as a corpse, and black about the eyes, the hair shedding from his head, and such a look in his countenance as a man may have when he is waiting for the gallows.

"Here it is, to be sure," thought Keawe, and so with this man he noways veiled his errand. "I am come to buy the bottle," said he.

At the word, the young Haole of Beritania Street reeled against the wall.

"The bottle!" he gasped. "To buy the bottle!" Then he seemed to choke, and seizing Keawe by the arm, carried him into a room and poured out wine in two glasses.

"Here is my respects," said Keawe, who had been much about with Haoles in his time. "Yes," he added, "I am come to buy the bottle. What is the price by now?"

At that word the young man let his glass slip through his fingers, and looked upon Keawe like a ghost.

"The price," says he; "the price! You do not know the price?"

"It is for that I am asking you," returned Keawe. "But why are you so much concerned? Is there anything wrong about the price?"

"It has dropped a great deal in value since your time, Mr Keawe," said the young man, stammering.

"Well, well, I shall have the less to pay for it," says Keawe. "How much did it cost you?"

The young man was as white as a sheet. "Two cents," said he.

"What!" cried Keawe, "two cents? Why, then, you can only sell it for one. And he who buys it——" The words died upon Keawe's tongue; he who bought it could never sell it again, the bottle and the bottle imp must abide with him until he died, and when he died must carry him to the red end of hell.

The young man of Beritania Street fell upon his knees. "For God's sake, buy it!" he cried. "You can have all my fortune in the bargain. I was mad when I bought it at that price. I had embezzled money at my store; I was lost else; I must have gone to jail."

"Poor creature," said Keawe, "you would risk your soul upon so desperate an adventure, and to avoid the proper punishment of your own disgrace; and you think I could hesitate with love in front of me. Give me the bottle, and the change which I make sure you have all ready. Here is a five-cent piece."

It was as Keawe supposed; the young man had the change

ready in a drawer; the bottle changed hands, and Keawe's fingers were no sooner clasped upon the stalk than he had breathed his wish to be a clean man. And sure enough, when he got home to his room, and stripped himself before a glass, his flesh was whole like an infant's. And here was the strange thing; he had no sooner seen this miracle than his mind was changed within him, and he cared naught for the Chinese Evil, and little enough for Kokua; and had but the one thought, that here he was bound to the bottle imp for time and for eternity, and had no better hope but to be a cinder for ever in the flames of hell. Away ahead of him he saw them blaze with his mind's eye, and his soul shrank, and darkness fell upon the light.

When Keawe came to himself a little, he was aware it was the night when the band played at the hotel. Thither he went, because he feared to be alone; and there, among happy faces, walked to and fro, and heard the tunes go up and down, and saw Berger beat the measure, and all the while he heard the flames crackle and saw the red fire burning in the bottomless pit. Of a sudden the band played *Hiki-ao-ao*; that was a song that he had sung with Kokua, and at the strain courage returned to him.

"It is done now," he thought, "and once more let me take the good along with the evil."

So it befell that he returned to Hawaii by the first steamer, and as soon as it could be managed he was wedded to Kokua, and carried her up the mountain-side to the Bright House.

Now it was so with these two, that when they were together Keawe's heart was stilled; but as soon as he was alone he fell into a brooding horror, and heard the flames crackle, and saw the red fire burn in the bottomless pit. The girl, indeed, had come to him wholly; her heart leaped in her side at sight of him, her hand clung to his; and she was so fashioned, from the hair upon her head to the nails upon her toes, that none could see her without joy. She was pleasant in her nature. She had the good word always. Full of song she was, and went to and fro in the Bright House, the brightest thing in its three storeys, carolling like the birds. And Keawe beheld and heard her with delight, and then must shrink upon one side, and weep and groan to think upon the price that he had paid for her; and then he must dry his eyes and wash his face, and go and sit with her on the broad balconies, joining in her songs, and, with a sick spirit, answering her smiles.

There came a day when her feet began to be heavy and her songs more rare; and now it was not Keawe only that would weep apart, but each would sunder from the other and sit in opposite balconies with the whole width of the Bright House betwixt. Keawe was so sunk in his despair he scarce observed the change, and was only glad he had more hours to sit alone and brood upon his destiny, and was not so frequently condemned to pull a smiling face on a sick heart. But one day, coming softly through the house, he heard the sound of a child sobbing, and there was Kokua rolling her face upon the balcony floor, and weeping like the lost.

"You do well to weep in this house, Kokua," he said. "And yet I would give the head off my body that you (at least) might have been happy."

"Happy!" she cried. "Keawe, when you lived alone in your Bright House you were the word of the island for a happy man; laughter and song were in your mouth, and your face was as bright as the sunrise. Then you wedded poor Kokua; and the good God knows what is amiss in her – but from that day you have not smiled. Oh!" she cried, "what ails me? I thought I was pretty, and I knew I loved him. What ails me, that I throw this cloud upon my husband?"

"Poor Kokua," said Keawe. He sat down by her side, and sought to take her hand; but that she plucked away. "Poor Kokua," he said again. "My poor child – my pretty. And I had thought all this while to spare you! Well, you shall know all. Then, at least, you will pity poor Keawe; then you will understand how much he loved you in the past – that he dared hell for your possession – and how much he loves you still (the poor condemned one), that he can yet call up a smile when he beholds you."

With that he told her all, even from the beginning.

"You have done this for me?" she cried. "Ah, well, then what do I care!" and she clasped and wept upon him.

"Ah, child!" said Keawe, "and yet, when I consider of the fire of hell, I care a good deal!"

"Never tell me," said she, "no man can be lost because he loved Kokua, and no other fault. I tell you, Keawe, I shall save you with these hands, or perish in your company. What! you loved me and gave your soul, and you think I will not die to save you in return?"

"Ah, my dear, you might die a hundred times: and what difference would that make?" he cried, "except to leave me lonely till the time comes for my damnation?"

"You know nothing," said she. "I was educated in a school in Honolulu; I am no common girl. And I tell you I shall save my lover. What is this you say about a cent? But all the world is not American. In England they have a piece they call a farthing, which is about half a cent. Ah! sorrow!" she cried, "that makes it scarcely better, for the buyer must be lost, and we shall find none so brave as my Keawe! But then, there is France; they have a small coin there which they call a centime, and these go five to the cent, or thereabout. We could not do better. Come, Keawe, let us go to the French islands; let us go to Tahiti, as fast as ships can bear us. There we have four centimes, three centimes, two centimes, one centime; four possible sales to come and go on; and two of us to push the bargain. Come, my Keawe! kiss me, and banish care. Kokua will defend you."

"Gift of God!" he cried. "I cannot think that God will punish me for desiring aught so good. Be it as you will, then, take me where you please; I put my life and my salvation in your hands."

Early the next day Kokua went about her preparations. She took Keawe's chest that he went with sailoring; and first she put the bottle in a corner, and then packed it with the richest of their clothes and the bravest of the knick-knacks in the house. "For," said she, "we must seem to be rich folks, or who would believe in the bottle?" All the time of her preparation she was as gay as a bird; only when she looked upon Keawe the tears would spring in her eye, and she must run and kiss him. As for Keawe, a weight was off his soul; now that he had his secret shared, and some hope in front of him, he seemed like a new man; his feet went lightly on the earth, and his breath was good to him again. Yet was terror still at his elbow; and ever and again, as the wind blows out a taper, hope died in him, and he saw the flame toss and the red fire burn in hell.

It was given out in the country they were gone pleasuring in the States, which was thought a strange thing, and yet not so strange as the truth, if any could have guessed it. So they went to Honolulu in the *Hall*, and thence in the *Umatilla* to San Francisco with a crowd of Haoles, and at San Francisco took their passage by the mail brigantine, the *Tropic Bird*, for Papeete, the chief place of the French in the south islands. Thither they came, after a pleasant voyage, on a fair day of the Trade Wind, and saw the reef with the surf breaking and Motuiti with its palms, and the schooner riding withinside, and the white houses of the town low down along the shore among green trees, and overhead the mountains and the clouds of Tahiti, the wise island.

It was judged the most wise to hire a house, which they did accordingly, opposite the British Consul's, to make a great parade of money, and themselves conspicuous with carriages and horses. This it was very easy to do so long as they had the bottle in their possession; for Kokua was more bold than Keawe, and, whenever she had a mind, called on the imp for twenty or a hundred dollars. At this rate they soon grew to be remarked in the town; and the strangers from Hawaii, their riding and their driving, the fine holokus, and the rich lace of Kokua, became the matter of much talk.

They got on well after the first with the Tahitian language, which is indeed like to the Hawaiian, with a change of certain letters; and as soon as they had any freedom of speech, began to push the bottle. You are to consider it was not an easy

subject to introduce; it is not easy to persuade people you are in earnest, when you offer to sell them for four centimes the spring of health and riches inexhaustible. It was necessary, besides, to explain the dangers of the bottle; and either people disbelieved the whole thing and laughed, or they thought the more of the darker part, became overcast with gravity, and drew away from Keawe and Kokua, as from persons who had dealings with the devil. So far from gaining ground, these two began to find they were avoided in the town; the children ran away from them screaming, a thing intolerable to Kokua; Catholics crossed themselves as they went by; and all persons began with one accord to disengage themselves from their advances.

Depression fell upon their spirits. They would sit at night in their new house, after a day's weariness, and not exchange one word, or the silence would be broken by Kokua bursting suddenly into sobs. Sometimes they would pray together; sometimes they would have the bottle out upon the floor, and sit all evening watching how the shadow hovered in the midst. At such times they would be afraid to go to rest. It was long ere slumber came to them, and, if either dozed off, it would be to wake and find the other silently weeping in the dark, or, perhaps, to wake alone, the other having fled from the house and the neighbourhood of that bottle, to pace under the bananas in the little garden, or to wander on the beach by moonlight.

One night it was so when Kokua awoke. Keawe was gone. She felt in the bed and his place was cold. Then fear fell upon her, and she sat up in bed. A little moonshine filtered through the shutters. The room was bright, and she could spy the bottle on the floor. Outside it blew high, the great trees of the avenue cried aloud, and the fallen leaves rattled in the veranda. In the midst of this Kokua was aware of another sound; whether of a beast or of a man she could scarce tell, but it was as sad as death, and cut her to the soul. Softly she arose, set the door ajar, and looked forth into the moonlit yard. There, under the bananas, lay Keawe, his mouth in the dust, and as he lay he moaned.

It was Kokua's first thought to run forward and console him; her second potently withheld her. Keawe had borne himself before his wife like a brave man; it became her little in the hour of weakness to intrude upon his shame. With the thought she drew back into the house.

"Heaven," she thought, "how careless have I been – how weak! It is he, not I that stands in this eternal peril; it was he, not I, that took the curse upon his soul. It is for my sake, and for the love of a creature of so little worth and such poor help, that he now beholds so close to him the flames of hell – aye, and smells the smoke of it, lying without there in the wind and moonlight. Am I so dull of spirit that never till now have I surmised my duty, or have I seen it before and turned aside? But now, at least, I take up my soul in both the hands of my affection; now I say farewell to the white steps of heaven and the waiting faces of my friends. A love for a love, and let mine be equalled with Keawe's! A soul for a soul, and be it mine to perish!"

She was a deft woman with her hands, and was soon apparelled. She took in her hands the change – the precious centimes they kept ever at their side; for this coin is little used, and they had made provision at a government office. When she was forth in the avenue clouds came on the wind, and the moon was blackened. The town slept, and she knew not whither to turn till she heard one coughing in the shadow of the trees.

"Old man," said Kokua, "what do you here abroad in the cold night?"

The old man could scarce express himself for coughing, but she made out that he was old and poor, and a stranger in the island.

"Will you do me a service?" said Kokua. "As one stranger to another, and as an old man to a young woman, will you help a daughter of Hawaii?"

"Ah," said the old man. "So you are the witch from the

Eight Islands, and even my old soul you seek to entangle. But I have heard of you, and defy your wickedness."

"Sit down here," said Kokua, "and let me tell you a tale." And she told him the story of Keawe from the beginning to the end.

"And now," said she, "I am his wife, whom he bought with his soul's welfare. And what should I do? If I went to him myself and offered to buy it, he will refuse. But if you go, he will sell it eagerly; I will await you here; you will buy it for four centimes, and I will buy it again for three. And the Lord strengthen a poor girl!"

"If you meant falsely," said the old man, "I think God would strike you dead."

"He would!" cried Kokua. "Be sure He would. I could not be so treacherous; God would not suffer it."

"Give me the four centimes and await me here," said the old man.

Now, when Kokua stood alone in the street, her spirit died. The wind roared in the trees, and it seemed to her the rushing of the flames of hell; the shadows towered in the light of the street lamp, and they seemed to her the snatching hands of evil ones. If she had had the strength, she must have run away, and if she had had the breath, she must have screamed aloud; but, in truth, she could do neither, and stood and trembled in the avenue, like an affrighted child.

Then she saw the old man returning, and he had the bottle in his hand.

"I have done your bidding," said he. "I left your husband weeping like a child; tonight he will sleep easy." And he held the bottle forth.

"Before you give it me," Kokua panted, "take the good with the evil – ask to be delivered from your cough."

"I am an old man," replied the other, "and too near the gate of the grave to take a favour from the devil. But what is this? Why do you not take the bottle? Do you hesitate?"

"Not hesitate!" cried Kokua. "I am only weak. Give me a

moment. It is my hand resists, my flesh shrinks back from the accursed thing. One moment only!"

The old man looked upon Kokua kindly. "Poor child!" said he, "you fear: your soul misgives you. Well, let me keep it. I am old, and can never more be happy in this world, and as for the next . . . "

"Give it me!" gasped Kokua. "There is your money. Do you think I am so base as that? Give me the bottle."

"God bless you, child," said the old man.

Kokua concealed the bottle under her holoku, said farewell to the old man, and walked off along the avenue, she cared not whither. For all roads were now the same to her, and led equally to hell. Sometimes she walked, and sometimes ran; sometimes she screamed out loud in the night, and sometimes lay by the wayside in the dust and wept. All that she had heard of hell came back to her; she saw the flames blaze, and she smelled the smoke, and her flesh withered on the coals.

Near day she came to her mind again, and returned to the house. It was even as the old man said – Keawe slumbered like a child. Kokua stood and gazed upon his face.

"Now, my husband," said she, "it is your turn to sleep. When you wake it will be your turn to sing and laugh. But for poor Kokua, alas! that meant no evil – for poor Kokua no more sleep, no more singing, no more delight, whether in earth or heaven."

With that she lay down in the bed by his side, and her misery was so extreme that she fell in a deep slumber instantly.

Late in the morning her husband woke her and gave her the good news. It seemed he was silly with delight, for he paid no heed to her distress, ill though she dissembled it. The words stuck in her mouth; it mattered not, Keawe did the speaking. She ate not a bite, but who was to observe it? For Keawe cleared the dish. Kokua saw and heard him, like some strange thing in a dream; there were times when she forgot or doubted, and put her hands to her brow; to know herself doomed and hear her husband's babble, seemed so monstrous.

All the while Keawe was eating and talking, and planning the time of their return, and thanking her for saving him and fondling her, and calling her the true helper after all. He laughed at the old man that was fool enough to buy that bottle.

"A worthy old man he seemed," Keawe said. "But no one can judge by appearances. For why did the old reprobate require the bottle?"

"My husband," said Kokua humbly, "his purpose may have been good."

Keawe laughed like an angry man.

"Fiddle-de-dee!" cried Keawe. "An old rogue, I tell you; and an old ass to boot. For the bottle was hard enough to sell at four centimes; and at three it will be quite impossible. The margin is not broad enough, the thing begins to smell of scorching – brrr!" said he, and shuddered. "It is true I bought it myself at a cent, when I knew not there were smaller coins. I was a fool for my pains; there will never be found another, and whoever has that bottle now will carry it to the pit."

"O my husband!" said Kokua. "Is it not a terrible thing to save oneself by the eternal ruin of another? It seems to me I could not laugh. I would be humbled. I would be filled with melancholy. I would pray for the poor holder."

Then Keawe, because he felt the truth of what she said, grew the more angry. "Heighty-teighty!" cried he. "You may be filled with melancholy if you please. It is not the mind of a good wife. If you thought at all of me, you would sit shamed."

Thereupon he went out, and Kokua was alone.

What chance had she to sell that bottle at two centimes? None, she perceived. And if she had any, here was her husband hurrying her away to a country where there was nothing lower than a cent. And here – on the morrow of her sacrifice – was her husband leaving her and blaming her.

She would not even try to profit by what time she had, but sat in the house, and now had the bottle out and viewed it with unutterable fear, and now, with loathing, hid it out of sight.

By-and-by Keawe came back, and would have her take a drive.

"My husband, I am ill." she said. "I am out of heart. Excuse me, I can take no pleasure."

Then was Keawe more wroth than ever. With her, because he thought she was brooding over the case of the old man; and with himself, because he thought she was right and was ashamed to be so happy.

"This is your truth," cried he, "and this your affection! Your husband is just saved from eternal ruin, which he encountered for the love of you – and you can take no pleasure! Kokua, you have a disloyal heart."

He went forth again furious, and wandered in the town all day. He met friends, and drank with them; they hired a carriage and drove into the country, and there drank again. All the time Keawe was ill at ease, because he was taking this pastime while his wife was sad, and because he knew in his heart that she was more right than he; and the knowledge made him drink the deeper.

Now there was an old brutal Haole drinking with him, one that had been a boatswain of a whaler – a runaway, a digger in gold mines, a convict in prisons. He had a low mind and a foul mouth; he loved to drink and to see others drunken; and he pressed the glass upon Keawe. Soon there was no more money in the company.

"Here you!" says the boatswain, "you are rich, you have been always saying. You have a bottle or some foolishness."

"Yes," says Keawe, "I am rich; I will go back and get some money from my wife, who keeps it."

"That's a bad idea, mate," said the boatswain. "Never you trust a petticoat with dollars. They're all as false as water; you keep an eye on her."

Now this word struck in Keawe's mind; for he was muddled with what he had been drinking.

"I should not wonder but she was false, indeed," thought he. "Why else should she be so cast down at my release? But I will show her I am not the man to be fooled. I will catch her in the act."

Accordingly, when they were back in town, Keawe bade the boatswain wait for him at the corner, by the old calaboose, and went forward up the avenue alone to the door of his house. The night had come again; there was a light within, but never a sound; and Keawe crept about the corner, opened the back door softly, and looked in.

There was Kokua on the floor, the lamp at her side; before her was a milk-white bottle, with a round belly and a long neck; and as she viewed it, Kokua wrung her hands.

A long time Keawe stood and looked in the doorway. At first he was struck stupid; and then fear fell upon him that the bargain had been made amiss, and the bottle had come back to him as it came at San Francisco; and at that his knees were loosened, and the fumes of the wine departed from his head like mists off a river in the morning. And then he had another thought; and it was a strange one, that made his cheeks to burn.

"I must make sure of this," thought he.

So he closed the door, and went softly round the corner again, and then came noisily in, as though he were but now returned. And, lo! by the time he opened the front door no bottle was to be seen; and Kokua sat in a chair and started up like one awakened out of sleep.

"I have been drinking all day and making merry," said Keawe. "I have been with good companions, and now I only came back for money, and return to drink and carouse with them again."

Both his face and voice were as stern as judgment, but Kokua was too troubled to observe.

"You do well to use your own, my husband," said she, and her words trembled.

"Oh, I do well in all things," said Keawe, and he went straight to the chest and took out money. But he looked beside in the corner where they kept the bottle, and there was the bottle there.

At that the chest heaved upon the floor like a sea-billow, and the house spun about him like a wreath of smoke, for he saw she was lost now, and there was no escape. "It is what I feared," he thought. "It is she who has bought it."

And then he came to himself a little and rose up; but the sweat streamed on his face as thick as the rain and cold as the well-water.

"Kokua," said he, "I said to you today what ill became me. Now I return to house with my jolly companions," and at that he laughed a little quietly. "I will take more pleasure in the cup if you forgive me."

She clasped his knees in a moment, she kissed his knees with flowing tears.

"Oh," she cried, "I ask but a kind word!"

"Let us never one think hardly of the other," said Keawe, and was gone out of the house.

Now, the money that Keawe had taken was only some of that store of centime pieces they had laid in at their arrival. It was very sure he had no mind to be drinking. His wife had given her soul for him, now he must give his for hers; no other thought was in the world with him.

At the corner, by the old calaboose, there was the boatswain waiting.

"My wife has the bottle," said Keawe, "and, unless you help me to recover it, there can be no more money and no more liquor tonight."

"You do not mean to say you are serious about that bottle?" cried the boatswain.

"There is the lamp," said Keawe. "Do I look as if I was jesting?"

"That is so," said the boatswain. "You look as serious as a ghost."

"Well, then," said Keawe, "here are two centimes; you

just go to my wife in the house, and offer her these for the bottle, which (if I am not much mistaken) she will give you instantly. Bring it to me here, and I will buy it back from you for one; for that is the law with this bottle, that it still must be sold for a less sum. But whatever you do, never breathe a word to her that you have come from me."

"Mate, I wonder are you making a fool of me?" asked the boatswain.

"It will do you no harm if I am," returned Keawe.

"That is so, mate," said the boatswain.

"And if you doubt me," added Keawe, "you can try. As soon as you are clear of the house, wish to have your pocket full of money, or a bottle of the best rum, or what you please, and you will see the virtue of the thing."

"Very well, Kanaka," says the boatswain. "I will try; but if you are having your fun out of me, I will take my fun out of you with a belaying-pin."

So the whaler-man went off up the avenue; and Keawe stood and waited. It was near the same spot where Kokua had waited the night before; but Keawe was more resolved, and never faltered in his purpose; only his soul was bitter with despair.

It seemed a long time he had to wait before he heard a voice singing in the darkness of the avenue. He knew the voice to be the boatswain's; but it was strange how drunken it appeared upon a sudden.

Next the man himself came stumbling into the light of the lamp. He had the devil's bottle buttoned in his coat; another bottle was in his hand; and even as he came in view he raised it to his mouth and drank.

"You have it," said Keawe. "I see that."

"Hands off!" cried the boatswain, jumping back. "Take a step near me, and I'll smash your mouth. You thought you could make a catspaw of me, did you?"

"What do you mean?" cried Keawe.

"Mean?" cried the boatswain. "This is a pretty good bottle, this is; that's what I mean. How I got it for two centimes I can't make out; but I am sure you shan't have it for one."

"You mean you won't sell?" gasped Keawe.

"No, sir," cried the boatswain. "But I'll give you a drink of the rum, if you like."

"I tell you," said Keawe, "the man who has that bottle goes to hell."

"I reckon I'm going anyway," returned the sailor; "and this bottle's the best thing to go with I've struck yet. No, sir!" he cried again, "this is my bottle now, and you can go and fish for another."

"Can this be true?" Keawe cried. "For your own sake, I beseech you, sell it me!"

"I don't value any of your talk," replied the boatswain. "You thought I was a flat, now you see I'm not; and there's an end. If you won't have a swallow of the rum, I'll have one myself. Here's your health, and good-night to you!"

So off he went down the avenue towards town, and there goes the bottle out of the story.

But Keawe ran to Kokua light as the wind; and great was their joy that night; and great, since then, has been the peace of all their days in the Bright House.

The Red Room

H. G. Wells

"I can assure you," said I, "that it will take a very tangible ghost to frighten me." And I stood up before the fire with my glass in my hand.

"It is your own choosing," said the man with the withered arm, and glanced at me askance.

"Eight-and-twenty years," said I, "I have lived, and never a ghost have I seen as yet."

The old woman sat staring hard into the fire, her pale eyes wide open. "Ay," she broke in; "and eight-and-twenty years you have lived and never seen the likes of this house, I reckon. There's many things to see, when one's still but eight-and-twenty." She swayed her head slowly from side to side. "A many things to see and sorrow for."

I half suspected the old people were trying to enhance the spiritual terrors of their house by their droning insistence. I put down my empty glass on the table and looked about the room, and caught a glimpse of myself, abbreviated and broadened to an impossible sturdiness, in the queer old mirror at the end of the room. "Well," I said, "if I see anything tonight, I shall be so much the wiser. For I come to the business with an open mind."

"It's your own choosing," said the man with the withered arm once more.

I heard the sound of a stick and a shambling step on the flags in the passage outside, and the door creaked on its hinges as a second old man entered, more bent, more wrinkled, more aged even than the first. He supported himself by a single crutch, his eyes were covered by a shade, and his lower lip, half-averted, hung pale and pink from his decaying yellow teeth. He made straight for an arm-chair on the opposite side of the table, sat down clumsily, and began to cough. The man with the withered arm gave this newcomer a short glance of positive dislike; the old woman took no notice of his arrival, but remained with her eyes fixed steadily on the fire.

"I said – it's your own choosing," said the man with the withered arm, when the coughing had ceased for a while.

"It's my own choosing," I answered.

The man with the shade became aware of my presence for the first time, and threw his head back for a moment and sideways, to see me. I caught a momentary glimpse of his eyes, small and bright and inflamed. Then he began to cough and splutter again.

"Why don't you drink?" said the man with the withered arm, pushing the beer towards him. The man with the shade poured out a glassful with a shaky arm that splashed half as much again on the deal table. A monstrous shadow of him crouched upon the wall and mocked his action as he poured and drank. I must confess I had scarce expected these grotesque custodians. There is to my mind something inhuman in senility, something crouching and atavistic; the human qualities seem to drop from old people insensibly day by day. The three of them made me feel uncomfortable, with their gaunt silences, their bent carriage, their evident unfriendliness to me and to one another.

"If," said I, "you will show me to this haunted room of yours, I will make myself comfortable there."

The old man with the cough jerked his head back so suddenly that it startled me, and shot another glance of his red eyes at me from under the shade; but no one answered me. I waited a minute, glancing from one to the other.

"If," I said a little louder, "if you will show me to this haunted room of yours, I will relieve you from the task of entertaining me."

"There's a candle on the slab outside the door," said the man with the withered arm, looking at my feet as he addressed me. "But if you go to the red room tonight . . ."

("This night of all nights!" said the old woman.)

"You go alone."

"Very well," I answered. "And which way do I go?"

"You go along the passage for a bit," said he, "until you come to a door, and through that is a spiral staircase, and half-way up that is a landing and another door covered with baize. Go through that and down the long corridor to the end, and the red room is on your left up the steps."

"Have I got that right?" I said, and repeated his directions. He corrected me in one particular.

"And are you really going?" said the man with the shade, looking at me again for the third time, with that queer, unnatural tilting of the face.

("This night of all nights!" said the old woman.)

"It is what I came for," I said, and moved towards the door. As I did so, the old man with the shade rose and staggered round the table, so as to be closer to the others and to the fire. At the door I turned and looked at them, and saw they were all close together, dark against the firelight, staring at me over their shoulders, with an intent expression on their ancient faces.

"Good-night," I said, setting the door open.

"It's your own choosing," said the man with the withered arm.

I left the door wide open until the candle was well alight, and then I shut them in and walked down the chilly, echoing passage.

I must confess that the oddness of these three old pensioners in whose charge her ladyship had left the castle, and the deep-toned, old-fashioned furniture of the housekeeper's room in which they forgathered, affected me in spite of my efforts to keep myself at a matter-of-fact phase. They seemed to belong to another age, an older age, an age when things spiritual were different from this of ours, less certain; an age when omens and witches were credible, and ghosts beyond denying. Their very existence was spectral; the cut of their clothing, fashions born in dead brains. The ornaments and conveniences of the room about them were ghostly – the thoughts of vanished men, which still haunted rather than participated in the world of today. But with an effort I sent such thoughts to the right-about. The long, draughty subterranean passage was chilly and dusty, and my candle flared and made the shadows cower and quiver. The echoes rang up and down the spiral staircase, and a shadow came sweeping up after me, and one fled before me into the darkness overhead. I came to the landing and stopped there for a moment, listening to a rustling that I fancied I heard; then, satisfied of the absolute silence, I pushed open the baize-covered door and stood in the corridor.

The effect was scarcely what I expected, for the moonlight coming in by the great window on the grand staircase picked out everything in vivid black shadow or silvery illumination. Everything was in its place; the house might have been deserted on the yesterday instead of eighteen months ago. There were candles in the sockets of the sconces, and whatever dust had gathered on the carpets or upon the polished flooring was distributed so evenly as to be invisible in the moonlight. I was about to advance, and stopped abruptly. A bronze group stood upon the landing, hidden from me by the corner of the wall, but its shadow fell with marvellous distinctness upon the white panelling and gave me the impression of some one crouching to waylay me. I stood rigid for half a minute perhaps. Then, with my hand in the pocket that held my revolver, I advanced, only to discover a Ganymede and Eagle glistening in the moonlight. That incident for a time restored my nerve, and a porcelain Chinaman on a buhl table, whose head rocked silently as I passed him, scarcely startled me.

The door to the red room and the steps up to it were in a shadowy corner. I moved my candle from side to side, in order to see clearly the nature of the recess in which I stood before opening the door. Here it was, thought I, that my predecessor was found, and the memory of that story gave me a sudden twinge of apprehension. I glanced over my shoulder at the Ganymede in the moonlight, and opened the door of the red room rather hastily, with my face half-turned to the pallid silence of the landing.

I entered, closed the door behind me at once, turned the key I found in the lock within, and stood with the candle held aloft, surveying the scene of my vigil, the great red room of Lorraine Castle, in which the young duke had died. Or, rather, in which he had begun his dying, for he had opened the door and fallen headlong down the steps I had just ascended. That had been the end of his vigil, of his gallant attempt to conquer the ghostly tradition of the place, and never, I thought, had apoplexy better served the ends of superstition. And there were other and older stories that clung to the room, back to the half-credible beginning of it all, the tale of a timid wife and the tragic end that came to her husband's jest of frightening her. And looking around that large sombre room, with its shadowy window bays, its recesses and alcoves, one could well understand the legends that had sprouted in its black corners, its germinating darkness. My candle was a little tongue of light in its vastness, that failed to pierce the opposite end of the room, and left an ocean of mystery and suggestion beyond its island of light.

I resolved to make a systematic examination of the place at once, and dispel the fanciful suggestions of its obscurity before they obtained a hold upon me. After satisfying myself of the fastening of the door, I began to walk about the room, peering round each article of furniture, tucking up the valances of the bed, and opening its curtains wide. I pulled up the blinds and examined the fastenings of the several windows before closing the shutters, leant forward and looked up the blackness of the wide chimney, and tapped the dark oak panelling for any secret opening. There were two big mirrors in the room, each with a pair of sconces bearing candles, and on the mantelshelf, too, were more candles in china candlesticks. All these I lit one after the other. The fire was laid, an unexpected consideration from the old housekeeper – and I lit it, to keep down any disposition to shiver, and when it was burning well, I stood round with my back to it and regarded the room again. I had pulled up a chintz-covered arm-chair and a table, to form a kind of barricade before me, and on this lay my revolver ready to hand. My precise examination had done me good, but I still found the remoter darkness of the place, and its perfect stillness, too stimulating for the imagination. The echoing of the stir and crackling of the fire was no sort of comfort to me. The shadow in the alcove at the end in particular had that undefinable quality of a presence, that odd suggestion of a lurking, living thing, that comes so easily in silence and solitude. At last, to reassure myself, I walked with a candle into it, and satisfied myself that there was nothing tangible there. I stood that candle upon the floor of the alcove, and left it in that position.

By this time I was in a state of considerable nervous tension, although to my reason there was no adequate cause for the condition. My mind, however, was perfectly clear. I postulated quite unreservedly that nothing supernatural could happen, and to pass the time I began to string some rhymes together, Ingoldsby fashion, of the original legend of the place. A few I spoke aloud, but the echoes were not pleasant. For the same reason I also abandoned, after a time, a conversation with myself upon the impossibility of ghosts and haunting. My mind reverted to the three old and distorted people downstairs, and I tried to keep it upon that topic. The sombre reds and blacks of the room troubled me; even with seven candles the place was merely dim. The one in the alcove flared in a draught, and the fire-flickering kept the shadows and penumbra perpetually shifting and stirring. Casting about for a remedy, I recalled the candles I had seen in the passage, and, with a slight effort, walked out into the moonlight, carrying a candle and leaving the door open, and presently returned with as many as ten. These I put in various knick-knacks of china with which the room was sparsely adorned, lit and placed where the shadows had lain deepest, some on the floor, some in the window recesses, until at last my seventeen candles were so arranged that not an inch of the room but had the direct light of at least one of them. It occurred to me that when the ghost came, I could warn him not to trip over them. The room was now quite brightly illuminated. There was something very cheery and reassuring in these little streaming flames, and snuffing them gave me an occupation, and afforded a helpful sense of the passage of time.

Even with that, however, the brooding expectation of the vigil weighed heavily upon me. It was after midnight that the candle in the alcove suddenly went out, and the black shadow sprang back to its place there. I did not see the candle go out; I simply turned and saw that the darkness was there, as one might start and see the unexpected presence of a stranger. "By Jove!" said I aloud; "that draught's a strong one!" and taking the matches from the table, I walked across the room in a leisurely manner to re-light the corner again. My first match would not strike, and as I succeeded with the second, something seemed to blink on the wall before me. I turned my head involuntarily, and saw that the two candles on the little table by the fireplace were extinguished. I rose at once to my feet.

"Odd!" I said. "Did I do that myself in a flash of absent-mindedness?"

I walked back, re-lit one, and as I did so, I saw the candle in the right sconce of one of the mirrors wink and go right out, and almost immediately its companion followed it. There was no mistake about it. The flame vanished, as if the wicks had been suddenly nipped between a finger and a thumb, leaving the wick neither glowing nor smoking, but black. While I stood gaping, the candle at the foot of the bed went out, and the shadows seemed to take another step towards me.

"This won't do!" said I, and first one and then another candle on the mantelshelf followed.

"What's up?" I cried, with a queer high note getting into my voice somehow. At that the candle on the wardrobe went out, and the one I had re-lit in the alcove followed.

"Steady on!" I said. "These candles are wanted," speaking with a half-hysterical facetiousness, and scratching away at a

match the while for the mantel candlesticks. My hands trembled so much that twice I missed the rough paper of the matchbox. As the mantel emerged from darkness again, two candles in the remoter end of the window were eclipsed. But with the same match I also re-lit the larger mirror candles, and those on the floor near the doorway, so that for the moment I seemed to gain on the extinctions. But then in a volley there vanished four lights at once in different corners of the room, and I struck another match in quivering haste, and stood hesitating whither to take it.

As I stood undecided, an invisible hand seemed to sweep out the two candles on the table. With a cry of terror, I dashed at the alcove, then into the corner, and then into the window, re-lighting three, as two more vanished by the fireplace; then, perceiving a better way, I dropped the matches on the iron-bound deedbox in the corner, and caught up the bedroom candle-stick. With this I avoided the delay of striking matches; but for all that the steady process of extinction went on, and the shadows I feared and fought against returned, and crept in upon me, first a step gained on this side of me and then on that. It was like a ragged storm-cloud sweeping out the stars. Now and then one returned for a minute, and was lost again. I was now almost frantic with the horror of the coming darkness, and my self-possession deserted me. I leaped panting and dishevelled from candle to candle in a vain struggle against that remorseless advance.

I bruised myself on the thigh against the table, I sent a chair headlong, I stumbled and fell and whisked the cloth from the table in my fall. My candle rolled away from me, and I snatched another as I rose. Abruptly this was blown out, as I swung it off the table by the wind of my sudden movement, and immediately the two remaining candles followed. But there was light still in the room, a red light that staved off the shadows from me. The fire! Of course I could still thrust my candle between the bars and re-light it!

I turned to where the flames were still dancing between the glowing coals, and splashing red reflections upon the furniture,

I made two steps towards the grate, and incontinently the flames dwindled and vanished, the glow vanished, the reflections rushed together and vanished, and as I thrust the candle between the bars darkness closed upon me like the shutting of an eye, wrapped about me in a stifling embrace, sealed my vision and crushed the last vestiges of reason from my brain. The candle fell from my hand. I flung out my arms in a vain effort to thrust that ponderous blackness away from me, and, lifting up my voice, screamed with all my might – once, twice, thrice. Then I think I must have staggered to my feet. I know I thought suddenly of the moonlit corridor, and, with my head bowed and my arms over my face, made a run for the door.

But I had forgotten the exact position of the door, and struck myself heavily against the corner of the bed. I staggered back, turned, and was either struck or struck myself against some other bulky furniture. I have a vague memory of battering myself thus, to and fro in the darkness, of a cramped struggle, and of my own wild crying as I darted to and fro, of a heavy blow at last upon my forehead, a horrible sensation of falling that lasted an age, of my last frantic effort to keep my footing, and then I remember no more.

I opened my eyes in daylight. My head was roughly bandaged, and the man with the withered arm was watching my face. I looked about me, trying to remember what had happened, and for a space I could not recollect. I rolled my eyes into the corner, and saw the old woman, no longer abstracted, pouring out some drops of medicine from a little blue phial into a glass. "Where am I?" I asked; "I seem to remember you, and yet I cannot remember who you are."

They told me then, and I heard of the haunted Red Room as one who hears a tale. "We found you at dawn," said he, "and there was blood on your forehead and lips."

It was very slowly I recovered my memory of my experience. "You believe now," said the old man, "that the room is haunted?" He spoke no longer as one who greets an intruder, but as one who grieves for a broken friend.

"Yes," said I; "the room is haunted."

"And you have seen it. And we, who have lived here all our lives, have never set eyes upon it. Because we have never dared . . . Tell us, is it truly the old earl who . . ."

"No," said I. "It is not."

"I told you so," said the old lady, with the glass in her hand. "It is his poor young countess who was frightened . . ."

"It is not," I said. "There is neither ghost of earl nor ghost of countess in that room, there is no ghost there at all; but worse, far worse . . ."

"Well?" they said.

"The worst of all the things that haunt poor mortal man," said I; "and that is, in all its nakedness – Fear! Fear that will not have light nor sound, that will not bear with reason, that deafens and darkens and overwhelms. It followed me through the corridor, it fought against me in the room . . ."

I stopped abruptly. There was an interval of silence. My hand went up to my bandages.

Then the man with the shade sighed and spoke. "That is it," said he. "I knew that was it. A power of darkness. To put such a curse upon a woman! It lurks there always. You can feel it even in the daytime, even of a bright summer's day, in the hangings, in the curtains, keeping behind you however you face about. In the dusk it creeps along the corridor and follows you, so that you dare not turn. There is Fear in that room of hers – black Fear, and there will be – so long as this house of sin endures."

The Haunted Dolls' House

M. R. James

"I suppose you get stuff of that kind through your hands pretty often?" said Mr Dillet, as he pointed with his stick to an object which shall be described when the time comes: and when he said it, he lied in his throat, and knew that he lied. Not once in twenty years – perhaps not once in a lifetime – could Mr Chittenden, skilled as he was in ferreting out the forgotten treasures of half a dozen counties, expect to handle such a specimen. It was collectors' palaver, and Mr Chittenden recognised it as such.

"Stuff of that kind, Mr Dillet! It's a museum piece, that is."

"Well, I suppose there are museums that'll take anything."

"I've seen one, not as good as that, years back," said Mr Chittenden thoughtfully. "But that's not likely to come into the market: and I'm told they 'ave some fine ones of the period over the water. No, I'm only telling you the truth, Mr Dillet, when I say that if you was to place an unlimited order with me for the very best that could be got – and you know I 'ave facilities for getting to know of such things, and a reputation to maintain – well, all I can say is, I should lead you straight up to that one and say, 'I can't do no better for you than that, sir'."

"Hear, hear!" said Mr Dillet, applauding ironically with the end of his stick on the floor of the shop. "How much are you sticking the innocent American buyer for it, eh?"

"Oh, I shan't be over hard on the buyer, American or otherwise. You see it stands this way, Mr Dillet – if I knew just a bit more about the pedigree . . ."

"Or just a bit less," Mr Dillet put in.

"Ha, ha! you will have your joke, sir. No, but as I was

saying, if I knew just a little more than what I do about the piece – though anyone can see for themselves it's a genuine thing, every last corner of it, and there's not been one of my men allowed to so much as touch it since it came into the shop – there'd be another figure in the price I'm asking."

"And what's that: five and twenty?"

"Multiply that by three and you've got it, sir. Seventy-five's my price."

"And fifty's mine," said Mr Dillet.

The point of agreement, was, of course, somewhere between the two, it does not matter exactly where – I think sixty guineas. But half an hour later the object was being packed, and within an hour Mr Dillet had called for it in his car and driven away. Mr Chittenden, holding the cheque in his hand, saw him off from the door with smiles, and returned, still smiling, into the parlour where his wife was making the tea. He stopped at the door.

"It's gone," he said.

"Thank God for that!" said Mrs Chittenden, putting down the teapot. "Mr Dillet, was it?"

"Yes it was."

"Well, I'd sooner it was him than another."

"Oh, I don't know; he ain't a bad feller, my dear."

"Maybe not, but in my opinion he'd be none the worse for a bit of a shake up."

"Well, if that's your opinion, it's my opinion he's putting himself into the way of getting one. Anyhow *we* shan't have no more of it, and that's something to be thankful for."

And so Mr and Mrs Chittenden sat down to tea.

And what of Mr Dillet and of his new acquisition? What it was, the title of this story will have told you. What it was like, I shall have to indicate as well as I can.

There was only just room enough for it in the car, and Mr Dillet had to sit with the driver: he had also to go slow, for though the rooms of the Dolls' House had all been stuffed carefully with soft cotton-wool, jolting was to be avoided, in view of the immense number of small objects which thronged them; and the ten-mile drive was an anxious time for him, in spite of all the precautions he insisted upon. At last his front door was reached, and Collins, the butler, came out.

"Look here, Collins, you must help me with this thing – it's a delicate job. We must get it out upright, see? It's full of little things that mustn't be displaced more than we can help. Let's see, where shall we have it?" (After a pause for consideration.) "Really, I think I shall have to put it in my own room, to begin with at any rate. On the big table – that's it."

It was conveyed – with much talking – to Mr Dillet's spacious room on the first floor, looking out on the drive. The sheeting was unwound from it, and the front thrown open, and for the next hour or two Mr Dillet was fully occupied in extracting the padding and setting in order the contents of the rooms.

When this thoroughly congenial task was finished, I must say that it would have been difficult to find a more perfect and attractive specimen of a Dolls' House in Strawberry Hill Gothic than that which now stood on Mr Dillet's large kneehole table, lighted up by the evening sun which came slanting through three tall sash-windows.

It was quite six feet long, including the Chapel or Oratory which flanked the front on the left as you faced it, and the stable on the right. The main block of the house was, as I have said, in the Gothic manner: that is to say, the windows had pointed arches and were surmounted by what are called ogival hoods, with crockets and finials such as we see on the canopies of tombs built into church walls. At the angles were absurd turrets covered with arched panels. The Chapel had pinnacles and buttresses, and a bell in the turret and coloured glass in the windows. When the front of the house was open you saw four large rooms, bedroom, dining-room, drawing-room and kitchen, each with its appropriate furniture in a very complete state.

The stable on the right was in two storeys, with its proper complement of horses, coaches and grooms, and with its clock and Gothic cupola for the clock bell.

Pages, of course, might be written on the outfit of the mansion – how many frying-pans, how many gilt chairs, what pictures, carpets, chandeliers, four-posters, table linen, glass, crockery and plate it possessed; but all this must be left to the imagination. I will only say that the base or plinth on which the house stood (for it was fitted with one of some depth which allowed of a flight of steps to the front door and a terrace, partly balustraded) contained a shallow drawer or drawers in which were neatly stored sets of embroidered curtains, changes of raiment for the inmates, and, in short, all the materials for an infinite series of variations and refittings of the most absorbing and delightful kind.

"Quintessence of Horace Walpole, that's what it is: he must have had something to do with the making of it." Such was Mr Dillet's murmured reflection as he knelt before it in a reverent ecstasy. "Simply wonderful! this is my day and no mistake. Five hundred pound coming in this morning for that cabinet which I never cared about, and now this tumbling into my hands for a tenth, at the very most, of what it would fetch in town. Well, well! It almost makes one afraid something'll happen to counter it. Let's have a look at the population, anyhow."

Accordingly, he set them before him in a row. Again, here is an opportunity, which some would snatch at, of making an inventory of costume: I am incapable of it.

There were a gentleman and lady, in blue satin and brocade respectively. There were two children, a boy and a girl. There was a cook, a nurse, a footman, and there were the stable servants, two postilions, a coachman, two grooms.

"Anyone else? Yes, possibly."

The curtains of the four-poster in the bedroom were closely drawn round all four sides of it, and he put his finger in between them and felt in the bed. He drew the finger back hastily, for it almost seemed to him as if something had – not stirred, perhaps, but yielded – in an odd live way as he pressed it. Then he put back the curtains, which ran on rods in the proper manner, and extracted from the bed a white-haired old gentleman in a long linen night-dress and cap, and laid him down by the rest. The tale was complete.

Dinner-time was now near, so Mr Dillet spent but five minutes in putting the lady and the children into the drawing-room, the gentleman into the dining-room, the servants into the kitchen and stables, and the old man back into his bed. He retired into his dressing-room next door, and we see and hear no more of him until something like eleven o'clock at night.

His whim was to sleep surrounded by some of the gems of his collection. The big room in which we have seen him contained his bed: bath, wardrobe, and all the appliances of dressing were in a commodious room adjoining: but his four-poster, which itself was a valued treasure, stood in the large room where he sometimes wrote, and often sat, and even received visitors.

Tonight he repaired to it in a highly complacent frame of mind.

There was no striking clock within earshot – none on the staircase, none in the stable, none in the distant church tower. Yet it is indubitable that Mr Dillet was startled out of a very pleasant slumber by a bell tolling one.

He was so much startled that he did not merely lie breathless with wide-open eyes, but actually sat up in his bed.

He never asked himself, till the morning hours how it was that, though there was no light at all in the room, the Dolls' House on the kneehole table stood out with complete clearness. But it was so. The effect was that of a bright harvest moon shining full on the front of a big white stone mansion – a quarter of a mile away it might be, and yet every detail was photographically sharp. There were trees about it, too – trees rising behind the chapel and the house. He seemed to be conscious of the scent of a cool still September night. He thought he could hear an occasional stamp and clink from the stables, as of horses stirring. And with another shock he realised that, above the house, he was looking, not at the wall of his room with its pictures, but into the profound blue of a night sky.

There were lights, more than one, in the windows, and he quickly saw that this was no four-roomed house with a movable front, but one of many rooms, and staircases – a real house, but seen as if through the wrong end of a telescope. "You mean to show me something," he muttered to himself,

and he gazed earnestly on the lighted windows. They would in real life have been shuttered or curtained, no doubt, he thought; but, as it was, there was nothing to intercept his view of what was being transacted inside the rooms.

Two rooms were lighted – one on the ground floor to the right of the door, one upstairs, on the left – the first brightly enough, the other rather dimly. The lower room was the dining-room: a table was laid, but the meal was over, and only wine and glasses were left on the table. The man of the blue satin and the woman of the brocade were alone in the room, and they were talking very earnestly, seated close together at the table, their elbows on it: every now and again stopping to listen, as it seemed. Once *he* rose, came to the window and opened it and put his head out and his hand to his ear. There was a lighted taper in a silver candlestick on a sideboard. When the man left the window he seemed to leave the room also; and the lady, taper in hand, remained standing and listening. The expression on her face was that of one striving her utmost to keep down a fear that threatened to master her – and succeeding. It was a hateful face, too; broad, flat and sly. Now the man came back and she took some small thing from him and hurried out of the room. He, too, disappeared, but only for a moment or two. The front door slowly opened and he stepped out and stood on the top of the perron, looking this way and that; then turned towards the upper window that was lighted, and shook his fist.

It was time to look at that upper window. Through it was seen a four-post bed: a nurse or other servant in an arm-chair, evidently sound asleep; in the bed an old man lying: awake, and, one would say, anxious, from the way in which he shifted about and moved his fingers, beating tunes on the coverlet. Beyond the bed a door opened. Light was seen on the ceiling, and the lady came in: she set down her candle on a table, came to the fireside and roused the nurse. In her hand she had an old-fashioned wine bottle, ready uncorked. The nurse took it, poured some of the contents into a little silver saucepan, added some spice and sugar from casters on the table, and set it to warm on the fire. Meanwhile the old man in the bed beckoned feebly to the lady, who came to him, smiling, took his wrist as if to feel his pulse, and bit her lip as if in consternation. He looked at her anxiously, and then pointed to the window, and spoke. She nodded, and did as the man below had done; opened the casement and listened – perhaps rather ostentatiously: then drew in her head and shook it, looking at the old man, who seemed to sigh.

By this time the posset on the fire was steaming, and the nurse poured it into a small two-handled silver bowl and brought it to the bedside. The old man seemed disinclined for it, and was waving it away, but the lady and the nurse together bent over him and evidently pressed it upon him. He must have yielded, for they supported him into a sitting position, and put it to his lips. He drank most of it, in several draughts, and they laid him down. The lady left the room, smiling good night to him, and took the bowl, the bottle and the silver saucepan with her. The nurse returned to the chair, and there was an interval of complete quiet.

Suddenly the old man started up in his bed – and he must have uttered some cry, for the nurse started out of her chair and made but one step of it to the bedside. He was a sad and terrible sight – flushed in the face, almost to blackness, the eyes glaring whitely, both hands clutching at his heart, foam at his lips.

For a moment the nurse left him, ran to the door, flung it wide open, and, one supposes, screamed aloud for help, then darted back to the bed and seemed to try feverishly to soothe him – to lay him down – anything. But as the lady, her husband, and several servants, rushed into the room with horrified faces, the old man collapsed under the nurse's hands and lay back, and the features, contorted with agony and rage, relaxed slowly into calm.

A few moments later, lights showed out to the left of the house, and a coach with flambeaux drove up to the door. A white-wigged man in black got nimbly out and ran up the steps, carrying a small leather trunk-shaped box. He was met in the doorway by the man and his wife, she with her handkerchief clutched between her hands, he with a tragic face, but retaining his self-control. They led the newcomer into the dining-room, where he set his box of papers on the table, and, turning to them, listened with a face of consternation at what they had to tell. He nodded his head again and again, threw out his hands slightly, declined, it seemed, offers of refreshment and lodging for the night, and within a few minutes came slowly down the steps, entering the coach and driving off the way he had come. As the man in blue watched him from the top of the steps, a smile not pleasant to see stole slowly over his fat white face. Darkness fell over the whole scene as the lights of the coach disappeared.

But Mr Dillet remained sitting up in the bed: he had rightly guessed that there would be a sequel. The house front glimmered out again before long. But now there was a difference. The lights were in other windows, one at the top of the house, the other illuminating the range of coloured windows of the chapel. How he saw through these is not quite obvious, but he did. The interior was as carefully furnished as the rest of the establishment, with its minute red cushions on the desks, its Gothic stall-canopies, and its western gallery and pinnacled organ with gold pipes. On the centre of the black and white pavement was a bier: four tall candles burned at the corners. On the bier was a coffin covered with a pall of black velvet.

As he looked the folds of the pall stirred. It seemed to rise at one end: it slid downwards: it fell away, exposing the black coffin with its silver handles and name-plate. One of the tall candlesticks swayed and toppled over. Ask no more, but turn, as Mr Dillet hastily did, and look in at the lighted window at the top of the house, where a boy and girl lay in two truckle-beds, and a four-poster for the nurse rose above them. The nurse was not visible for the moment; but the father and mother were there, dressed now in mourning, but with very little sign of mourning in their demeanour. Indeed, they were laughing and talking with a good deal of animation, sometimes to each other, and sometimes throwing a remark to one or other of the children, and again laughing at the answers. Then the father was seen to go on tiptoe out of the room, taking with him as he went a white garment that hung on a peg near the door. He shut the door after him. A minute or two later it was slowly opened again, and a muffled head poked round it. A bent form of sinister shape stepped across to the truckle-beds, and suddenly stopped, threw up its arms and revealed, of course, the father, laughing. The children were in agonies of terror, the boy with the bedclothes over his head, the girl throwing herself out of bed into her mother's arms. Attempts at consolation followed – the parents took the children on their laps, patted them, picked up the white gown and showed there was no harm in it, and so forth; and at last putting the children back into bed, left the room with encouraging waves of the hand. As they left it, the nurse came in, and soon the light died down.

Still Mr Dillet watched immovable.

A new sort of light – not of lamp or candle – a pale ugly light, began to dawn around the door-case at the back of the room. The door was opening again. The seer does not like to dwell upon what he saw entering the room: he says it might be described as a frog – the size of a man – but it had scanty white hair about its head. It was busy about the truckle-beds, but not for long. The sound of cries – faint, as if coming out of a vast distance – but, even so, infinitely appalling, reached the ear.

There were signs of a hideous commotion all over the house: lights moved along and up, and doors opened and shut, and running figures passed within the windows. The clock in the stable turret tolled one, and darkness fell again.

It was only dispelled once more, to show the house front. At the bottom of the steps dark figures were drawn up in two lines, holding flaming torches. More dark figures came down the steps, bearing, first one, then another small coffin. And the lines of torch-bearers with the coffins between them moved silently onward to the left.

The hours of night passed on – never so slowly, Mr Dillet thought. Gradually he sank down from sitting to lying in his bed – but he did not close an eye: and early next morning he sent for the doctor.

The doctor found him in a disquieting state of nerves, and recommended sea-air. To a quiet place on the East Coast he accordingly repaired by easy stages in his car.

One of the first people he met on the sea front was Mr Chittenden, who, it appeared, had likewise been advised to take his wife away for a bit of a change.

Mr Chittenden looked somewhat askance upon him when they met: and not without cause.

"Well, I don't wonder at you being a bit upset, Mr Dillet. What? yes, well, I might say 'orrible upset, to be sure, seeing what me and my poor wife went through ourselves. But I put it to you, Mr Dillet, one of two things: was I going to scrap a lovely piece like that on the one 'and, or was I going to tell customers: 'I'm selling you a regular picture-palace-dramar in reel life of the olden time, billed to perform regular at one o'clock a.m.'? Why, what would you 'ave said yourself? And next thing you know, two Justices of the Peace in the back parlour, and pore Mr and Mrs Chittenden off in a spring cart to the County Asylum and everyone in the street saying, 'Ah, I thought it 'ud come to that. Look at the way the man drank!' – and me next door, or next door but one, to a total abstainer, as you know. Well, there was my position. What? Me 'ave it back in the shop? Well, what do *you* think? No, but I'll tell you what I will do. You shall have your money back, bar the ten pound I paid for it, and you make what you can."

Later in the day, in what is offensively called the "smoke-room" of the hotel, a murmured conversation between the two went on for some time.

"How much do you really know about that thing, and where it came from?"

"Honest, Mr Dillet, I don't know the 'ouse. Of course it came out of the lumber room of a country 'ouse – that anyone could guess. But I'll go as far as say this, that I believe it's not a hundred miles from this place. Which direction and how far I've no notion. I'm only judging by guess-work. The man as I actually paid the cheque to ain't one of my regular men, and I've lost sight of him; but I 'ave the idea that this part of the country was his beat, and that's every word I can tell you. But now, Mr Dillet, there's one thing that rather physicks me. That old chap – I suppose you saw him drive up to the door – I thought so: now, would he have been the medical man, do you take it? My wife would have it so, but I stuck to it that he was the lawyer, because he had papers with him, and one he took out was folded up."

"I agree," said Mr Dillet. "Thinking it over, I came to the conclusion that was the old man's will, ready to be signed."

"Just what I thought," said Mr Chittenden, "and I took it that will would have cut out the young people, eh? Well, well! It's been a lesson to me, I know that. I shan't buy no more dolls' houses, nor waste more money on the pictures – and as to this business of poisonin' grandpa, well, if I know myself I never 'ad much of a turn for that. Live and let live: that's bin my motto throughout life, and I ain't found it a bad one."

Filled with these elevated sentiments, Mr Chittenden retired to his lodgings. Mr Dillet next day repaired to the Local Institute, where he hoped to find some clue to the riddle that absorbed him. He gazed in despair at a long file of the Canterbury and York Society's publications of the Parish Registers of the district. No print resembling the house of his nightmare was among those that hung on the staircase and in the passages. Disconsolate, he found himself at last in a derelict room, staring at a dusty model of a church in a dusty glass case: Model of St. Stephen's Church, Coxham. Presented by J. Merewether, Esq. of Ilbridge House, 1877. The work of his ancestor James Merewether, d. 1786. There was something in the fashion of it that reminded him dimly of his horror. He retraced his steps to a wall map he had noticed, and made out that Ilbridge House was in Coxham Parish. Coxham, was, as it happened, one of the parishes of which he had retained the name when he glanced over the file of printed registers, and it was not long before he found in them the record of the burial of Roger Milford, aged 76 on the 11th of September, 1757, and of Roger and Elizabeth Merewether, aged 9 and 7, on the 19th of the same month. It seemed worth while to follow up this clue, frail as it was; and in the afternoon he drove out to Coxham. The east end of the north aisle of the church is a Milford chapel, and on its north wall are tablets to the same persons; Roger, the elder, it seems, was distinguished by all the qualities which adorn "the Father, the Magistrate and the Man"; the memorial was erected by his attached daughter Elizabeth, "who did not long survive the loss of a parent ever solicitous for her welfare, and of two amiable children." The last sentence was plainly an addition to the original inscription.

A yet later slab told of James Merewether, husband of Elizabeth, "who in the dawn of life practised, not without success, those arts which, had he continued their exercise, might in the opinion of the most competent judges have earned for him the name of the British Vitruvius: but who, overwhelmed by the visitation which deprived him of an affectionate partner and a blooming offspring, passed his Prime and Age in a secluded yet elegant Retirement: his grateful Nephew and Heir indulges a pious sorrow by this too brief recital of his excellences."

The children were more simply commemorated. Both died on the night of the 12th of September.

Mr Dillet felt sure that in Ilbridge House he had found the scene of his drama. In some old sketch-book, possibly in some old print, he may yet find convincing evidence that he is right. But the Ilbridge House of today is not that which he sought; it is an Elizabethan erection of the forties, in red brick with stone quoins and dressings. A quarter of a mile from it, in a low part of the park, backed by ancient, stag-horned, ivy-strangled trees and thick undergrowth, are marks of a terraced platform overgrown with rough grass. A few stone balusters lie here and there, and a heap or two, covered with nettles and ivy, of wrought stones with badly-carved crockets. This, someone told Mr Dillet, was the site of an older house.

As he drove out of the village, the hall clock struck four, and Mr Dillet started up and clapped his hands to his ears. It was not the first time he had heard that bell.

Awaiting an offer from the other side of the Atlantic, the Dolls' House still reposes, carefully sheeted, in a loft over Mr

Dillet's stables, whither Collins conveyed it on the day when Mr Dillet started for the sea coast.

(*It will be said, perhaps, and not unjustly, that this is no more than a variation on a former story of mine called* The Mezzotint. *I can only hope that there is enough of variation in the setting to make the repetition of the motif tolerable.*)

His Own Number

William Croft Dickinson

"What do you gain by putting a man into space?" asked Johnson, somewhat aggressively. "Instruments are far more efficient."

"But," protested Hamilton, our Professor of Mathematical Physics, "an astronaut can make use of instruments which don't respond to remote control. Also, he can bring the right instruments into work at exactly the right time in flight."

"Maybe so," returned Johnson. "But what if he gets excited? The advantage of the instrument is that it never gets excited. It has no emotions. Its response is purely automatic."

"Can you be sure of that?" asked Munro, from his chair by the fire. And, by the way he spoke, we could sense that there was something behind his question.

"If it is in perfect order, why not?" persisted Johnson.

"I don't know," Munro replied slowly. "But I can tell you a tale of an electronic computer that was in perfect order and yet three times gave the same answer to an unfortunate technician."

"Something like a wrist-watch which is affected by the pulse-beat of the wearer?" suggested Hayles.

"Something more than that," said Munro. "A great deal more. But what that 'something' was, I simply don't know. Or can an instrument have 'second sight,' or respond to forces that are beyond our reckoning? I wish I knew the answer to that. However, I'll tell you my tale, and then each of you can try to explain it to his own satisfaction."

*

As you probably know, when I first came here I came to a

Research Fellowship in the Department of Mathematics. And, as it happened, one of the problems upon which I was engaged necessitated the use of an electronic computer. There were several in the Department, but the one which I normally used was quite a simple instrument, little more than an advanced calculator. I could 'programme' a number of calculations, feed them into it, and, in less than a minute, out would come the answer which it would have taken me perhaps a month to work out by myself. Just that, and no more. And I wish I could say it was always: 'Just that, and no more.' For here comes my tale.

One afternoon, being somewhat rushed – for I had been invited to a sherry party in the Senate Room – I asked one of the technicians if he'd feed my calculations into the computer, and leave the result on my desk. By pure chance the man I asked to do the job for me was called Murdoch Finlayson, a Highlander from somewhere up in Wester Ross. He was a good fellow in every way, and as honest and conscientious as they make them. I say 'by pure chance;' but perhaps it was all foreordained that I should pick on Finlayson. Certainly it seemed so, in the end. But, at the time, all I wanted to do was to get away to a sherry party; Finlayson happened to be near at hand; and I knew that I could trust him.

I thought, when I asked him to do the job, and when I indicated the computer I wanted him to use, that he looked strangely hesitant, and even backed away a bit. I remember wondering if he had been wanting to leave early, and here was I keeping him tied to his work. But, just when I was about to say that there was no real hurry, and that I'd attend to it myself in the morning, he seemed to pull himself together, reached out for my calculations, and with an odd look in his eyes, murmured something that sounded like "the third time."

I was a little puzzled by his reaction to what I thought was a simple request, and even more puzzled by that murmured remark about "the third time;" but, being in a hurry, gave the matter no second thought and dashed off.

My sherry party lasted somewhat longer than I had expected and, when I returned to the Department, I found it deserted. Everyone had gone home. I walked over to my desk, and then stood there, dumbfounded. Instead of the somewhat complex formula I had expected, I saw one of the computer's sheets bearing a simple number. A simple line of six digits. I won't give you the exact number on that sheet, but it was something like

585244

and underneath the number was a short note:

It's come for the third time.

I recognized Finlayson's handwriting. But what did he mean by that cryptic statement? First of all, he had murmured something about "the third time;" and now he had left a message saying: "It's come for the third time." And what was that simple line of digits, anyway? If it was supposed to be the answer to my series of calculations, it was no answer at all.

At first I felt slightly angry. What was Finlayson playing at? Then a vague feeling of uneasiness supervened. Finlayson was too sound and solid to be playing tricks with me: had it perhaps been fear? What could that number mean? As a line of digits, a six-figure number, I could see nothing unusual about it. It was a simple number, and nothing more. Then, for a time, I played with it. I cubed it; but I was no wiser. I added up the digits and cubed the total; I multiplied by three and tried again; and so forth and so on till I admitted that I was simply wasting my time. I could make nothing of it.

Unfortunately I didn't know where Finlayson lived, so perforce I had to contain my curiosity until the next morning. Also I had to contain that vague feeling of uneasiness which still persisted. But the next morning, as soon as I had entered the Department, I sought him out.

"This is an extraordinary result, Finlayson," I said, holding out the computer sheet which he had left on my desk.

"Aye, sir."

"But surely the computer must have gone completely haywire."

"The computer's all right, sir. But yon's the result it gave me, and I'm no' liking it at all."

"The computer can't be right," I persisted. "And your note seems to say that this is the third time you've received this result from it. Do you really mean that on three separate occasions, whatever the calculations you have put into this computer, it has each time returned this same number – 585244?"

"It has that, sir. And it's unchancy. I'm no' liking a machine that gives me yon same number three times. I'm thinking that maybe it's my own number. And now I'm afeared o' it. I'm for handing in my papers and leaving, sir. I'll away to my brother's to help with the sheep. 'Tis safer feeding a flock of ewes than tending a machine that aye gives you a queer number."

"Nonsense," I retorted. "There's something wrong with the computer, or with the way in which you set it and fed in the calculations."

"Maybe aye and maybe no, sir. But maybe I've been given my own number, and I'm no liking it at all. I'm wanting to leave."

I realised that I was up against some form of Highland superstition. Finlayson had been given a simple number three times, and that was enough for him. Maybe it was "his own number" – whatever that might mean. I realized, too, that he had made up his mind to go, and that nothing I could say would dissuade him. Sheep were safer than electronic computers.

"All right," I said to him. "I'll speak to the Dean. And if it is any comfort to you, I won't ask you to operate that computer again."

He thanked me for what he called my "consideration", and went back to his work. I, in turn, went straight to the Dean.

"What an extraordinary business," said the Dean, when I had recounted the circumstances to him. "I wouldn't have believed it of Finlayson. I would have said he was far too intelligent to let anything like that upset him. There's surely something wrong with that computer. It's a very old instrument. Let's have a look at it."

And, naturally, "having a look at it" included feeding in the calculations which I had previously given to Finlayson. The computer quickly gave us the result. And it was a result far different from Finlayson's simple number, 585244. Although it would have taken me days to check it, the result was a complex formula like the one I had expected.

The Dean muttered something to himself and then turned to me. "We'll try it again. I have some calculations of my own to which I know the answer."

He went to his room, came back with his calculations and fed them into the machine. A few seconds later, out came the computer's sheet bearing the answer.

"Perfectly correct," said the Dean, crisply. "Finlayson must have been imagining things. Or else, for some unknown reason, he has three times fed a wrong programme into the computer. Even then, he couldn't get an answer like 585244."

"I don't know, "I replied, slowly. "He's too good a technician to make mistakes. And carelessness is no explanation. He's convinced he has received that six-figure number on the last three occasions on which he has used this machine. I'm beginning to think he did – though don't ask me why. But he's also convinced that there's some premonition in it. 'His own number' has turned up three times. And 'the third time' is a kind of final summons. Superstition if you like, but I'm beginning to feel for him. I think we should let him go."

"Very well," returned the Dean with a sigh of resignation. "Have it your own way. I'll tell him he can leave at the end of the week. But you know as well as I do how difficult it is to get good technicians."

We sought out Finlayson and the Dean told him that if he was determined to go he could be released at the end of the week. The man's eyes lit up at the news, and his relief was obvious.

"I'll away to my brother's," he said, delightedly. "He'll be glad of my help, and I'll be glad to be helping him. Not that I've been unhappy in my work here, sir. I would not be saying that. But I'm kind of feared to be staying. And if ye had not said I could go, I doubt I would have been going all the same. Though it would not be like me to be doing a thing like that."

"Where does your brother live?" the Dean asked, quickly changing the conversation.

"In Glen Ogle, sir, on the road from Lochearnhead to Killin."

"A beautiful stretch of country," I put in. "Do you know, I'll drive you there on Saturday morning if you like. It will be a lovely run. Where shall I pick you up?"

He accepted my offer with alacrity, and gave me the address of his lodgings.

I did not tell him of the two tests of the computer which the Dean and I had carried out.

*

The Saturday morning was fine and clear. I called for him at the address he had given me, and found him waiting, with his possessions packed into a large grip.

Once we had passed through Stirling and had reached the foothills of the Highlands, the beauty of the country seized hold of me. Finlayson's desire to join his brother amid these browns and purples, golds, blues and greens, seemed the most sensible thing in all the world. The sun made the hills a glory; Ben Ledi and Ben Vorlich raised their heads in the distance; and, as we left Callander, the long-continuing Falls of Leny cascaded over their rocks by the side of the road. Finlayson's thrice-recurring number was surely a blessing and not a curse.

We had run through Lochearnhead and had entered Glen Ogle when, just as I was about to ask Finlayson for the whereabouts of his brother's farm, the car suddenly slowed down and stopped. I knew the tank was practically full, for I had just put in eight gallons at Callander. My first thought was carburettor trouble, or possibly a blocked feed. I loosened the bonnet-catch, got out, raised the bonnet, and went through all the usual checks. But, to my annoyance, I could find nothing wrong. The tank was full; feed, pump and carburettor were all functioning properly. I gave myself a few minor shocks as I tested the electrical circuits. Nothing wrong there. Coil, battery, distributor, plugs were all in order. I reached over to the fascia board and pressed the self-starter. The starter-motor whirred noisily in the stillness, but the engine did not respond. Once more I tested every connection and every part. Again I pressed the self-starter, and again with no effect. Thoroughly exasperated, I turned to Finlayson who had joined me in this exhaustive check and who was as puzzled as I was.

"Well, and what do we do now?" I asked.

"I'll walk the two-three miles to my brother's," he said. "He has the tractor, and can tow us to the farm. Then maybe we can find out what has gone wrong."

"Excellent!" I agreed, "Off you go."

I sat down on the grass and I watched him striding away until he disappeared round a bend in the road. A little later I got up, closed the bonnet of the car, and took a road map from one of the door-pockets. Perhaps there was an alternative route for my way back.

I had barely opened the map and laid it on top of the bonnet when a car came tearing round the bend ahead. As soon as the driver saw me, he pulled up with a screech of his brakes and jumped out.

"For God's sake, come back with me," he cried. "I've killed a man, just up the road. He walked right into me."

For a moment the shock of his words stunned me, and I stood irresolute.

"Quick!" he continued. "We'll take your car. It will save the time of reversing mine."

Without further ado, he jumped into the driver's seat of my car, pressed the self-starter and impatiently signalled to me to get in beside him.

So Finlayson was dead. Somehow I knew it was Finlayson. Dead in Glen Ogle where sheep were safer than machines. He had walked from my useless car to meet his death round the bend in the road.

My useless car! With a sudden tremor of every nerve I realised that the engine was turning over as smoothly as it had ever done.

Had the whole world turned upside down?

Mechanically I got in and sat down beside the man. He drove a short distance round the bend and then slowly came to a halt. I saw at once that my fears were only too true. Finlayson was dead. The man had lifted him on to the grass that verged the road. I got out and bent over him. There was nothing I could do.

"I saw him walking on his own side of the road," I heard the man saying to me. "And I was on my own side too. But he couldn't have seen me or heard me. Just when I should have passed him, he suddenly crossed over. My God! He crossed right in front of me! Do you think he was deaf? Or perhaps he was thinking of something. Absent-minded. How else could he walk right into me?"

The man was talking on and on. Later, I realised he had to talk. It was the only relief for him. But I was not listening. Finlayson lay there, broken, still. Seeking life, he had found death. His "number" had "come up" three times. It was "unchancy." To hell with his number! What had that to do with this?

*

At the subsequent inquiry, the driver of the car was completely exonerated. In a moment of absent-mindedness Finlayson had stepped across the road right into the path of the oncoming car. The finding was clear and definite. Yet for me, I could not forget that the unhappy man had felt some premonition of mischance. He had decided to cheat mischance and seek safety amid the hills. And mischance and death had met him there. Yet what possible connection could there be between "his number," 585244, and his death?

At first I thought that Finlayson had possibly seen "his number" on a telegraph pole, or perhaps on a pylon, and, startled, had crossed the road to look at it more clearly. I made a special journey to Lochearnhead, parked my car there, and examined every bit of the road from the place where my car had "broken down" to the place where Finlayson had been killed. But I could find nothing to substantiate my theory.

And why had my car so mysteriously broken down and then so mysteriously started again? Could it be that the fates had decreed the time and place of the death of Murdoch Finlayson and had used the puny machines of man's invention for their decree's fulfilment? An electronic computer that could be made to give the one number, and an internal combustion engine that could be brought to a halt. And why that number? Why that number?

That one question so dominated my mind that it ruined my work by day and my rest by night. And then, perhaps a fortnight after Finlayson's death, I was given an answer; yet it was an answer that still left everything unexplained. I had gone over to the Staff House for lunch, and had joined a table where, too late, I found an animated discussion in progress to the effect that members of the Faculty of Arts were too ignorant of elementary science, and members of the Faculty of Science too ignorant of the arts. I was in no mood to join in the discussion, though politeness demanded that occasionally I should put in my word. The table gradually emptied until only Crossland, the Professor of Geography, and I were left.

"Neither Science nor Arts can answer some of our questions," I said to him, bitterly.

"I know," he replied. "It must have been a terrible shock for you. I suppose we shall never know why that computer returned the one number to Finlayson three times. That is, if it did. And what was the number, by the way? I never heard."

"A simple line of six digits – 585244."

"Sounds just like a normal national grid reference," Crossland commented.

"A normal national grid reference?" I queried.

"Yes. Surely you know our national grid system for map-references. Or," he continued with a smile, "is this a case of the scientist knowing too little of the work in the Faculty of Arts?"

"You've scored a point there," I replied. "I'm afraid I'm completely ignorant of this grid system of yours."

"Probably you've been using motoring-maps too much," he conceded. "But the grid is quite simple. If you look at any sheet of the Ordnance Survey you will see that it is divided into kilometre squares by grid lines, numbered from 0 to 99, running west to east, and 0 to 99, running south to north. Then, within each kilometre square, a closer definition is obtained by measuring in tenths between the grid lines. Thus a particular spot, say a farm-steading or a spinney, can be pin-pointed on the map, within its numbered square, by a grid reference which runs to six figures: three, west to east; and three, south to north. A six-figure number, which is known as the 'normal national grid reference'."

For a minute or so I digested this in silence.

"Can we go over to your map-room?" I asked.

"Surely," he said, a little surprised. "And see on a map how it works?"

"Yes."

We went over to Crossland's department.

"Any particular map?" he asked.

"Yes. A map of Western Perthshire."

Crossland produced the Ordnance Survey Sheet. I looked at it almost with reluctance.

Taking out a pencil, I pointed to the place on the map where, as near as I could judge, Finlayson had met his death. "What would be the grid reference for that particular spot?" I asked, and wondered at the strangeness of my voice.

Crossland picked up a transparent slide and bent over the map. I heard him take in his breath. He straightened himself, and when he turned to look at me his eyes were troubled and questioning.

*

"Yes," concluded Munro. "I needn't tell you what that grid reference was. But can anyone tell me why Finlayson was given that number three times on an electronic computer? Or why my car 'broke down', so that he would walk of his own accord to that very spot?"

The Apple of Trouble

Joan Aiken

It was a black day for the Armitage family when Great-Uncle Gavin retired. In fact, as Mark pointed out, Uncle Gavin did not exactly retire; he was pushed. He had been High Commissioner of Mbutam-Mbuta-land, which had suddenly decided it needed a High Commissioner no longer, but would instead become the Republic of Mbutambutala. So Sir Gavin Armitage K.C.M.G., O.B.E., D.S.O. and so forth, was suddenly turned loose on the world, and because he had expected to continue living at the High Commissioner's Residence for years to come, and had no home of his own, he moved in with the parents of Mark and Harriet.

The first disadvantage was that he had to sleep in the ghost's room. Mr Peake was nice about it, he said he quite understood, and they would probably shake down together very well, he had been used to all sorts of odd company in his three hundred years. But after a few weeks of Great-Uncle Gavin's keep-fit exercises, coughing, thumping, harrumphing, snoring, and blazing open windows, Mr Peake became quite thin and pale (for a ghost); he migrated through the wall into the room next door, explaining apologetically that he wasn't getting a wink of sleep. Unfortunately the room next door was a bathroom, and though Mark didn't mind, Mr Armitage complained that it gave him the jumps to see a ghostly face suddenly loom up beside his in the mirror when he was shaving, while Harriet and her mother had to take to the downstairs bathroom. Great-Uncle Gavin never noticed Mr Peake at all. He was not sensitive. Besides he had other things to think about.

One of his main topics of thought was how disgracefully the children had been brought up. He was horrified at the way they were allowed to live all over the house, instead of being pent in some upstairs nursery.

"Little gels should be seen and not heard," he boomed at Harriet whenever she opened her mouth. To get her out from underfoot during the holidays he insisted on her enrolling in a domestic science course run by a Professor Grimalkin who had recently come to live in the village.

As for Mark, he had hardly a minute's peace.

"God bless my soul, boy" – nearly all Great-Uncle Gavin's remarks began with this request – "God bless my soul, what are you doing now? Reading? God bless my soul, do you want to grow up a muff?"

"A muff, Great-Uncle? What is a muff, exactly?" And Mark pulled out the notebook in which he was keeping a glossary of Great-Uncle Gavin.

"A muff, why, a muff is a – a funk, sir, a duffer, a frowst, a tug, a swot, a miserable litle sneaking milksop!"

Mark was so busy writing down all these words that he forgot to be annoyed.

"You ought to be out of doors, sir, ought to be out playin' footer."

"But you need twenty-two people for that," Mark pointed out, "and there's only Harriet and me. Besides it's summer. And Harriet's a bit of a duffer at French cricket."

"Don't be impident, boy! Gad, when I was your age I'd have been out collectin' birds' eggs."

"Birds' eggs," said Mark, scandalised. "But I'm a subscribing member of the Royal Society for the Protection of Birds."

"Butterflies, then," growled his great-uncle.

"I read a book, Great-Uncle, that said all the butterflies were being killed by indiscriminate use of pesticides and what's left ought to be carefully preserved."

Sir Gavin was turning eggplant colour and seemed likely to explode.

"Boy's a regular sea-lawyer," he said furiously. "Grow up into one of those confounded trade-union johnnies. Why don't you go out on your velocipede, then, sir? At your age I was as keen as mustard, by gad; used to ride miles on my penny-farthing, rain or shine."

"No bike," said Mark. "Only the unicorn, and he's got a swelled fetlock; we're fomenting it."

"Unicorn! Never heard such namby-pamby balderdash in my life! Here," Great-Uncle Gavin said, "what's your weekly allowance when your pater's at home?"

With the disturbed family ghost and the prospect of Uncle Gavin's indefinite stay to depress them, Mr and Mrs Armitage had rather meanly decided that they were in need of three weeks in Madeira, and had left the day before.

"Half a crown a week," said Mark. "I've had three weeks in advance."

"How much does a bike cost nowadays?"

"Oh, I dare say you could pick one up for thirty-five pounds."

"What?" Great-Uncle Gavin nearly fell out of his chair, but then, rallying, he pulled seven five-pound notes out of his ample wallet. "Here, then, boy; this is an advance on yer allowance for the next two hundred and eighty weeks. I'll collect it from your governor when he comes home. Cut along, now, and buy a bicycle, an' go for a topping spin and don't let me see your face again till suppertime."

"But I don't want a bicycle," Mark said.

"Be off, boy, make yourself scarce, don't argue! – On second thoughts, 'spose I'd better come with you, to make sure you don't spend the money on some appallin' book about nature."

So Great-Uncle Gavin stood over Mark while the latter unwillingly and furiously purchased a super-excellent low-slung bicycle with independent suspension, disc brakes, three-inch tyres, five-speed, and an outboard motor. None of which assets did Mark want in the least, as who would when they had a perfectly good unicorn to ride?

"Now be off with you and see how quickly you can get to Brighton and back."

Day after day thereafter, no sooner had breakfast been eaten than Mark was hounded from the house by his relentless great-uncle and urged to try and better his yesterday's time to Brighton.

"Gosh, he must have led those Mbutam-Mbutas a life," Mark muttered darkly in the privacy of Harriet's room.

"I suppose he's old and we ought to be patient with him," Harriet said. She was pounding herbs in a mortar for her domestic science homework.

The trouble was, concluded Mark, gloomily pedalling along one afternoon through a heavy summer downpour, that during his forty years among the simple savages Great-Uncle Gavin had acquired the habit of command; it was almost impossible not to obey his orders.

Almost impossible; not quite. Presently the rain increased to a cloudburst.

"Drat Great-Uncle Gavin! I'm not going all the way to Brighton in this," Mark decided. "Anyway, why *should* I go to Brighton?"

And he climbed a stile and dashed up a short grassy path to a small nearby church which had a convenient and dry-looking porch. He left his bike on the other side of the stile, for that is another disadvantage of bikes; you can never take them all the way to where you want to go.

The church proved to be chilly and not very interesting so Mark, who always carried a paperback in his pocket, settled on the porch bench to read until the rain abated. After a while, hearing footsteps, he looked up and saw that a smallish, darkish, foreign-looking man had joined him.

"Nasty afternoon," Mark said civilly.

"Eh? Yes? Yes, indeed." The man seemed nervous; he kept glancing over his shoulder down the path.

"Is your bicycle, boy, by wall yonder?" he asked by and by.

"Yes it is."

"Is a fine one," the man said. "Very fine one. Would go lickety-spit fast, I dare say?"

"An average of twenty m.p.h." Mark said gloomily.

"Will it? Will it so?"

The little man fell silent, glancing out uneasily once more at the rainy dusk, while Mark strained his eyes to see the print of his book. He noticed that his companion seemed to be shuffling about, taking a pack off his back and rummaging among the contents; presently Mark realised that something was being held out to him. He looked up from the page and saw a golden apple – quite a large one, about the size of a Bramley. On one side the gold had a reddish bloom, as if the sun had ripened it. The other side was paler. Somebody had taken two bites out of the red side; Mark wondered what it had done to their teeth. Near the stalk was a dark-brown stain, like a patch of rust.

"Nice, eh?" the little man said, giving the apple to Mark, who nearly dropped it on the flagged floor. It must have weighed at least four pounds.

"Is it real gold all through?" he asked. "Must be quite valuable?"

"Valuable?" the man said impressively. "Such apple is beyond price. You of course well-educated, familiar with Old Testament tale of Adam and Eve?"

"W-why yes," Mark said, stammering a little. "But you – you don't mean to say that apple . . . ?"

"Selfsame one," the little man said, nodding his head. "Original bite marks of Adam and Eve before apple carried out of Eden. Then – see stain? Blood of Abel. Cain killed him for apple. Stain will never wash off."

"Goodness," Mark said.

"Not all, however – not at all all! Apple of Discord – golden apple same which began Trojan War – have heard of such?"

"Why, yes. But – but you're not telling me . . ."

"Identical apple," the little man said proudly. "Apples of

Asgard, too? Heard of? Scandinavian golden apples of perpetual youth, guarded by Idhunn?"

"Yes, but you don't . . ."

"Such was one of those. Not to mention Apples of Hesperides, stolen by Hercules."

"Hold on – surely it couldn't have been both?"

"Could," the little man said. "Was. William Tell's apple – familiar story? – same apple. Newton – apple fell on head, letting in dangerous principle of gravity. This. Atalanta – apple thrown by Venus to stop her winning race. Also. Prince Ahmed's apple . . ."

"Stop, stop!" said Mark. "I don't understand how it could possibly be all those."

But somehow, as he held the heavy, shining thing in his hand, he did believe the little man's story. There was a peculiar, rather nasty fascination about the apple. It scared him, and yet he wanted it.

"So, see," the little man said, nodding more than ever, "worth millions pounds. No lie – millions. And yet I give to you . . ."

"Now, wait a minute . . ."

"Give in exchange for bicycle, Yes? Okay?"

"Well, but – but why? Why don't you want the apple?"

"Want bicycle more." He glanced down the road again, and now Mark guessed.

"Someone's after you – the police? You stole the apple?"

"Not stole, no, no, no! Did swap, like with bicycle, you agree, yes?"

He was already half-way down the path. Hypnotised, Mark watched him climb the style and mount the bike, wobbling. Suddenly Mark found his voice and called,

"What did you swap for it?"

"Drink of water – in desert, see?"

"Who's chasing you, then?"

By now the little man was chugging down the road and his last word, indistinct, floated back through the rain, something ending in -ese; it might have been Greek for all Mark could make of it.

He put the apple in his pocket, which sagged under the weight, and, since the shower was slackening, walked to the road to flag a lift home in the next lorry.

Great-Uncle Gavin nearly burst a blood vessel when he learned that Mark had exchanged his new bicycle for an apple, albeit a gold one.

"Did what – merciful providence – an apple? – Hesperides? Eden? Asgard? Never heard such a pack of moonshine in all me born – let's see it then. Where is it?"

Mark produced the apple and a curious gleam lit up Uncle Gavin's eye.

"Mind," he said, "don't believe a word of the feller's tale, but plain that's val'ble; far too val'ble an article to be in your hands, boy. Better give it here at once. I'll get Christies to value it. And of course we must advertise in *The Times* for the wallah who palmed it off on you – highly illegal transaction, I dare say."

Mark felt curiously relieved to be rid of the apple, as if a load had been lifted from his mind as well as his pocket.

He ran upstairs whistling. Harriet, as usual, was up in her room mixing things in retorts and crucibles. When Uncle Gavin, as in duty bound, asked each evening what she had been learning that day in her domestic science course, she always replied briefly, "Spelling." "Spellin', gel? Rum notion of housekeepin' the johnny seems to have. Still, dare say it keeps you out of mischief." In fact, as Harriet had confided to Mark, Professor Grimalkin was a retired alchemist who, having failed to find the Philosopher's Stone, was obliged to take in pupils to make ends meet. He was not a very good teacher; his heart wasn't in it. Mark watched Harriet toss a pinch of green powder into a boiling beaker. Half a peach tree shot up, wavered, sagged, and then collapsed. Impatiently Harriet tipped the frothing liquid out of the window and put some more water on to boil.

Then she returned to the window and peered out into the dark.

"Funny," she said. "There seem to be some people waiting outside the front door. Can't think why they didn't ring the bell. Could you let them in, Mark? My hands are all covered with prussic acid. I expect they're friends of Uncle Gavin's."

Mark went down and opened the door. Outside, dimly illuminated by the light from the porch, he saw three ladies. They seemed to be dressed in old-fashioned clothes, drainpipe skirts down to their ankles, and cloaks and bonnets rather like those of Salvation Army lasses; the bonnets were perched on thick, lank masses of hair. Mark didn't somehow care for their faces which resembled those of dogs – but not tame domestic dogs so much as starved, wild, slightly mad dogs; they stared at Mark hungrily.

"Er – I'm so sorry. Did you ring? Have you been waiting long?" he said.

"A long, long time. Since the world-tree was but a seed in darkness. We are the daughters of Night," one of them hollowly replied. She moved forward with a leathery rustle.

"Oh." Mark noticed that she had bat's wings. He stepped back a little. "Do you want to see Great-Uncle – Sir Gavin Armitage? Won't you come in?"

"Nay. We are the watchers by the threshold. Our place is here."

"Oh, all right. What name shall I say?"

To this question they replied in a sort of gloomy chant, taking it in turns to speak.

"We are the avengers of blood."

"Sisters of the nymph with the apple-bough, Nemesis."

"We punish the sin of child against parent . . ."

"Youth against age . . ."

"Brother against brother . . ."

"We are the Erinnyes, the Kindly Ones . . ." (But their expressions were far from kindly, Mark thought.)

"Tisiphone . . ."

"Alecto . . ."

"And Megaera."

"And what did you wish to see Sir Gavin about?" Mark knew his great-uncle hated to be disturbed once he was settled in the evening with a glass of port and *The Times*.

"We attend him who holds the apple."

"There is blood on it – a brother's blood, shed by a brother."

"It cries for vengeance."

"Oh, I see!" said Mark, beginning to take in the situation. Now he understood why the little man had been so anxious for a bicycle. "But, look here, dash it all, Uncle Gavin hasn't shed any blood. That was Cain, and it was a long time ago. I don't see why Uncle should be responsible."

"He holds the apple."

"He must bear the guilt."

"The sins of the fathers are visited on the children."

"Blood calls for blood."

Then the three wolfish ladies disconcertingly burst into a sort of hymn, shaking tambourines and beating on them with brass-studded rods which they pulled out from among their draperies:

"We are the daughters
Of darkness and time
We follow the guilty
We punish the crime
Nothing but bloodshed
Will settle old scores
So blood has to flow and
That blood must be yours!"

When they had finished they fixed their ravenous eyes on Mark again and the one called Alecto said,

"Where is he?"

Mark felt greatly relieved that Uncle Gavin had taken the apple away from him and was therefore apparently responsible for its load of guilt, but as this was a mean thought he tried to stifle it. Turning (not that he liked having the ladies behind his back) he went into the sitting-room where Uncle Gavin was sitting snug by the fire and said,

"There are some callers asking for you, Great-Uncle."

"God bless my soul, at this time of the evenin'? Who the deuce . . ."

Great-Uncle Gavin crossly stumped out to the porch, saying over his shoulder, "Why didn't you ask 'em in, boy? Not very polite to leave 'em standing . . ."

Then he saw the ladies and his attitude changed. He said sharply, "Didn't you see the notice on the gate, my good women? It says No Hawkers or Circulars. I give handsome cheques to charity each year at Christmas and make it a rule never to contribute to door-to-door collections. So be off, if you please!"

"We do not seek money," Tisiphone hungrily replied.

"Milk-bottle-tops, jumble, old gold, it's all the same. Pack of meddlesome old maids – I've no time for you!" snapped Sir Gavin. "Good night!" And he shut the door smartly in their faces.

"Have to be firm with that sort of customer," he told Mark. "Become a thorough nuisance otherwise – tiresome old harpies. Got wind of that golden apple, I dare say – shows what happens when you mix with such people. Shockin' mistake. Take the apple to Christies tomorrow. Now, please see I'm not disturbed again." And he returned to the sitting-room.

Mark looked uneasily at the front door but it remained shut; evidently the three Kindly Ones were content to wait outside. But there they stayed; when Mark returned to Harriet's room he looked out of the window and saw them, sombre and immovable, in the shadows outside the porch, evidently prepared to sit out the night.

"Not very nice if they're going to picket our front door from now on," he remarked gloomily to Harriet. "Goodness knows what the postman will think. And *I* don't fancy 'em above half. Wonder how we can get rid of them."

"I've an idea," Harriet said. "Professor Grimalkin was talking about them the other day. They are the Furies. But it's awfully hard to shake them off once they're after you."

"That's gay."

"There are various things you can do: biting off your finger . . ."

"Some hope of Uncle Gavin doing that!"

"Or shaving your head."

"Wouldn't be much use, since he's bald as a bean already."

"You can bathe seven times in running water or the blood of pigs . . ."

"He always does take a lot of cold baths and we had pork for supper, so plainly that's no go."

"Well, you can go into exile for a year," Harriet said.

"I only wish he would."

"Or build them a grotto, nice and dark, preferably under an ilex tree, and make suitable offerings."

"Such as what?"

"Anything black, or they rather go for iris flowers. Milk and honey too. And they can be shot with a bow of horn, but that doesn't seem to be very successful as a rule."

"Oh well, let's try the milk-and-honey and something black for now," Mark said. "And I'll make a bow of horn tomorrow – I've got Candleberry's last year's horn in my room somewhere." Candleberry was the unicorn.

Harriet therefore collected a black velvet pincushion and a bowl of milk and honey. These she put out on the front step, politely wishing the Daughters of Night good evening, to which their only response was a baleful silence.

Next morning the milk and honey was still there. So were the Furies. Evidently they did not intend to be placated so easily. By daylight they were even less prepossessing, having black claws, bloodshot eyes, and snakes for hair. However, slipping down early to remove the saucer in case the postman tripped over it, Harriet did notice that all the pins had been removed from the pincushion. And eaten? This was encouraging. So was the fact that when the postman arrived with a card from parents in Madeira – *Having wonderful time hope you are behaving yourselves* – he walked clean through the Furies without noticing them at all. Evidently his conscience at least was clear.

"Perhaps they're only visible to relatives of their victim," Harriet suggested to Mark, who was working on the unicorn horn with emery paper.

"I hope they've taken the pins to stick in Uncle Gavin," he growled. In default of bicycle exercise Great-Uncle Gavin had made Mark do five hundred press-ups before breakfast and had personally supervised the operation. Mark felt it would be far, far better to shoot Uncle Gavin than the Furies who, after all, were only doing their duty.

The most annoying thing of all was that, after his initial interview with them, Uncle Gavin seemed not to notice the avenging spirits at all ("He only sees what he chooses to," Harriet guessed) and walked past them quite as unconcernedly as the postman had. He packed up the golden apple in a cigar-box, rang for a taxi, and departed to London. The Furies followed him in a black, muttering group, and were seen no more for several hours; Mark and Harriet heaved sighs of relief. Prematurely, though; at teatime the Furies reappeared, even blacker, muttering still more, and took up their post once more by the front door.

"Lost the old boy somewhere in London," Mark diagnosed. "Or perhaps they were chucked out of Christies."

The unwanted guests were certainly in a bad mood. This time they were accompanied by a smallish thickset winged serpent or dragon who seemed to be called Ladon. Harriet heard them saying, "Down, Ladon! Behave yourself, and soon you shall sup on blood." Ladon too seemed to have a snappish disposition, and nearly took off Harriet's hand when she stooped to pat him on returning home from her domestic science lesson.

"What a beautiful green his wings are. Is he yours?" she said to the Furies politely.

"He is the guardian of the apple; he but waits for his own," Tisiphone replied dourly.

Ladon did not share the Furies' scruples about coming indoors; evidently he was used to a warmer clime and found the doorstep too draughty. He followed Harriet into the kitchen and flopped his bulky length in front of the stove, hissing cantankerously at anyone who came near, and thoroughly upsetting Walrus, the cat.

Walrus was not the only one.

"Miss Harriet! Get that nasty beast out of here at once!" exclaimed Mrs Epis the cook when she came back from shopping. "And what those black ladies are doing out on the front door step I'm sure I don't know; I've two or three times give them a hint to be off but they won't take it."

Evidently Mrs Epis counted as one of the family or else she, too, had a guilty conscience. Mark and Harriet soon found that visitors to the house who had episodes in their past of which they had cause to be ashamed were apt to notice the Erinnyes in a patchy, nervous way and hurry away with uneasy glances behind them, or else break into sudden and embarrassing confessions.

And Ladon was a thorough nuisance. So long as Harriet kept on the fan heater in her room he would lie in front of it, rolling luxuriously on his back and only snapping if anyone approached him. But at bedtime when she turned the fan off – for she hated a warm room at night – he became fretful and roamed snarling and clanking about the house. Even Uncle Gavin tripped over him then and blamed the children furiously for leaving what he thought was a rolled-up tent lying in the passage.

"Things can't go on like this," Mark said despondently.

"We've certainly got to get rid of them all somehow before Mother and Father come home next week," Harriet agreed. "And Uncle Gavin's plainly going to be no help at all."

Uncle Gavin was even more tetchy than usual. Christies had sent him a letter saying that in view of the apple's unique historical interest it was virtually impossible to put a price on it, but in their opinion it was certainly worth well over a million pounds. They would return the apple by the next registered post pending further instructions. And the advertisement which appeared in *The Times* every day, "Will person who persuaded young boy to exchange valuable new bicycle for metal apple on August 20 please contact Box—" was producing no replies.

"Nor likely to," Mark said. "That chap knows when he's well out of trouble."

During that day Mark finished his horn bow and tried shooting at the Furies with it. The operation was a total failure. The arrows, which he had decided to make from a fallow-deer's antler (brow, bay, and tray) were curved, and flew on a bias, like bowls, missing the visitors nine times out of ten. If they did hit they merely passed clean through and, as Mark told Harriet later, he felt a fool having to pick them up under the malign snaky-and-bonneted gaze of Alecto, Megaera, and Tisiphone.

Harriet, however, came home in good spirits. She pulled out and showed Mark a paper covered with Professor Grimalkin's atrocious handwriting.

"What is it?" he asked.

"Recipe for a friendship philtre. You've heard of a love philtre? This is like that, only milder. I'm going to try it in their milk. Now don't interrupt, while I make it up."

She put her crucible on to bubble. Mark curled up at the end of her bed and read his bird book, only coming out when Harriet tripped over Ladon and dratted him, or asked Mark's opinion about the professor's handwriting.

"Is this verdigris or verjuice, do you think? And is that Add sugar, or Allow to simmer?"

"It'll be a miracle if the stuff turns out all right," Mark said pessimistically. "Anyway, do we want the Furies friendly?"

"Of course we do, it'll be a tremendous help. Where was I now? Add bad egg, and brown under grill."

Finally the potion was finished and put in a cough-mixture bottle. ("It smells awful," Mark said, sniffing. "Never mind, how do we know what *they* like?") A spoonful of the noxious stuff was divided between three bowls of milk, which were placed on the front step, at the feet of the unresponsive Erinnyes.

However, after a moment or two they began to snuff the air like bloodhounds on the track of a malefactor, and as Harriet tactfully retired she had the pleasure of seeing all three of them lapping hungrily at the mixture. So far, at least, the spell had worked. Harriet went hopefully to bed.

Next morning she was woken by a handful of earth flung at her window.

"Miss Harriet!" It was Mrs Epis on the lawn. "Miss

Harriets you'll have to make the breakfast yourself. I'm taking a week's holiday. And things had better be different when I come back or I'll give in my notice; you can tell your Ma it was me broke the Crown Derby teapot and I'm sorry about it, but there's some things a body can't bear. Now I'm off home."

Sleepy and mystified, Harriet went to the kitchen to put on the kettle for Great-Uncle Gavin's tea. There, to her dismay, she found the Furies, who greeted her with toothy smiles. They were at ease in basket chairs round the stove, with their long skirts turned back so as to toast their skinny legs and feet, which rested on Ladon. Roused by the indoor warmth, the snakes on their heads were in a state of disagreeable squirm and writhe which Harriet too found hard to bear, particularly before breakfast; she quite sympathised with the cook's departure.

"Oh, good morning," she said, however, stoutly controlling her qualms. "Would you like some more milk?" She mixed another brew with potion (which was graciously accepted) and took up a tray of breakfast to Great-Uncle Gavin, explaining that Mrs Epis had been called away. By the time she returned, Mark was in the kitchen, glumly taking stock of the situation.

"Feel like a boiled egg?" Harriet said.

"I'll do it, thanks, I've had enough of your domestic science."

They ate their boiled eggs in the garden. But they had taken only a bite or two when they were startled by hysterical screams from the window-cleaner who, having arrived early and started work on the kitchen window, had looked through the glass and was now on his knees in the flowerbed, confessing to anyone who would listen that he had pinched a diamond brooch from an upstairs bedroom in West Croydon. Before he was pacified they had also to deal with the man who came to mend the fridge, who seemed frightfully upset about something he had done to a person called Elsie, as well as a French onion-seller who dropped eight strings of onions in the back doorway and fled, crying, "Mon Dieu, mon Dieu, mon crime est découvert! Je suis perdu!"

"This won't do," said Mark, as he returned from escorting the sobbing electrician to the gate. Exhaustedly mopping his brow he didn't look where he was going, barked his shins painfully on Ladon, who was stalking the cat, and let out an oath. It went unheard; the Furies, much cheered by their breakfast and a night spent in the snug kitchen, were singing their bloodthirsty hymn fortissimo, with much clashing of tambourines. Ladon and the cat seemed all set for a duel to the death; and Great-Uncle Gavin was bawling down the stairs for less row while a man was breakfastin', dammit!

"It's all right," Harriet soothed Mark. "I knew the potion would work wonders. Now, your Kindlinesses," she said to the Erinnyes, "we've got a beautiful grotto ready for you, just the sort of place you like, except I'm sorry there isn't an ilex tree, if you wouldn't mind stepping this way," and she led them to the coal-cellar, which, being peaceful and dark, met with their entire approval.

"I dare say they'll be glad of a nap," she remarked, shutting the door thankfully on them. "After all, they've been unusually busy lately."

"That's all very well," said Mark. "They'd better not stay there long. I'm the one that fetches the coal. And there's still beastly Ladon to dispose of."

Ladon, unlike his mistresses, was not tempted by milk containing a friendship potion. His nature remained as intractable as ever. He now had the cat Walrus treed on the banister post at the top of the stairs, and was coiled in a baleful bronze-and-green heap just below, hissing like a pressure-cooker.

"Perhaps bone arrows will work on him," said Mark, and dashed to his bedroom.

As he reappeared a lot of things happened at once.

The postman rang the front-door bell and handed Harriet a letter for Uncle Gavin and a registered parcel labelled GOLD WITH CARE. Ladon made a dart at the cat, who countered with a faster-than-light left hook, all claws extended. It caught the dragon in his gills and he let out a screech like the whistle of a steam locomotive which fetched the Furies from their grotto at the double, brass-studded batons out and snakes ready to strike.

At the same moment Mark let fly with his bow and arrow and Uncle Gavin burst from his bedroom exclaiming, "I will not have this bedlam while I'm digestin' my breakfast!" He received the arrow intended for Ladon full in his slippered heel and gave a yell which quite drowned the noise made by the cat and dragon.

"Who did that? Who fired that damned thing?" Enraged, hopping, Uncle Gavin pulled out the bone dart. "What's that cat doin' up there? Why's this confounded reptile in the house? Who are those people down there? *What the devil's going on around here?*"

Harriet gave a shout of joy.

"Look, quick!" she called to the Furies. "Look at his heel! It's bleeding!" (It was indeed). "You said blood had to flow and now it has, so you've done your job and can leave with clear consciences! Quick, Mark, open the parcel and give that wretched dragon his apple and they can all leave. Poor Uncle Gavin, is your foot very painful? Mark didn't mean to hit you. I'll bandage it up in two shakes."

Mark tore the parcel undone and tossed the golden apple to Ladon, who caught it with a snap of his jaws and was gone in a flash through the landing window. (It was shut, but no matter.) At the same moment the Furies, their lust for vengeance appeased by the sight of Uncle Gavin's gore, departed with more dignity by the front door.

Alecto even turned and gave Harriet a ghastly smile.

"Thank you for having us, child," she said. "We enjoyed our visit."

"Don't mention it," Harriet mechanically replied, and only just stopped herself from adding, "Come again."

Then she sat her great-uncle in the kitchen arm-chair and bathed his heel. The wound, luckily, proved to be no more than a scratch. While she bandaged it he read his letter, and suddenly gave a curious grunt of pleasure and astonishment.

"God bless my soul! They want me back! Would you believe it!"

"Who want you back, Great-Uncle?" Harriet asked, tying the ends of the bandage in a knot.

"The Mbutam-Mbutas, bless 'em! They want me to go and help 'em as Military and Economic Adviser. I've always said there's good in the black feller and I say so yet! Well, well, well! Don't know when I've been so pleased." He gave his nose a tremendous blow and wiped his eyes.

"Oh, Uncle Gavin, how perfectly splendid!" Harriet gave him a hug. "When do they want you to go?"

"Three weeks' time. Bless my soul I'll have a bustle getting me kit ready."

"Oh, we'll all help like mad. I'll run down the road now and fetch Mrs Epis; I'm sure she'll be glad to come back for such an emergency."

Mrs Epis had no objection at all, once she was assured the intruders were gone from the house.

Harriet had one startled moment when they got back.

"Uncle Gavin!" she called, and ran upstairs. The old gentleman had out his tin tropical trunk and was inspecting a pith helmet. "Yes, m'dear, what is it?" he said absently.

"The little brown bottle on the kitchen table. Was it – did you . . . ?"

"Oh, that? My cough mixture? Yes, I finished it and threw the bottle away. Why, though, bless my soul – *there's* my cough mixture! What the deuce have I been an' taken, then, gel? Anything harmful?"

"Oh no, perfectly harmless," Harriet hastily reassured him. "Now, you give me anything you want mended and I'll be getting on with it."

" 'Pon me soul," Uncle Gavin said, pulling out a bundle of spotless white ducks and a dress jacket with tremendous epaulettes and fringes, " 'pon me soul, I believe I'll miss you young ones when I'm back in the tropics. Come and visit me sometimes, m'dear? Young Mark too. Where is the young rogue? Ho, ho, can't help laughing when I think how he hit me in the heel. Who'd have thought he had it in him?"

"He's gone apple-picking at the farm down the road," Harriet explained. "He wants to earn enough to pay back that thirty-five pounds."

"Good lad, good lad!" Uncle Gavin exclaimed approvingly. "Not that he need have bothered, mark you."

And in fact, when Mark tried to press the money on Uncle Gavin at his departure, he would have none of it.

"No, no, bless your little hearts, split it between you." He chucked Harriet under the chin and earnestly shook Mark's hand. "I'd never have thought I'd cotton to young 'uns as I have to you two – 'mazing thing. So you keep the money and buy something pretty to remind you of my visit."

But Mark and Harriet thought they would remember his visit quite easily without that – especially as the Furies had taken quite a fancy to the coal-cellar and frequently came back to occupy it on chilly winter nights.